Also by Kathy Reichs

Déjà Dead

Death du Jour

Deadly Décisions

FATAL VOYAGE

KATHY REICHS

SCRIBNER

NEW YORK   LONDON   TORONTO
SYDNEY   SINGAPORE

SCRIBNER
1230 Avenue of the Americas
New York, NY 10020

SCRIBNER and design are trademarks of Macmillan Library Reference USA, Inc., used under license by Simon & Schuster, the publisher of this work. For information regarding special discounts for bulk purchases, please contact Simon & Schuster Special Sales at 1-800-456-6798 or business@simonandschuster.com

Manufactured in the United States of America

1 3 5 7 9 10 8 6 4 2

Library of Congress Cataloging-in-Publication Data
Reichs, Kathleen J.
Fatal voyage/Kathy Reichs
p. cm.
1. Brennan, Temperance (Fictitious character)—Fiction.
2. Forensic anthropology—Fiction. 3. Women anthropologists—Fiction. 4. Montréal (Québec)—Fiction. I. Title.
PS3568.E476345 F37 2001   813'.54—dc21   2001020171
ISBN 0-7432-1662-8

Dedicated with button-bursting pride to:

Kerry Elisabeth Reichs, J.D., M.P.P.,
Duke University,
Class of 2000

Courtney Anne Reichs, B.A.,
University of Georgia,
Class of 2000

Brendan Christopher Reichs, B.A. (*cum laude*),
Wake Forest University,
Class of 2000

Yippee!!!

ACKNOWLEDGMENTS

As always, I owe many thanks to many people:

To Ira J. Stimson, P.E., and Captain John Gallagher (retired), for input on aircraft design and accident investigation. To Hughes Cicoine, C.F.E.I., for advice on fire and explosion investigation. Your patience was amazing.

To Paul Sledzik, M.S., National Museum of Health and Medicine, Armed Forces Institute of Pathology, on the history, structure, and operation of the DMORT system; Frank A. Ciaccio, M.P.A., Office of Government, Public, and Family Affairs, United States National Transportation Safety Board, for information on DMORT, the NTSB, and the Family Assistance Plan.

To Arpad Vass, Ph.D., Research Scientist, Oak Ridge National Laboratories, for a crash course on volatile fatty acids.

To Special Agent Jim Corcoran, Federal Bureau of Investigation, Charlotte Division, for outlining the workings of the FBI in North Carolina; Detective Ross Trudel (retired), Communauté Urbaine de Montréal Police, for information on explosives and their regulation; Sergent-détective Stephen Rudman (retired), Communauté Urbaine de Montréal Police, for details on police funerals.

To Janet Levy, Ph.D., University of North Carolina-Charlotte, for specifics on the North Carolina Department of Cultural Resources, and answers to questions archaeological; Rachel Bonney, Ph.D., University of North Carolina-Charlotte, and Barry Hipps, Cherokee Historical Association, for knowledge about the Cherokee.

To John Butts, M.D., Chief Medical Examiner, State of North Carolina; Michael Sullivan, M.D., Mecklenburg County Medical Examiner; and Roger Thompson, Director, Charlotte-Mecklenburg Police Department Crime Laboratory.

To Marilyn Steely, M.A., for pointing me to the Hell Fire Club; Jack C. Morgan Jr., M.A.I., C.R.E., for enlightening me on property deeds, maps, and tax records; Irene Bacznsky, for help with airline names.

To Anne Fletcher, for accompanying me on our Smoky Mountain adventure.

A special thanks to the people of Bryson City, North Carolina, including Faye Bumgarner, Beverly Means, and Donna Rowland at the Bryson City library; Ruth Anne Sitton and Bess Ledford at the Swain County Tax and Land Records Office; Linda Cable, Swain County Administrator; Susan Cutshaw and Dick Schaddelee at the Swain County Chamber of Commerce; Monica Brown, Marty Martin and Misty Brooks at the Fryemont Inn; and, especially,

ACKNOWLEDGMENTS

Chief Deputy Jackie Fortner, Swain County Sheriff's Department.

Merci to M. Yves St. Marie, Dr. André Lauzon, and to all my colleagues at the Laboratoire de Sciences Judiciaires et de Médecine Légale; Chancellor James Woodward at the University of North Carolina-Charlotte. Your continued support is greatly appreciated.

To Paul Reichs, for his valuable comments on the manuscript.

To my superb editors, Susanne Kirk and Lynne Drew.

And, of course, to my miracle-worker agent, Jennifer Rudolph Walsh.

My stories could not be what they are without the help of friends and colleagues. I thank them. As always, all mistakes are of my making.

FATAL VOYAGE

1

I STARED AT THE WOMAN FLYING THROUGH THE TREES. Her head was forward, chin raised, arms flung backward like the tiny chrome goddess on the hood of a Rolls-Royce. But the tree lady was naked, and her body ended at the waist. Blood-coated leaves and branches imprisoned her lifeless torso.

Lowering my eyes, I looked around. Except for the narrow gravel road on which I was parked, there was nothing but dense forest. The trees were mostly pine, the few hardwoods like wreaths marking the death of summer, their foliage every shade of red, orange, and yellow.

Though it was hot in Charlotte, at this elevation the early October weather was pleasant. But it would soon grow cool. I took a windbreaker from the backseat, stood still, and listened.

Birdsong. Wind. The scurrying of a small animal.

Then, in the distance, one man calling to another. A muffled response.

Tying the jacket around my waist, I locked the car and set off toward the voices, my feet swishing through dead leaves and pine needles.

Ten yards into the woods I passed a seated figure leaning against a mossy stone, knees flexed to his chest, laptop computer at his side. He was missing both arms, and a small china pitcher protruded from his left temple.

On the computer lay a face, teeth laced with ortho- dontic wiring, one brow pierced by a delicate gold ring. The eyes were open, the pupils dilated, giving the face an expression of alarm. I felt a tremor beneath my tongue, and quickly moved on.

Within yards I saw a leg, the foot still bound in its hiking boot. The limb had been torn off at the hip, and I wondered if it belonged to the Rolls-Royce torso.

Beyond the leg, two men rested side by side, seat belts fastened, necks mushrooming into red blos- soms. One man sat with legs crossed, as if reading a magazine.

I picked my way deeper into the forest, now and then hearing disconnected shouts, carried to me at the wind's whim. Brushing back branches and climbing over rocks and fallen logs, I continued on.

Luggage and pieces of metal lay among the trees. Most suitcases had burst, spewing their contents in random patterns. Clothing, curling irons, and electric shavers were jumbled with containers of hand lotion, shampoo, aftershave, and perfume. One small carry-on had disgorged hundreds of pilfered hotel toiletries. The smell of drugstore products and airplane fuel mingled with the scent of pine and mountain air. And from far off, a hint of smoke.

I was moving through a steep-walled gully whose thick canopy allowed only mottled sunlight to reach the ground. It was cool in the shadows, but sweat dampened my hairline and glued my clothing to my skin. I caught my foot on a backpack and went hurtling forward, tearing my sleeve on a jagged bough truncated by falling debris.

I lay a moment, hands trembling, breath coming in ragged gulps. Though I'd trained myself to hide emotion, I could feel despair rising in me. So much death. Dear God, how many would there be?

Closing my eyes, I centered myself mentally, then pushed to my feet.

Aeons later, I stepped over a rotting log, circled a stand of rhododendron, and, seeming no closer to the distant voices, stopped to get my bearings. The muted wail of a siren told me the rescue operation was gathering somewhere over a ridge to the east.

Way to get directions, Brennan.

But there hadn't been time to ask questions. First responders to airline crashes or other disasters are usually well intentioned, but woefully ill-prepared to deal with mass fatalities. I'd been on my way from Charlotte to Knoxville, nearing the state line, when I'd been asked to get to the scene as quickly as possible. Doubling back on I-40, I'd cut south toward Waynesville, then west through Bryson City, a North Carolina hamlet approximately 175 miles west of Charlotte, 50 miles east of Tennessee, and 50 miles north of Georgia. I'd followed county blacktop to the point where state maintenance ended, then proceeded on gravel to a Forest Service road that snaked up the mountain.

Though the instructions I'd been given had been accurate, I suspected there was a better route, perhaps a small logging trail that allowed a closer approach to the adjacent valley. I debated returning to the car, decided to press on. Perhaps those already at the site had trekked overland, as I was doing. The Forest Service road had looked like it was going nowhere beyond where I'd left the car.

After an exhausting uphill scramble, I grabbed the trunk of a Douglas fir, planted one foot, and heaved myself onto a ridge. Straightening, I stared into the button eyes of Raggedy Ann. The doll was dangling upside down, her dress entangled in the fir's lower branches.

An image of my daughter's Raggedy flashed to mind, and I reached out.

Stop!

I lowered my arm, knowing that every item must be mapped and recorded before removal. Only then could someone claim the sad memento.

From my position on the ridge I had a clear view of what was probably the main crash site. I could see an engine, half buried in dirt and debris, and what looked like pieces of wing flap. A portion of fuselage lay with the bottom peeled back, like a diagram in an instructional manual for model planes. Through the windows I could see seats, some occupied, most empty.

Wreckage and body parts covered the landscape like refuse discarded at a dump. From where I stood, the skin-covered body portions looked starkly pale against the backdrop of forest floor, viscera, and airplane parts. Articles dangled from trees or lay snarled in the leaves and branches. Fabric. Wiring. Sheet metal. Insulation. Molded plastic.

The locals had arrived and were securing the site and checking for survivors. Figures searched among the trees, others stretched tape around the perimeter of the debris field. They wore yellow jackets with *Swain County Sheriff's Department* printed on the back. Still others just wandered or stood in clumps, smoking, talking, or staring aimlessly.

Way off through the trees I noticed the flashing of red, blue, and yellow lights, marking the location of the access route I'd failed to find. In my mind I saw the police cruisers, fire engines, rescue trucks, ambulances, and vehicles of citizen volunteers that would clog that road by tomorrow morning.

The wind shifted and the smell of smoke grew stronger. I turned and saw a thin, black plume curling upward just beyond the next ridge. My stomach tightened, for I was close enough now to detect another odor mingling with the sharp, acrid scent.

Being a forensic anthropologist, it is my job to investigate violent death. I have examined hundreds of fire victims for coroners and medical examiners, and know the smell of charred flesh. One gorge over, people were burning.

I swallowed hard and refocused on the rescue operation. Some who had been inactive were now moving across the site. I watched a sheriff's deputy bend and inspect debris at his feet. He straightened, and an object flashed in his left hand. Another deputy had begun stacking debris.

"Shit!"

I started picking my way downward, clinging to underbrush and zigzagging between trees and boulders to control my balance. The gradient was steep, and a stumble could turn into a headlong plunge.

Ten yards from the bottom I stepped on a sheet of metal that slid and sent me into the air like a snowboarder on a major wipeout. I landed hard and began to half roll, half slide down the slope, bringing with me an avalanche of pebbles, branches, leaves, and pinecones.

To stop my fall, I grabbed for a handhold, skinning my palms and tearing my nails before my left hand struck something solid and my fingers closed around it. My wrist jerked painfully as it took the weight of my body, breaking my downward momentum.

I hung there a moment, then rolled onto my side, pulled with both hands, and scooched myself to a sitting position. Never easing my grasp, I looked up.

The object I clutched was a long metal bar, angling skyward from a rock at my hip to a truncated tree a yard upslope. I planted my feet, tested for traction, and worked my way to a standing position. Wiping bleeding hands on my pants, I retied my jacket and continued downward to level ground.

At the bottom, I quickened my pace. Though my *terra* felt far from *firma,* at least gravity was now on my side. At the cordoned-off area, I lifted the tape and ducked under.

"Whoa, lady. Not so fast."

I stopped and turned. The man who had spoken wore a Swain County Sheriff's Department jacket.

"I'm with DMORT."

"What the hell is DMORT?" Gruff.

"Is the sheriff on site?"

"Who's asking?" The deputy's face was rigid, his mouth compressed into a hard, tight line. An orange hunting cap rested low over his eyes.

"Dr. Temperance Brennan."

"We ain't gonna need no doctor here."

"I'll be identifying the victims."

"Got proof?"

In mass disasters, each government agency has specific responsibilities. The Office of Emergency Preparedness, OEP, manages and directs the National Disaster Medical System, NDMS, which provides medical response and victim identification and mortuary services in the event of a mass fatality incident.

To meet its mission, NDMS created the Disaster

Mortuary Operational Response Team, DMORT, and Disaster Medical Assistance Team, DMAT, systems. In officially declared disasters, DMAT looks after the needs of the living, while DMORT deals with the dead.

I dug out and extended my NDMS identification.

The deputy studied the card, then tipped his head in the direction of the fuselage.

"Sheriff's with the fire chiefs." His voice cracked and he wiped a hand across his mouth. Then he dropped his eyes and walked away, embarrassed to have shown emotion.

I was not surprised at the deputy's demeanor. The toughest and most capable of cops and rescue workers, no matter how extensive their training or experience, are never psychologically prepared for their first major.

Majors. That's what the National Transportation Safety Board dubbed these crashes. I wasn't sure what was required to qualify as a major, but I'd worked several and knew one thing with certainty: Each was a horror. I was never prepared, either, and shared his anguish. I'd just learned not to show it.

Threading toward the fuselage, I passed a deputy covering a body.

"Take that off," I ordered.

"What?"

"Don't blanket them."

"Who says?"

I showed my ID again.

"But they're lying in the open." His voice sounded flat, like a computer recording.

"Everything must remain in place."

"We've got to do something. It's getting dark. Bears are gonna scent on these"—he stumbled for a word—"people."

I'd seen what *Ursus* could do to a corpse and sympathized with the man's concerns. Nevertheless, I had to stop him.

"Everything must be photographed and recorded before it can be touched."

He bunched the blanket with both hands, his face pinched with pain. I knew exactly what he was feeling. The need to do something, the uncertainty as to what. The sense of helplessness in the midst of overwhelming tragedy.

"Please spread the word that everything has to stay put. Then search for survivors."

"You've got to be kidding." His eyes swept the scene around us. "No one could survive this."

"If anyone *is* alive they've got more to fear from bears than these folks do." I indicated the body at his feet.

"And wolves," he added in a hollow voice.

"What's the sheriff's name?"

"Crowe."

"Which one?"

He glanced toward a group near the fuselage.

"Tall one in the green jacket."

I left him and hurried toward Crowe.

The sheriff was examining a map with a half dozen volunteer firefighters whose gear suggested they'd come from several jurisdictions. Even with head bent, Crowe was the tallest in the group. Under the jacket his shoulders looked broad and hard, suggesting regular workouts. I hoped I would not find myself at cross purposes with Sheriff Mountain Macho.

When I drew close the firemen stopped listening and looked in my direction.

"Sheriff Crowe?"

Crowe turned, and I realized that macho would not be an issue.

Her cheeks were high and broad, her skin cinnamon. The hair escaping her flat-brimmed hat was frizzy and carrot red. But what held my attention were her eyes. The irises were the color of glass in old Coke bottles. Highlighted by orange lashes and brows, and set against the tawny skin, the pale green was extraordinary. I guessed her age at around forty.

"And you are?" The voice was deep and gravelly, and suggested its owner wanted no nonsense.

"Dr. Temperance Brennan."

"And you have reason to be at this site?"

"I'm with DMORT."

Again the ID. She studied the card and handed it back.

"I heard a crash bulletin while driving from Charlotte to Knoxville. When I phoned Earl Bliss, who's leader of the Region Four team, he asked me to divert over, see if you need anything."

A bit more diplomatic than Earl's actual comments.

For a moment the woman did not reply. Then she turned back to the firefighters, spoke a few words, and the men dispersed. Closing the gap between us, she held out her hand. The grip could injure.

"Lucy Crowe."

"Please call me Tempe."

She spread her feet, crossed her arms, and regarded me with the Coke-bottle eyes.

"I don't believe any of these poor souls will be needing medical attention."

"I'm a forensic anthropologist, not a medical doctor. You've searched for survivors?"

She nodded with a single upward jerk of her head, the type of gesture I'd seen in India. "I thought something like this would be the ME's baby."

"It's everybody's baby. Is the NTSB here yet?" I knew the National Transportation Safety Board never took long to arrive.

"They're coming. I've heard from every agency on the planet. NTSB, FBI, ATF, Red Cross, FAA, Forest Service, TVA, Department of the Interior. I wouldn't be surprised if the pope himself came riding over Wolf Knob there."

"Interior and TVA?"

"The feds own most of this county; about eighty-five percent as national forest, five percent as reservation." She extended a hand at shoulder level, moved it in a clockwise circle. "We're on what's called Big Laurel. Bryson City's off to the northwest, Great Smoky Mountains National Park's beyond that. The Cherokee Indian Reservation lies to the north, the Nantahala Game Land and National Forest to the south."

I swallowed to relieve the pressure inside my ears.

"What's the elevation here?"

"We're at forty-two hundred feet."

"I don't want to tell you how to do your job, Sheriff, but there are a few folks you might want to keep ou—"

"The insurance man and the snake-bellied lawyer. Lucy Crowe may live on a mountain, but she's been off it once or twice."

I didn't doubt that. I was also certain that no one gave lip to Lucy Crowe.

"Probably good to keep the press out, too."

"Probably."

"You're right about the ME, Sheriff. He'll be here. But the North Carolina emergency plan calls for DMORT involvement for a major."

I heard a muffled boom, followed by shouted orders. Crowe removed her hat and ran the back of her sleeve across her forehead.

"How many fires are still burning?"

"Four. We're getting them out, but it's dicey. The mountain's mighty dry this time of year." She tapped the hat against a thigh as muscular as her shoulders.

"I'm sure your crews are doing their best. They've secured the area and they're dealing with the fires. If there are no survivors, there's nothing else to be done."

"They're not really trained for this kind of thing."

Over Crowe's shoulder an old man in a Cherokee Volunteer PD jacket poked through a pile of debris. I decided on tact.

"I'm sure you've told your people that crash scenes must be treated like crime scenes. Nothing should be disturbed."

She gave her peculiar down-up nod.

"They're probably feeling frustrated, wanting to be useful but unsure what to do. A reminder never hurts."

I indicated the poker.

Crowe swore softly, then crossed to the volunteer, her strides powerful as an Olympic runner's. The man moved off, and in a moment the sheriff was back.

"This is never easy," I said. "When the NTSB arrives they'll assume responsibility for the whole operation."

"Yeah."

At that moment Crowe's cell phone rang. I waited as she spoke.

"Another precinct heard from," she said, hooking the handset to her belt. "Charles Hanover, CEO of Air TransSouth."

Though I'd never flown it, I'd heard of the airline, a small, regional carrier connecting about a dozen cities in the Carolinas, Georgia, and Tennessee with Washington, D.C.

"This is one of theirs?"

"Flight 228 was late leaving Atlanta for Washington, D.C. Sat on the runway forty minutes, took off at twelve forty-five P.M. The plane was at about twenty-five thousand feet when it disappeared from radar at one oh seven. My office got the 911 call around two."

"How many on board?"

"The plane was a Fokker-100 carrying eighty-two passengers and six crew. But that's not the worst of it."

Her next words foretold the horror of the coming days.

2

"THE UGA SOCCER TEAMS?"

Crowe nodded. "Hanover said both the men and women were traveling to matches somewhere near Washington."

"Jesus." Images popped like flashbulbs. A severed leg. Teeth with braces. A young woman caught in a tree.

A sudden stab of fear.

My daughter, Katy, was a student in Virginia, but often visited her best friend in Athens, home of the University of Georgia. Lija was on athletic scholarship. Was it soccer?

Oh, God. My mind raced. Had Katy mentioned a trip? When was her semester break? I resisted the impulse to grab my cell phone.

"How many students?"

"Forty-two passengers booked through the university. Hanover thought most of those were students.

Besides the athletes there would be coaches, trainers, girlfriends, boyfriends. Some fans." She ran a hand across her mouth. "The usual."

The usual. My heart ached at the loss of so many young lives. Then another thought.

"This will be a media nightmare."

"Hanover opened with that concern." Crowe's voice dripped with sarcasm.

"When the NTSB takes over they'll deal with the press."

And with the families, I didn't add. They, too, would be here, moaning and huddling for comfort, some watching with frightened eyes, some demanding immediate answers, belligerence masking their unbearable grief.

At that moment blades whumped, and we saw a helicopter come in low over the trees. I spotted a familiar figure beside the pilot, another silhouette in the rear. The chopper circled twice, then headed in the opposite direction from where I assumed the road to be.

"Where are they going?"

"Hell if I know. We're not oversupplied with landing pads up here." Crowe lowered her gaze and replaced her hat, tucking in frizz with a backhand gesture.

"Coffee?"

Thirty minutes later the chief medical examiner of the State of North Carolina walked into the site from the west, followed by the state's lieutenant governor. The former wore the basic deployment uniform of boots and khaki, the latter a business suit. I watched them pick their way through the debris, the pathologist looking around, assessing, the politician with head bowed, glancing neither left nor right, holding himself gathered tightly, as if contact with his surroundings might draw him in as a participant rather than an observer. At one point they stopped and the ME spoke to a deputy. The man pointed in our direction, and the pair angled toward us.

"Hot damn. A superb photo op." Said with the same sarcasm she'd directed toward Charles Hanover, the Air TransSouth CEO.

Crowe crumpled her Styrofoam cup and jammed it into a thermos bag. I handed her mine, wondering at the vehemence of her disapproval. Did she disagree with the lieutenant governor's politics, or was there personal history between Lucy Crowe and Parker Davenport?

When the men drew close the ME showed ID. Crowe waved it aside.

"No need for that, Doc. I know who you are."

So did I, having worked with Larke Tyrell since his appointment as North Carolina's chief medical examiner in the mid-1980s. Larke was cynical, dictatorial, and one of the best pathologist-administrators in the country. Working with an inadequate budget and a disinterested legislature, he had taken an office in chaos and turned it into one of the most efficient death investigative systems in North America.

My forensic career was in its infancy at the time of Larke's appointment, and I had just qualified for certification by the American Board of Forensic Anthropology. We met through work I was doing for the North Carolina State Bureau of Investigation, reassembling and identifying the corpses of two drug dealers murdered and dismembered by outlaw bikers. I was one of Larke's first hires as a consulting specialist, and had handled the skeletal, the decomposed, the mummified, the burned, and the mutilated dead of North Carolina ever since.

The lieutenant governor extended one hand, pressed a hankie to his mouth with the other. His face was the color of a frog's belly. He said nothing as we shook.

"Glad you're in country, Tempe," said Larke, also crushing my fingers in his grip. I was rethinking this whole handshake business.

Larke's "in country" idiom was Vietnam-era military, his dialect pure Carolina. Born in the low country, Larke grew up in a Marine Corps family, then did two hitches of his own before heading off to medical school. He spoke and looked like a spit-and-polish version of Andy Griffith.

"When do you head north?"

"Next week is fall break," I responded.

Larke's eyes narrowed as he did another sweep of the site.

"I'm afraid Quebec may have to do without its anthropologist this autumn."

A decade back I'd participated in a faculty exchange with McGill University. While in Montreal I'd begun consulting to the Laboratoire de Sciences Judiciaires et de Médecine Légale, Quebec's central crime and medico-legal lab. At the end of my year, recognizing the need for a staff forensic anthropologist, the provincial government had funded a position, equipped a lab, and signed me up on a permanent consultant basis.

I'd been commuting between Quebec and North Carolina, teaching physical anthropology at UNC-Charlotte and consulting to the two jurisdictions, ever since. Because my cases usually involved the less-than-recent dead, this arrangement had worked well. But there was an understanding on both ends that I would be immediately available for court testimony and in crisis situations.

An aviation disaster definitely qualified as a crisis situation. I assured Larke that I would cancel my October trip to Montreal.

"How did you get here so quickly?"

Again I explained my trip to Knoxville and the phone conversation with the DMORT leader.

"I've already talked to Earl. He'll deploy a team up here tomorrow morning." Larke looked at Crowe. "The NTSB boys will be rolling in tonight. Until then everything stays put."

"I've given that order," Crowe said. "This location is pretty inaccessible, but I'll post extra security. Animals will probably be the biggest problem. Especially when these bodies start to go."

The lieutenant governor made an odd sound, spun, and lurched off. I watched him brace against a mountain laurel, bend, and vomit.

Larke fixed us with a sincere Sheriff of Mayberry gaze, shifting his eyes from Crowe to me.

"You ladies are making a very difficult job infinitely easier. Words can't express how much I appreciate your professionalism."

Shift.

"Sheriff, you keep things squared away here."

Shift.

"Tempe, you go on and give your lecture in Knoxville. Then pick up whatever supplies you'll need and report back tomorrow. You're going to be here awhile, so inform the university. We'll secure a bunk for you."

Fifteen minutes later a deputy was dropping me at my car. I'd been right about a better route. A quarter mile up from where I'd parked, a dirt track cut off from the Forest Service road. Once used for hauling timber, the tiny trail meandered around the mountain, allowing access to within a hundred yards of the main crash site.

Vehicles now lined both sides of the logging trail, and we'd passed newcomers on our way downhill. By sunrise both the Forest Service and county roads would be jammed.

As soon as I was behind the wheel I grabbed my cell phone. Dead.

I did a three-point turn and headed down toward the county road. Once on Highway 74, I tried again. The signal was back, so I punched in Katy's number. A machine picked up after four rings.

Uneasy, I left a message, then set the tape in my head to play the "don't-be-an-idiot-mother" lecture. For the next hour I tried to focus on my upcoming presentation, pushing away thoughts of the carnage I'd left behind and the horror I'd face the following day. It was no go. Images of floating faces and severed limbs shattered my concentration.

I tried the radio. Every station carried accounts of the crash. Broadcasters reverently talked of the death of young athletes and solemnly hypothesized as to cause. Since weather did not seem to be a factor, sabotage and mechanical failure were the favored theories.

Hiking out behind Crowe's deputy, I'd spotted a line of sheared-off trees oriented opposite my point of entrance. Though I knew the damage marked the plane's final descent path, I refused to join in the speculation.

I entered I-40, switched stations for the hundredth time, and caught a journalist reporting from overhead a warehouse fire. Chopper sounds reminded me of Larke, and I realized I hadn't asked where he and the lieutenant governor had landed. I stored the question in the back of my brain.

At nine, I redialed Katy.

Still no answer. I rewound the mind tape.

Arriving in Knoxville, I checked in, contacted my host, then ate the Bojangles' chicken I'd picked up on the outskirts of town. I phoned my estranged husband in Charlotte to request care for Birdie. Pete agreed, saying I'd be billed for cat transport and feeding. He hadn't talked to Katy for several days. After delivering a mini-version of my own lecture, he promised to try to reach her.

Next, I phoned Pierre LaManche, my boss at the Laboratoire de Sciences Judiciaires et de Médecine Légale, to report that I would not be in Montreal the following week. He'd heard reports of the crash and was expecting my call. Last, I rang my department chair at UNC-Charlotte.

Responsibilities covered, I spent an hour selecting slides and placing them into carousel trays, then showered and tried Katy again. No go.

I glanced at the clock. Eleven-forty.

She's fine. She's gone out for pizza. Or she's at the library. Yes. The library. I'd used that one many times when I was in school.

It took a very long time to fall asleep.

By morning, Katy hadn't called and was still not picking up. I tried Lija's number in Athens. Another robotic voice requested a message.

I drove to the only anthropology department in America located in a football stadium, and gave one of the more disjointed talks of my career. The host of the guest lecture series listed my DMORT affiliation

« 34 »

in his introduction and mentioned that I would be working the Air TransSouth recovery. Though I could supply little information, follow-up queries largely ignored my presentation and focused on the crash. The question-and-answer period lasted forever.

As the crowd finally milled toward the exits, a scarecrow man in a bow tie and cardigan made straight for the podium, half-moon glasses swinging across his chest. Being in a profession with relatively few members, most anthropologists know one another, and our paths cross and recross at meetings, seminars, and conferences. I'd met Simon Midkiff on several occasions, and knew it would be a long session if I wasn't firm. Looking pointedly at my watch, I gathered my notes, stuffed my briefcase, and descended from the platform.

"How are you, Simon?"

"Excellent." His lips were cracked, his skin dry and flaky, like that of a dead fish lying in the sun. Tiny veins laced the whites of eyes overshadowed by bushy brows.

"How is the archaeology business?"

"Excellent, as well. Since one must eat, I am engaged in several projects for the cultural resources department in Raleigh. But mainly I spend my days organizing data." He gave a high-pitched laugh and tapped a hand to one cheek. "It seems I've collected an extraordinary amount of data throughout my career."

Simon Midkiff earned a doctorate at Oxford in 1955, then came to the United States to accept a position at Duke. But the archaeology superstar published nothing and was denied tenure six years later. Midkiff was given a second chance by the University of Tennessee, again failed to produce publications, and again was let go.

Unable to obtain a permanent faculty position, for thirty years Midkiff had hung around the periphery of academia, doing contract archaeology and teaching courses as replacement instructors were needed at colleges and universities in the Carolinas and Tennessee. He was notorious for excavating sites, filing the requisite reports, then failing to publish his findings.

"I'd love to hear about it, Simon, but I'm afraid I have to run."

"Yes, indeed. Such a terrible tragedy. So many young lives." His head moved sadly from side to side. "Where exactly is the crash?"

"Swain County. And I really must get back." I started to move on, but Midkiff made a subtle shift, blocking my path with a size-thirteen Hush Puppy.

"Where in Swain County?"

"South of Bryson City."

"Perhaps you could be a bit more specific?"

"I can't give you coordinates." I did not mask my irritation.

"Please forgive my beastly rudeness. I've been excavating in Swain County, and I was worried about damage to the site. How selfish of me." Again the giggle. "I apologize."

At that moment my host joined us.

"May I?" He waggled a small Nikon.

"Sure."

I assumed the Kodak smile.

"It's for the departmental newsletter. Our students seem to enjoy it."

He thanked me for the lecture and wished me well with the recovery. I thanked him for the accommodations, excused myself to both men, collected my slide carousels, and hurried from the auditorium.

Before leaving Knoxville I located a sporting goods store and purchased boots, socks, and three pairs of khakis, one of which I put on. At an adjoining pharmacy I grabbed two packages of Hanes Her Way cotton bikinis. Not my brand, but they would do. Shoving the panties and extra khakis into my overnighter, I pointed myself east.

Born in the hills of Newfoundland, the Appalachians parallel the East Coast on their plunge from north to south, splitting near Harpers Ferry, West Virginia, to form the Great Smoky and Blue Ridge chains. One of the world's oldest upland regions, the Great Smoky Mountains rise to over 6,600 feet at Clingmans Dome on the North Carolina–Tennessee border.

Less than an hour out of Knoxville, I'd traversed the Tennessee towns of Sevierville, Pigeon Forge, and Gatlinburg, and was passing east of the dome, awed, as always, by the surreal beauty of the place. Molded by aeons of wind and rain, the Great Smokies roll across the south as a series of gentle valleys and peaks. The forest cover is luxuriant, much of it preserved as national land. The Nantahala. The Pisgah. The Cherokee. The Great Smoky Mountains National Park. The soft, mohair greens and smokelike haze for which these highlands are named create an unparalleled allure. The earth at its best.

Death and destruction amid such dreamlike loveliness was a stark contrast.

Just outside Cherokee, on the North Carolina side, I made another call to Katy. Bad idea. Again, her voice mail answered. Again I left a message: *Phone your mother.*

I kept my mind miles from the task ahead. I thought about the pandas at the Atlanta zoo, the fall lineup on NBC, luggage retrieval at the Charlotte airport. Why was it always so slow?

I thought about Simon Midkiff. What an odd duck. What were the chances a plane would drop precisely on his dig?

Avoiding the radio, I slipped in a CD of Kiri Te Kanawa, and listened to the diva sing Irving Berlin.

It was almost two when I approached the site. A pair of cruisers now blocked the county road just below its junction with the Forest Service road. A National Guardsman directed traffic, sending some motorists up the mountain, ordering others back down. I produced ID, and the guardsman checked his clipboard.

"Yes, ma'am. You're on the list. Park on up at the holding area."

He stepped aside, and I squeezed through a gap between the cruisers.

A holding area had been created from an overlook built to accommodate a fire tower and a small field on the other side of the road. The cliff face had been stripped back to increase the size of the inside tract, and gravel had been spread as a precaution against rain. It was at this location that briefings would take place and relatives counseled until a family assistance center could be established.

Scores of people and vehicles filled both sides of the road. Red Cross trailers. Television vans with satellite dishes. SUVs. Pickups. A hazardous-materials truck. I squeezed my Mazda between a Dodge Durango and a Ford Bronco on the uphill side, grabbed my overnighter, and wove toward the blacktop.

Emerging opposite the overlook, I could see a collapsible school table at the base of the tower, outside one of the Red Cross trailers. A convention-sized coffeemaker gleamed in the sun. Family members huddled around it, hugging and leaning on one another, some crying, others stiffly silent. Many clutched Styrofoam cups, a few spoke into cell phones.

A priest circulated among the mourners, stroking shoulders and squeezing hands. I watched him bend to speak to an elderly woman. With his hunched posture, bald head, and hooked nose he resembled the carrion-eating birds I'd seen on the plains of East Africa, an unfair comparison.

I remembered another priest. Another death watch. That man's sympathetic hovering had extinguished any hope I'd sustained that my grandmother would recover. I recalled the agony of that vigil, and my heart went out to those gathering to claim their dead.

Reporters, cameramen, and soundmen jockeyed for position along the low stone wall bordering the overlook, each team seeking the choicest backdrop for its coverage. As with the 1999 Swissair crash in Peggy's Cove, Nova Scotia, I was certain that scenic panoramas would feature prominently in every broadcast.

Shouldering my bag, I headed downhill. Another guardsman allowed me onto the logging trail, which had been converted overnight to a two-lane gravel road. An access route now led from the expanded trail into the crash site. Gravel crunched underfoot as I walked through the freshly cut tunnel of trees, the scent of pine tainted by the faint odor of early stage putrefaction.

Decontamination trailers and Porta-Johns lined barricades blocking access to the primary site, and an Incident Command Center had been set up inside the restricted area. I could see the familiar NTSB trailer, with its satellite dish and generator shed. Refrigerated trucks were parked beside it, and stacks of body bags lay on the ground. This temporary morgue would be the staging site for transfer of remains to a more permanent incident morgue.

Backhoes, cherry pickers, dump trucks, fire engines, and squad cars were scattered here and there. The solitary ambulance told me that the operation had officially changed from "search and rescue" to "search and recovery." Its vigil was now for injured workers.

Lucy Crowe stood inside the barricades talking with Larke Tyrell.

"How's it going?" I asked.

"My phone never stops." Crowe sounded exhausted. "Almost turned the damn thing off last night."

Over her shoulder I could see the debris field where searchers in masks and Tyvek jumpsuits moved in straight lines, eyes to the ground. Occasionally someone squatted, inspected an item, then marked the spot. Behind the team, red, blue, and yellow flags dotted the landscape like colored pins on a city map.

Other white-suited workers milled around the fuselage, wing tip, and engine, taking pictures, jotting notes, and speaking into tiny Dictaphones. Blue caps identified them as NTSB.

"The gang's all here," I said.

"NTSB, FBI, SBI, FAA, ATF, CBS, ABC. And, of course, the CEO. If they've got letters, they're here."

"This is nothing," said Larke. "Give it a day or two." He peeled back a latex glove and checked his watch.

"Most of the DMORTs are at a briefing at the incident morgue, Tempe, so there's no sense you suiting up now. Let's head in."

I started to object but Larke cut me off.

"We'll walk back together."

While Larke went to decontamination, Lucy gave me directions to the incident morgue. It wasn't necessary. I'd spotted the activity while driving up the county road.

"Alarka Fire Department's about eight miles back. Used to be a school. You'll see swing sets and slides, and the engines parked in a field next door."

On our hike up to the holding area the ME filled me in on recent developments. Foremost among them, the FBI had received an anonymous tip of an onboard bomb.

"Good citizen was kind enough to share this information with CNN. The media are slathering like hounds with a brisket."

"Forty-two dead students is going to make this a Pulitzer event."

"There's the other bad news. Forty-two may be a low number. Turns out more than fifty booked through UGA."

"Have you seen the passenger list?" I could barely get the question out.

"They'll have it at the briefing."

I felt icy cold.

"Yessir," Larke went on. "We screw up on this one, the press will eat us alive."

We separated and hurried to our cars. Somewhere

along the road I drove into a pocket of reception, and my phone beeped. I hit the brakes, afraid of losing the signal.

The message was barely discernible through the static.

"Dr. Brennan, this is Haley Graham, Katy's room-mate. Um. I played your messages, four of them, I think. And Katy's dad. He called a couple of times. Anyway, then I heard about the crash, and"—Rattling—*"well, here's the thing. Katy left for the week-end, and I'm not sure where she is. I know Lija phoned a couple of times earlier this week, so I'm kinda worried that maybe Katy went to visit her. I'm sure that's stupid, but I thought I'd call and ask if you'd talked to her. Well"*—More rattling. *"Anyway. I sound like a geek, but I'd feel better if I knew where Katy was. O.K. 'Bye."*

I punched the autodial for Pete's number. He still had not spoken to our daughter. I dialed again. Lija still did not answer her phone.

The cold fear spread through my chest and curled around my breastbone.

A pickup honked me out of the way.

I continued down the mountain, craving but dreading the upcoming meeting, certain of my first request.

ONE OF DMORT'S FIRST DUTIES IN A MASS DISASTER is the establishment of an incident morgue as close to the scene as possible. Favored sites include coroner and medical examiner offices, hospitals, mortuaries, funeral homes, hangars, warehouses, and National Guard armories.

When I arrived at the Alarka Fire Department, chosen to receive the bodies from Air TransSouth 228, the front lot was already packed, and a score of cars waited at the entrance. I got in line and crept forward, drumming my fingers and looking around.

The back lot had been set aside for the refrigerated trucks that would transport victims. I watched a pair of middle-aged women drape the fence with opaque sheeting in anticipation of photographers, both professional and amateur, who would arrive to violate the privacy of the dead. A breeze twisted and snapped the plastic as they struggled to secure it to the chain linking.

I finally reached the guard, showed ID, and was allowed to park. Inside, dozens of workers were setting up tables, portable X-ray units and developers, computers, generators, and hot water heaters. Bathrooms were being scrubbed and sanitized, and a staff break room and changing areas were being constructed. A conference room had been created in one rear corner. A computer center and the X-ray station were going up in another.

The briefing was in progress when I entered. People lined the makeshift walls and sat around portable tables pushed together in the center of the "room." Fluorescent lights hung by wires from the ceiling, casting a blue tint on tense, pale faces. I slipped to the back and took a seat.

The NTSB investigator in charge, Magnus Jackson, was finishing an Incident Command System overview. The IIC, as Jackson was called, was lean and hard as a Doberman pinscher, with skin almost as dark. He wore oval wire-rimmed glasses; his graying hair was cropped close to his head.

Jackson was describing the NTSB "go team" system. One by one he introduced those heading the investigative groups under his command: structures, systems, power plants, human performance, fire and explosion, meteorology, radar data, event recorders, and witness statements. Investigators, each in a cap and shirt marked *NTSB* in bold yellow letters, rose or waved as Jackson ran down the roster.

Though I knew these men and women would determine why Air TransSouth 228 fell from the sky, the hollow feeling in my chest would not go away, making it hard to concentrate on anything but the passenger list.

A question snapped me back.

"Have the CVR and FDR been located?"

"Not yet."

The cockpit voice recorder captures radio transmissions and sounds in the cockpit, including the pilots' voices and engine noise. The flight data recorder monitors flight operating conditions, such as altitude, airspeed, and heading. Each would play an important role in determining probable cause.

When Jackson finished, an NTSB family affairs specialist discussed the Federal Family Assistance Plan for Aviation Disasters. He explained that the NTSB would serve as liaison between Air TransSouth and the victims' families. A family assistance center was being established at the Sleep Inn in Bryson City to serve as the collecting point for antemortem identification information, facts that family members would provide to help identify remains as those of a son or daughter. Despite myself, I shivered.

Charles Hanover stood next. He looked strikingly ordinary, like a pharmacist and member of the Elks rather than the CEO of a regional airline. His face was ashen and his hands trembled. A tic pulled his left eye, another the corner of his mouth, and one side of his face jumped when the two fired simultaneously. There was something benign and sad about the man, and I wondered how Crowe could have found him offensive.

Hanover reported that Air TransSouth had set up a toll-free number to handle public inquiries. Phones were being installed in the family assistance center, and personnel had been appointed to meet regularly with family members who were present, and to maintain contact with those who were not. Arrangements had been made for mental health and spiritual support.

My agitation grew as the briefing dragged on. I'd heard it all before, and I wanted to see that list.

A representative of the Federal Emergency Management Agency discussed communications. NTSB headquarters, the command center at the crash site, and the incident morgue were now linked, and FEMA would assist the NTSB in the dissemination of public information.

Earl Bliss spoke about DMORT. He was a tall, angular man with thinning brown hair slicked back and severely parted. As a high school student, Earl had taken a part-time job picking up bodies on weekends. Within ten years, he'd purchased his own funeral home. Named Early because of his premature arrival into the world, Earl had lived his entire forty-nine years in Nashville, Tennessee. When not deployed on mass fatality incidents, he favored string ties and played banjo in a country-and-western band.

Earl reminded the representatives of the other agencies that each DMORT team was composed of private citizens with particular expertise, including pathologists, anthropologists, dentists, fingerprint specialists, funeral directors, medical records technicians and transcribers, X-ray technicians, mental health specialists, and security, administrative, and support personnel.

One of the ten regional DMORT teams was activated at the request of local officials for natural disasters, aircraft and other transportation accidents, fires, bombings, terrorist attacks, and incidents of mass murder/suicide. Earl mentioned recent deployments. The bombing of the Murrah Federal Building, Oklahoma City, 1995. The Amtrak derailment, Bourbonnais, Illinois, 1999. Commuter aircraft accidents, Quincy, Illinois, 1996, and Monroe, Michigan, 1997. Korean Air Flight 801, Guam, 1997; Egypt Air Flight 990, Rhode Island, 1999; and Alaska Airlines Flight 261, California, 2000.

I listened as Earl described the modular design of the incident morgue, and explained how remains would move through it. All victims and personal effects would be tagged, coded, photographed, and X-rayed in the remains identification section. Disaster victim packets, DVPs, would be created, and human bodies, body parts, and tissue would be sent on to the postmortem data collection section for autopsy, including anthropological, dental, and fingerprint examination.

All postmortem findings would be computerized in the identification section. Records provided by families would also be entered there, and antemortem and postmortem information would be compared. Following analysis, remains would be sent to a holding area to await release.

Larke Tyrell was the last to take the floor. The medical examiner thanked Earl, drew a deep breath, and surveyed the room.

"Ladies and gentlemen, we've got a lot of grieving families out there searching for peace of mind. Magnus and his boys are going to help them by figuring out what knocked this plane out of the sky. We'll contribute to that process, but our main job here will be victim identification. Having something to bury speeds the healing, and we're going to try our damndest to send a casket home to each and every family."

I remembered my hike through the woods, and knew what many of those coffins would hold. In the coming weeks DMORT, local, and state personnel would go to extraordinary lengths to identify every scrap of tissue associated with the crash. Fingerprints, dental and medical records, DNA, tattoos, and family photos would be the main sources of information, and the team anthropologists would be intimately involved in the ID process. Despite our best efforts, little would be left to put in some caskets. A severed limb. A charred molar crown. A cranial fragment. In many cases, what went home would weigh only grams.

"Once site processing is complete, all remains will be brought here from the temporary morgue," Larke continued. "We expect transport to start in the next few hours. That's when the real work begins for us. You all know your jobs, so I've got just a few reminders, then I'll shut up."

"That'll be a first."

Mild laughter.

"Don't separate any personal effects from any set of remains until they're fully photographed and written up."

My mind slid to Raggedy Ann.

"Not every set of remains will go through every stage of processing. The folks doing intake will decide what goes where. But if a station is skipped, indicate that clearly in the disaster victim packet. I don't want to be guessing later if dental wasn't done because there weren't any teeth, or because that station got overlooked. Put something on every sheet in the packet. And be sure that information stays with the body. We want full documentation on every ID.

"One more thing. As I'm sure you've heard, the FBI received a call about an explosive device. Be alert for blast effects. Check X rays for bomb parts and shrapnel. Examine lungs and eardrums for pressure damage. Look for peppering and flash burns on the skin. You know the drill."

Larke paused and looked around the room.

"Some of you are first-timers, others have done this before. I don't have to tell any of you how hard the next few weeks are going to be. Take breaks. No one works more than twelve hours per day. If you feel overwhelmed, talk to a counselor. There's no weakness in that. These folks are here for your benefit. Use them."

Larke clipped his pen to the legal pad he was holding.

"Guess that about does it, except for thanking my staff and Earl's DMORT folks for getting here so quickly. As for the rest of you, clear out of my morgue."

As the room emptied, I crossed to Larke, determined to ask about the passenger list. Magnus Jackson arrived at the same moment and nodded a greeting. I'd met the IIC while working a commuter crash some years back, and knew he was not one for trading pleasantries.

"Howdy, Tempe," Larke said to me, then turned to Jackson.

"I see you've brought a full team."

"There's going to be a lot of pressure on this one. We'll have close to fifty on site by tomorrow."

I knew that only superficial examination of the wreckage would be done in situ. Once photographed and recorded, the plane's parts would be removed and taken to a permanent location for reassembly and analysis.

"Anything else on the bomb?" Larke asked.

"Hell, it's probably a crank, but the media already has this thing wrapped up slicker than snail spit. CNN's calling him the Blue Ridge Bomber, geography be damned. ABC floated the Soccer Bomber, but it just doesn't have the alliterative ring."

"The FBI's coming on board?" Larke asked.

"They're here, pawing at the fence, so it may not be long."

I broke in, unable to wait another moment.

"Do we have a passenger list?"

The ME slid a printout from his pad and handed it to me.

I experienced a kind of fear I'd rarely felt in my life.

Please, God.

The world receded as I raced through the names. Anderson. Beacham. Bertrand. Caccioli. Daignault. Larke spoke, but his words didn't penetrate.

A lifetime later, I unclamped the teeth from my lower lip and resumed breathing.

Neither Katy Brennan Petersons nor Lija Feldman was on the list.

I closed my eyes and inhaled deeply.

I opened them to questioning looks. Offering no explanation, I returned the printout, the profound relief already blunted by a sense of guilt. My daughter was alive, but the children of others lay dead on a mountain. I wanted to work.

"What would you like me to do?" I asked Larke.

"Earl has the morgue under control. Go work

recovery. But once transport starts I'll need you here."

Back at the site, I went directly to a decontamination trailer and donned mask, gloves, and jumpsuit. Looking more like a spaceman than an anthropologist, I nodded to the guard, circled the barricade, and crossed to the temporary morgue for an update.

The exact location of every flagged item was being entered into a CAD-type program using technology called Total Station. The position of airplane parts, personal effects, and human remains would later be plotted onto virtual grids and printed out as hard copy. Since the technique was far quicker and less labor-intensive than the traditional system of mapping with strings and grids, the removal of remains had already begun. I headed out across the debris field.

The sun was arcing toward the tree line, and delicate shadows spiderwebbed the carnage. Klieg lights had been set up, and the smell of putrefaction had strengthened. Otherwise, little had changed in the time I'd been gone.

For the next three hours I assisted my colleagues in tagging, photographing, and packaging what was left of the passengers of Air TransSouth 228. Complete corpses, limbs, and torsos went into large body bags, fragments into small ones. The bags were then hauled uphill and placed on racks in refrigerated trailers.

The temperature was warm, and I perspired inside my suit and gloves. Flies swarmed, attracted by the rotting flesh. Several times I had to fight nausea as I scraped up entrails or brain tissue. Eventually, my nose and mind numbed. I didn't notice when the sky went red and the lights clicked on.

Then I came to the girl. She lay face up, legs bent backward in the middle of her shins. Her features had been gnawed, and the exposed bone glowed crimson in the sunset.

I straightened, wrapped my arms around my middle, and drew several steadying breaths. In, out. In, out.

Dear God. Wasn't a thirty-thousand-foot plunge enough? Must creatures degrade what remained?

These children had danced, played tennis, ridden the roller coaster, checked their e-mail. They represented the dreams of their parents. But no longer. Now they would be framed photos resting on closed caskets.

I felt a hand on my shoulder.

"Time for a break, Tempe."

Earl Bliss's eyes peered at me from the slit between his mask and cap.

"I'm fine."

"Take a break. That's an order."

"O.K."

"At least an hour."

Halfway to the NTSB command center I stopped, dreading the chaos I knew I'd find. I needed serenity. Life. Birds singing, squirrels chasing, and air that was free of the smell of death. I reversed direction and walked toward the woods.

Skirting the edge of the debris field, I spotted a

break in the trees and remembered that Larke and the lieutenant governor had appeared at that point, coming from their helicopter. Up close, I could see the route they had probably taken. Perhaps a trail or streambed at one time, it was now a meandering, treeless passage littered with rocks and bordered by scrub. Stripping off mask and gloves, I headed into the forest.

As I moved deeper into the trees the organized hubbub around the wreckage receded, and forest sounds took over. Thirty yards in, I climbed onto a fallen sourwood, drew my feet to my bum, and gazed up at the sky. Yellow and rose now streaked the red as nightfall crawled toward the horizon. It would soon be dark. I couldn't stay long.

I let my brain cells pick their topic.

The girl with the ravaged face.

No. New category.

The cells chose living people.

Katy. My daughter was over twenty now, moving off on a life of her own. It was what I wanted, of course, but the severing of ties was hard. The child Katy had passed through my life and disappeared. I was now meeting the young woman Katy, and liking her very much.

But where is she? the cells asked.

Next.

Pete. We were better friends separated than we'd ever been married. On occasion, he actually talked to me and listened to me. Should I ask for a divorce and move on, or roll with the status quo?

The cells had no answer.

Andrew Ryan. I'd been thinking of him a lot lately. Ryan was a homicide detective with the provincial police in Montreal. Though we'd known each other for nearly a decade, it was only last year that I'd agreed to date him.

Date. I had my usual cringe reaction. There had to be a better term for singles over forty.

The cells had no suggestion.

Nomenclature aside, Ryan and I had never pulled it off. Before our first official social outing, he had gone undercover, and I hadn't seen him in months. At times like this, I missed him intensely.

I heard rustling in the underbrush and held my breath to listen. The woods were quiet. Seconds later I heard it again, this time on my other side. The movement sounded too large for a rabbit or squirrel.

The brain cells sounded a low-level alarm.

Thinking perhaps Earl had followed me, I stood up and looked around. I was alone.

For a full minute nothing moved, then the rhododendron to my right jiggled, and I heard a low growl. I whirled but saw only leaves and bushes. Eyes probing into the shrubbery, I slipped off the log and planted my feet.

Moments later there was another growl, followed by a high-pitched keening.

The cells called in the limbic guys, and adrenaline shot to every part of my body.

Slowly, I squatted and reached for a rock. Hearing movement behind me, I pivoted in that direction.

My eyes met other eyes, black and gleaming. Lips curled back over teeth pale and slick in the deepening twilight. Between the teeth, something horrifyingly familiar.

A foot.

The cells struggled for meaning.

The teeth were embedded in a human foot.

The cells linked to recently stored memories. A mangled face. A deputy's comment.

Oh, God! A wolf? I was unarmed. What to do? Threaten?

The animal stared at me, its body feral and emaciated.

Run?

No. I had to get the foot. It belonged to a person. A person with family and friends. I wouldn't abandon it to scavengers.

Then a second wolf emerged and positioned itself behind the first, teeth bared, saliva darkening the fur around its mouth. It snarled and the lips quivered. Slowly, I stood and raised the rock.

"Back!"

Both animals halted, and the first wolf dropped the foot. Sniffing the air, the ground, the air again, it lowered its head, raised its tail, took a step in my direction, then sidled away a few feet and stopped, motionless and watching. The other wolf followed. Were they uncertain or did they have a plan? I started to retreat, heard a snap, and turned to see three more animals at my back. They appeared to be slowly circling.

"Stop!"

I screamed and threw the rock, catching the closest animal near its eye. He yelped and twisted, scampering backward. The others froze for a moment, then resumed circling.

Placing my back to the fallen tree, I twisted a branch from side to side, trying to detach it.

The circle was getting smaller. I could hear their panting, smell their bodies. One of the group took a step inside the circle, then another, flicking its tail up, down. It stood staring, soundless.

The branch broke, and at the sound the wolf jumped back, then stood again and stared.

Grasping my branch like a baseball bat, I screamed, "Beat it, you scavengers. Get out of here," and lunged at the lead wolf, swinging my club.

The wolf easily jumped out of the way, retreated a few feet, then resumed circling and snarling. As I was readying my lungs for the loudest yell that had ever escaped them, someone beat me to it.

"Scram, you goddamn fur balls. Yo! Haul ass!"

Then one missile followed by another landed near the lead wolf.

The wolf scented, snarled, then spun and loped off into the underbrush. The others hesitated, then moved off behind him.

Hands trembling, I dropped the branch and braced myself against the fallen sourwood.

A figure in Tyvek and mask ran toward me and heaved another rock in the direction of the disappearing wolves. Then a hand went up and removed the mask. Though barely visible in the twilight gloom, I recognized the face.

But it couldn't be. This was too improbable to be real.

4

"Nice swing. You looked like Sammy Sosa."

"The goddamn thing was getting ready to go for my throat!" It was almost a shriek.

"They don't attack live people. They were only trying to drive you away from their dinner."

"Did one of them explain that to you personally?"

Andrew Ryan plucked a leaf from my hair.

But Ryan was underground somewhere in Quebec.

"What in hell are you doing here?" Slightly calmer.

"Is that a thank-you, Goldilocks? Maybe Riding Hood would be more appropriate, given the circumstances."

"Thanks," I mumbled, brushing bangs off my forehead. Though I *was* grateful for the intervention, I preferred not to cast it as a rescue.

"Nice do."

He reached for my hair again, and I parried the

move. As usual when our paths crossed, I was not looking my best.

"I'm scraping up quarts of brain matter, and a wolf pack was just sizing me up as a candidate for joining the dismembered, and you find fault with my styling gel?"

"Is there a reason you're out here by yourself?"

His paternalism irritated me. "Is there a reason you're here at all?"

The lines in his face tensed. Such nice lines, each placed exactly where it ought to be.

"Bertrand was on the plane."

"Jean?"

The passenger list. Bertrand. It was a common name, so I'd never thought of Ryan's partner.

"He was escorting a prisoner." Ryan drew air through his nostrils, exhaled. "They were connecting to an Air Canada flight at Dulles."

"Oh, God. Oh, my God. I am so sorry."

We stood mute, unsure what to say, until the silence was pierced by an eerie, quavering sound, followed by a series of high-pitched yips. Were our friends challenging us to a rematch?

"We'd better get back," Ryan said.

"No argument here."

Ryan unzipped his jumpsuit, took a flashlight from his belt, flicked the switch, and raised it to shoulder level.

"After you."

"Wait. Let me have the light."

He handed it to me, and I crossed to the spot where I'd first seen the wolf.

Ryan followed.

"If you're hunting mushrooms, this is not a good time."

He stopped when he saw what lay on the ground.

The foot looked macabre in the yellow beam, its flesh ending in a crushed mass just above the ankle. Shadows danced in and out of the grooves and pits left by carnivore teeth.

Pulling fresh gloves from my pocket, I snapped one on and picked up the foot. Then I marked the spot with another glove and secured it with a rock.

"Shouldn't it be mapped?"

"We can't tell where the pack found this. Besides, if we leave the thing here it's puppy chow."

"You're the boss."

I followed Ryan out of the woods, holding the foot as far from my body as possible.

When we got back to the command center, Ryan went into the NTSB trailer and I took my find to the temporary morgue. After hearing my explanation of its provenance and why I'd collected it, the intake team assigned it a number, bagged it, and sent it to one of the refrigerated trucks. I rejoined the recovery operation.

Two hours later Earl found me and delivered a note: *Report to the morgue. 7 A.M. LT.*

He produced an address and told me I was done for

the day. No amount of argument would change his mind.

I went to decontamination, showered under scalding water for as long as I could take it, and put on fresh clothes. I left the trailer with Christmas-bow skin, but at least the smell was gone.

Clomping down the steps, as exhausted as I'd ever been, I noticed Ryan leaning against a bubble-top cruiser ten feet up the access road, talking with Lucy Crowe.

"You look beat," said Crowe when I drew near.

"I'm good," I said. "Earl pulled me in."

"How's it going out there?"

"It's going."

I felt like a midget talking to them. Both Ryan and Crowe topped six feet, though she had him beat in shoulder breadth. He looked like a point guard; she was a power forward.

Not in a mood to chat, I asked Crowe for directions and excused myself.

"Hold it, Brennan."

I allowed Ryan to catch up, then gave him a "don't bring it up" look. I did not want to discuss wolves.

As we walked, I thought of Jean Bertrand, with his designer jackets, matching ties, and earnest face. Bertrand always gave the impression he was trying too hard, listening too closely, afraid to miss an important clue or nuance. I could hear him, flipping from French to English in his own personal brand of

Franglais, laughing at his own jokes, unaware that others weren't.

I remembered the first time I'd met Bertrand. Shortly after arriving in Montreal, I'd gone to a Christmas party hosted by the SQ homicide unit. Bertrand was there, mildly drunk, and newly partnered with Andrew Ryan. The hotshot detective was already something of a legend, and Bertrand's veneration flowed undisguised. By evening's end the hero worship had grown embarrassing for everyone. Especially Ryan.

"How old was he?" I voiced the question without thinking.

"Thirty-seven." Ryan was right there in the middle of my thoughts.

"Jesus."

We reached the county road and headed uphill.

"Whom was he escorting?"

"A guy named Rémi Petricelli, known to his friends as Pepper."

I knew the name. Petricelli was a bigwig in the Quebec Hells Angels, reputed to have ties to organized crime. The Canadian and American governments had been investigating him for years.

"What was Pepper doing in Georgia?"

"About two months ago a small-time trafficker named Jacques Fontana ended up charcoal in a Subaru Outback. When every road led to his door, Pepper decided to sample the hospitality of his brothers in Dixie. Long story short, Pepper was spotted in a bar in Atlanta, the locals nailed him, and last week Georgia agreed to extradite. Bertrand was hauling his ass back to Quebec."

We'd arrived at my car. Across at the overlook, a spotlighted man held a mike while an assistant powdered his face.

"Which brings more players to the table," Ryan went on, his voice leaden.

"Meaning?"

"Pepper had juice. If he'd decided to deal, a lot of his friends would be in deep-dish shit."

"I'm not following."

"Some powerful people probably wanted Pepper dead."

"Enough to kill eighty-seven other people?"

"Without a hitch in their breathing."

"But that plane was full of kids."

"These guys aren't the Jesuits."

I was too shocked to respond.

Seeing my face, Ryan switched tacks. "Hungry?"

"I need to sleep."

"You need to eat."

"I'll stop for a burger," I lied.

Ryan stepped back. I unlocked my door and drove off, too tired and heartsick to say good night.

Since every room in the area had been grabbed by the press and NTSB, I was booked into a small B & B on the outskirts of Bryson City. It took several wrong turns and two inquiries to find it.

True to its name, High Ridge House sat atop a summit at the end of a long, narrow lane. It was a two-story white farmhouse with intricate woodwork on the doors and windows, and on the beams, banisters, and railings of a wide veranda wrapping around the front and sides. In the porch light I could see wooden rockers, wicker planters, ferns. Very Victorian.

I added my car to a half dozen others in a postage-stamp lot to the left of the house, and followed a flag-stone path flanked by metal lawn chairs. Bells jangled as I opened the front door. Inside, the house smelled of wood polish, Pine-Sol, and simmering lamb.

Irish stew is perhaps my favorite dish. As usual, it brought Gran to mind. Twice in two days? Maybe the old girl was looking down.

In moments a woman appeared. She was middle-aged, about five feet tall, with no makeup and thick gray hair pulled into an odd sausage roll on the top of her head. She wore a long denim skirt and a red sweatshirt with *Praise the Lord* scrolled across her chest.

Before I could speak, the woman embraced me. Surprised, I stood angled down with hands out, trying not to strike her with my overnighter or laptop.

After a decade the woman stepped back and gazed at me with the intensity of a player receiving serve at Wimbledon.

"Dr. Brennan."

"Tempe."

"It's the Lord's work you're doing for these poor dead children."

I nodded.

"Precious in the sight of the Lord is the death of his saints. He tells us that in the Book of Psalms."

Oh, boy.

"I'm Ruby McCready, and I'm honored to have you at High Ridge House. I intend to look after each and every one of you."

I wondered who else was quartered there, but said nothing. I would find out soon enough.

"Thank you, Ruby."

"Let me take that." She reached for my bag. "I'll show you to your room."

My hostess led me past a parlor and dining room, up a carved wooden staircase, and down a corridor with closed doors on either side, each bearing a small hand-painted plaque. We made a ninety-degree turn at the far end of the hall and stopped in front of a single door. Its nameplate said *Magnolia.*

"Since you're the only lady, I put you in Magnolia." Though we were alone, Ruby's voice had become a whisper, her tone conspiratorial. "It's the only one with its own WC. I reckoned you'd appreciate the privacy."

WC? Where in the world did they still refer to bathrooms as water closets?

Ruby followed me in, placed my satchel on the

bed, and began fluffing pillows and lowering shades like a bellman at the Ritz.

The fabric and wallpaper explained the floral appellation. The window was draped, the tables skirted, and ruffles adorned every edge in the room. The maple rocker and bed were stacked with pillows, and a million figurines filled a glass-fronted cabinet. On top sat ceramic renderings of Little Orphan Annie and her dog, Sandy, Shirley Temple dressed as Heidi, and a collie I assumed to be Lassie.

My taste in home furnishings tends toward the simple. Though I have never cared for the starkness of modern, give me Shaker or Hepplewhite and I am happy. Surround me with clutter and I start to get itchy.

"It's lovely," I said.

"I'll leave you to yourself now. Dinner's at six, so you missed that, but I left stew to simmerin'. Would you like a bowl?"

"No, thank you. I'm going to turn in."

"Have you eaten dinner?"

"I'm not very hungr—"

"Look at you, you're thin as the broth at a homeless shelter. You can't go with nothin' on your stomach."

Why was everyone so concerned with my diet?

"I'll bring up a tray."

"Thank you, Ruby."

"I don't need thankin'. One last thing. We've got no locks here at High Ridge House, so you come and go as you like."

Though I'd showered at the site, I unpacked my few things and took a long, hot bath. Like rape victims, those who clean up after mass fatalities often overbathe, driven by a need to purge mind and body.

I came out of the bathroom to stew, brown bread, and a mug of milk. My cell phone rang as I was poking at a turnip. Fearing the messaging service would kick in, I lunged for my purse, dumped its contents onto the bed, and fished through hair spray, wallet, passport, organizer, sunglasses, keys, and makeup. I finally found the phone and clicked on, praying the caller was Katy.

It was. My daughter's voice triggered such emotion in me, I had to struggle to keep my voice steady.

Though evasive about her whereabouts, she sounded happy and healthy. I gave her the number at High Ridge House. She told me she was with a friend and would return to Charlottesville on Sunday night. I didn't request, nor did she offer, the gender specifics of her pal.

The soap and water, combined with the long-awaited call from my daughter, had done the trick. Almost giddy with relief, I was suddenly famished. I devoured Ruby's stew, set my travel alarm, and fell into bed.

Maybe the House of Chintz wouldn't be so bad.

The next morning I rose at six, put on clean khakis, brushed my teeth, dabbed on blush, and drew my hair up under a Charlotte Hornets' cap. Good enough.

I headed downstairs, intending to ask Ruby about laundry arrangements.

Andrew Ryan occupied a bench at a long pine table in the dining room. I took a chair opposite, returned Ruby's cheery "Good morning," and waited while she poured coffee. When the kitchen door swung closed behind her, I spoke.

"What are you doing here?"

"Is that all you ever say to me?"

I waited.

"The sheriff recommended this place."

"Above all others."

"It's nice," he said, gesturing around the room. "Loving." He raised his mug to a message above our heads: *Jesus Is Love* had been burned into knotty pine and varnished for posterity.

"How did you know I was here?"

"Cynicism causes wrinkles."

"It doesn't. Who told you?"

"Crowe."

"What's wrong with the Comfort Inn?"

"Full."

"Who else is here?"

"There are a couple of NTSB boys upstairs and a special agent from the FBI. What makes them special?"

I ignored that.

"I'm looking forward to guy-bonding in the bathroom. Two others are on the main floor, and I hear there are some journalists squeezed into a bonus room in the basement."

"How did you get a room here?"

The Viking blues went little-boy innocent. "Must have been lucky timing. Or maybe Crowe has pull."

"Don't even think about using my bathroom."

"Cynicism."

Ruby arrived with ham, eggs, fried potatoes, and toast. Though my normal routine is cereal and coffee, I dug in like a recruit at boot camp.

Ryan and I ate in silence while I did some mental sorting. His presence annoyed me, but why? Was it his supreme self-confidence? His custodial attitude? His invasion of my turf? The fact that less than a year ago he'd prioritized the job over me and disappeared from my life? Or the fact that he'd reappeared exactly when I'd needed help?

As I reached for toast I realized he'd said nothing about his stint undercover. Fair enough. Let him bring it up.

"Jam, please."

He passed it.

Ryan *had* gotten me out of a nasty spot.

I spread blackberry preserves thicker than lava.

The wolves weren't Ryan's fault. Nor was the crash.

Ruby poured refills.

And the man *has* just lost his partner, for God's sake.

Compassion overrode irritation.

"Thanks for your help with the wolf thing."

"They weren't wolves."

"What?" Irritation boomeranged back.

"They weren't wolves."

"I suppose it was a pack of cocker spaniels."

"There are no wolves in North Carolina."

"Crowe's deputy talked about wolves."

"The guy probably wouldn't know a wombat from a caribou."

"Wolves have been reintroduced into North Carolina." I was sure I'd read that somewhere.

"Those are red wolves and they're on a reserve down east, not in the mountains."

"I suppose you're an expert on North Carolina wildlife."

"How did they hold their tails?"

"What?"

"Did the animals hold their tails up or down?"

I had to think.

"Down."

"A wolf holds its tail straight out. A coyote keeps its tail low, raises it to horizontal when threatening."

I pictured the animal sniffing, then raising its tail and locking me into its gaze.

"You're telling me those were coyotes?"

"Or wild dogs."

"There are coyotes in Appalachia?"

"There are coyotes all over North America."

"So what?" I made a mental vow to check.

"So nothing. I just thought you might want to know."

"It was still terrifying."

"Damn right. But it's not the worst thing you've ever been through."

Ryan was right. Though frightening, the coyote incident was not my worst experience. But the days that followed were contenders. I spent every waking moment up to my elbows in shattered flesh, separating commingled remains and reassociating body parts. As part of a team of pathologists, dentists, and other anthropologists, I determined age, sex, race, and height, analyzed X rays, compared antemortem and postmortem skeletal features, and interpreted injury patterns. It was a gruesome task, made even grimmer by the youth of most of those being analyzed.

For many, the stress was too much. Some hung in, running on the rim until tremors, tears, or unbearable nightmares finally won out. These were the ones who would require extensive counseling. Others simply packed up and slipped back home.

But for most, the mind adjusted and the unthinkable became the ordinary. We mentally detached and did what needed doing. Each night as I lay in bed, lonely and exhausted, I was comforted by the day's progress. I thought of the families, and assured myself that the system was working. We would grant them closure of sorts.

Then specimen number 387 arrived at my station.

5

I'D FORGOTTEN THE FOOT UNTIL A BODY TRACKER brought it to me.

Ryan and I had rarely crossed paths since our first breakfast. I'd been up and gone each day before seven, returning to High Ridge House long after dark to shower and collapse into bed. We'd exchanged only "Good morning" or "Have a good one," and we'd yet to discuss his time undercover or his role in the crash investigation. Because a Quebec law officer had been on the plane, the Canadian government had asked that Ryan be involved. All I knew was that the request had been granted.

Blocking thoughts of Ryan and coyotes, I emptied the body bag onto my table. In recent days I'd processed dozens of severed limbs and appendages, and the foot no longer seemed macabre. In fact, the frequency of lower leg and ankle trauma was so high it had been discussed at that morning's meeting. The pathologists and anthropologists agreed that the injury pattern was disturbing.

There is little one can say from eyeballing a foot. This one had thickened yellow nails, a large bunion, and lateral displacement of the big toe, indicating an older adult. The size suggested female gender. Though the skin was the color of toast, I knew this meant nothing since even short-term exposure can bleach or darken flesh.

I popped the X rays onto a light box. Unlike many of the films I'd viewed, these revealed no foreign objects embedded in the foot. I noted that on a form in the disaster victim packet.

The cortical bone was thin, and I could see remodeling at many of the phalangeal joints.

O.K. The lady was old. Arthritis and bone loss fit with the bunion.

Then I got my first surprise. The X ray showed tiny white clouds floating among the toe bones, and scooped-out lesions at the margins of the first and second metatarso-phalangeal joints. I recognized the symptoms immediately.

Gout results from inadequate uric acid metabolism, leading to the deposition of urate crystals, particularly in the hands and feet. Nodules form adjacent to joints, and, in chronic cases, the underlying bone is eroded. The condition is not life-threatening, but those affected experience intermittent periods of pain and swelling. Gout is relatively common, with 90 percent of all cases occurring in men.

So why was I seeing it in a female?

I returned to the table, picked up a scalpel, and got my second surprise.

Though refrigeration can cause drying and shrinkage, the foot looked different from the remains I'd been seeing. Even in the charred bodies and body parts I'd examined, the deep tissue remained firm and red. But the flesh inside the foot was soupy and discolored, as though something had accelerated its rate of decomposition. I made a note, planning to seek other opinions.

Using my scalpel, I teased back muscle and tendon until I could position my calipers directly against the largest bone, the calcaneus. I measured its length and breadth, then the length of a metatarsal, and jotted the figures onto a form in the disaster victim packet, and onto a page in a spiral pad.

Stripping off my gloves, I washed, then took the tablet to my laptop in the staff lounge. I called up a program called Fordisc 2.0, entered the data, and asked for a discriminant function analysis using the two calcaneal measurements.

The foot classified as that of a black male, though the typicality and posterior probabilities indicated the results were meaningless. I tried a male–female comparison, independent of ancestry, and the program again placed the foot in the male range.

O.K. Jockey shorts fit with gout. Maybe the guy was small. Atypical size could explain the weakness of the racial classification.

Returning for the packet, I crossed to the identification section, where a dozen computers sat on tables, and bundled wires snaked across the floor. A records specialist worked at each terminal, entering data obtained from the family assistance center and information provided by the forensic specialists, including fingerprint, X ray, anthropology, pathology, and dental details.

I spotted a familiar figure, half-moon glasses on the end of her nose, upper teeth nibbling her lower lip. Primrose Hobbs had been an ER nurse for over thirty years when she switched from defibrillators to data sets and moved to the medical records department at Presbyterian Hospital in Charlotte. But she hadn't severed herself completely from the world of traumatic injury. When I joined DMORT, Primrose was already a seasoned member of the Region Four team. Past sixty, she was patient, efficient, and shocked by absolutely nothing.

"Can we run one?" I asked, dragging a folding chair next to hers.

"Hang on, baby." Primrose continued to type, her face illuminated by the screen's glow. Then she closed a folder and turned to me.

"What have you got?"

"A left foot. Definitely old. Probably male. Possibly black."

"Let's see who needs a foot."

DMORT relies on a software package called VIP, which tracks the progress of remains, stores all data, and facilitates the comparison of antemortem and postmortem information. The program handles more than 750 unique identifiers for each victim, and stores digital records such as photographs and radiographs. For each positive identification, VIP creates a document containing all parameters used.

Primrose worked the keys and a postmortem grid appeared. The first column showed a list of case numbers. She moved sideways through the grid to a column headed "Body Parts Not Recovered" and scrolled down. To date, four bodies had been logged without a left foot. Primrose moved through the grid, highlighting each.

Number 19 was a white male with an estimated age of thirty. Number 38 was a white female, with an estimated age of twenty. Number 41 was an African-American female with an estimated age of twenty-five. Number 52 was a male lower torso, African American, with an estimated age of forty-five.

"It could be fifty-two," I said.

Primrose scrolled to the height and weight columns. The gentleman tagged as number 52 was estimated to have stood six feet two inches and weighed two hundred and fifty pounds.

"No way," I corrected myself. "This is not a sumo tootsie."

Primrose leaned back and removed her glasses. Frizzy gray hairs spiraled out at her forehead and temples, escapees from the bun atop her head.

"This event is more dental than DNA, but I've logged

quite a few isolated body parts." She let the glasses drop onto a chain around her neck. "So far we've had few matches. That will improve as more bodies flow through, but you may have to wait for DNA."

"I know. I hoped we might get lucky."

"You're sure it's male?"

I explained the discriminant function analysis.

"So the program takes your unknown and compares it to groups for whom measurements have been recorded."

"Exactly."

"And this foot fell in with the boys."

"Yes."

"Maybe the computer got it wrong."

"That's very possible since I'm not sure about the race."

"That matters?"

"Sure. Some populations are smaller than others. Look at the Mbuti."

She raised gray eyebrows.

"The pygmies of the Ituri rain forest," I explained.

"We've got no pygmies here, sugar."

"No. But there might have been Asians on board. Some Asian populations are smaller than Westerners, so they'd tend to have smaller feet."

"Not like my dainty size tens." She lifted a booted foot and laughed.

"What I do feel certain about is the age. This person was over fifty. Quite a bit over, I think."

"Let's check the passenger list."

She replaced the glasses, hit keys, and an ante-mortem grid appeared on the screen. This spread sheet was similar to the postmortem grid except that most of its cells contained information. There were columns for first name, last name, date of birth, blood type, sex, race, weight, height, and myriad other variables. Primrose clicked to the age column and asked the program to sort by that criterion.

Air TransSouth 228 had carried only six passengers over the age of fifty.

"So young for the good Lord to be callin' 'em home."

"Yeah," I said, staring at the screen.

We were silent a moment, then Primrose moved the cursor and we both leaned in.

Four males. Two females. All white.

"Let's sort by race."

The antemortem grid showed sixty-eight whites, ten African Americans, two Hispanics, and two Asians among the passengers. The entire cabin crew and both pilots were white. None of the blacks was over forty. Both Asians were in their early twenties, probably students. Masako Takaguchi had been lucky. She'd died in one piece and was already identified.

"I guess I'd better try another approach. For now you can enter an age estimate of fifty plus. And the victim had gout."

"My ex has gout. Only human thing about that man." Another laugh, straight from the belly.

"Mmm. Could I ask one other favor?"

"Sure, baby."

"Check Jean Bertrand."

She found the row and moved the cursor to the status column.

To date, Bertrand's body had not been identified.

"I'll be back when I know more on this one," I said, collecting the packet for number 387.

Returning to the foot, I removed and tagged a small plug of bone. If a reference sample could be found, an old gallstone, a Pap smear, hair or dandruff from a brush or comb, DNA might prove useful in establishing identity. If not, DNA testing could determine gender, or could link the foot to other body parts, and a tattoo or dental crown might send the victim home.

As I sealed the specimen bag and made notes in the file, something bothered me. Was the computer in error? Could I have been right in my initial impression that the foot belonged to a woman? Very possible. It happened all the time. But what about age? I was certain these were the bones of an older person, yet no one on the plane fit that profile. Could some pathology other than gout be skewing my assessment?

And what about the advanced putrefaction?

I cut a second slice of bone from the highest intact point on the tibia, tagged and sealed it. If the foot remained unidentified, I would attempt a more precise age estimate using histological features. But microscopic analysis would have to wait. Slides were being made at the ME facility in Charlotte, and the backlog was monumental.

I rebagged the foot, returned it to the body tracker in charge of the case, and moved on, continuing with a day identical to the previous four. Hour after hour I sorted bodies and body parts, probing their most intimate details. I didn't notice when others came and went, or when daylight dimmed in the windows high above our heads.

I'd lost all track of time when I glanced up to see Ryan rounding a stack of pine caskets at the far end of the fire station. He walked to my table, his face as tense as I'd ever seen it.

"How's it going?" I asked, lowering my mask.

"It'll be a bloody decade before this is sorted out."

His eyes were dark and shadowed, his face as pale as the flesh that lay between us. I was shocked by the change. Then, realization. While my grief was for strangers, Ryan's pain was personal. He and Bertrand had partnered for almost a decade.

I wanted to say something comforting, but all I could think of was "I'm so sorry about Jean."

He nodded.

"Are you all right?" I asked gently.

His jaw muscles bulged, relaxed.

I reached across the table, wanting to take his hand, and we both looked at my bloody glove.

"Whoa, Quincy, no gestures of sympathy."

The comment broke the tension.

"I was afraid you'd pocket the scalpel," I said, snatching up the implement.

"Tyrell says you're done for the day."

"But I—"

"It's eight o'clock. You've been here thirteen hours."

I looked at my watch.

"Meet me back at the temple of love and I'll update you on the investigation."

My back and neck ached, and my eyelids felt like they'd been lined with sand. I placed both hands on my hips and arched backward.

"Or I could help you"—When I returned to vertical Ryan's eyes locked onto mine and his brows flicked up and down—"relax."

"I'll be asleep before I hit the pillow."

"You've got to eat."

"Jesus, Ryan, what is this concern with my nutrition? You're worse than my mother."

At that moment I spotted Larke Tyrell waving at me. He pointed to his watch then made a slicing movement across his throat. I nodded and gave him a thumbs-up.

Telling Ryan that I'd take the briefing, and only the briefing, I zipped the remains into their pouch, made notes in the disaster victim packet, and returned everything to the body tracker. Stripping down to my street clothes, I washed and headed out.

Forty minutes later Ryan and I sat with meat loaf sandwiches in the kitchen of High Ridge House. He'd just voiced his third complaint concerning the absence of beer.

"The drunkard and the glutton shall come to poverty," I replied, pounding on a ketchup bottle.

"Says who?"

"According to Ruby, the Book of Proverbs."

"I will make it a felony to drink small beer." The weather had cooled and Ryan was wearing a ski sweater, the cornflower blue a perfect match for his eyes.

"Did Ruby say that?"

"Shakespeare. *Henry VI.*"

"Your point being?"

"Like the king, Ruby is being autocratic."

"Tell me about the investigation." I took a bite of my sandwich.

"What do you want to know?"

"Have the black boxes been recovered?"

"They're orange. You have ketchup on your chin."

"Have the flight recorders been found?" I blotted my face, wondering how a man could be so attractive and so annoying at the same time.

"Yes."

"And?"

"They've been sent to the NTSB lab in Washington, but I've listened to a copy of the cockpit voice recording. Worst twenty-two minutes I've ever spent."

I waited.

"The FAA has a sterile cockpit rule below ten thousand feet, so for the first eight minutes or so the pilots are all business. After that they're more relaxed, responding to air traffic controllers, chatting about their kids, their lunch, their golf games. Suddenly there's a pop, and everything changes. They're breathing hard and shouting to each other."

He swallowed.

"In the background you hear beeps then chirps then wails. A member of the recorders group identified each sound as we listened. Autopilot disconnect. Overspeed. Altitude alert. Apparently that meant they'd managed to level off for a while. You hear all this and you picture those guys struggling to save their plane. Shit."

He swallowed again.

"Then there's this chilling whooping noise. The ground proximity warning. Then a loud crunch. Then nothing."

Somewhere in the house a door slammed, then water ran through pipes.

"You know how it is when you watch nature films? You've got no doubt that the lion is going to gut that gazelle, but you hang in anyway, then feel awful when it happens. It's like that. You hear these people moving from normalcy into nightmare, knowing they're going to die and there's not a damn thing you can do about it."

"What about the flight data recorder?"

"That'll take weeks, maybe even months. The fact that the voice recorder worked as long as it did says something about break-up sequence, since power is lost to the recorders once the engines and generator go. But all they're saying now is that input ceased abruptly during a seemingly normal flight. That could indicate a midair disaster."

"An explosion?"

"Possibly."

"Bomb or mechanical failure?"

"Yes."

I gave him a withering look.

"The repair records indicate there were minor problems with the plane over the past two years. Normal parts were reworked, and some sort of switch was replaced twice. But the maintenance records group is saying it looks pretty routine."

"Any progress on the tipster?"

"The calls were made from a pay phone in Atlanta. Both CNN and the FBI have tapes, and voice analysis is being done."

Ryan swigged his lemonade, made a face, set it on the table.

"What's the word from the body teams?"

"This is strictly between us, Ryan. Anything official has to come from Tyrell."

He curled his fingers in a "go on" gesture.

"We're finding penetrations and a lot of lower leg and ankle fractures. That's not typical of ground impact."

I flashed back to the gouty foot, and again felt puzzled. Ryan must have read my face.

"What now, buttercup?"

"Can I bounce something off you?"

"Shoot."

"This is going to sound weird."

"As opposed to your normally conventional views."

More withering eye action.

"Remember the foot we rescued from the coyotes?"

He nodded.

"It doesn't match any passenger."

"What doesn't fit?"

"Mainly age, and I feel pretty confident in my estimate. There was no one that old on the plane. Could someone have boarded without being listed?"

"I can look into it. We used to hitch rides in the military, but I suspect that would be pretty tough on a commercial flight. Airline employees sometimes ride free. It's called deadheading. But they'd be listed on the manifest."

"You were in the military?"

"Crimean War."

I ignored that.

"Could someone have given a ticket away? Or sold it?"

"You're required to show a picture ID."

"What if the ticketed passenger checks in, shows ID, then passes the ticket to someone else?"

"I'll ask."

I finished my pickle.

"Or could someone have been transporting a biological specimen? This foot looks muckier than the stuff I've been processing."

He looked at me skeptically. "Muckier?"

"The tissue breakdown seems more advanced."

"Isn't decay rate affected by the environment?"

"Of course it is."

I dabbed up ketchup and popped the last of my sandwich into my mouth.

"I think biological specimens have to be reported," Ryan said.

I recalled times I'd flown with bones, boarding with them as carry-ons. In at least one instance I'd transported tissue sealed in Tupperware so I could study saw marks left by a serial killer. I wasn't convinced.

"Maybe the coyotes got the foot someplace else," I suggested.

"Such as?"

"An old cemetery."

"Air TransSouth 228 nosed into a cemetery?"

"Not directly into one." I remembered my encounter with Simon Midkiff and his worry about his dig, and realized how absurd I must sound. Nevertheless, Ryan's skepticism irked me. "You're the expert on canids. Surely you're aware that they drag things around."

"Maybe the foot took a jolt in life that makes it look older than its actual age."

I had to admit that was possible.

"And more decomposed."

"Maybe."

I gathered napkins and utensils and carried our plates to the sink.

"Look, how 'bout we stroll Coyote Canyon tomor-
row, see if anyone's pushing up daisies?"
I turned to look at him.
"Really?"
"Anything to ease your troubled mind, cupcake."
That's not how it went.

6

I SPENT THE NEXT MORNING SEPARATING FLESH INTO four individuals. Case number 432 came from a burned segment of fuselage that lay in a valley north of the main crash site. Inside the body bag I found one relatively intact corpse missing the top of the skull and the lower arms. The bag also contained a partial head and a complete right arm with a portion of mandible embedded in the triceps muscle. Everything was congealed into a single charred mass.

I determined that the corpse was that of a black female in her early twenties who stood five feet seven at the time of death. Her X rays showed healed fractures of the right humerus and scapula. I classified number 432 as fragmented human remains, recorded my observations, and sent the body on to odontology.

The partial head, a white male in his late teens, became number 432A, and was also forwarded for dental analysis. The jaw fragment belonged to someone older than number 432A, probably a female, and went on to the dentists as number 432C. The state of bone development suggested that the unrelated arm came from an adult over twenty. I calculated upper and lower limits for stature, but was unable to determine gender since all hand and arm bone measurements fell into the overlap range for males and females. I sent the arm to the fingerprint section as case number 432D.

It was twelve-fifteen when I looked at my watch. I had to hurry.

I spotted Ryan through a small window in the morgue's back door. He was sitting on the steps, one long leg outstretched, the other raised to support an elbow as he spoke into a cell phone. Opening the door, I could hear that his words were English, his tone agitated, and I suspected the business was other than official.

"Well, that's the way it's going to be."

He turned a shoulder when he saw me, and his answers grew terse.

"Do what you want, Danielle."

I waited until he had disconnected, then joined him on the porch.

"Sorry I'm late."

"No problemo."

He flipped the cover and slid the phone into his pocket, his movements stiff and jerky.

"Problems on the home front?"

"What's your pleasure for lunch? Fish or fowl?"

"Nice dodge," I said, smiling. "And about as subtle as a full court press."

"The home front is not your concern. Subtle enough?"

Though my mouth opened, no words emerged.

"It's just a personal disagreement."

"Have a lovers' spat with the Archbishop of Canterbury for all I care, just don't treat me to the performance." Heat flamed my cheeks.

"Since when are you curious about my love life?"

"I couldn't care less about your love life," I snapped.

"Thus the inquisition."

"What?"

"Let's forget it." Ryan reached out, but I stepped back.

"You *did* ask me to meet you here."

"Look, this investigation has us both on edge."

"But I don't take cheap shots at you."

"What I don't need is more browbeating," he said, lowering the shades from the top of his head.

"Browbeating?" I exploded.

Ryan repeated his question. "Fish or fowl?"

"Go fowl your own fish."

I whirled and lunged for the doorknob, my face burning with anger. Or was it humiliation? Or hurt?

Inside, I slammed then leaned against the door. From the lot I heard an engine, then the squeal of brakes as a truck arrived with twenty more cases. Rolling my head, I saw Ryan kick a heel at the ground, then cross to his rental car.

Why had he made me so furious? I'd spent a lot of time thinking of the man during his months under-cover. But distancing myself from Ryan had become so routine, I'd never considered the possibility that someone else might enter his life. Was that now the case? While I wanted to know, I sure as hell wasn't going to ask.

I turned back to find Larke Tyrell regarding me intently.

"You need some R and R."

"I'm taking two hours this afternoon." I'd requested the break so Ryan and I could search the area where I'd found the foot. Now I'd have to do it alone.

"Sandwich?" Larke tilted his chin toward the staff lounge.

"Sure."

Minutes later we were seated at one of the folding tables.

"Squashed subs and pulverized chips," he said.

"My usual order."

"How's LaManche?" Larke had selected what looked like tuna on wheat.

"Back to his usual cantankerous self."

Being the director of the medico-legal unit, Pierre LaManche was Larke Tyrell's counterpart at the lab in Montreal. My two bosses had known each other for years through membership in the National Association of Medical Examiners and the American Academy of Forensic Sciences. LaManche had suffered a heart attack the previous spring but was fully recovered and back to work.

"Mighty glad to hear that."

As we peeled cellophane and popped sodas, I remembered the ME's first appearance at the site.

"Can I ask you something?"

"Sure." He watched me carefully, his eyes chestnut in the sunlight angling down from an overhead window.

"Jesus, Larke, I'm fine, so quit with the stress assessment. Lieutenant-Detective Ryan just happens to be a horse's ass."

"Noted. You sleeping O.K.?"

"Like Custer after Little Bighorn." I avoided the impulse to roll my eyes.

"What's your question?"

"When you and the lieutenant governor arrived last week, where did the chopper land?"

I upended my chip bag and poured fragments into my hand.

"There's a house a spit west of the crash site. The pilot liked the lay of the land so that's where he put us down."

"There's a landing strip?"

"Hell, no, just a small clearing. I thought Davenport was gonna soil his Calvin Kleins, he was so scared." Larke chuckled. "It was like a scene out of *M*A*S*H*. Triggs kept insisting we head back out, and the pilot kept saying, 'Yes, sir, yes, sir,' then put that bird exactly where he wanted."

I palmed the chips into my mouth.

"Then we just worked our way toward the site. I'd say it was maybe a quarter mile."

"It's a house?"

"An old cabin or something. I didn't pay much attention."

"Did you see a road?"

He shook his head. "Why the questions?"

I told him about the foot.

"I didn't notice a cemetery, but there's no harm poking around out there. You sure these were coyotes?"

"No."

"Be safe; take a radio and a can of Mace."

"Do coyotes hunt during the day?"

"Coyotes hunt whenever they feel like it."

Great.

North Carolina's official tree is the longleaf pine, its official flower the dogwood. The shad boat, the salt-water bass, and the Eastern box turtle have been similarly honored. The state boasts wild ponies on the Shackleford Banks and the nation's highest suspension bridge at Grandfather Mountain. The Old North State flows from the peaks of the southern Appalachians in the west, across the hills of the piedmont, to the marshlands, beaches, and barrier islands along its eastern shore. It is Mount Mitchell and the Outer

Banks. Blowing Rock and Cape Fear. Linville Gorge and Bald Head Island.

North Carolina's geography splits its residents along ideological lines. The high-country crowd plays recreational roulette mountain biking, hang gliding, whitewater kayaking, rock climbing, and, in winter, downhill skiing and snowboarding. The less reckless go in for golf, antiques, bluegrass music, and the viewing of foliage.

Fans of the low country favor salt air, warm sand, ocean fishing, and Atlantic breakers. Temperatures are mild. The locals have never owned mittens or snow tires. Except for the occasional shark or renegade gator, the fauna is nonthreatening. Golf, of course, also permeates the low country.

While I am awed by the beauty of foaming rivers, cascading falls, and towering trees, my allegiance has always been to the sea. I prefer ecozones where shorts and sundresses suffice, and only one layer is needed. Give me a swimsuit catalog and forget Eddie Bauer. All things considered, I'd rather be at the beach.

These thoughts drifted through my mind as I circled the debris field. The day was clear but breezy, the smell of decay less apparent. Though victim recovery was well along, and fewer bodies littered the ground, the big picture looked relatively unchanged. Bio-suited figures still wandered about and crawled through the wreckage, though some now wore caps marked *FBI*.

I found Larke's opening and cut into the woods. Though the high-altitude sunlight was warm, the temperature dropped appreciably when I moved into shadow. I followed the trail I'd taken the week before, now and then stopping to listen. Branches tapped and scraped, and dead leaves tumbled across the ground with soft ticking sounds. Overhead, a wood-pecker drummed a staccato tattoo, paused, repeated itself.

I was wearing a bright yellow jacket, wanting to surprise no one, and hoping the Tommy Hilfiger colors would suggest avoidance to the coyote mind. If not, I'd zap the furry buggers. Inside my pocket I clutched a small can of Mace.

At the fallen sourwood, I dropped to one knee and scanned the forest floor. Then I rose and looked around. Other than my Louisville Slugger branch, there was no hint of my canid adventure.

I continued along the subtle passageway. The ground was slightly concave, and I had to take care not to turn an ankle on a rock hidden beneath leaves. Though lower than the surrounding scrub, the vege-tation at times rose almost to my knees.

I kept my eyes roving, watching for critters or signs of interment. Larke's house meant human settlement, and I knew that old farmsteads often included family burials. One summer I'd directed a dig at the top of Chimney Rock. Intending to excavate only the cabin, we'd uncovered a tiny graveyard, unlisted on any document. Also timber rattlers and water moccasins, I suddenly remembered.

I pressed on through cool, dark shade, thorns and twigs tugging my clothes and insects dive-bombing my face. Gusts sent shadows dancing, changing shape around me. Then, without warning, the trees gave way to a small clearing. As I emerged into sunlight a white-tailed deer raised its head, stared, then disappeared.

Ahead sat a house, its back snugged to a sheer rock cliff that rose straight up for several hundred feet. The structure had a thick-walled foundation, dormer windows, and a sloping roof with wide eaves. A covered porch hid the front, and an odd stone wall peeked from behind the left side.

I waved. Waited. Called out. Waved again.

No challenging voice or bark. Nor any sound of welcome.

I shouted again, hoping a *Deliverance* redneck did not have me in his crosshairs.

Silence.

Banjos dueling in my head, I started across the meadow. Though it was blindingly bright away from the trees, I left my sunglasses in my pocket. In addition to your run-of-the-mill holler rustics, these mountains sheltered white-supremacist, paramilitary types. Strangers were not encouraged to visit.

I could see that the grounds largely had been taken back by nature. What had once been lawn or garden was now overgrown with stunted white alder, sourwood, Carolina silverbell, and numerous shrubs I didn't recognize. Beyond the bushes, big-tooth aspen, Fraser magnolia, poplar, maple, oak, beech, and Eastern white pine mixed with unfamiliar trees. Kudzu draped everything in tangled webs of green.

As I walked to the front steps, goose bumps spread along my arms and a sense of uneasiness wrapped around me like a cold, wet shawl. A feeling of menace hung over the place. Was it born of the dark, weathered wood, the blind, boarded windows, or the jungle of vegetation that kept the dwelling in perpetual gloom?

"Hello?" My heartbeat quickened.

Still no dogs or mountain men.

One look told me the house had not been thrown up quickly. Or recently. The construction was as solid as London's Newgate prison. Though I doubted George Dance drew the plans, this designer shared the prison architect's distrust of portals on to the world. There were no expanses of glass to maximize the mountain view. No skylights. No widow's walks. Constructed of rock and thick, unstained planking, the place had clearly been built for function. I couldn't tell if it had last been visited at the end of the summer or at the end of the Great Depression.

Or if someone was inside now, watching my movements through a crack or gun hole.

"Is anyone home?"

Nothing.

I climbed to the porch and knocked.

"Hello?"

No sounds of movement.

Sidestepping to a window, I brought my eyes close to the shutters. Heavy, dark material hid the interior. I twisted and turned my head, angling for a view, until the feathery brush of a spider sent me jumping backward.

I descended the steps, circled the house on an overgrown flagstone path, and stepped through an arch into a gloomy little courtyard. The enclosure was surrounded by eight-foot stone walls overhung by lilac bushes, their leaves dark against the greens and yellows of the forest beyond. Except for moss, nothing grew on the hard-packed, moist ground. The dank little quadrangle seemed completely incapable of sustaining life.

I turned my gaze back to the house. A crow circled and settled on a nearby branch, a small black silhouette against brilliant blue. The bird cawed twice, clicked its beak, then lowered its head in my direction.

"Tell the mistress I stopped by," I said with more self-assurance than I felt.

The crow regarded me briefly, then flapped into the air.

Turning, I caught a flicker, like sunlight glinting off broken glass. I froze. Had I seen movement in an upstairs window? I waited a full minute. Nothing stirred.

The yard had only one entrance, so I retraced my

steps and surveyed the far side of the property. Brush filled the space between forest and house, ending in a jungle of dead hollyhocks crowding the foundation. I walked the area, but saw no evidence of burials, disturbed or intact. My only discovery was a broken metal bar.

Frustrated, I returned to the front porch, inserted the bar between the shutters, and pried gently. There was no give. I applied more pressure, curious, but not wanting to cause damage. The wood was solid and would not budge.

I looked at my watch. Two forty-five. This was useless. And stupid, if the property wasn't abandoned. If proprietors existed, they were away, or wanted it to seem so. I was tired, sweaty, and itchy from thousands of tiny scratches.

And I had to admit, the place creeped me out. Though I knew my reaction was irrational, I felt a sense of evil pervading the grounds. Deciding to make inquiries in town, I dropped the bar and headed back to the crash site.

Driving toward the morgue, I pondered the mysterious lodge. Who had built it? Why? What was it about the place that made me so uneasy?

R YAN WAS LYING IN WAIT WHEN I ARRIVED AT HIGH
Ridge House shortly after nine. I didn't see him until
he spoke.

"Looks like we've got an explosion."

I paused, one hand on the screen door handle.

"Not now, Ryan."

"Jackson's going to make a statement tomorrow."

I turned in the direction of the porch swing. Ryan
had one heel on the banister and was pushing himself
slowly back and forth. When he drew on his cigarette,
a tiny red glow lighted his face.

"It's certain?"

"As Madonna's lost virginity."

I hesitated, wanting news of the investigation, but
wary of the bearer.

"It's been a sincerely fucked-up day, Brennan. I
apologize for any misbehavior."

Though I'd had little time to dwell on it, the noontime confrontation had led me to a decision. I was ending the circle of disaster that had been my relationship with Ryan. From now on our interactions would be strictly professional.

"Tell me."

Ryan patted the swing.

I crossed to him but remained standing.

"Why an explosion?"

"Sit."

"If this is a come-on, you can—"

"There's cratering and fiber penetration."

In the half-light of the overhead bulb Ryan's face looked drained of life. He inhaled deeply, then flicked his butt into Ruby's ferns. I watched sparks comet through the dark, imagining the plunge of Air TransSouth 228.

"Do you want to hear this?"

Placing my pack between us, I dropped onto the swing.

"What's cratering?"

"Cratering is caused when a solid or liquid is suddenly converted to a gas."

"As in a detonation."

"Yes. An explosion rockets the temperature thousands of degrees and sends out shock waves that create a gas wash effect on metal surfaces. That's how the explosives group experts described it. They showed slides at today's briefing. It looks kind of like an orange peel."

"They're finding cratering?"

"They've spotted it on fragments. Rolled edges, too, which is another indicator."

He gave the swing a gentle push.

"What's fiber penetration?"

"They're seeing the fibers of some materials driven through other, undamaged materials. All under high-powered microscopes, of course. They're also finding heat fractures and flash melting at the ends of some fibers."

Another oscillation, and I tasted the Greek salad I'd wolfed down after leaving the morgue.

"Don't rock the swing."

"Some of the blow-up photos are amazing."

I zipped my jacket and tucked my hands into the pockets. Though the days were still warm, the nights were growing crisp.

"So cratering and rolled edges on metal, and flash melting and penetration of fibers mean an explosion. Our lower leg injuries fit with that."

"So does the fact that a large part of the fuselage landed intact."

I planted a foot to stop our forward motion.

"It all adds up to an explosion."

"Caused by?"

"Bomb. Missile. Mechanical failure. The FAA's Aviation Explosives Security Unit will conduct chromatographic analysis to determine what chemicals might be present, and radiophotography and X-ray diffraction to identify molecular species. And one other. Oh, yeah. Infrared spectrophotometry. Not sure what that one's for, but it has a nice ring. That is, if they can arm-wrestle the job away from the FBI crime lab."

"Missile?" It was the first I'd heard of that possibility.

"Not likely, but it's been suggested. Remember all the hoopla about a missile bringing down TWA 800? Pierre Salinger bet his nuts the navy was to blame."

I nodded.

"And these hills are home to a number of militia groups. Maybe Eric Rudolph's white-trash buds got into the arms market and bought a new toy."

Rudolph was wanted in connection with a number of abortion clinic attacks and as a suspect in the bombing at the 1996 Olympic Games in Atlanta. Rumors persisted that he'd fled to these hills.

"Any idea where this explosion was centered?"

"It's too early to tell. The cabin-interior documentation group is compiling a seat damage chart that'll help pinpoint the blast."

Ryan pushed with his toes, but I held the swing firm.

"Our group is doing the same for wounds and fractures. Right now it looks like the worst injuries occurred in the back of the plane." The anthropologists and pathologists were diagramming the distribution of trauma by seat location. "What about the radar group?"

"Nothing unexpected. Following takeoff, the flight routed northeast from the airport toward Athens. The

Atlanta air traffic control center is in charge up to Winston-Salem, where Washington takes over, so the plane never left Atlanta ATC. The radar shows an emergency call by the pilot twenty minutes and thirty seconds into the flight. Approximately ninety seconds later the target broke into two, possibly three pieces, and disappeared from the screen."

Headlights appeared far down the mountain. Ryan and I watched them climb through the dark, swing onto the drive, then cut out in the lot to the left of the house. Moments later a figure materialized on the path. When it crossed in front of us, Ryan spoke.

"Long day?"

"Who's that?" The man was barely an imprint against the black of the sky.

"Andy Ryan."

"Well, *bonsoir,* sir. I'd forgotten you were billeted here." The voice sounded like years of whiskey. All I could make of its owner was a burly man in a dozer cap.

"The lilac shower gel is mine."

"I've been respecting that, Detective Ryan."

"I'd buy you a beer but the bar just closed."

The man climbed to the porch, dragged a chair opposite the swing, placed an athletic bag beside it, and sat. The dim light revealed a fleshy nose and cheeks mottled with broken veins.

When introduced, FBI Special Agent Byron McMahon removed the hat and bowed in my direction. I saw thick white hair, centered and splayed like a cockscomb.

"This one's on me." Unzipping the bag, McMahon produced a six-pack of Coors.

"Devil liquor," said Ryan, pulling a beer from the plastic web.

"Yes," agreed McMahon. "Bless him." He waggled a can at me.

I wanted that beer as much as I'd wanted anything in a long time. I remembered the feel of booze filtering through my veins, the warmth rising inside me as the molecules of alcohol blended with my own. The sense of relief, well-being.

But I'd learned some things about myself. It had taken years, but I now understood that every double helix in me carries a pledge to Bacchus. Though craving the release, I knew the euphoria would be temporary, the anger and self-loathing would last a long time. I could not drink.

"No, thanks."

"There's plenty where this came from."

"That's the problem."

McMahon smiled, freed a can, and dropped the others into his bag.

"So what's the thinking at the FBI?" Ryan asked.

"Some son of a bitch blew a plane out of the sky."

"Who does the Bureau like?"

"Your biker buddies score high on a lot of dance cards. This Petricelli was a lowlife sleaze with soup for brains, but he was well connected."

"And?"

"Could be a professional hit."

A breeze swayed Ruby's baskets, and black shadows danced on the banisters and floorboards.

"Here's another script. Mrs. Martha Simington was seated in 1A. Three months ago Haskell Simington insured his wife for two million big ones."

"That's a chunk of change."

"Goes a long way toward easing hubby through his pain. Oh, and I forgot to mention. The couple have been living apart for four years."

"Is Simington enough of a mutant to cap eighty-eight people?" Ryan drained his Coors and tossed the empty into McMahon's athletic bag.

"We're getting to know Simington real well."

McMahon mimicked Ryan's performance with his empty can.

"Here's another scenario: 12F was occupied by a nineteen-year-old named Anurudha Mahendran. The kid was a foreign student from Sri Lanka and played goalie on the soccer team."

McMahon released two more beers and handed one to Ryan.

"Back home, Anurudha's uncle works for Voice of Tigers Radio."

"As in Tamil Tigers?"

"Yes, ma'am. The guy's a loudmouth, undoubtedly slots high on the government's wish list for terminal illness."

"You suspect the Sri Lankan government?" I was astounded.

"No. But there are extremists on both sides."

"If you can't persuade unc, go for the kid. Send a message."

Ryan popped the new beer.

"It may be a long shot, but we have to consider it. Not forgetting our local resources, of course."

"Local resources?" I asked.

"Two country preachers who live near here. The Reverend Isaiah Claiborne swears the Reverend Luke Bowman shot the plane down." Another pop. "They're rival snake handlers."

"Snake handlers?"

I ignored Ryan's question. "Claiborne witnessed something?"

"He insists he saw a white streak shoot from behind Bowman's house, followed by an explosion."

"Is the FBI taking him seriously?"

McMahon shrugged. "The time tallies. The location would be right with regard to the flight path."

"What snakes?" Ryan persisted.

"Any word on the voice tapes?" I segued to another subject, not wanting further commentary on the spiritual fervor of our mountain neighbors.

"The calls were made by a white American male with no distinguishable accent."

"That narrows the field to how many million?"

I caught movement in McMahon's eyes, as though he were seriously considering the question.

"A few."

McMahon drained his beer, crumpled the can, and added it to his collection. Rising, he wished us both a good evening, and headed for the door. The bell jangled, and moments later a light went on in an upstairs window.

Save for the creak of Ruby's planters, the porch was totally quiet. Ryan lit a cigarette, then, "Did you do coyote patrol?"

"Yes."

"And?"

"No coyotes. No exposed coffins."

"Did you find anything interesting?"

"A house."

"Who lives there?"

"Hansel and Gretel and the cannibal witch." I stood. "How the hell should I know?"

"Was anyone home?"

"No one rushed out to offer me tea."

"Is the place abandoned?"

I slung my pack over one shoulder and considered the question.

"I'm not sure. There were gardens once, but those have gone to hell. The house is so well built it's hard to know if it's being maintained or if it's just impervious to damage."

He waited.

"There is one peculiar thing. From the front, the place is just another unpainted mountain lodge. But around back it has a walled enclosure and a courtyard."

Ryan's face went apricot, receded into the darkness.

"Tell me about these snake handlers. You have snake handlers in North Carolina?"

I was about to decline when the bell tinkled again. I looked, expecting to see McMahon, but no one appeared.

"Another time."

Opening the outer screen, I found the heavy wooden door ajar. Once inside, I pushed it tight and tested the handle, hoping Ryan would do the same. Then I trudged to Magnolia, intent on a shower and bed. I was barely in the room when someone tapped softly.

Thinking it was Ryan, I set my face in the hard stare and cracked the door.

Ruby stood in the hall, her features looking solemn and deeply creased. She wore a gray flannel robe, pink socks, and brown slippers shaped like paws. Her hands were clasped at chest level, fingers tightly interlaced.

"I'm about to turn in." I smiled.

She gazed at me gravely.

"I've had dinner," I added.

One hand rose, as if to pluck something from the air. It trembled slightly.

"What is it, Ruby?"

"The devil assumes many forms."

"Yes." I wanted desperately to bathe and sleep. "But I'm sure you're way ahead of him."

I reached out to touch her shoulder, but she stepped back and the hands found each other again.

"They fly with Lucifer in the face of divinity. They blaspheme."

"Who does?"

"They've grasped the keys of Hades and of death. Just like it says in Revelations."

"Ruby, please speak to me in plain English."

Her eyes were wide, the nodes in the corners pink and shiny with moisture.

"You're from foreign parts so you can't be knowing."

"Knowing what?" Irritation curled the edges of my voice. I was not in a mood for parables.

"There's evil here."

The beer?

"Detective Ryan an—"

"Wicked men scoff at the Almighty."

This was going nowhere.

"Let's talk about this tomorrow."

I grasped the doorknob, but a hand flew out and clutched my arm. Calluses scratched the sleeve of my nylon jacket.

"The Lord God has sent a sign."

She drew even closer.

"Death!"

Gently prying loose the bony fingers, I squeezed Ruby's hand and stepped back. I watched her through the gap as the door swung shut, her small body frozen, the sausage curl crawling her skull like a dull, gray serpent.

8

THE NEXT DAY HONORED SOMEONE. CHRISTOPHER Columbus, I think. By midmorning it had turned into a nightmare.

I drove to the morgue through mist so thick it obliterated the mountains, and worked until ten-thirty. When I broke for coffee, Larke Tyrell was in the staff room. He waited while I filled a cup with industrial sludge and added white powder.

"There's something we need to talk about."

"Sure."

"Not here." He looked at me a long time. The look meant something, and I felt a prick of anxiety.

"What is it, Larke?"

"Come on."

Taking my arm, he propelled me out the back door.

"Tempe, I don't know how to say this." He swirled his coffee, and iridescent clouds slid across the surface.

"Just say it." I kept my voice low and level.

"There's been a complaint."

I waited.

"I feel terrible about this." He studied his cup a few more seconds, then raised his eyes to mine. "It's about you."

"Me?" I was incredulous.

He nodded.

"What did I do?"

"The complaint cites unprofessional behavior of a nature sufficient to compromise the investigation."

"Such as?"

"Entering the site without authority and mishandling evidence."

I stared at him in disbelief.

"And trespass."

"Trespass?" A cold fist was closing around my gut.

"Did you poke around that property we talked about?"

"It wasn't trespass. I wanted to talk to the owners."

"Did you try to break in?"

"Of course not!"

I flashed on myself prying a shutter with a rusty bar.

"And I had authorization to enter the crash site last week."

"Whose?"

"Earl Bliss sent me there. You know that."

"See, here's the problem, Tempe." Larke rubbed a hand across his chin. "At that point DMORT hadn't been requested."

I was stunned.

"In what way did I mishandle evidence?"

"I hate to even ask this." The hand went back to the chin. "Tempe—"

"Just ask."

"Did you pick up remains that hadn't been logged?" The foot.

"I told you about that." Stay calm. "I made a judgment call."

He said nothing.

"Had I left that foot, it would now be coyote dung. Talk to Andrew Ryan. He was there."

"I'll do that."

Larke reached out and squeezed my arm.

"We'll sort this out."

"You're taking this seriously?"

"I have no choice."

"Why is that?"

"You know the press are snapping at my backside. They're gonna jump on this like a hound with a one-eyed hare."

"Who made this complaint?" I blinked back tears.

"I can't tell you that."

He dropped his hand and stared off at the mist. It was lifting now, revealing the landscape in a slow, upward peel. When he turned back, there was an odd expression on his face.

"But I will tell you that powerful people are involved."

"The Dalai Lama? The Joint Chiefs of Staff?" Anger hardened my voice.

"Don't be mad at me, Tempe. This investigation is big news. If problems develop, no one's going to want to own them."

"So I'm being set up in case a scapegoat is needed."

"It's nothing like that. I just have to go through proper procedures."

I took a deep breath.

"What happens now?"

He looked straight at me and his voice softened.

"I'm going to have to ask you to leave."

"When?"

"Now."

It was my turn to stare into the mist.

High Ridge House was deserted in the middle of the day. I left a note for Ruby, thanking her and apologizing for my abrupt departure and for my coolness the night before. Then I gathered my belongings, tossed them into my Mazda, and drove off so fast the tires threw up a gravel spray.

All the way home to Charlotte I stopped and started hard, screeching from lights then weaving from lane to lane once I reached the highway. For three hours I crawled up bumpers and rode the horn. I talked to myself, trying out words. *Vile. Despicable. Vicious.* Other drivers avoided my eyes and gave me lots of space.

I was irate and depressed at the same time. The injustice of an anonymous accusation. The helplessness. For a week I'd been working under brutal conditions, seeing, smelling, and feeling death. I'd dropped everything, devoted myself to the effort, then been dismissed like a servant suspected of stealing. No hearing. No opportunity for explanation. No thank-you. Pack and go.

Besides the professional humiliation, there was the personal letdown. Though we'd been friends for years, and Larke knew I was scrupulous about professional ethics, he hadn't defended me. Larke was not a cowardly man. I had expected more of him.

The wild driving served its purpose. By the outskirts of Charlotte my cascading fury had congealed into cold resolve. I'd done nothing inappropriate and I would clear my name. I would find out what this grievance was, quash it, and finish my work. And I would confront the accuser.

My empty town house destroyed that resolve. No one to greet me. No one to hold me and tell me I'd be fine. Ryan was quibbling with a distant Danielle, whoever she was. Ryan had told me it was none of my business. Katy was with her friend, gender unspecified, and Birdie and Pete were far across town. I threw down my bags, flung myself on the sofa, and dissolved into tears.

Ten minutes later I lay quietly, chest heaving, feeling like a kid coming off a tantrum. I'd accomplished nothing and felt drained. Dragging myself to the bathroom, I blew my nose, then checked my phone messages.

Zero to brighten my mood. A student. Salesmen.

My sister, Harry, calling from Texas. A query from my friend Anne: Could we get together for lunch since she and Ted were leaving for London?

Great. They were probably dining at the Savoy as I erased her words. I decided to collect Birdie. At least he would purr in my lap.

Pete still lives in the house we shared for almost twenty years. Though it is worth hundreds of thousands of dollars, the fence is mended with a wooden block, and a makeshift goal sags in the backyard, testimonial to Katy's soccer years. The house is painted, the gutters cleaned, the lawn mowed by professionals. A maid maintains the inside. But beyond normal upkeep, my estranged husband believes in laissez-faire and the quick patch. He feels no obligation to protect area real estate values. I used to worry about neighborhood protests. The separation relieved me of that.

A furry brown face watched through the fence as I swung onto the drive. When I climbed from the car, it crinkled and gave a low "rrup!"

"Is he here?" I asked, slamming the door.

The dog lowered its head, and a purple tongue dropped from its mouth.

I circled to the front and rang. No response.

I rang again. A key still hung from my chain, but I wouldn't use it. Though we'd been living apart for over two years, Pete and I were still stepping carefully in establishing the new order between us. The sharing of keys involved an intimacy I didn't want to imply.

But it was Thursday afternoon and Pete would be at the office. And I wanted my cat.

I was digging in my purse, when the door opened.

"Hello, attractive stranger. Need a place to sleep?" said Pete, surveying me from top to bottom.

I was wearing the khakis and Doc Martens I'd donned for the morgue at six that morning. Pete was perfect in a three-piece suit and Gucci loafers.

"I thought you'd be at work."

I wiped knuckles across the mascara smears on my lower lids, and took a quick peek inside the house. If I spotted a woman I'd die of humiliation.

"Why *aren't* you at work?"

He glanced left, then right, lowered his voice, and gestured me close, as if imparting secure information. "Rendezvous with the plumber."

I didn't want to contemplate what had gone so wrong that Mr. Fix It would call in an expert.

"I came for Birdie."

"I think he's free." Pete stepped back. I entered a foyer lighted by my great-aunt's chandelier.

"How about a drink?"

I drilled him a look that could slice feldspar. Pete had witnessed many of my Academy Award performances, and knew better.

"You know what I mean."

"A Diet Coke would be nice."

While Pete rattled glassware and ice cubes in the

kitchen, I called up the stairs to Birdie. No cat. I tried the parlor, dining room, and den.

Once upon a time, Pete and I had lived together in these rooms, reading, talking, listening to music, making love. We'd nurtured Katy from infant to toddler to adolescent, redecorating her room and adjusting our lives with each passage. I'd watch the honeysuckle come and go through the window over the kitchen sink, welcoming every season. Those had been fairy-tale days, a time when the American dream seemed real and attainable.

Pete reappeared, transformed from attorney-chic to yuppie-casual. The jacket and vest were gone, the tie loosened, the shirtsleeves rolled to below the elbows. He looked good.

"Where's Bird?" I asked.

"He's been keeping to the upper decks since Boyd checked in."

He handed me a mug with *Uz to mums atkal jaiedzer!* scrolled around the glass. "To that we must drink again!" in Latvian.

"Boyd's the dog?"

A nod.

"Yours?"

"Interesting point. Have a seat and I'll share with you the saga of Boyd."

Pete got pretzels from the kitchen and joined me on the couch.

"Boyd belongs to one Harvey Alexander Dineen, a gentleman recently in need of pro bono defense.

Completely surprised by his arrest, and lacking family, Harvey requested that I look after his dog until the misunderstanding with the state was cleared up."

"And you agreed?"

"I appreciated his confidence in me."

Pete licked salt from a pretzel, bit off the large loop, and washed it down with beer.

"And?"

"Boyd's on his own for a minimum of ten and a maximum of twenty. I figured he'd get hungry."

"What is he?"

"He thinks of himself as an entrepreneur. The judge called him a con man and career criminal."

"I meant the dog."

"Boyd's a chow. Or at least most of him is. We'd need DNA testing to clarify the rest."

He ate the other half of the pretzel.

"Been out with any good corpses lately?"

"Very funny." My face must have suggested that it was not.

"Sorry. Must be grim up there."

"We're getting through it."

We made small talk for a while, then Pete invited me for dinner. Our usual routine. He asked, I refused. Today I thought of Larke's allegations, Anne and Ted's London adventure, and my empty condo.

"What are you serving?"

His eyebrows shot up in surprise.

"Linguini con sauce vongole."

A Pete specialty. Canned clams on overcooked pasta.

"Why don't I pick up steaks while you deal with the plumber. When the pipes are flowing, we can grill the meat."

"It's an upstairs toilet."

"Whatever."

"It will be good for Bird to see that we're friends. I think he still blames himself."

Pure Pete.

Boyd joined us at dinner, sitting beside the table, eyes glued to the New York strips, now and then pawing a knee to remind us of his presence.

Pete and I talked about Katy, about old friends, and about old times. He discussed some current litigation, and I described one of my recent cases, a student found hanging in his grandmother's barn nine months after his disappearance. I was pleased that we'd reached a comfort level at which normal conversation was possible. Time flew, and Larke and his complaint receded from my thoughts.

After a dessert of strawberries on vanilla ice cream, we took coffee to the den and switched on the news. The Air TransSouth crash was the lead story.

A grim-faced woman stood at the overlook, the Great Smoky Mountains rolling behind her, and talked of a meet in which thirty-four athletes would never compete. She reported that the cause of the crash was still unclear, although a midair explosion was now almost certain. To date forty-seven victims had been identified, and the investigation was continuing around the clock.

"It's smart they're giving you time off," Pete said.

I didn't answer.

"Or did they send you down here on a secret mission?"

I felt a tremor in my chest and kept my eyes on my Doc Martens.

Pete slid close and raised my chin with an index finger.

"Hey, babe, I'm only kidding. Are you O.K.?"

I nodded, not trusting myself to speak.

"You don't look too O.K."

"I'm fine."

"Do you want to tell me about it?"

I must have, for the words poured out. I told him about the days of gore, about the coyotes and my attempts to pinpoint the foot's origin, about the anonymous complaint and my dismissal. I left out nothing but Andrew Ryan. When I finally wound down my feet were curled beneath me, and I was clutching a throw pillow to my chest. Pete was regarding me intently.

For a few moments neither of us spoke. The schoolhouse clock ticked loudly from the den wall, and I wondered idly who kept it wound.

Tick. Tick. Tick.

"Well, this has been fun," I said, unwinding my legs.

Pete took my hand, his eyes still steady on my face.

"What are you going to do about it?"

"What can I do?" I said irritably, pulling free. I was already embarrassed by my outpouring and dreaded what I knew was coming. Pete always gave the same advice when aggravated by others. "Fuck 'em."

He surprised me.

"Your DMORT commander will clear up the issue of entering the site. The foot is central to the rest. Was anyone around when you picked the thing up?"

"There was a cop nearby." I focused on the pillow.

"Local?"

I shook my head.

"Did he see the coyotes?"

"Yes."

"Do you know who he is?"

Oh yes.

I nodded.

"That should settle that. Have this cop contact Tyrell and describe the situation." He leaned back. "The trespass is going to be tougher."

"I wasn't trespassing," I said hotly.

"How strongly do you feel about this foot?"

"I don't think it fits with anyone on the passenger list. That's why I was snooping around."

"Because of the age."

"Largely. It also looked more decomposed."

"Can you prove the age?"

"What do you mean?"

"Are you absolutely certain the foot donor was that old?"

"No."

"Is there any other test that can more firmly establish your age estimate?" Pete, the lawyer.

"I'll check the histology once the samples are processed."

"When is that?"

"Slide preparation is taking forev—"

"Go there tomorrow. Get your slides bumped. Don't quit until you know the guy's collar size and the name of his bookie."

"I could try."

"Do it."

Pete was right. I was being a pansy.

"Then ID Foot Man and shove it up Tyrell's ass."

"How do I do that?"

"If your foot didn't come from the plane, it must be local."

I waited.

"Start by finding out who owns that property."

"How do I do *that*?"

"Has the FBI checked the place out?"

"They're involved in the crash investigation, but until there's proof of sabotage, the Bureau isn't officially in charge. Besides, given my current status, I doubt they're going to share their thoughts with me."

"Then find out on your own."

"How?"

"Check the title to the property and the tax rolls at the county courthouse."

"Can you walk me through that?"

I took notes as he talked. By the time he finished, my resolve was back. No more whining and self-pity. I'd probe that foot until I knew every detail of its owner's life. Then I'd find out where it came from, nail an ID, and paste it to Larke Tyrell's forehead.

"Thank you so much, Pete."

I leaned over and kissed him on the cheek. Without hesitating, he drew me in. Before I could pull back, he returned my cheek kiss, then another, then his lips slid to my neck, my ear, my mouth. I smelled the familiar mix of sweat and Aramis, and a million images burst in my brain. I felt the arms and chest I'd known for two decades, that had once held only me.

I loved making love with Pete. I always had, from that first earthquake magic in his tiny room on Clarke Avenue in Champaign, Illinois, to the later years, when it became slower, deeper, a melody I knew as well as the curves of my own body. Making love with Pete was all-encompassing. It was pure sensation and total detachment. I needed that now. I needed the familiar and comforting, the shattering of my consciousness, the stopping of time.

I thought of my silent apartment. I thought of Larke and his "powerful people," of Ryan and the unknown Danielle, of separation and distance. Then Pete's hand slid to my breast.

"Fuck 'em," I thought.

Then I thought of nothing else.

9

I AWOKE TO THE SOUND OF A PHONE. PETE HAD DRAWN
the shades, and the room was so dim I needed several
rings to locate it.

"Meet me at Providence Road Sundries tonight
and I'll buy you a burger."

"Pete, I—"

"You drive a hard bargain. Meet me at Bijoux."

"It's not the restaurant."

"Tomorrow night?"

"I don't think so."

The line hummed.

"Remember when I wrecked the Volkswagen and
insisted we push on?"

"Georgia to Illinois with no headlights."

"You didn't speak to me for six hundred miles."

"It's not like that, Pete."

"Didn't you enjoy last night?"

I loved last night.

"It's not that."

I heard voices in the background and looked at the clock. Eight-ten.

"Are you at work?"

"Yes, ma'am."

"Why are you phoning?"

"You asked me to wake you."

"Oh." An old routine. "Thanks."

"No problem."

"And thanks for keeping Birdie."

"Has he made an appearance?"

"Briefly. He looked edgy."

"The old Bird has become set in his ways."

"Birdie never liked dogs."

"Or change."

"Or change."

"Some change is good."

"Yes."

"I have changed."

I'd heard that from Pete. He'd said it after his tryst with a court reporter three years earlier, again following a Realtor episode. I hadn't waited for the trifecta.

"That was a bad time for me," he went on.

"Yeah. Me, too."

I hung up and took a long shower, reflecting on our failings. Pete was where I'd always turned for advice, comfort, support. He'd been my safety net, the calm I'd seek after a day of tempest. The breakup had been devastating, but it had also brought out strength I'd never known I had.

Or ever used.

When I'd toweled off and wrapped my hair, I studied myself in the mirror.

Question: What was I thinking last night?

Answer: I wasn't. I was angry, hurt, vulnerable, and alone. And I hadn't had sex in a very long time.

Question: Would it happen again?

Answer: No.

Question: Why not?

Why not? I still loved Pete. I had since first laying eyes on him, barefoot and bare-chested on the steps of the law school library. I'd loved him as he lied about Judy, then Ellen. I'd loved him as I packed and left two years ago.

And I obviously still found him sexy as hell.

My sister, Harry, has a Texas expression. Flat ass stupid. Though I love Pete, and find him sexy, I am not flat ass stupid. *That's* why it would not happen again.

I wiped steam from the glass, remembering the old me looking back from that same mirror. My hair was blond when we first moved in, long and straight to my shoulders. It's short now, and I've abandoned the golden surfer look. But gray hairs are sneaking in, and I'll soon be checking out the Clairol browns. The lines have increased and deepened around my eyes, but my jawline is firm and my upper lids have stayed put.

Pete always said my butt was my best feature. That, too, has remained in place, though effort is now required. But, unlike many of my contemporaries, I own no spandex and have never hired a personal trainer. I possess no treadmill, step machine, or stationary bike. I do not enroll in aerobics or kickboxing classes, and have not run in an organized race in over five years. I go to the gym in T-shirts and FBI shorts, tied at the waist with a drawstring. I jog or swim, lift, then leave. When the weather is nice, I run outside.

I've also tried to tighten up on what I eat. Daily vitamins. Red meat no more than three times a week. Junk food no more than five.

I was positioning my panties when my cell phone rang. Racing to the bedroom, I upended my purse, retrieved the phone, and hit the button.

"Where have you disappeared to?"

Ryan's voice was completely unexpected. I hesitated, panties in one hand, phone in the other, unable to think of a thing to say.

"Hello?"

"I'm here."

"Here where?"

"I'm in Charlotte."

There was a pause. Ryan broke it.

"This whole thing is a crock of sh—"

"Have you talked to Tyrell?"

"Briefly."

"Did you describe the coyote scene?"

"Vividly."

"And he said?"

"Thank ya, sir." Ryan mimicked the ME's drawl.

"This isn't Tyrell's idea."

"There's something off center about the whole thing."

"What do you mean?"

"I'm not sure."

"What's off center?"

"Tyrell was jumpy. I've only known him a week, but jumpy is not normal demeanor for him. Something is making him squirm. He knows you didn't tamper with remains, and he knows Earl Bliss ordered you up here last week."

"So who's behind the complaint?"

"I don't know, but I sure as hell intend to find out."

"It's not your problem, Ryan."

"No."

"Any developments in the investigation?" I switched the subject.

I heard a match flare, then a deep inhalation.

"Simington is starting to look like a good choice."

"The guy with the heavily insured wife?"

"It's better than that. The new widower owns a company that does highway construction."

"So?"

"Easy access to plastic X."

"Plastic X?"

"Plastic explosive. The stuff was used in Vietnam, but now it's sold to private industry for construction, mining, demolition. Hell, farmers can get it to blast out tree stumps."

"Aren't explosives tightly controlled?"

"Yes and no. The regs for transport are tighter than those for storage and use. If a highway is under construction, for example, you need a special truck with escorts and a prescribed route bypassing congested areas. But once the stuff is on-site it's usually stored in a mobile vault in the middle of a field with the word *explosive* written on it in large letters.

"The company hires some old geezer as guard and pays him minimum wage, mainly to meet insurance requirements. Vaults can be burgled, misplaced, or simply disappear."

Ryan drew on his cigarette, exhaled.

"The military is supposed to account for every ounce of plastic explosive, but construction crews don't have to ledger up that precisely. Say a blaster gets ten sticks, uses three quarters of each, and pockets the rest. No one's the wiser. All the guy needs is a detonator and he's in business. Or he can sell the stuff black market. Explosives are always in demand."

"Assuming Simington filched explosives, could he have gotten them on board?"

"Apparently it's not all that hard. Terrorists used to take plastique, flatten it to the thickness of a wad of bills, and put it in their wallets. How many security guards check the bills in your wallet? And you can get an electrical detonator the size of a watchcase these days. The Libyan terrorists that blew up Pan Am 103 over Lockerbie slipped the stuff on in a cassette case. Simington could have found a way."

"Jesus."

"I've also had news from *la belle province*. Earlier this week a group of homeowners got suspicious about a Ferrari parked on their street. It seems sports cars costing over a hundred thousand dollars don't commonly overnight in that part of Montreal. Turned out to be a good call. Police found the owner, one Alain 'the Fox' Barboli, stuffed in the trunk with two bullets in his head. Barboli was a member of the Rock Machine and had ties to the Sicilian Mafia. Carcajou's got it."

Opération Carcajou was a multiagency task force devoted to the investigation of outlaw bikers in Quebec province. I'd worked with them on a number of murders.

"Does Carcajou think Barboli was revenge for Petricelli?"

"Or Barboli was involved in the Petricelli hit and the big boys are sanitizing the witness list. If there *was* a hit."

"If Simington could get his hands on explosives, the Hells Angels would have no problem."

"Like buying Cheez Whiz at the 7-Eleven. Look, why don't you get back up here and tell this Tyrell—"

"I want to check some bone samples to make sure I'm right on my age estimate. If that foot didn't come from the plane, the tampering charges will be irrelevant."

"I mentioned your suspicions about the foot to Tyrell."

"And?"

"And nothing. He brushed it off."

Again I felt the flush of anger.

"Have you turned up any unlisted passengers?"

"Nope. Hanover swears deadheading is strictly regulated. No paper, no ride. The Air TransSouth employees we've interviewed confirm their CEO's claim."

"Anyone who might have been transporting body parts?"

"No anatomists, anthropologists, podiatrists, orthopedic surgeons, or corrective footwear salesmen. And Jeffrey Dahmer isn't flying these days."

"You're a scream, Ryan."

I hesitated.

"Has Jean been identified?"

"He and Petricelli remain among the missing."

"They'll find him."

"Yeah."

"You all right?"

"Tough as nails. How 'bout you? Feeling lonely all by yourself?"

"I'm fine," I said, staring at the bed I'd just vacated.

North Carolina has a centralized medical examiner system, with headquarters in Chapel Hill and regional offices in Winston-Salem, Greenville, and Charlotte. Due to geography, and to its physical layout, the Charlotte branch, dubbed the Mecklenburg County Medical Examiner, was chosen for the processing of specimens collected at the incident morgue in Bryson

City. A technician had been loaned from Chapel Hill, and a temporary histology unit had been set up.

The Mecklenburg County Medical Examiner is part of the Harold R. "Hal" Marshall County Services Center, which takes up both sides of College Street between Ninth and Tenth, just on the edge of uptown. The facility's home was once a Sears Garden Center. Though an architectural orphan, it is modern and efficient.

But Hal's tenure may be threatened. Shunned for years, the land on which the center sits, with its views of condos, shops, and bistros, has caught the interest of developers as more fitting for mixed-use commercial expansion than for use as county offices, parking lots, and a morgue. American Express gold cards, cappuccino makers, and Hornets and Panthers club seats may soon flourish where scalpels, gurneys, and autopsy tables used to hold sway.

Twenty minutes after finally donning the panties, I pulled into the MCME lot. Across College, the homeless were being served hot dogs and lemonade from folding tables. Blankets covered the moss strip between sidewalk and curb, displaying shoes, shirts, and socks for the taking. A score of indigents milled about, nowhere to go, in no hurry to get there.

Locking the car, I walked to the low-rise redbrick structure and was buzzed through the glass doors. After greeting the ladies up front, I checked in with Tim Larabee, the Mecklenburg County ME. He led me to a computer that had been set aside for crash victim processing and pulled up case number 387. It was probably violating the terms of my banishment, but I had to take the chance.

DNA testing was being done at the Charlotte-Mecklenburg crime laboratory, and those results were not yet available. But the histology was ready. The samples I'd cut from the ankle and foot bones had been shaved into slivers less than one hundred microns thick, processed, stained, and placed on slides. I got them and settled at a microscope.

Bone is a miniature universe in which birth and death occur constantly. The basic unit is the osteon, composed of concentric loops of bone, a canal, osteocytes, vessels, and nerves. In living tissue osteons are born, nourished, and eventually replaced by newer units.

When magnified and viewed under polarized light, osteons resemble tiny volcanoes, ovoid cones with central craters and flanks that spread out to flatlands of primary bone. The number of volcanoes increases with age, as does the count of abandoned calderas. By determining the density of these features one arrives at an age estimate.

First I looked for signs of abnormality. In the cross-section of a long bone, thinning of the shaft, scalloping of its inner or outer edges, or abnormal deposition of woven bone can indicate problems, including fracture healing or unusually rapid remodeling. I saw no such anomalies.

Satisfied that a realistic age estimate was possible,

I increased the magnification to one hundred and inserted a ruled ocular micrometer into the eyepiece. The grid contained one hundred squares, with each side measuring one millimeter at the level of the section. Moving from slide to slide, I studied the miniature landscapes, carefully counting and recording the features within each grid. When I'd finished and plugged my totals into the proper formulae, I had my answer.

The owner of the foot had been at least sixty-five, probably nearer to seventy.

I leaned back and considered that. No one on the manifest was close to that age range. What were the options?

One. An unlisted traveler was on board. A septuagenarian deadheader? A senior citizen stowaway? Unlikely.

Two. A passenger had carried the foot on board. Ryan said they'd found no one whose profile suggested an interest in body parts.

Three. The foot was unrelated to Air TransSouth 228.

Then where did it come from?

I dug a card from my purse, checked the number, and dialed.

"Swain County Sheriff's Department."

"Lucy Crowe, please."

"Who's calling."

I gave my name and waited. Moments later I heard the gravelly voice.

"I probably shouldn't be talking to you."

"You've heard."

"I've heard."

"I could try to explain, but I don't think I understand the situation myself."

"I don't know you well enough to judge."

"Why *are* you talking to me?"

"Gut instinct."

"I'm working to clear this up."

"That'd be good. You've got 'em buzzing at the top of the heap."

"What do you mean?"

"I just had a call from Parker Davenport."

"The lieutenant governor?"

"Himself. Ordered me to keep you off the crash site."

"Doesn't he have better things to worry about?"

"Apparently you're a hot topic. My deputy took a call this morning. Fellow wanted to know where you live and where you were staying up here."

"Who was he?"

"Wouldn't give a name, hung up when my deputy insisted."

"Was he press?"

"We're pretty good at spotting that."

"There's something you can do for me, Sheriff."

I heard the sound of long-distance air.

"Sheriff?"

"I'm listening."

I described the foot, and my reasons for doubting its association with the crash.

"Could you check on missing persons for Swain and the surrounding counties?"

"Got any descriptors besides age?"

"Sixty-three to sixty-six inches in height, with bad feet. When the DNA's in I'll know the gender."

"Time frame?"

Despite the soft tissue preservation, I decided on broad parameters.

"One year."

"I know we've got some here in Swain. I'll pull those up. And I suppose there's no harm in sending out a few queries."

When we'd disconnected, I sealed the slide case and returned it to the technician. As I drove toward home new questions burned in my brain, fanned by feelings of anger and humiliation.

Why wasn't Larke Tyrell defending me? He knew the commitment I felt to my work, knew I'd never compromise an investigation.

Could Parker Davenport be Tyrell's "powerful people"? Larke was an appointed official. Could the lieutenant governor be putting pressure on his chief medical examiner? Why?

Could Lucy Crowe's reaction to Davenport be accurate? Was the lieutenant governor concerned with his image and planning to use me for publicity purposes?

I remembered him at the crash site, hanky to his mouth, eyes down to avoid the carnage.

Or was it me he was avoiding? An unpleasant feeling shifted inside me, and I tried to erase the image. It was no good. My mind was like a computer with no delete button.

I thought of Ryan's advice. Pete's. Both were saying the same thing.

I dialed Information, then placed a call.

Ruby answered after two rings.

I identified myself and asked if Magnolia was available.

"The room's empty, but I offered it to one of the downstairs boarders."

"I'd like to check back in."

"They told me you were gone for good. Cleared the bill."

"I'll pay you for a week in advance."

"Must be the Lord's will the other 'un hasn't moved up there yet."

"Yes," I answered, with an enthusiasm I didn't feel. "The Lord's will."

10

CHARLOTTE IS A POSTER CHILD FOR MULTIPLE PER-sonality disorder, the Sybil of cities. It is the New South, proud of its skyscrapers, airport, university, NBA Hornets, NFL Panthers, and NASCAR racing. Headquarters to Bank of America and First Union, it is the nation's second largest financial center. It is home to the University of North Carolina at Charlotte. It yearns to be a world-class city.

Yet Charlotte remains nostalgic for the Old South. In its affluent southeast quadrant, it is stately homes and tidy bungalows garnished by azaleas, dogwoods, rhododendrons, redbuds, and magnolias. It is winding streets, front porch swings, and more trees per square mile than any burg on the planet. In spring, Charlotte is a kaleidoscope of pink, white, violet, and red. In fall it blazes with yellow and orange. It has a church on every corner and people attend them. The erosion of the genteel life is a constant topic of conversation, but the same folks lamenting its passage keep one eye on the stock market.

I live at Sharon Hall, a turn-of-the-century estate in the elegant old neighborhood of Myers Park. Once a graceful Georgian manor, the Hall had fallen into disrepair by the 1950s and was donated to a local college. In the mid-eighties the two-and-a-half-acre property was purchased by developers, upfitted, and reincarnated as a modern condominium complex.

While most of the Hall's residents occupy the main house, or one of its recently constructed wings, my condo is a tiny structure on the western edge of the property. Records indicate the building started life as an addition to the coach house, but no document describes its original function. For lack of a better term it is simply called the Annex.

Though cramped, my two stories are bright and sunny, and my small patio is perfect for geraniums, one of the few species able to survive my horticultural ministrations. The Annex has been home since my marital breakup, and it suits me perfectly.

The sky was resolutely blue as I entered the gates and circled the grounds. The petunias and marigolds smelled of autumn, their perfume mingling with the scent of drying leaves. Sunshine warmed the bricks of the Hall's buildings, walks, and perimeter wall.

Rounding the Annex, I was surprised to see Pete's Porsche parked next to my patio, Boyd's head protruding from the passenger side. Spotting me, the dog pricked his ears, pulled in his tongue, then let it dangle again.

Through the back window I could see Birdie in his travel cage. My cat did not look pleased with the transport arrangements.

As I pulled parallel to Pete's car, he rounded the building.

"Jesus, am I glad I caught you." His face looked anxious.

"What is it?"

"A client's knitting plant just went up in flames. The case is certain to become a matter of litigation, and I've got to get out there with some experts before would-be fire inspectors muck things up."

"Out where?"

"Indianapolis. I was hoping you'd take Boyd for a couple of days."

The tongue disappeared, dropped again.

"I'm leaving for Bryson City."

"Boyd loves the highlands. He'd be great company."

"Look at him."

Boyd's chin now rested on the window ledge, and saliva trickled down the car's outside panel.

"He'd be protection."

"That's a stretch."

"Really. Harvey didn't like unexpected visitors, so he trained Boyd to sniff out strangers."

"Especially those in uniform."

"The good, the bad, the ugly, even the beautiful. Boyd makes no distinctions."

"Isn't there a kennel where he can board?"

"It's full." He glanced at his watch, then gave me his most beguiling choirboy look. "And my flight leaves in an hour."

Pete had never refused when I'd needed help with Birdie.

"Go. I'll figure something out."

"You're sure?"

"I'll find a kennel."

Pete squeezed both my arms.

"You're my hero."

There are twenty-three kennels in the greater Charlotte area. It took an hour to establish that fourteen were fully booked, five did not answer, two could not accommodate a dog over fifty pounds, and two would take no dog without a personal interview.

"Now what?"

Boyd raised and cocked his head, then went back to licking my kitchen floor.

Desperate, I made another call.

Ruby was less fastidious. For three dollars a day the dog was welcome, no personal audience required.

My neighbor took Birdie, and the chow and I hit the road.

Halloween has its roots in the pagan festival of Samhain. Held at the onset of winter and the beginning of the Celtic New Year, Samhain was the time when the veil between living and dead was thinnest, and spirits roamed the land of mortals. Fires were extinguished and rekindled, and people dressed up to frighten away the unfriendly departed.

Though the holiday was still two weeks off, the residents of Bryson City were into the concept in a big way. Ghouls, bats, and spiders were everywhere. Scarecrows and tombstones had been erected in front yards, and skeletons, black cats, witches, and ghosts dangled from trees and porch lights. Jack-o'-lanterns leered from every window in town. A couple of cars had rather realistic replicas of human feet protruding from their trunks. Good time to actually dispose of a body, I thought.

By five I'd settled Boyd into a run behind High Ridge House, and myself into Magnolia. Then I drove to the sheriff's headquarters.

Lucy Crowe was on the phone when I appeared in her doorway. She waved me into her office, and I took one of two chairs. Her desk filled most of the small space, looking like something at which a Confederate general might have penned military orders. Her chair was also ancient, brown leather and studded, with stuffing oozing from the left arm.

"Nice desk," I said when she'd hung up.

"I think it's ash." The sea-foam eyes were just as startling as on our first meeting. "It was made by my predecessor's grandfather."

She leaned back, and the chair squeaked musically.

"Tell me what I've missed."

"They say you've damaged the investigation."

"Sometimes you get bad press."

Her head did a j-stroke. "What have you got?"

"That foot was walking the earth at least sixty-five years. No one on the plane had that privilege. I need to establish that this was not crash evidence."

The sheriff opened a folder and spread its contents on her blotter.

"I've got three missing persons. Had four, but one turned up."

"Shoot."

"Jeremiah Mitchell, black male, age seventy-two. Disappeared from Waynesville eight months ago. According to patrons at the Mighty High Tap, Mitchell left the bar around midnight to buy hooch. That was February fifteenth. Mitchell's neighbor reported him missing ten days later. He hasn't been seen since."

"No family?"

"None listed. Mitchell was a loner."

"Why the neighbor's concern?"

"Mitchell had his ax and the guy wanted it back. Visited the house several times, finally got tired of waiting, went to see if Mitchell was in the drunk tank. He wasn't, so the neighbor filed an MP report, thinking a police search might flush him."

"And his ax."

"A man's nothing without his tools."

"Height?"

She ran a finger down one of the papers.

"Five foot six."

"That fits. Was he driving?"

"Mitchell was a heavy drinker, traveled by foot. Folks figure he got himself lost and died of exposure."

"Who else?"

"George Adair." She read from another form. "White male, age sixty-seven. Lived over to Unahala, disappeared two weeks ago. Wife said he went fishing with a buddy and never came back."

"What was the buddy's story?"

"Woke one morning and Adair wasn't in the tent. Waited a day, then packed up and went home."

"Where was this fatal fishing trip?"

"The Little Tennessee." She swiveled and stabbed at a spot on a wall map behind her. "Up the Nantahala Mountains."

"Where's Unahala?"

Her finger moved a fraction toward the northeast.

"And where's the crash site?"

Her finger barely moved.

"Who's contestant number three?"

When she turned back, the chair sang another verse.

"Daniel Wahnetah, age sixty-nine, Cherokee from the reservation. Failed to show up for his grandson's birthday on July twenty-seventh. Family reported him missing on August twenty-sixth when he pulled a no-show for his own party." Her eyes moved down the paper. "No height reported."

"The family waited a month?"

"Except in winter, Daniel spends most of his time out in the woods. He has a string of camps, works a circuit hunting and fishing."

She leaned back, and the chair squeaked a tune I didn't know.

"Looks like Jesse Jackson's Rainbow Coalition. If it's one of these guys, nail the race and you've got your man."

"That's it?"

"Folks pretty much stay put up here. Like the idea of dying in their beds."

"See if any of these guys had foot problems. Or if they left shoes at home. Sole imprints could be useful. And start thinking about DNA. Head hair. Extracted teeth. Even a toothbrush might be a source if it hasn't been cleaned or reused. If there's nothing left from the victim we could work with a comparison sample from a blood relative."

She jotted a note.

"And be discreet. If the rest of the body is out there and someone's responsible, we don't want to tip them into finishing what the coyotes began."

"I hadn't thought of that," she said, her voice chalky.

"Sorry."

Again the head movement.

"Sheriff, do you know who owns property about a quarter mile west of the crash site? A house with a walled garden?"

She gazed at me, the eyes like pale green marbles.

"I was born in these mountains, been sheriffing

here almost seven years. Until you came along I had no idea there was anything up that hollow but pine."

"I don't suppose we could get a warrant, have a look inside."

"Don't suppose."

"Isn't it odd that no one knows about the place?"

"Folks keep to themselves up here."

"And die in their beds."

Back at High Ridge House, I took Boyd for a long walk. Or he took me. The chow was psyched, sniffing and baptizing every plant and rock along the road. I enjoyed myself on the downhill lap, awed by soft-focus mountains rolling to the horizon like a Monet landscape. The air was cool and moist, smelling of pine, and loam, and traces of smoke. The trees were alive with the twitter of birds settling in for the night.

The uphill run was another story. Still enthused, Boyd continued to pull on the leash like White Fang mushing across the Arctic. By the time we reached his pen my right arm was dead and my calves ached.

I was closing the gate when I heard Ryan's voice.

"Who's your friend?"

"Boyd. And he's seriously vicious." I was still out of breath, and the words came out chopped and ragged.

"In training for extreme dog walking?"

"Have a good night, boy," I said to the dog.

Boyd concentrated on crunching small brown pellets that looked like petrified jerky.

"You talk to dogs, but not to your old partner?"

I turned and looked at him.

"How ya doing, little fella?"

"Don't even think of scratching my ears. I'm doing well. And yourself?"

"Splendid. We were never partners."

"Did you do your age thing?"

"I was right on."

I checked the lock, then turned to face him.

"Sheriff Crowe's got three elderly MPs. Any scoop on the Bates Motel?"

"Nada. No one knows the place exists. If anyone's using it, they must beam themselves in and out. Either that or no one's talking."

"I'm going to check the tax rolls as soon as the courthouse opens tomorrow. Crowe's following up on the MPs."

"Tomorrow's Saturday."

"Damn." I avoided the impulse to slap my forehead.

Preoccupied with Larke's dismissal of me, I'd lost all track of the days. Government buildings are closed on weekends.

"Damn," I repeated for emphasis, and turned back toward the house. Ryan fell into step beside me.

"Interesting briefing today."

"Oh?"

"The NTSB has compiled preliminary damage diagrams. Come to headquarters tomorrow and I'll pull them up for you."

"Will my presence cause you problems?"

"Call me crazy."

The investigation had taken over much of the Bryson City area. Up on Big Laurel, work continued at the NTSB command center and temporary morgue established at the crash site. Victim identification was progressing at the incident morgue housed in the Alarka Fire Department, and a family assistance center had been set up at the Sleep Inn on Veterans' Boulevard.

In addition, the federal government had rented space in the Bryson City Fire Department and allotted portions to the FBI, NTSB, ATF, and other organizations. At ten the next morning Ryan and I were seated at a desktop computer in one of the tiny cubicles honeycombing the building's upper floor. Between us were Jeff Lowrey, of the NTSB's cabin-interior documentation group, and Susan Katzenberg of the structures group.

As Katzenberg explained her group's preliminary ground-wreckage diagram, I kept a wary eye out for Larke Tyrell. Though I was with the feds, and not really in violation of Larke's banishment, I didn't want a confrontation.

"Here's the wreckage triangle. The apex is at the crash site, then the trail extends back along the flight path for almost four miles. That's consistent with a parabolic descent from twenty-four thousand feet at approximately four miles per minute climbing to pure vertically down."

"I processed bodies recovered more than a mile from the primary wreckage field," I said.

"The pressure hull was breached in midair, permitting the bodies to fall out in flight."

"Where were the flight recorders?" I asked.

"They were found with pieces of the aft fuselage, about halfway along the wreckage trail." She pointed at the screen. "In the F-100 the recorders are located in the unpressurized fuselage aft of the rear pressure bulkhead. They went early when something blew out aft and up."

"So the wreckage pattern is consistent with a midair disintegration sequence?"

"Yes. Anything without wings, that is, without aerodynamic lift generation, falls in a ballistic trajectory, with the heavier stuff going farther horizontally."

She indicated a large cluster of items, then moved her finger along the trail.

"The initial wreckage on the ground would be the small, light stuff."

She pushed back from the computer and turned to Ryan and me.

"I hope that helps. Gotta run."

Lowery took over when she'd gone. The monitor's glow deepened the lines in his face as he bent over the keyboard. He entered commands, and a new pattern filled the screen, looking like a Seurat in primary colors.

"First we established a set of general guidelines to describe the condition of the recovered seats and seat units."

He pointed out colors in the pattern.

"Seats with minimal damage are indicated by light blue, those with moderate damage by dark blue, those with severe damage by green. Seats classified as 'destroyed' are shown in yellow, those classified as 'fragmented' in red."

"What do the categories mean?" I asked.

"Light blue means the seat legs, back, pan, and armrest are intact, as is the safety belt restraint system. Dark blue means there's minor deformation to one or more of those components. Green means both fractures and deformation are present. Yellow indicates a seat with at least two of the five components fractured or missing, and red indicates damage to three or more components."

The diagram showed a plane interior with lavatory, galleys, and closets behind the cockpit, eight seats in first class and eighteen rows in coach, double on port, triple on starboard. Behind the last row, which was double on both sides, was another set of galleys and lavatories.

A child could have interpreted the pattern. The colors flowed from cool blue to flaming red as they spread from forward to aft, indicating that seats closest to the cockpit were largely intact, those in midcabin more damaged, those behind the wings largely demolished. The highest concentration of red was at the rear left of the plane.

Lowery hit the keys and a new chart came up.

"This shows passenger seat assignments, though the aircraft wasn't full and people might have moved around. The cockpit voice recorder indicates that the captain had not turned off the 'Fasten Seat Belt' sign, so most passengers should have been seated with their belts fastened. The voice recorder also indicates that the captain had released the flight attendants to begin cabin service, so they could have been anywhere."

"Will you ever be able to tell who was seated and who wasn't?"

"Recovered seats will be examined for evidence of belt restraint, things like belt loading, belt cuts, occupant-related deformation. With data from the medical/anthropology group we'll try to correlate seat damage with body fragmentation."

I listened, knowing the bodies would be coded, just as the seats had been. Green: body intact. Yellow: crushed head or loss of one extremity. Blue: loss of two extremities with or without crushed head. Red: loss of three or more extremities or complete transection of body.

"The autopsy reports will also show where passengers with penetrating materials, thermal burns, or chemical burns were seated within the cabin," Lowery went on. "We'll also try to correlate right-versus-left-side injury patterns with right-versus-left-seat deformation."

"What does that tell you?" Ryan asked.

"A high degree of correlation would suggest that passengers remained seated through most of the crash sequence. A poor correlation would mean either they were not in their assigned seats, or they became separated from their seats fairly early in the sequence."

I felt a chill thinking of the terror-filled final moments of those passengers.

"The docs will also give us data on anterior-versus-posterior injuries, which we'll correlate to fore-versus-aft seat deformation."

"Why?" Ryan.

"It's assumed that the forward motion of the plane combined with the protective effect of the seat at the occupant's back result in predominantly anterior injuries."

"Unless the passenger is separated from the seat."

"Exactly. Also, in crashes with forward velocity, forward-facing seats are deformed in the forward direction. In midair breakups, that pattern may not occur, since portions of the plane may have tumbled prior to impact."

"And?"

"Of the seats recovered so far, over seventy percent show detectable deformation in the fore-aft plane. Of those, less than forty percent were deformed in the forward direction."

"Meaning in-flight destruction."

"No doubt about it. Susan's group is still studying the mode of breakup. They'll try to reconstruct the exact sequence of failure, but it's pretty clear there was a sudden, catastrophic midair event. That means that parts of the fuselage tumbled prior to ground impact. I'm a little surprised there isn't more variation among the various sections, but these things never follow the book. What is clear is that the seats in each section show nearly identical impact loading."

He worked the keys, and the original diagram filled the screen.

"And there's little doubt where the blast occurred." He pointed to the splotch of fiery red at the left rear of the cabin.

"An explosion doesn't necessarily mean a bomb."

We swiveled to see Magnus Jackson standing at the cubicle entrance. He looked at me a long time but said nothing. The screen glowed rainbow bright behind us.

"The rocket scenario has been given some new credibility," Jackson said.

We all waited.

"There are now three witnesses claiming to have seen an object shoot into the sky."

Ryan crooked an arm over the back of his chair. "I've talked to the Right Reverends Mr. Claiborne and Mr. Bowman, and I'd estimate a combined IQ in the woolly worm range."

I wondered how Ryan knew about woolly worms but didn't ask.

"All three witnesses give times and descriptions that are virtually identical."

"Like their genetic codes," Ryan quipped.

"Will these witnesses take lie detector tests?" I asked.

"They probably think a microwave will fry their genitals," Ryan said.

Jackson almost smiled, but Ryan's jokes were beginning to annoy me.

"You're right," Jackson said. "There's a healthy suspicion of authority and science in the rural areas up here. The witnesses refuse to submit to polygraphs on the grounds that the government could use the technology to alter their brains."

"Give them upgrades?"

Jackson did smile briefly. Then the investigator in charge studied me again, and left without another word.

"Can we go back to the seating chart?" I asked.

Lowery entered a sequence of keystrokes and the diagram filled the screen.

"Can you superimpose the seat damage over that?"

Another few keys and the Seurat was in place.

"Where was Martha Simington seated?"

Lowery pointed to the first row in first class: "1A."

Pale blue.

"And the Sri Lankan exchange student?"

"Anurudha Mahendran—12F, just forward of the right wing."

Dark blue.

"Where were Jean Bertrand and Rémi Petricelli?"

Lowery's finger moved to the last row on the left.

"Twenty-three A and B."

Fiery red.

Ground zero.

11

Following the briefing, Ryan and I bought lunch at Hot Dog Heaven and watched tourists at the Great Smoky Mountains Railroad Depot as we ate. The weather had warmed, and at one-thirty in the afternoon the temperature was in the low eighties. The sun was bright, the wind barely a whisper. Indian summer in Cherokee country.

Ryan promised to ask about progress in victim identification, and I promised to dine with him that night. As he drove off I felt like a housewife whose children had just started full-day school: a long after-noon of yawning until the troops reappeared.

Returning to High Ridge House, I took Boyd for another walk. Though the dog was delighted, the outing was really for me. I was restless and edgy and needed physical exertion. Crowe hadn't called, and I couldn't get into the courthouse until Monday. As I was barred from the morgue and persona non grata with my colleagues, further research into the foot was at a standstill.

I then tried reading but by three-thirty could take it no longer. Grabbing purse and keys, I set out, going somewhere.

I'd hardly left Bryson City when I passed a mile marker for Cherokee.

Daniel Wahnetah was Cherokee. Was he living on the reservation at the time of his disappearance? I couldn't remember.

In fifteen minutes I was there.

The Cherokee Nation once ruled 135,000 square miles of North America, including parts of what are now eight states. Unlike the Plains Indians, so popular with producers of Western movies, the Cherokee lived in log cabins, wore turbans, and adopted the European style of dress. With Sequoyah's alphabet, their language became transcribable in the 1820s.

In 1838, in one of the more infamous betrayals in modern history, the Cherokee were forced from their homes and driven 1,200 miles west to Oklahoma on a death march christened the Trail of Tears. The survivors came to be known as the Western Band Cherokee. The Eastern Band is composed of the descendants of those who hid out and remained in the Smoky Mountains.

As I drove past signs for the Oconaluftee Indian Village, the Museum of the Cherokee Indian, and the outdoor drama *Unto These Hills,* I experienced my usual anger at the arrogance and cruelty of manifest destiny.

Though geared toward the dollar, these contemporary enterprises were also attempts at heritage preservation, and demonstrated the tenacity of another people screwed over by my noble pioneer ancestors.

Billboards plugged Harrah's Casino and the Cherokee Hilton, living proof that Sequoyah's descendants shared his aptitude for cultural borrowing.

So did downtown Cherokee, where T-shirt, leather, knife, and moccasin stores elbowed for space with gift and souvenir emporiums, fudge shops, ice cream parlors, and fast-food joints. The Indian Store. The Spotted Pony. The Tomahawk Mini-Mall. The Buck and Squaw. Teepees sprouted from roofs and painted totem poles flanked entrances. Aboriginal kitsch extraordinaire.

After several unsuccessful passes up and down Highway 19, I parked in a small lot several blocks off the main drag. For the next hour I joined the tourist mass swarming walkways and businesses. I appraised genuine Cherokee ashtrays, key chains, back scratchers, and tom-toms. I inspected authentic wooden tomahawks, ceramic buffalo, acrylic blankets, and plastic arrows, and marveled at the ringing of the cash registers. Had there ever been buffalo in North Carolina?

Now who's screwing whom? I thought, watching a young boy hand over seven dollars for a neon-feathered headdress.

Despite the culture of commercialism, I enjoyed stepping back from my normal world: Women with bite marks on their breasts. Toddlers with vaginal abrasions. Drifters with bellies full of antifreeze. A severed foot. Goosefeather headdresses are preferable to violence and death.

It was also a relief to step out of the emotional quagmire of puzzling relationships. I bought post-cards. Peanut butter fudge. A caramel apple. My problems with Larke Tyrell and my confusion about Pete and Ryan receded to another galaxy.

Walking past the Boot Hill Leather Shop, I had a sudden impulse. Beside Pete's bed I'd noticed the slippers that Katy had given him when she was six years old. I'd buy him moccasins as a thank-you for boosting my spirits.

Or whatever it was that he had boosted.

As I was poking through bins, another thought struck me: Perhaps genuine imitation Native-American footwear would cheer Ryan's spirits over the loss of his partner. O.K. Two for one.

Pete was easy. Eleven D translates to "large" in moccasin. What the hell did Ryan wear?

I was comparing sizes, debating whether an extra large would fit a six-foot-three Irish-Canadian from Nova Scotia, when a series of synapses fired in my brain.

Foot bones. Soldiers in Southeast Asia. Formulae for distinguishing Asian remains from those of American blacks and whites.

Could it work?

Had I taken the necessary measurements?

Grabbing one large and one extra large, I paid and raced for the parking lot, anxious to return to Magnolia to check my spiral notebook.

I was approaching my car when I heard an engine, glanced up, and saw a black Volvo moving in my direction. At first my mind didn't register danger, but the car kept coming. Fast. Too fast for a parking lot.

My mental computer. Velocity. Trajectory.

The car was speeding directly toward me!

Move!

I didn't know which way to throw myself. I guessed left and hit the ground. In seconds the Volvo flashed by, showering me with dirt and gravel. I felt a blast of wind, gears shifted close to my head, and the smell of exhaust filled my lungs.

The engine sounds receded.

I lay flat on the ground, listening to my pounding heart.

My mind connected. Look up!

When I turned my head the Volvo was rounding a corner. The sun was low and straight in my eyes, so I caught only a glimpse of the driver. He was hunched forward, and a cap hid most of his face.

I rolled and pushed myself to a sitting position, brushed dirt from my clothes, and glanced around. I was alone in the lot.

Rising on shaky legs, I threw my purse and package into the backseat, slid behind the wheel, and hit the locks. Then I sat a moment massaging my throbbing shoulder.

What the hell had just happened?

All the way to High Ridge House I replayed the scene. Was I becoming paranoid, or had someone tried to run me down? Was the driver drunk? Blind? Stupid?

Should I report the incident? To Crowe? To McMahon?

Had the silhouette seemed familiar? I'd automatically thought "he," but was it a man?

I decided to ask Ryan's opinion at dinner.

Back in Ruby's kitchen, I made tea and drank it slowly. By the time I'd climbed to Magnolia, my nerves had calmed and my hands were steady. I made a call to the university in Charlotte, not really expecting an answer. My assistant picked up on the first ring.

"What are you doing at the lab on Saturday?"

"Grading."

"Right. I appreciate your dedication, Alex."

"Grading exercises is part of my job. Where are you?"

"Bryson City."

"I thought you were finished there. I mean, your job was finished. I mean . . ." She trailed off, unsure what to say.

Her embarrassment told me that news of my dismissal had reached the university.

"I'll explain when I get back."

"You go, girl." Lamely.

"Listen, can you grab the lab copy of my book?"

"Eighty-six or ninety-eight?"

I'd been the editor of a book on forensic techniques that had become a leading text in its field, largely due to the excellent work of the contributing authors I had managed to assemble, but including a couple of my own chapters as well. After twelve years it had been updated with a second, entirely new edition.

"The first one."

"Hold on."

In seconds she was back.

"What do you need?"

"There's a chapter on population differences in the calcaneus. Flip to that."

"Got it."

"What's the percentage of correct classification when comparing Mongoloid, black, and white foot bones?"

There was a long pause. I could picture her scanning the text, forehead creasing, glasses creeping down her nose.

"Just below eighty percent."

"Not great."

"But wait." Another pause. "That's because the whites and blacks don't separate well. The Mongoloids could be distinguished with eighty-three to ninety-nine percent accuracy. That's not too bad."

"O.K. Give me the list of measurements."

I had a sinking feeling as I wrote them down.

"Now see if there's a table that gives the unstandardized canonical discriminant function coefficients for American Indians, blacks, and whites." I would need these figures for comparison to coefficients I would derive from the unknown foot.

Pause.

"Table Four."

"Will you fax that chapter to me?"

"Sure."

I gave her Primrose Hobbs's name and the fax number at the incident morgue in Bryson City. Hanging up, I dug out the notes I'd taken on case number 397.

When I punched another number and asked for Primrose Hobbs a voice told me she was not there, but asked if I would like her number at the Riverbank Inn.

Primrose also answered on the first ring. This was my lucky day.

"Hey, sweetie pie, how you doin'?"

"I'm good, Primrose."

"Don't you let these slanders get you down. God will do what God will do, and he knows it's all bunk."

"I'm not."

"One day we're going to sit down, play us some more bid whit, and laugh at all this."

"I know."

"Though I must say, for a smart woman, Tempe Brennan, you are the sorriest bid whit player I've ever sat a table with." She laughed her deep, throaty laugh.

"I'm not very good at card games."

"You sure got that right."

Again the laugh.

"Primrose, I need a favor."

"Just ask, sugar."

I gave a condensed version of the history of the foot, and Primrose agreed to go to the morgue early Sunday morning. She would read the fax, call me, and I would walk her through the missing measurements. She commented again on the charges against me, and suggested anatomical locations in which Larke Tyrell could store them.

I thanked her for her loyalty and disconnected.

Ryan chose Injun Joe's Chili Joint for dinner. I chose The Misty Mountain Café, featuring nouvelle cuisine and spectacular views of Balsam Mountain and Maggie Valley. When reasonable discussion failed to resolve the impasse, we flipped a coin.

The Misty Mountain looked more like a ski lodge than a café, built of logs, with high ceilings, fireplaces, and lots of glass. Upon our arrival we were informed that a table would be available in ninety minutes, but wine could be served on the patio immediately.

Joe seated us without delay. Even when I win, I lose.

One look told me *le joint* catered to a different market than *le café*. A half dozen TVs broadcast a college football game, and men in dozer caps lined the bar. Couples and groups occupied tables and booths, denimed and booted, most looking like a haircut or shave had not played a part in their recent past. Mixed into the crowd were tourists in brightly colored windbreakers, and a few faces I recognized from the investigation.

Two men worked the bar, pulling taps, scooping ice, and pouring liquor from bottles in front of a dingy mirror. Each had pasty skin and lank brown hair tied in a ponytail and secured with a bandanna. Neither looked Injun, and neither shopped at Armani. One wore a T-shirt plugging Johnson's Brown Ale, the other a group called Bitchin' Tits.

On a platform in back, across from a pool table and pinball machines, members of a band adjusted equipment, directed by a woman in black leather pants and Cruella makeup. Every few seconds we'd hear the amplified tap of her finger, then a count from one to four. Her sound tests barely overrode the TV play-by-play and the clicks and dings of the pinball machines.

Nevertheless, the band looked like it had enough acoustic power to reach Buenos Aires. I suggested we order.

Ryan scanned the room and made a hand gesture. A woman, maybe forty or so, with overmoussed hair and an out-of-season tan, appeared at our table. A plastic badge gave her name as Tammi. With an *i*.

"Whatillitbe?" Tammi poised pencil over pad.

"May I have a menu?" I asked.

Tammi sighed, retrieved two menus from the bar, and slapped them on the table. Then she looked at me with forbidding patience.

Click. Click. Click. Ding. Ding. Ding. Ding.

My decision did not take long. Injun Joe offered nine types of chili, four burgers, a hot dog, and mountain meat loaf.

I requested the Climbingbear Burger and a Diet Coke.

"I've heard you make killer chili here." Ryan showed Tammi a lot of teeth.

"Best in the west." Tammi showed Ryan even more.

Tap. Tap. Tap. Tap. One. Two. Three. Four.

"It must be hard to wait on so many people at the same time. I don't know how you do it."

"Personal charm." Tammi tilted her chin and threw out one hip.

"How's the Walkingstick Chili?"

"Hot. Like me."

I fought a gag impulse.

"I'll go for it. And a bottle of Carolina Pale."

"Coming atcha, cowboy."

Click. Click. Click. Click. Ding. Ding. Ding. Ding. Ding.

Tap. Tap. One. Two. Three. Four.

I waited until Tammi was out of earshot, which, given the din, was about two steps.

"Nice choice."

"One should mingle with the locals."

"You were pretty critical of the locals this morning."

"One must keep a finger on the pulse of the common man."

"And woman." *Tap. Tap.* "Cowboy."

Tammi returned with a beer, a Diet Coke, and a million miles of teeth. I smiled her back to the kitchen.

"Anything new since this morning?" I asked when she'd gone.

"Seems Haskell Simington may not be such a hot pick. Turns out he's worth zillions, so a two mill policy on his wife isn't that unusual. Besides being worth megabucks, the guy named their kids as beneficiaries."

"That's it?"

Ryan waited out another sound check.

"The structures group reported that three quarters of the plane has been trucked down the mountain. They're reassembling in a hangar near Asheville."

Tap. Tap. Tap. One. Screeeeeeech. Two. Three. Four.

Ryan's eyes drifted to a TV behind my head.

"That's it?"

"That's it. Why the orange paw prints?"

"It's a Clemson home game."

He looked a question at me.

"Never mind."

Tammi was back after three downs.

"I gave you extra cheese," she purred, bending low to give Ryan a spectacular view of cleavage.

"I love cheese." Ryan gave her another blinding smile, and Tammi held position.

Tap. Tap. One. Two. Three. Four.

I glared at Tammi's breasts, and she removed them from my line of vision.

"Will that be all?"

"Ketchup." I picked up a French fry.

"Any talk about my visit to headquarters this morning?"

When I lifted my burger a cheese umbilicus clung to the plate.

"Special Agent McMahon said you looked good in jeans."

"I didn't see McMahon there." The bun was raining soggy clumps onto the cheese connector.

"He saw *you*. At least from the back."

"What's the FBI position on my dismissal?"

"I can't speak for the entire Bureau, but I know McMahon isn't fond of your state's second in command."

"I don't know for certain that Davenport is behind the complaint."

"Whether he is or not, McMahon has no time for him. He called Davenport a brainless buttwipe." Ryan spooned chili into his mouth, followed it with beer. "We Irish are poets at heart."

"That brainless buttwipe can probably have you invited back to Canada."

"How was your afternoon?"

"I went to the reservation."

"Did you see Tonto?"

"How did I know you would ask that?"

I reached into my bag and produced the moccasins.

"I wanted you to have something from my native land."

"To atone for the way you've been treating me lately?"

"I've been treating you as a colleague."

"A colleague who'd like to suck your toes."

My stomach did that little flippy thing.

"Open the package."

He did.

"These are kickin'."

Resting an ankle on one knee, Ryan replaced a deck shoe with a moccasin. A big-haired deb at the bar stopped peeling the label from her Coors to watch him.

"Made by Sitting Bull himself?"

"Sitting Bull was Sioux. These were probably made by Wang Chou Lee."

He reversed, and did the other foot. The deb jabbed an elbow at her companion.

"You may not want to wear them here."

"Certainly I do. They were a gift from a colleague."

He wrapped the deck shoes in the moccasin bag and went back to his chili.

"Meet any interesting aboriginals?"

I wanted to say no. "Actually, I did."

He looked up with eyes blue enough to blend in with a village full of Finns.

"Or, I might have."

I told him about the Volvo incident.

"Jesus, Brennan. How do—"

"I know. How do I get myself into these situations. Do you think I should worry about it?" I was hoping he would say no.

Ding. Ding. Ding. Ding.

Tap. Tap. One. Two. Three. Four.

Chili.

Beer.

Fragments of conversations.

"The deconstructionists tell us that nothing is real, but I've discovered one or two truisms in life. The first is, when attacked by a Volvo, take it seriously."

"I'm not sure the guy meant to run me down. Maybe he didn't see me."

"Did you think so at the time?"

"That's how it felt."

"Second truism: Volvo first impressions are generally correct."

We'd finished eating and Ryan was in the men's room when I noticed Lucy Crowe enter and make her way toward the bar. She was in uniform and looked armed and deadly.

I waved but Crowe didn't notice. I stood and waved again, and a voice bellowed, "You're blocking the game. Park it or haul it."

Ignoring the suggestion, I flapped both arms. Crowe saw me, nodded, and held up an index finger. As I sat, the bartender handed her a glass, then leaned forward to whisper something.

"Hey, sweet cheeks!"

A redneck scorned is never pretty. I continued to ignore, he continued to taunt.

"Hey, you with the windmill act."

The redneck was ratcheting up when he spotted the sheriff moving in my direction. Realizing his error, he swigged his beer and reengaged with the game.

Ryan and Crowe reached the booth simultaneously. Noticing Ryan's feet, the sheriff looked at me.

"He's Canadian."

Ryan let it pass and resumed his seat.

Crowe set her 7UP on the table and joined us.

"Dr. Brennan has a story she wants to share," said Ryan, pulling out his cigarettes.

I looked icicles at him. I would have preferred a lifetime of tax audits to telling Crowe of the Volvo incident.

She listened without interrupting.

"Did you get the license number?"

"No."

"Can you describe the driver?"

"Wearing a cap."

"What kind of cap?"

"I couldn't tell." I could feel my cheeks flush with humiliation.

"Was anyone else present?"

"No. I checked. Look, the whole thing may have been an accident. Maybe it was a kid peeling out in Daddy's Volvo."

"Is that what you think?" The celery eyes were locked on mine.

"No. I don't know."

I placed my hands on the tabletop, pulled them back, and wiped spilled beer onto my jeans.

"While I was on the reservation I thought of something that might be helpful," I said, changing the subject.

"Oh?"

I described the foot bone research and explained how the measurements could be used to determine racial background.

"So I may be able to sort out your rainbow coalition."

"I'll talk with Daniel Wahnetah's kin tomorrow."

She swirled the ice in her 7UP.

"But I unearthed some interesting facts about George Adair."

"The missing angler?"

A Crowe nod.

"Adair saw his doctor twelve times during the past year. Seven of those visits were for throat problems. The other five were for pain in his feet."

"Hot dog."

"It gets better. Adair's only gone one week, his grieving widow takes a trip to Las Vegas with the next-door neighbor."

I waited while she drained her 7UP.

"The neighbor is George Adair's best friend."

"And fishing buddy?"

"You've got it."

12

THE NEXT MORNING I SLEPT UNTIL EIGHT, FED BOYD, and overdosed on one of Ruby's mountain breakfasts. My hostess had bonded with the dog, and that day's Scripture lauded the fish of the sea, the fowl of the air, and things that creepeth upon the earth. I wondered if Boyd qualified as a creeper but didn't ask.

Ryan hadn't appeared by the time I left the dining room. Either he was out early, sacking in, or passing up the hotcakes, bacon, and grits. We'd returned from Injun Joe's around eleven the previous night, and he'd proffered his usual invitation. I'd left him on the front porch, swinging without me.

I was climbing to Magnolia when my cell phone rang. It was Primrose, calling from the incident morgue.

"You must have risen with the birds."

"Have you been outside?" she asked.

"Not yet."

"It's a great gettin'-up morning out there."

"Did you get the fax?"

"I surely did. Studied the descriptions and dia-grams and took every measurement."

"You're amazing, Primrose."

I double-stepped the last few stairs, raced to my room, and opened the file on case number 387. After jotting down the new figures, we compared Prim-rose's data with that which I'd already collected.

"Each of your measurements is within one mil-limeter of mine," I said. "You're good."

"You got that right."

Confident that inter-observer error would not be a problem, I thanked her, and asked when I could get the chapter. She suggested I meet her at the parking lot gate in twenty minutes. In her opinion, entry into the morgue was not yet an option for me.

Primrose must have been watching, for as soon as I left the highway she emerged through the morgue's back door and began picking her way across the lot, cane in one hand, plastic grocery bag in the other.

Meanwhile, the guard came forward, read my license plate, and checked a clipboard. Then he shook his head, held one hand in a halt gesture, and signaled me to reverse direction with the other. Primrose approached him and said a few words.

The guard continued to signal and shake his head. Primrose leaned close and spoke again, old black woman to young black man. The guard rolled his eyes, then folded his hands across his chest and watched her continue toward my car, a five-star general in boots, fatigues, and granny bun.

Leaning on her cane, she handed the bag through the driver's-side window. Her face was serious a moment, then a smile lighted her eyes, and she patted me on the shoulder.

"Don't you pay this trouble no mind, Tempe. You haven't done any of those things and they'll see that soon."

"Thanks, Primrose. You're right, but it's hard."

"Course it is. But I'm keeping you in my prayers."

Her voice was as soothing as a Brandenburg Concerto.

"In the meantime, you just take one day at a time. One damn day at a time."

With that she turned and set off toward the morgue.

I'd rarely heard Primrose Hobbs curse.

Back in my room, I pulled out the chapter, flipped to Table IV, plugged in the measurements, and did the math.

The foot classified as American Indian.

I calculated again, using a second function.

Though closer to the cluster for African Americans, the foot still fell with the Native Americans.

George Adair was white, Jeremiah Mitchell was black. So much for the missing fisherman and the man who'd borrowed his neighbor's ax.

Unless he'd wandered back to the reservation, Daniel Wahnetah was looking like a match.

I checked my watch. Ten forty-five. Late enough.

The sheriff was not in. No. They would not phone her at home. No. They would not give out her pager number. Was this an emergency? They would relay the message that I had called.

Damn. Why hadn't I gotten Crowe's pager number?

For the next two hours I engaged in irrelevant activity, directed by the brain for tension relief rather than goal attainment. Behaviorists call it displacement.

Following a laundry session involving panties in the bathroom sink, I sorted and organized the contents of my briefcase, deleted temporary files from my laptop, balanced my checkbook, and rearranged Ruby's glass animal collection. I then phoned my daughter, sister, and estranged husband.

Pete did not answer, and I assumed he was still in Indiana. Katy did not answer, and I made no assumptions. Harry kept me on the phone for forty minutes. She was quitting her job, having trouble with her teeth, and dating a man named Alvin from Denton. Or was it Denton from Alvin?

I was testing the ring options on my phone when a strange baying arose from the yard, like a hound in a Bela Lugosi movie. Peering through the screen, I saw Boyd seated in the middle of his run, head thrown back, a wail rising from his throat.

"Boyd."

He stopped howling and looked around. Far down the mountain I heard a siren.

"I'm up here."

The dog stood and cocked his head, then the purple tongue slid out.

"Look up, boy."

Reverse cock.

"Up!" I clapped my hands.

The chow spun, ran to the end of the pen, sat, and resumed his love song to the ambulance.

The first thing one notices on meeting Boyd is his disproportionately large head. It was becoming clear that the dog's cranial capacity was in no way related to the size of his intellect.

Grabbing jacket and leash, I headed out.

The temperature was still warm, but the sky was slowly filling with dark-centered clouds. Wind flapped my jacket and gusted leaves and pine needles across the gravel road.

This time we did the uphill lap first, Boyd charging ahead, huffing and coughing as the collar tightened across his larynx. He raced from tree to tree, sniffing and squirting, while I gazed into the valley below, each of us enjoying the mountain in our own way.

We'd gone perhaps a half mile when Boyd froze and his head shot up. The fur went stiff along his spine, his mouth half opened, and a growl rose from the back of his throat, a sound quite different from the siren display.

"What is it, boy?"

Ignoring my question, the dog lunged, ripping the leash from my grip, and charged into the woods.

"Boyd!"

I stamped my foot and rubbed my palm.

"Damn!"

I could hear him through the trees, barking like he was on scrap yard sentry duty.

"Boyd, come back here!"

The barking continued.

Cursing at least one creature that creepeth, I left the road and followed the noise. I found him ten yards in, dashing back and forth, yapping at the base of a white oak.

"Boyd!"

He continued running, barking, and snapping at the oak.

"BOYD!"

He skidded to a stop and looked in my direction.

Dogs have fixed facial musculature, making them incapable of expression. They cannot smile, frown, grimace, or sneer. Nevertheless, Boyd's eyebrows made a movement that clearly communicated his disbelief.

Are you crazy?

"Boyd, sit!" I pointed a finger and held it on him.

He looked at the oak, back at me, then sat. Never lowering the finger, I picked my way to him and regained the leash.

"Come on, dog breath," I said, patting his head, then tugging him toward the road.

Boyd twisted and yipped at the oak, then turned back and did the eyebrow thing.

"What *is* it?"

Rrrrup. Rup. Rup.

"O.K. Show me."

I gave him some leash, and he dragged me toward the tree. Two feet from it, he barked and whipped around, eyes shining with excitement. I parted the vegetation with a boot.

A dead squirrel lay among the sow thistle, orbits empty, brown tissue sheathing its bones like a dark, leathery shroud.

I looked at the dog.

"Is this what's got your fur in a twist?"

He dropped on front paws, rump in the air, then rose and took two hops backward.

"It's dead, Boyd."

The head cocked, and the eyebrow hairs rotated.

"Let's go, mighty tracker."

The rest of the walk was uneventful. Boyd found no more corpses, and we clocked a much better time on the downhill run. Rounding the last curve I was surprised to see a cruiser parked under the trees at High Ridge House, a Swain County Sheriff's Department shield on its side.

Lucy Crowe stood on the front steps, a Dr Pepper in one hand, Smokey hat in the other. Boyd went right to her, tail wagging, tongue drooping like a purple eel. The sheriff set her hat on the railing and ruffled the dog's fur. He nuzzled and licked her hand, then curled on the porch, chin on forepaws, and closed his eyes. Boyd the Deadly.

"Nice dog," said Crowe, wiping a hand on the seat of her pants.

"I'm minding him for a few days."

"Dogs are good company."

"Um."

Obviously, she'd never spent time with Boyd.

"I had a talk with the Wahnetah family. Daniel still hasn't returned."

I waited while she sipped her soda.

"They say he stood about five-seven."

"Did he complain about his feet?"

"Apparently he never complained about anything. Didn't talk much at all, liked to be alone. But here's an interesting sidebar. One of Daniel's campsites was out at Running Goat Branch."

"Where's Running Goat Branch?"

"Spit and a half from your walled enclosure."

"No shit."

"No shit."

"Was he there when he went missing?"

"The family wasn't sure, but that was the first place they checked."

"I've got another sidebar," I said, my excitement growing.

I told her about the discriminant function classification placing the foot bones closest to those of Native Americans.

"Now can you get a warrant?" I asked.

"Based on what?"

I ticked off points by raising fingers.

"An elderly Native American went missing in your county. I have a body part fitting that profile. This body part was recovered in proximity to a location frequented by your missing person."

She cocked an eyebrow, then did her own ticking.

"A body part that might or might not be related to an aviation disaster. An old man who might or might not be dead. A property that might or might not be implicated in either situation."

The hunch of an anthropologist who might or might not be the spawn of Satan. I didn't say it.

"Let's at least go to his camp and look around," I pushed.

She thought a moment, then looked at her watch.

"That I can do."

"Give me five minutes." I gestured at Boyd.

She nodded.

"Come on, boy."

The head came up and the eyebrows puckered.

A ping in my mind. The dead squirrel. My line of work makes me unusually sensitive to the smell of putrefaction, yet I hadn't detected a trace. Boyd went ballistic at ten yards.

"Could the dog ride along?" I asked. "He's not cadaver-trained, but he's pretty good at sniffing out carrion."

"He sits in back."

I opened the door and whistled. Boyd bounded over and leaped in.

Eleven days had passed since the Air TransSouth crash. All remains had been taken to the morgue, and the last of the wreckage was being hauled down the mountain. The recovery operation was winding down, and the change was evident.

The county road was now open, though a sheriff's deputy protected the entrance to the Forest Service road. The families and press were gone, and only a handful of vehicles occupied the overlook holding area.

Crowe cut the engine where the road ended, about a half mile beyond the cutoff to the crash site. A large granite outcropping lay to the right. Clipping a radio to her belt, she crossed the gravel track and walked the uphill side, carefully studying the tree line.

I leashed Boyd and followed, keeping him as close to me as I could. After a full five minutes the sheriff cut left and disappeared up the embankment into the trees. I gave Boyd his head, and was dragged along in her wake.

The land climbed steeply, leveled off, then shot downward into a valley. As we moved farther and farther from the road, the trees closed around us, and everything started to look the same. But the landmarks given by the Wahnetah family made sense to the sheriff. She found the path they'd described, and from it a small dirt road. I couldn't tell if it was the same logging trail that passed by the wreckage field or another similar to it.

It took Crowe forty minutes to locate Daniel's cabin, set among beech and pine at the edge of a small creek. I probably would have walked right past it.

The camp looked as though it had been thrown up in an afternoon. The shack was wood, the floor dirt, the roof corrugated tin, extended in front to provide shelter for a makeshift bench beside the door. A wooden table and another bench sat to the left front of the shanty, a tree stump to the right. Out back I could see a pile of bottles, cans, tires, and other refuse.

"How do you suppose the tires got here?" I asked.

Crowe shrugged.

Gingerly, I cracked the door and stuck my head inside. In the gloom I could make out a cot, an aluminum lawn chair, and a collapsible table holding a rusty camp stove and a collection of plastic dishes and cups. Fishing gear, a bucket, a shovel, and a lantern hung from nails. Kerosene cans lined the floor. That was it.

"Would the old man leave his fishing gear if he planned to move on?"

Another shrug.

Lacking a real plan, Crowe and I decided to split up. She searched the creek bank while I walked the surrounding woods. My canine companion sniffed and peed contentedly.

Returning to the shack, I secured Boyd to a table leg, swung the door wide, and propped it with a rock. Inside, the air smelled of mildew, kerosene, and muscatel. Millipedes skittered as I shifted objects, and at one point a daddy longlegs high-stepped up my arm. I found nothing to indicate where Daniel Wahnetah had gone or when he'd left. Or why.

Crowe reappeared as I was poking through the refuse heap. After toeing over dozens of wine bottles, cracker tins, and Dinty Moore beef stew cans, I gave up and picked my way out to join her.

Trees whispered in the wind. Leaves sailed across the ground in a colorful regatta, and a corner of the corrugated tin rose and fell with a scraping sound. Though the air felt dense and heavy, there was movement all around us.

Crowe knew what I was thinking. Without a word she pulled a small spiral-bound atlas from her jacket and flipped through the pages.

"Show me," she said, handing me the book.

The map she'd chosen was a close-up of the piece of Swain County in which we stood. Using elevation lines, the county road, and the logging trails, I located the crash site. Then I estimated the position of the courtyard house and pointed to it.

"Here."

Crowe studied the topography around my finger.

"You're sure there's a structure back in there?" I heard doubt in her voice.

"Yes."

"It's less than a mile."

"By foot?"

She nodded, a slower motion than usual.

"There's no road I know of, so we might as well go overland."

"Can you find it?"

"I can find it."

We spent an hour threading our way through trees and brush, up one ridge and down another, following a track that was clear to Crowe but invisible to me. Then, at an ancient pine, its trunk knotted and worn, we emerged onto a path that even I could recognize.

We came to a high wall, vaguely familiar from my previous visit. Every sense sharpened as we moved along the mossy stone. A jay cawed, shrill and strident, and my skin seemed to tighten on my body. There was something here. I knew it.

Boyd continued to amble and snuffle, oblivious to my tension. I wrapped the leash around my palm, tightened my grasp.

Within yards, the wall made a ninety-degree turn. Crowe rounded the corner and I followed, my grip so tight I felt my nails dig into my palm.

The trees ended three quarters of the distance up the wall. Crowe stopped at the verge of the woods and Boyd and I caught up.

Ahead and to the left I spotted another walled enclosure, the rock face rising in the distance beyond. I had my bearings. We'd approached from the rear of the property; the house lay ahead of us, its back to the escarpment. The wall we'd been skirting surrounded a larger area I hadn't noted on my first visit. The courtyard was within the larger enclosure.

"I'll be damned." Crowe reached down and released the safety on her gun.

She called out as I had done. Called again.

Eyes and ears alert, we proceeded to the house and climbed the steps. The shutters were still closed, the windows still draped. I was gripped by the same sense of foreboding as on my first visit.

Crowe stepped to the side of the door and gestured with an arm. When Boyd and I had moved behind her, she knocked. Still no answer.

She knocked again, identified herself. Silence.

Crowe raised her eyes and looked around.

"No phone lines. No power lines."

"Cell phone and generator."

"Could be. Or the place could be deserted."

"Do you want to see the courtyard?"

"Not without a warrant I don't."

"But, Sheriff—"

"No warrant, no entry." She looked at me, her eyes unblinking. "Let's go. I'll buy you a Dr Pepper."

At that moment, a light rain began to fall. I listened to drops tick softly on the porch roof, frustration seething in me. She was right. It was nothing but a hunch. But every cell in my being was telling me that something important lay close at hand. Something evil.

"Could I run Boyd around the property, see if he has any thoughts?"

"Keep him outside the walls, I've got no objection. I'll check for vehicular access. If folks are coming here, they must be driving."

For fifteen minutes Boyd and I crisscrossed the brush to the west of the house, much as I had on my first trip. The dog showed no reaction. Though I was beginning to suspect the squirrel hit had been a fluke, I decided to make one last sweep, skirting the edge of the forest up to its terminus at the second enclosure. This would be virgin territory.

We were twenty feet from the wall when Boyd's head snapped up. His body tensed, and the hair prickled along his back. He rotated his snout, testing the air, then growled in a way I'd heard only once, deep and feral and vicious. Then he lunged, choking and barking as though possessed.

I staggered, barely able to hold him.

"Boyd! Stop!"

Spreading my feet, I grabbed the leash with both hands. The dog continued to pull, muscles straining, forefeet scrabbling inches above the ground.

"What is it, boy?"

We both knew.

I hesitated, heart pounding. Then I unwrapped the leash and let it fall.

Boyd flew to the wall and exploded in a frenzy of barking, approximately six feet south of the back corner. I could see that the mortar was crumbling at that point, and that a dozen stones had tumbled free, leaving a gap between the ground and the wall's foundation.

I ran to the dog, crouched at his shoulder, and inspected the gap. The soil was moist and discolored. Overturning a fallen stone, I saw a dozen tiny brown objects.

Instantly, I knew what Boyd had found.

I DID NOT GO TO THE SWAIN COUNTY COURTHOUSE on Monday. Instead, I recrossed the mountains west to Tennessee, and by midmorning was approximately thirty miles northwest of Knoxville, approaching the entrance to the Oak Ridge National Laboratory. The day was wet and gloomy, and my wipers slapped a steady cadence back and forth, clearing two fans on the misty windshield.

Through the side window I could see an old woman and toddler feeding swans on the bank of a small lagoon. At the age of ten I'd had a run-in with an ugly duckling that could have taken out a commando force. I questioned the wisdom of their outing.

After showing ID at a guardhouse, I drove across a vast parking area to the reception center. My host was waiting, signed me in, and we returned to the car. Another hundred yards, and my new ORNL badge and license plates were verified at a third checkpoint before I was allowed to pass through a chain-link fence surrounding the compound.

"Pretty tight security. I thought this was Department of Energy."

"It is. Most of the work involves energy conservation, computers and robotics, biomedical and environmental conservation, medical radioisotope development, that sort of thing. We maintain security to protect DOE intellectual property and physical equipment. There's also a high-flux isotope reactor on-site."

Laslo Sparkes was in his thirties but already nurturing a stout paunch. He had short, slightly bowed limbs and a round face, pockmarked on the cheeks.

Oak Ridge began as a World War II wonder baby, constructed in just three short months in 1943. Thousands were dying in Europe and Asia, and Enrico Fermi and his colleagues had just achieved nuclear fission in a squash court under the stands of the football stadium at the University of Chicago. Oak Ridge's mission had been simple: build the atomic bomb.

Laslo directed me through a labyrinth of narrow streets. Turn right here. Left. Left. Right. Except for its vast size, the complex looked like an apartment project in the Bronx.

Laslo indicated a dark brick building identical to a score of other dark brick buildings.

"Park here," he said.

I pulled over and cut the engine.

"I really appreciate your doing this on such short notice."

"You were there when I asked for help."

Years earlier, Laslo had needed bone for his master's research in anthropology, and I'd provided samples. We'd kept in touch throughout his doctoral work and during the decade he'd been a research scientist at Oak Ridge.

Laslo waited while I retrieved a small cooler from the trunk, then led me into the building and up the stairs to his lab. The room was small and windowless, every millimeter crammed with battered steel desks, computers, printers, refrigerators, and a million machines that glowed and hummed. Glass vials, water containers, stainless-steel instruments, and boxes of latex gloves lined the countertops, and cardboard cartons and plastic buckets were stacked below.

Laslo led me to a work space in back and reached for the cooler. When I handed it to him, he removed a plastic bag, peeled off the tape, and peeked inside.

"Give this to me again," he said, sniffing the bag's contents.

As I explained my trek with Lucy Crowe, Laslo poured dirt from the bag into a glass container. Then he began entering information onto a blank form.

"Where did you sample?"

"I collected where the dog indicated, under the wall and under the stones that had fallen out. I figured that soil would be most protected."

"Good thinking. Normally the corpse acts as a shield for the soil, but stones would have had the same effect."

"Does rain create problems?"

"In a protected environment the heavy, mucoidlike secretions produced from anaerobic fermentation bind the soil together, making dilutional factors from rainfall insignificant."

He sounded like he was reading from one of his articles in the *Journal of Forensic Sciences*.

"Keep it simple, please. This is way off my field."

"You spotted the decomp stain."

"Actually, my dog did." I indicated a plastic vial. "The pupae are what tipped me."

Laslo withdrew the jar, twisted off the lid, and shook a number of casings into the palm of his hand. Each looked like a miniature football.

"So maggot migration had taken place."

"*If* the stain is from a decomp espisode." I'd had all night to worry over Boyd's discovery. Though I was sure his nose and my instincts were correct, I wanted proof.

"Maggot pupae definitely suggest the presence of a corpse." He replaced the casings. "I think your dog was right on."

"Can you determine if it was an animal?"

"The amount of volatile fatty acids will tell us if the body was over one hundred pounds. Very few mammals get that big."

"What about hunting? A deer or bear could get that big."

"Did you find any hairs?"

I shook my head.

"Decaying animals leave behind tons of hair. And bones, of course."

When an organism dies, scavengers, insects, and microbes take an immediate interest, some munching from the outside, others from within, until the body is reduced to bone. This is known as decomposition.

Ruby would talk in terms of dust to dust, but the process is much more complicated than that.

Muscle, comprising 40 to 50 percent of the weight of a human body, is composed of protein, which is composed of amino acids. At death, the fermentation of fat and protein yields volatile fatty acids, or VFAs, through bacterial action. Inside the gut, other microbes do their part. As putrefaction advances, liquids ooze from the body, carrying with them the VFAs. Death investigators call the mixture soup.

Laslo's research focused at the microbial level, analyzing organic components contained in the dirt under and around a body. Years of work had demonstrated a correlation between the decay process and VFA production.

I watched him filter soil through a stainless-steel sieve.

"Exactly what do you look for in the dirt?"

"I don't use soil, I use soil solution."

I must have looked blank.

"The liquid component between soil particles. But first I have to clean it."

He weighed the sample.

"As body fluids flow through, the organic matter becomes bound to the soil. I can't use chemical extractants for separation, because that would partially dissolve the volatile fatty acids from the decomposing body."

"And alter their measurements."

"Exactly."

He placed the soil in a centrifuge tube and added water.

"I use deionized water in a ratio of two to one."

The tube went onto a vortex for one minute to mix the solution. Then he transferred it to a centrifuge and closed the lid.

"The temperature inside is held at five degrees. I'll centrifuge for forty minutes, then filter the sample to remove any remaining microorganisms. After that it's simple. I'll check the pH, acidify with a formic acid solution, and pop the thing into the gas chromatograph."

"How about a crash course."

Laslo finished adjusting settings, then gestured to a desk and we both sat.

"O.K. As you know, I'm looking at the products of muscle and fat breakdown called volatile fatty acids. Are you familiar with the four stages of decomposition?"

Anthropologists and death investigators think of corpses as being in one of four broad stages: fresh, bloated, decayed, or skeletal.

I nodded.

"There's little change in VFAs in a fresh corpse. In the second stage, a body bloats due to anaerobic fermentation, primarily in the gut. This causes skin breakage and the leakage of fermentation by-products rich in butyric acids."

"Butyric acids?"

"Volatile fatty acids include forty-one different organic compounds, of which butyric acid is one. Butyric, formic, acetic, propionic, valeric, caproic, and heptanoic are detectable in soil solution because they're soluble in water. Two of them, formic and acetic, are too abundant in nature to be of much use."

"Formic is the one that causes pain from ant bites, right?"

"That's the one. Caproic and heptanoic are only found in significant amounts during the colder months. Propionic, butyric, and valeric are my boys. They're released from a decomposing corpse and deposited in soil solutions in specific ratios."

I felt like I was back in Biochem 101.

"Since butyric and propionic acids are formed by anaerobic bacteria in the gut, the levels are high during the bloat stage."

I nodded.

"Later, during decay, aerobic bacteria join the act."

"So at stage three there's a surge in all VFA formation."

"Yes. Then there's a rapid fall-off at the onset of stage four."

"No flesh, no bacteria."

"The soup kitchen closes."

Behind us the centrifuge hummed softly.

"I've also found that all fatty acid values are highest just after maggot migration."

"When larvae abandon the corpse to pupate."

"Yes. Until that point the presence of the insects tends to restrict the flow of body fluids into the soil."

"Doesn't pupation occur at approximately four hundred ADD?" ADD stands for "accumulated degree days," a figure calculated by summing average daily temperatures.

"With some variation. Which brings up a good point. VFA production is temperature dependent. That's why it can be used to determine time since death."

"Because a corpse will produce the same ratios of propionic, butyric, and valeric acids for any given accumulated degree days."

"Exactly. So the volatile fatty acid profile can provide an estimate of TSD." TSD is the investigator's shorthand for "time since death."

"Did you get the National Weather Service data?"

He went to a set of shelves and returned with a printout.

"It was amazingly fast. Normally it takes much longer. But we do have a slight problem. For a really accurate TSD estimate I need three things. First, the specific fatty acid ratios."

He pointed at a computer screen linked to the gas chromatograph.

"We'll have those shortly. Second, the National Weather Service data at the location where the corpse was found."

He held up the printout.

"Third, information on the weight and condition of the corpse. And you ain't got no body." He sang the last.

"Everyone's a comedian."

"Two variables are important: the amount of moisture in the soil, and the weight of the body prior to decomposition. Because everyone has a different ratio of fat and muscle tissue, if I don't have a body, I use a standard of one hundred fifty pounds, then apply a correction factor. I think we're safe in assuming your deceased weighed between one hundred and three hundred pounds?"

"Yes. But in doing this, our range broadens, right?"

"Unfortunately. Did you try a rule-of-thumb estimate?"

Since volatile fatty acid liberation ceases at accumulated degree days 1,285 plus or minus 110, it is possible to obtain a rough estimate of time since death by dividing the average daily temperature on the day a corpse is found into 1,285. I'd done this for

Lucy Crowe. Yesterday's average temperature in Bryson City was 18°C (64°F), yielding a maximum time since death of seventy-one days.

"That would be the date on which full skeletonization had taken place, and no more VFAs would be detectable."

Laslo looked at the wall clock.

"Let's see how accurate you were."

He rose, filtered and vortexed the soil solution sample, tested its acidity, then placed the tube into the gas chromatograph. After closing and sealing the chamber, and adjusting the settings, he turned back to me.

"Let's give this a few minutes. Coffee?"

When we returned the screen showed a series of peaks in varying colors, and a list of components and their concentrations.

"Each curve shows the concentration of a volatile fatty acid per gram of dry weight of soil. First I'll correct for dilution and soil moisture."

He hit a few keys.

"Now I can calculate an ADD for each VFA."

He started with butyric acid.

"Seven hundred accumulated degree days."

He performed more calculations, using each acid. With one exception the ADDs fell within the 675 to 775 range.

"Now I'll use the National Weather Service data to determine the number of days needed to obtain 675 to 775 accumulated degree days. We may have to adjust later if the readings at your body site differ from the officially recorded temperatures. Normally, I like to know that in advance, but it's not a major problem."

A few more keystrokes. I held my breath.

"Forty-one to forty-eight days. That's your range. According to your calculation, full skeletonization would have taken place in seventy-one days."

"So death occurred six to seven weeks ago."

He nodded. "But keep in mind that this time frame is based on an estimated, not an actual, predeath weight."

"And at the time the stain was produced, the body was fleshed and actively decomposing."

He nodded.

"But I ain't got no body."

"And nobody cares for me."

I drove straight to Lucy Crowe's office. The rain had stopped, but dark clouds shouldered each other low over the mountains, jockeying for position with their heavy loads.

I found the sheriff eating a corn dog behind the Civil War desk. Seeing me, she wiped crumbs from her mouth, then arced the stick and wrapper into a trash can across the room.

"Two points," I said.

"All net. No rim."

I laid hard copy in front of her and took a chair. She studied the VFA profile a full minute, elbows splayed on the desktop, fingers on her temples. Then she looked up.

"I know you're going to explain this."

"Volatile fatty acids."

"Meaning?"

"A body decomposed inside that wall."

"Whose?"

"The VFA ratios suggest a time since death of six to seven weeks. Daniel Wahnetah was last seen in late July, reported missing in August. It's now October. Do the math."

"Assuming I accept that premise, which I don't necessarily, how did Wahnetah's foot get to the crash scene?"

"If Boyd smelled decomposition, so could coyotes. They probably dragged the foot from under the wall. There's room where the foundation has crumbled."

"And left the rest of him?"

"They probably couldn't detach anything else."

"And how did Wahnetah get inside the courtyard?"

I shrugged.

"And how did he die?"

"That's sheriffing. I do the science."

Down the hall Hank Williams crooned the "Long-Gone Lonesome Blues." Static made the music sound like it was coming from another era.

"Is this enough for a warrant?" I asked.

The sheriff studied the paper for another full minute. Finally she looked up, the eyes to die for hard on mine. Then she reached for the phone.

* * *

By the time I left the sheriff's office a light rain was falling. Headlights, stoplights, and neon signs twinkled and shimmered in the dusk of early evening. The air was heavy with the smell of skunk.

Outside at High Ridge House, Boyd lay in his doghouse, chin on paws, gazing at the raindrops. He raised his head when I called and gave me a look to indicate I should do something. Seeing that I wasn't, he sighed noisily and settled back down. I filled his dish and left him to ponder his sodden world.

Inside, the house was still. I climbed the stairs to the slow *tick-tick-tick* of Ruby's hall clock. No sound came from any bedroom.

Rounding the corner at my end of the hall, I was surprised to see the door to Magnolia slightly ajar. I pushed it inward. And froze.

The drawers in my room had been rifled, the bed stripped. My briefcase had been emptied, and papers and manila folders lay scattered across the floor.

My mind locked on one word.

No! No! No!

I tossed my purse on the bed, flew to the wardrobe, and threw open the doors.

My laptop sat tucked in back, exactly as I'd left it. I pulled it out and clicked it on, my mind still racing.

What was in the room? What was in the room? What was in the room?

Quick mental inventory. Car keys. Credit cards. Driver's license. Passport. All had been with me.

Why? Why? Why?

A quick ransack for valuables, or was someone after something specific? What was there that anyone would want?

What? What? What?

When the computer booted I checked a few files. Everything seemed fine.

I went to the bathroom and splashed cold water on my face. Then I closed my eyes and played a childhood game I knew would calm me. Silently, I ran through the lyrics of the first song to come to mind. "Honky Tonk Women."

The time-out with Mick and the Stones worked. Steadier, I returned and began gathering papers.

I was still filing when I heard a knock, and opened the door to Andrew Ryan. He held two DoveBars in his right hand.

Ryan's eyes swept the mess.

"What the fuck went on in here?"

I just looked at him, not trusting my voice.

"Is anything missing?"

I swallowed.

"The only thing of value was the computer, and they left that."

"Pretty much rules out robbery."

"Unless the intruder was interrupted."

"Looks like they tossed the place looking for something."

"Or just to be ornery."

Why?

"Ice cream?" Ryan offered.

We ate our DoveBars and considered possible explanations. None was persuasive. The two most likely were someone looking for money or someone letting me know he or she didn't care for me.

When Ryan had gone, I stacked the remaining folders and went to run a bath. Throwing back the shower curtain, I got my next shock.

Ruby's ceramic figurine of Orphan Annie lay at the bottom of the tub, her face smashed, her limbs shattered. Sandy dangled from the showerhead, a makeshift noose tight around his neck.

Again, my mind flew, my hands trembled. This message had nothing to do with money. Someone clearly didn't care for me.

Suddenly, I remembered the Volvo. Was that episode a threat? Was this intrusion another? I fought the impulse to run down the hall to Ryan's room.

I considered the lockless doors and thought about bringing Boyd inside. Then who would be threatened?

An hour later, lying in bed and somewhat more logical, I reflected on the strength of my reaction to the invasion of my space. Had it been anger or fear that had sent me over the edge? At whom should I be angry? What should I fear?

Sleep did not come easily.

14

WHEN I CAME DOWNSTAIRS THE NEXT MORNING, Ryan was questioning Ruby about my intruder. Byron McMahon sat across from him, dividing his attention between the interrogation and a trio of fried eggs.

Ruby had one comment.

"Satan's minions are among us."

I was annoyed by her nonchalance toward the rifling of my possessions, but let it go.

"Was anything taken?" asked McMahon. Good. The FBI was on my case.

"I don't think so."

"Been irritating someone?"

"I suspect my dog has. Dogs bark." I described what had been done to Annie and Sandy.

Ryan looked at me oddly but said nothing.

"This place isn't exactly Los Alamos. Anyone could walk in and out of here." McMahon forked up fried potatoes. "What else have you been up to lately? I haven't seen you around."

I told him about the foot and the courtyard house, ending with the VFA profile I'd gotten the day before. I did not tell him about my current status in the crash investigation, but left that gap for him to fill. As I spoke, his grin slowly dissolved.

"So Crowe is going for a warrant?" he asked, cop cool.

I was about to answer when my cell phone sounded the *William Tell* Overture. The men looked at each other as I clicked it on.

The call was from Laslo Sparkes at Oak Ridge. I listened, thanked him, and rang off.

"Rossini calling?" Ryan asked.

"I was testing the ring options and forgot to change it back." I jabbed my egg and yolk spurted onto the table. "I wouldn't have pegged *you* as an opera buff."

"Zinger." McMahon reached for a slice of toast.

"It was the anthropologist at Oak Ridge."

"Let me guess. He's profiled the soup, and the missing body is D. B. Cooper."

Ryan was on a roll. Ignoring him, I directed my response to McMahon.

"He found something while filtering the remaining soil."

"What's that?"

"He didn't say. Just that the item might be useful. He's going to stop by Bryson City sometime later in the week on his way to Asheville."

Ruby returned, cleared plates, left.

"So you're off to the courthouse?" Ryan.

"Yes." Terse.

"Sounds like detecting."

"Somebody's got to do it."

"It can't hurt to know who owns that property." McMahon drained his cup. "After today's briefing I have to shoot down to Charlotte to interview some asswipe claiming to have information about a militia group up here in Swain. Otherwise, I'd tag along."

He drew a card from his wallet and placed it in front of me.

"If they're uncooperative at the courthouse, wave this. Sometimes the acronym induces a mood swing."

"Thanks." I pocketed the card.

McMahon excused himself, leaving Ryan and me and three empty mugs.

"Who do you think tossed your room?"

"I don't know."

"Why?"

"They were looking for your shower gel."

"I wouldn't belittle this. How about I poke around, ask a few questions?"

"You know that'd be a journey into pointlessness. These things are never solved."

"It would let folks know that someone is curious."

"I'll talk with Crowe."

I rose to leave and he took my arm.

"Do you want backup at the courthouse?"

"In case of an armed attack by the recorder of deeds?"

He looked away, back at me.

"Would you like *company* at the courthouse?"

"Aren't you going to the NTSB briefing?"

"McMahon can fill me in. But there's one condition."

I waited.

"Change your phone."

"Hi-Ho, Silver," I said.

The Swain County Administration Building and Courthouse replaced its predecessor in 1982. It is a rectangular concrete building, with a low-angled roof of red galvanized metal, that sits on the bank of the Tuckasegee River. Though lacking the charm of the old domed courthouse at Everett and Main, the structure is bright, clean, and efficient.

The tax office is located on the ground floor, immediately off a tiled octagonal lobby. When Ryan and I entered, four women looked up from computers, two behind a counter directly ahead, two behind a counter to our left.

I explained what we wanted. Woman number three pointed to a door at the back of the room.

"Land Records Department," she said.

Eight eyes traveled with us across the floor.

"Must be where they archive the classified stuff," Ryan whispered as I opened the door.

We entered to find another counter, this one

guarded by a tall, thin woman with an angular face. It brought to mind my father's old picture of Stan Musial.

"May I help you?"

"We'd like to look at the county tax index map."

The woman put a hand to her mouth, as though the question startled her.

"The tax map?"

I began to suspect my request was a first. Taking Byron McMahon's card from my pocket, I walked to the counter and handed it to her.

Madam Musial eyeballed the card. "Is this, like, the actual FBI?"

When she looked up, I nodded.

"Byron?"

"It's a family name." I smiled winningly.

"Do you have a gun?"

"Not here." Not anywhere, but that would tarnish the image.

"Does this have to do with the airplane crash?"

I leaned close. She smelled of mint and overperfumed shampoo. "What we're looking for could be critical to the investigation."

Behind me, I heard Ryan's feet shift.

"My name is Dorothy." She handed back the card. "I'll get it."

Dorothy went to a map case, pulled out a drawer approximately two inches high, withdrew a large sheet, and spread it on the counter.

Ryan and I bent over the map. Using township

boundaries, roads, and other markers, we pinpointed the section containing the courtyard house. Dorothy observed from her side of the divide, vigilant as an Egyptologist displaying a papyrus.

"Now we'd like section map six-two-one, please."

Dorothy smiled to indicate she was part of the sting, went to another case, and returned with the document.

Earlier in my career as an anthropologist, when I had done some archaeology, I'd spent hours with U.S. Geological Survey maps and knew how to interpret symbols and features. The experience came in handy. Using elevations, creeks, and roads, Ryan and I were able to zero in on the house.

"Section map six twenty-one, parcel four."

Keeping my finger on the spot, I looked up. Dorothy's face was inches from mine.

"How long will it take to pull up the tax records for this property?"

"About a minute."

I must have looked surprised.

"Swain County is not a pumpkin patch. We *are* computerized."

Dorothy went to a rear corner in her "secure" area and lifted a plastic cover from a monitor and keyboard. Ryan and I waited as she fastidiously folded the plastic, placed it on an overhead shelf, and booted the computer. When the program was up and running she keyed in a number of commands. Seconds passed. Finally, she entered the tax number and the screen filled with information.

"Do you want hard copy?"

"Please."

She unveiled a Hewlett-Packard bubble-jet printer similar to the first one I'd ever owned. Again we waited while she folded and stored the plastic cover, took one sheet of paper from a drawer, and placed it in the feeder tray.

Finally, she hit a key, the printer whirred, and the paper disappeared then oozed out.

"I hope this helps," she said, handing it to me.

The printout gave a vague description of the property and its buildings, its assessed value, the owner's name and mailing address, and the address to which the tax bills were being sent.

I passed it to Ryan, feeling deflated.

"'H&F Investment Group, LLP,'" he read aloud. "The mailing address is a PO box in New York."

He looked at me.

"Who the hell is the H&F Investment Group?"

I shrugged.

"What's LLP?"

"Limited liability partnership," I said.

"You could try the deed room."

We both turned to Dorothy. A touch of pink had sprouted on each cheek.

"You could look up the date that H&F bought the property, and the name of the previous owner."

"They'd have that?"

She nodded.

. . .

We found the register of deeds around the corner from the tax office. The records room was situated behind the obligatory counter, through a set of slatted swinging doors. Shelves lining the walls and filling free-standing cases held deed books spanning hundreds of years. Recent ones were square and red, their numbers stated in plain gold lettering. Older volumes were ornately decorated, like leather-bound volumes of first editions.

It was like a treasure hunt, with each deed sending us backward in time. We learned the following:

The H&F Investment Group was an LLP registered in Delaware. Ownership of tax parcel number four transferred to the partnership in 1949 from one Edward E. Arthur. The description of the property was charming, but a bit loose by modern standards. I read it aloud to Ryan.

"'The property begins at a Spanish oak on a knob, the corner of state grant 11807, and runs north ninety poles to the Bellingford line, then up the ridge as it meanders with Bellingford's line to a chestnut in the line of the S. Q. Barker tract—'"

"Where did Arthur get it?"

I skipped the rest of the survey and read on.

"Do you want to hear the 'party of the first part' bits?"

"No."

"'. . . having the same land conveyed by deed from Victor T. Livingstone and wife J. E. Clampett, dated March 26, 1933, and recorded in Deed Book number 52, page 315, Records of Swain County, North Carolina.'"

I went to the shelf and pulled the older volume.

Arthur had obtained the property from one Victor T. Livingstone in 1933. Livingstone must have purchased it from God, since there were no records before that time.

"At least we know how the happy homeowners got in and out."

The Livingstone and Arthur deeds both described an entrance road.

"Or *get* in and out." I was still not convinced the property was abandoned. "While we were there Crowe found a track leading from the house to a logging trail. The turnoff at the trail is obscured by a makeshift gate completely overgrown with kudzu. When she showed me the entrance I couldn't believe it. You could walk or drive past it a million times without ever seeing it."

Ryan said nothing.

"Now what?"

"Now we wait for Crowe's warrant."

"And in the meantime?"

Ryan grinned, and his eyes crinkled at the corners.

"In the meantime we talk to the attorney general of the great state of Delaware, find out what we can about the H&F Investment Group."

Boyd and I were sharing a club sandwich and fries on the porch at High Ridge House when Lucy Crowe's squad car appeared on the road below. I watched her wind upward toward the driveway. Boyd continued to watch the sandwich.

"Spending quality time?" Crowe asked when she'd reached the stairs.

"He says I've been neglecting him."

I held out a slice of ham. Boyd tipped his head and took it gently with his front teeth. Then he lowered his snout, dropped the ham on the porch, licked it twice, and wolfed it down. In seconds his chin was back on my knee.

"They're just like kids."

"Mmm. Did you get the warrant?"

Boyd's eyes moved as my hand moved, alert for lunch meat or fries.

"I had a real heart-to-heart with the magistrate."

"And?"

She sighed and removed her hat.

"He says it's not enough."

"Evidence of a body?" I was shocked. "Daniel Wahnetah could be decomposing in that courtyard even as we speak."

"Are you familiar with the term junk science? I am. It was thrown at me at least a dozen times this morning. I think old Frank is going to start his own support group. Junk Science Victims Anonymous."

"Is the guy an idiot?"

"He's never going to Sweden to collect a prize, but he's usually reasonable."

Boyd raised his head and blew air through his

nose. I put my hand down and he sniffed, then gave
it a lick.

"You're neglecting him, again."

I offered a slice of egg. Boyd dropped it, licked it,
sniffed, licked again, then left it on the porch.

"I don't care for egg in club sandwiches, either,"
Crowe said to Boyd. The dog moved his ear slightly,
to indicate that he'd heard, but kept his eyes on my
plate.

"It gets worse," Crowe went on.

Why not?

"There have been additional complaints."

"About me?"

She nodded.

"By whom?"

"The magistrate wouldn't share that information.
But if you go anywhere near the site, the morgue, or
any crash-related record, item, or family member, I
am to arrest you for obstruction of justice. That
includes this courtyard property."

"What the hell is going on?" My stomach tightened in anger.

Crowe shrugged. "I'm not sure. But you're out of
that investigation."

"Am I allowed to go to the public library?" I spat.

The sheriff rubbed the back of her neck and rested
a boot on the bottom step. Beneath her jacket I could
see the bulge of a gun.

"There's something very wrong here, Sheriff."

"I'm listening."

"My room was ransacked yesterday."

"Theories?"

I told her about the figurines in the bathtub.

"Not exactly a Hallmark greeting."

"It's probably that Boyd's annoying someone." I said it hopefully, but didn't really believe my own words.

Boyd's ears shot forward at the sound of his name. I gave him a slice of bacon.

"Is he a barker?"

"Not really. I asked Ruby if he makes noise when I'm away. She said he howls a bit, but nothing extraordinary."

"What does Ruby say about it?"

"Satan's minions."

"Maybe you have something that someone wants."

"Nothing was taken, though all my files were thrown around. The whole room was trashed."

"Did you keep notes on this foot?"

"I'd taken them with me to Oak Ridge."

She looked at me a full five seconds, then nodded her nod.

"Makes that Volvo episode a little more suspect. You watch yourself."

Oh yes.

Crowe leaned over and brushed off the toe of her boot, then looked at her watch.

"I'll see if I can get the DA to push harder."

At that moment Ryan's rental car appeared in the valley. The driver's-side window was open and his silhouette looked dark against the car's interior. We watched him climb the mountain and turn into the drive. Moments later he strode up the path, his face looking drawn and tense.

"What is it?"

I heard Crowe's hat brush the top of her thigh.

Ryan hesitated a beat, then, "There's still no sign of Jean's body."

I could read naked misery in his demeanor. And more. Self-imposed guilt. The conviction that his absence from the partnership had caused Bertrand to be on that plane. Detectives without partners are limited in what they can investigate. That makes them available for courier duty.

"They'll find him," I said softly.

Ryan let his eyes rove the horizon, his back rigid, his neck muscles tight as twisted ropes. After a full minute, he shook out and lit a cigarette, cupping the flame in both hands.

"How did your afternoon go?" He flicked the match.

I told him about Crowe's meeting with the magistrate.

"Your foot may be a dead issue."

"What do you mean?"

He blew smoke through his nostrils, then pulled something from his jacket pocket.

"They also found this."

He unfolded a paper and handed it to me.

15

I STARED, FIRST IN CONFUSION, THEN IN DAWNING comprehension.

Ryan had given me a composite produced on a color printer. There were three images, each showing a fragment of plastic. In the first I could make out the letters *b-i-o-h-a-z*. In the second, a truncated phrase: *-aboratory servic-*. A red symbol practically leaped from the third picture. I'd seen dozens at the lab, and recognized it instantly.

I looked at Ryan.

"It's a biohazard container."

He nodded.

"Which wasn't on the manifest."

"No."

"And everyone thinks it held a foot."

"Opinion is running in that direction."

Boyd nudged my hand, and I absently held out the rest of the sandwich. He looked at me, as though assuring himself there was no mistake, then took the booty and moved off, opting for distance in case it was a misunderstanding, after all.

"So they're admitting that the foot does not belong to any passenger."

"Not exactly. But they're opening up to the possibility."

"What does this do to the warrant?" I asked Crowe.

"It won't help."

She pushed back from the step, stood with feet apart, and replaced her hat.

"But something's reeking under that wall, and I intend to find out what."

She gave her Sheriff Crowe head dip, turned, and walked up the path. Moments later we saw her bubble top wending down the mountain.

I felt Ryan's stare and brought my gaze back to him.

"Why did the magistrate nix the warrant?"

"Apparently the guy's a candidate for the Flat Earth Society. On top of that, he'll issue a warrant for obstruction if I so much as shed a skin cell." My cheeks burned with anger.

Boyd crossed the porch, snout down, head moving from side to side. Reaching the swing, he sniffed up my leg, then sat and stared at me with his tongue out.

Ryan drew on his cigarette, flicked it onto the lawn. Boyd's eyes shifted sideways, then back to me.

"Did you find out about H&F?"

Ryan had gone to his "office" to phone Delaware.

"I thought the request might be processed more

expeditiously if it came from the FBI, so I asked McMahon to make the call. I'll be at the reassembly site all afternoon but I can ask him tonight."

Reassembly. The piecing together of the airplane as it had been before the event. Total reassembly is a tremendous drain on time, money, and manpower, of which the NTSB had precious little. They do not attempt it in every major, do so reluctantly when public clamor demands. They undertook it with TWA 800 because the Brits had done it with Pan Am 102, and they didn't want to be outperformed.

With fifty dead students, reassembly was a given.

For the past two weeks trucks had been carrying the wreckage from Air TransSouth 228 across the mountains to a rented hangar at the Asheville airport. Parts were being laid out on grids corresponding to their positions on the Fokker-100. Parts that could not be associated with specific sections of the plane were being sorted according to structure type. Unidentifiable parts were being sorted according to position of recovery at the crash site.

Eventually, every scrap would be cataloged and subjected to a range of tests, then reassembled around a wood-and-wire frame. Over time an aircraft would take shape, like a slow-motion reverse, with a million fragments drawing together to form a recognizable object.

I'd visited reassembly sites on other crashes, and could picture the tedious scene. In this case the process would move more quickly since Air Trans-

South 228 had not been driven into the ground. The plane had come apart in midair and plummeted to earth in large pieces.

But I would not see it. I was exiled. My face must have registered my despondency.

"I can put off the meeting." Ryan laid a hand on my shoulder.

"I'm O.K."

"What are you going to do this afternoon?"

"I'm going to sit here and finish my lunch with Boyd. Then I'm going to drive into town and buy dog food, razors, and shampoo."

"Will you be all right?"

"I may have trouble finding the ones with double blades. But I'll persevere."

"You can be a pain in the ass, Brennan."

"See. I'm fine."

I managed a weak smile.

"Go to your meeting."

When he'd gone, I gave Boyd the last of the fries.

"Any preferred brands?" I asked.

He didn't answer.

I suspected Boyd would eat just about anything but boiled eggs.

I was stuffing wrappers into the carry-out bag when Ruby shot out the front door and grabbed my arm.

"Quick! Come quick!"

"What is—"

She dragged me off the swing and into the house.

Boyd danced along, nipping at my jeans. I wasn't sure if it was Ruby's urgency that excited him or his entry onto forbidden turf.

Ruby pulled me straight to the kitchen, where an ironing board stood with a pair of Levi's draped across it. A wicker basket rested below, heaped to the rim with crumpled laundry. Neatly pressed garments hung from cabinet knobs around the room.

Ruby pointed to a twelve-inch black-and-white TV on a counter opposite the board. A ribbon at the bottom of the screen announced fast-breaking news. A newscaster spoke above the graphic, his face grim, his voice serene. Though reception was poor, I had no trouble identifying the figure over his left shoulder.

The room receded around me. I was aware of nothing but the voice and the snowy picture.

". . . an inside source revealed that the anthropologist has been dismissed, and that an investigation is under way. Charges have not yet been filed, and it is unclear if the crash investigation has been compromised, or if victim identifications have been affected. When contacted, Dr. Larke Tyrell, North Carolina's chief medical examiner, had no comment. In other news . . ."

"That's you, isn't it?"
Ruby brought me back.
"Yes," I said.
Boyd had stopped racing around the kitchen and

was sniffing the floor below the sink. His head came up when I spoke.

"What's he saying?" Ruby's eyes were the size of Frisbees.

Something snapped, and I rolled over her like a tsunami.

"It's a mistake! A goddamn mistake!" It was my voice, shrill and harsh, though I hadn't consciously formed the words.

The room felt hot, the smell of steam and fabric softener cloying. I spun and rushed for the door.

Boyd flew after me, paws jumbling the carpet runner as we raced down the hall. I burst out the door and across the lawn, the bell jangling in my wake. Ruby must have thought I was possessed by the Archfiend himself.

When I opened the car Boyd bounded in and centered himself in back, his head protruding through the gap between the seats. I hadn't the will to stop him.

Sliding behind the wheel, I did some deep breathing, hoping to turn a page in my mind. My heartbeat normalized. I began to feel guilty about my outburst, but couldn't force myself to return to the kitchen to apologize.

Boyd chose that moment to lick my ear.

At least the chow doesn't question my integrity, I thought.

"Let's go."

.   .   .

During the ride into Bryson City, I answered call after call on my cell phone, each a reporter. After seven "no comments," I turned it off.

Boyd shifted between his center spot and the left rear window, reacting with the same low growl to cars, pedestrians, and other animals. After a time he ceased serving notice on everyone of just who he was, and stared placidly as the sights and sounds of the mountains flashed by.

I found everything I needed at an Ingles supermarket on the southern edge of town. Herbal Essence and Gillette Good News for me, Kibbles 'n Bits for Boyd. I even sprang for a box of Milk-Bone jumbos.

Buoyed by finding the razors, I decided on an outing.

Approximately three miles beyond the Bryson City line, Everett Street becomes a scenic roadway that snakes through the Great Smoky Mountains National Park above the north shore of Lake Fontana. Officially the highway is called Lakeview Drive. To locals it is known as the Road to Nowhere.

In the 1940s, a two-lane blacktop led from Bryson City along the Tuckasegee and Little Tennessee Rivers to Deal's Gap near the Tennessee state line. Realizing the creation of Lake Fontana would flood the highway, the TVA promised a new north-shore road. Construction began in 1943, and a 1,200-foot tunnel was eventually built. Then everything stopped, leaving Swain County with a road and tunnel to nowhere, and with wounded feelings as to its low rank in the universal order of things.

"Want to take a ride, boy?"

Boyd showed enthusiasm by placing his chin on my right shoulder and running his tongue up the side of my face. One thing I admired about him was his agreeable nature.

The drive was beautiful, the tunnel a perfect monument to federal folly. Boyd enjoyed racing from end to end while I stood in the middle and watched.

Though the outing cheered me, the improvement in my mood was short-lived. Just after leaving the park, my engine gave an odd ping. Two miles before the town line it pinged again, chunked repeatedly, then segued into a loud, ratchety, persistent noise.

Veering onto the shoulder, I cut the motor, draped my arms around the steering wheel, and rested my forehead on them, my temporary lift in spirits replaced by a sense of despondency and anxiety.

Was this ordinary car trouble, or had someone tampered with my engine?

Boyd laid his chin on my shoulder, indicating that he, too, found it a disturbing question, and not entirely paranoid.

We'd been like that a few minutes when Boyd growled without raising his head. I ignored this, assuming he'd spotted a squirrel or a Chevy. Then he shot to his feet and gave three sharp woofs, an impressive sound inside a Mazda.

I looked up to see a man approaching my car from the highway side. He was small, maybe five foot three, with dark hair combed straight back. He wore a black suit, perfectly fitted, but probably new in the early sixties.

Drawing close, the man raised knuckles to tap the glass, but pulled back as Boyd erupted again.

"Easy, boy."

I could see an old pickup angled onto the shoulder across the road, the driver's door open. The truck looked empty.

"Let's see what the gentleman has to say."

I cracked my window.

"Are you ill, ma'am?" The voice was rich and resonant, seeming to come from deeper inside than the small stature allowed. The man had a hooked nose and intense dark eyes, and reminded me of someone, though I couldn't recall whom. From his tone I could tell Boyd was thinking Caligula.

"I may have thrown a rod." I had no idea what that meant, but it seemed like an engine noise sort of thing to say.

"May I offer assistance?"

Boyd growled suspiciously.

"I'm on my way into town. It would be no trouble to drop you at a repair shop, ma'am."

Sudden synapse. The man looked and sounded like a miniature Johnny Cash.

"If there's a garage you can recommend, I'll call ahead and ask for a tow."

"Yes, of course. There's one right up the road. I have the number in my glove compartment."

Boyd was having none of it.

KATHY REICHS

"Shh." I reached back and stroked his head.

The man crossed to his truck, rummaged, then returned with a slip of thin yellow paper. Holding my cell phone in clear view, I lowered the window another few inches and accepted it.

The form looked like the carbon copy of a repair bill. The writing was almost illegible, but a header identified the garage as P & T Auto Repair, and gave an address and phone number in Bryson City. I tried to make out the customer signature, but the ink was too smeary.

When I turned on my cell, the screen told me I had missed eleven calls. Scrolling through, I recognized none of the numbers. I dialed the auto repair shop.

When the phone was answered I explained my situation and asked for towing.

How would I be paying?

Visa.

Where are you?

I gave the location.

Can you find transportation?

Yes.

Come on in and leave the car. They'd send a truck within the hour.

I told the voice at the other end that P & T had been recommended by a passerby, and that I would be riding to the garage with this man. Then I read off the bill number, hoping that P or T was writing it down.

With that call completed, I lowered the window,

smiled at Johnny Cash, and dialed again. Speaking loudly, I left Lieutenant-Detective Ryan a message, detailing my intended whereabouts. Then I looked at Boyd. He was looking at the man in the dark suit.

Closing the window, I grabbed my purse and the grocery bag.

"How could things possibly get worse?"

Boyd did the eyebrow thing but said nothing.

Dropping the bag behind the seat, I took the middle position and gave Boyd the window. When our Samaritan slammed the door, the dog stuck his head out and tracked his movement to the driver's side. Then a pickup truck whizzed by with a pair of weimaraners in the bed, and Boyd's interest shifted. When he tried to rise, I pushed down on his haunches.

"That's a fine dog, ma'am."

"Yes."

"No one's going to bother you with that big fella around."

"He can be vicious when he's being protective."

We drove in silence. The phone rang. I checked the number, ignored the call. After a while, my rescuer spoke.

"I saw you on TV, didn't I?"

"Did you?"

"I've got trouble with stillness, turn the set on when I'm home alone. I don't pay it much mind, just look up now and again. It's kind of like having company."

He grinned, acknowledging his own foolishness.

"But I do have a knack for faces. It's mighty useful in my line of work."

He pointed in my direction. I noticed that the hand was gray and unnaturally smooth, as though the flesh had ballooned, then contracted with only a vague memory of its original form.

"I'm sure I saw you today." The hand returned to the steering wheel. The hawk eyes shifted from the road to me and back again. "You're with the air crash investigation."

I smiled. Either he hadn't listened to the story, or he was being polite.

The hand came toward me.

"Name's Bowman."

We shook. His grip was steel.

"Temperance Brennan."

"That's a powerful name, young lady."

"Thank you."

"Are you anti-saloon?"

"I'm sorry?"

"I am among those who see intoxicating liquor as the main cause of crime, poverty, and violence in this great nation. Fermented liquor is the greatest threat to the nuclear family ever spawned by Lucifer." He pronounced it *nucular.*

The name Bowman suddenly clicked.

"Are you Luke Bowman?"

"I am."

"The Reverend Luke Bowman?"

"You've heard of me?"

"I'm staying with Ruby McCready at High Ridge House." It was irrelevant but seemed safe.

"Sister McCready is not one of my flock, but she's a good woman. Keeps a fine Christian house."

"Is there a Mr. McCready?" I'd been curious for some time but had never asked.

Now the eyes remained on the road. Seconds passed. I thought he wasn't going to answer.

"I'm gonna leave that question alone, ma'am. Best to let Sister McCready tell the tale as she sees fit."

Ruby had a tale?

"What's the name of your church?"

"The Eternal Light Holiness-Pentecostal House of God."

The southern Appalachians are home to a fundamentalist Christian sect known as the Church of God with Signs Following, or the Holiness Church. Inspired by biblical passages, adherents seek the power of the Holy Ghost by repenting their sins and leading godly lives. Only thus is one anointed, and thereby able to follow the signs. These signs include speaking in tongues, casting out demons, healing the sick, handling serpents, and ingesting toxic substances.

In more populated areas preachers establish permanent congregations. Elsewhere, they work a circuit. Services last hours, the centerpiece sometimes being the drinking of strychnine and the handling of poisonous snakes. Preachers accumulate fame and followers based on their oratorical skills and immunity to venom. Each year someone dies.

The distorted hand now made sense. Bowman had been bitten more than once.

Bowman turned left a few blocks past the supermarket where I'd made my purchases, then right onto a rutted side street. P & T Auto Repair was situated between businesses offering glass replacement and small-appliance repair. The reverend pulled in and cut the engine.

The garage was a blue aluminum-sided rectangle with an office at one end. Through the open door I made out a cash register, counter, and trio of heads in dozer caps.

The other end of the building held a work bay in which a battered Chevy station wagon was pedestaled on a hydraulic lift, its doors flung wide. The car looked as though it were taking flight.

An old Pinto and two pickups were parked outside the office. I did not see a tow truck.

As Bowman got out, Boyd began what I knew was not a Pinto growl. Following his line of vision I spotted a black-and-brown dog lying inside the office door. It looked pure pit bull.

The flesh on Boyd's snout compressed against his gums. His body tensed. The growl deepened.

Damn. Why hadn't I brought the leash?

Wrapping my fingers around Boyd's collar, I opened the door and we both jumped down. Bowman met us with a length of rope.

"Had this in back," he said. "Flush can be peevish."

I thanked him and tied the rope to Boyd's collar. Boyd remained focused on the other dog.

"I'd be glad to hold him while you talk with the mechanic."

I looked at Boyd. He was staring fixedly at Flush, thinking flank steak.

"Thanks. That might be wise."

Crossing the lot, I stepped through the door and circled Flush. An ear twitched, but he didn't look up. Maybe pit bulls are calm because they are secure in the belief that they can kill anyone or anything that provokes them. I hoped Boyd would keep quiet and keep his distance.

The office had the usual tasteful garage appointments. A calendar with a photo of the Grand Canyon and tear-off sheets for each month. A cigarette machine. A glass case containing flashlights, maps, and an assortment of automotive paraphernalia. Three kitchen chairs. A pit bull.

A pair of geezers occupied two of the chairs. In the third sat a middle-aged man in an oil-stained work shirt and pants. The men stopped talking when I entered, but no one rose.

Assuming the younger man was either P or T, I introduced myself and asked about the tow.

He answered that the wrecker was on its way, should be back in twenty minutes. He'd look at my car as soon as he finished the Chevy.

How long would that be?

He couldn't say, but offered me the chair if I wanted to wait.

The air inside was packed tight with smells. Gas, oil, cigarette smoke, geezers, dog. I elected to wait outside.

Returning to Luke Bowman, I thanked him for his kindness and reclaimed my dog. Boyd was straining at his collar, every fiber focused on the pit bull. Flush was either sleeping or playing possum, waiting for the chow to approach.

"You'll be all right by yourself?"

"My car will be here any minute. And there's a detective on his way over. If it's going to take long he can give me a lift back to High Ridge House. But thank you again. You've been a lifesaver."

My phone rang again. I checked the number, ignored the call. Bowman watched. He seemed reluctant to leave.

"Sister McCready is housing quite a few crash investigation folks up there, i'n't she?"

"Some are there."

"That air crash is nasty business." He pinched his nostrils then shook his head.

I said nothing.

"Do they have any idea what brought that plane down?"

He must have seen something in my face.

"You didn't hear my name from Ruby McCready, did you, Miss Temperance?"

"It came up in a briefing."

"Lord God Almighty."

The dark eyes seemed to grow darker for an instant. Then he dropped his chin, reached up, and massaged his temples.

"I've sinned, and my Savior wants confession."

Oh boy.

When Bowman looked back up his eyes were moist. His voice cracked as he spoke the next sentence.

"And the Lord God sent you to bear witness."

16

BACK IN THE TRUCK, IT TOOK LUKE BOWMAN A FULL half hour to unburden his soul. During that time I had four calls from the media. I finally turned the unit off.

As Bowman talked, the phrase "obstruction of justice" floated through my mind. The rain started again. I watched fat drops wriggle through the windshield film and pockmark puddles in the lot. Boyd lay curled at my feet, persuaded at last that leaving Flush undisturbed was a better plan.

My car arrived, rolling behind the wrecker like sea salvage. Bowman continued his strange narrative.

The station wagon was lowered and moved to join the Pinto and pickups. The man in the oil-stained clothing opened a door and steer-pushed my Mazda into the bay. Then he raised the hood and peered under.

Bowman talked on, seeking absolution.

Finally the reverend stopped, his tale finished, a

place near his god reestablished. It was then that Ryan swung into the lot.

When Ryan got out of his car, I lowered my window and called out. Crossing to the truck, he leaned down and spread his forearms on my window ledge.

I introduced Bowman.

"We've met." Moisture glistened like a halo around the perimeter of Ryan's hair.

"The reverend has just relayed an interesting story."

"Has he?" The iceberg eyes studied Bowman.

"It may translate into something helpful to you, Detective. It may not. But it's God's honest truth."

"Feeling the devil's riding crop, brother?"

Bowman looked at his watch.

"I'll let this fine lady tell it to you."

He turned the key and Boyd raised his head. When Ryan stepped back and opened my door, the chow stretched and hopped out, looking slightly annoyed.

"Thank you, again."

"It was my pleasure." He looked at Ryan. "You know where to find me."

I watched the pickup lurch across the lot, its tires shooting spray from the water-filled ruts.

I'd never known Bowman's brand of faith. Why had he told me what he had? Fear? Guilt? A desire to cover his ass? Where were his thoughts now? On eternity? On repentance? On the pork chops he'd defrosted for tonight's dinner?

"What's the status of your car?" Ryan's question brought me back.

"Hold on to Boyd while I go check."

I ran to the work bay, where P/T was still under my hood. He thought the problem might be a water pump, would know tomorrow. I gave him my cell phone number and told him I was staying with Ruby McCready.

When I returned to the car, Ryan and Boyd were already inside. I joined them, brushing rain from my hair.

"Would a broken water pump make a loud noise?" I asked.

Ryan shrugged.

"How come you're back from Asheville so early?"

"Something else came up. Listen, I'm meeting McMahon for dinner. You can entertain us both with Bowman's parable."

"Let's drop Rinty off first."

I hoped we weren't going to Injun Joe's.

We didn't.

After settling Boyd at High Ridge House, we drove to the Bryson City Diner. The place was long and narrow like a railroad car. Chrome booths jutted from one side, each with its own condiment tray, napkin holder, and miniature jukebox. A chrome counter ran the length of the other, faced by stools bolted to the floor at precise intervals. Red vinyl upholstery. Plastic-domed cake bins. Coat rack at the door. Rest rooms in back.

I liked the place. No promise of a mountain view

or ethnic experience. No confusing acronym. No misspelling for alliterative cuteness. It was a diner and the name said that.

We were early for the dinner crowd, even in the mountains. A few customers sat at the counter, grumbling over the weather or talking about their problems at work. When we entered, most glanced up.

Or were they talking about me? As we moved to the corner booth I felt eyes on my back, sensed nudges directing attention toward me. Was it my imagination?

We'd no sooner sat than a middle-aged woman in a white apron and pink dress approached and issued handwritten menus sheathed in plastic. The name "Cynthia" was embroidered over her left breast.

I chose pot roast. Ryan and McMahon went for meat loaf.

"Drinks?"

"Iced tea, please. Unsweetened."

"Same here." McMahon.

"Lemonade." Ryan stayed deadpan, but I knew what he was thinking.

Cynthia looked at me a long time after jotting our order, then tucked the pencil above her ear. Circling the counter, she tore off the sheet and pinned it to a wire above the service window.

"Two sixes and a four," she bellowed, then turned to look at me again.

The paranoia flared anew.

Ryan waited until Cynthia brought drinks, then told McMahon I had a statement from Luke Bowman.

"What the hell were you doing with Bowman?" There was concern in his voice. I wondered if it was there out of worry for my safety, or out of knowledge that meddling in the investigation could get me arrested.

"My car broke down. Bowman gave me a lift. Don't ask me why that inspired the baring of his soul."

I unsheathed a straw and jammed it into my tea.

"Do you want to hear this?"

"Go ahead."

"It seems the reverends Bowman and Claiborne have been slugging it out over ministerial boundaries for some time. The Holiness movement isn't what it once was, and the parsons are forced to compete for followers from a dwindling pool. This takes showmanship."

"Could we back up? We're talking snakes here, right?" Ryan asked.

I nodded.

"What do snakes have to do with holiness?"

This time I did not ignore Ryan's question.

"Holiness followers interpret the Bible literally, and cite specific passages that mandate the handling of snakes."

"What passages?" Ryan's voice dripped with scorn.

"'In my name shall they cast out devils; they shall speak with new tongues. They shall take up serpents; and if they drink any deadly thing, it shall not hurt them.' The Gospel of Mark, chapter sixteen, verses seventeen and eighteen."

Ryan and I stared at McMahon.

"'Behold I give unto you the power to tread on serpents and scorpions, and over all the power of the enemy; and nothing by any means shall hurt you.' Luke, chapter ten, verse nineteen," McMahon continued.

"How do you know that?" Ryan said.

"We all carry baggage."

"I thought you trained in engineering."

"I did."

Ryan circled back to the reptiles.

"Are the snakes tamed in some way? Are they accustomed to being handled, or have their fangs been pulled, or their venom milked?"

"Apparently not," McMahon said. "They use diamondbacks and water moccasins caught in the hills. Quite a few handlers have died."

"Isn't it illegal?"

"Yes," said McMahon. "But in North Carolina snake handling is merely a misdemeanor, and rarely enforced."

Cynthia arrived with our meals, left. Ryan and I shook salt and pepper. McMahon covered everything on his plate with gravy.

"Go on, Tempe," he said.

"I'll try to reconstruct this as best I can."

I tested a green bean. It was perfect, sweet and greasy after hours of cooking with sugar and bacon fat. God bless Dixie. I had several more.

"Though he denied it in his interview with the

NTSB, Bowman *was* outside his house that day. And he *was* launching things into the sky."

I halted for a bite of pot roast. It was equal to the beans.

"But not rockets."

The men waited while I forked another piece of meat, swallowed. Chewing was hardly necessary.

"This is really good."

"What was he launching?"

"Doves."

Ryan's fork stopped in midair.

"As in birds?"

I nodded. "It seems the reverend relies on special effects to keep the faithful interested."

"Sleight of hand?"

"He prefers to think of it as theater for the Lord. Anyway, he says he was experimenting the afternoon Air TransSouth 228 went down."

Ryan urged me on with a gesture of his fork.

"Bowman was working up a sermon on the Ten Commandments. He planned to wave a clay model of the tablets, and finish with a replay of Moses destroying the originals in anger over the Hebrew people's abandonment of their faith. As a finale, he'd dash the mock-ups to the ground, and admonish the congregation to repent. When they begged forgiveness, he'd hit a couple of levers and a flock of doves would rise up in a cloud of smoke. He thought it would be effective."

"Mind-blowing," said Ryan.

"So that's his tell-all tabloid confession? He was in the backyard playing with pigeons and smoke?" said McMahon.

"That's his story."

"Does he do this type of thing regularly?"

"He likes spectacle."

"And he lied when questioned because he couldn't risk his parishioners finding out they were being duped?"

"So he says. But then the Almighty tapped him on the shoulder, and he began to fear the loss of his soul."

"Or fear a bump in federal prison." Ryan's scorn had increased.

I finished my green beans.

"It actually makes sense," McMahon said. "The other witnesses, including Claiborne, stated they saw something shoot into the sky. Knowing the reliably unreliable nature of eyewitnesses, pigeons and smoke would tally."

"Doves," I corrected. "They're more papal."

"The NTSB has pretty much ruled out the rocket theory, anyway," McMahon went on.

"Oh?"

"For a number of reasons."

"Give me one."

"There's not been a single trace of a missile found anywhere within a five-mile radius of the wreckage field."

McMahon spread mashed potatoes on a forkful of meat loaf.

"And there's no twinning."

"What's twinning?"

"Basically, it involves cracking in the crystalline structure of metals such as copper, iron, or steel. Twinning requires forces greater than eight thousand meters per second. Typically, that means a military explosive. Things like RDC or C4."

"And twinning is absent?"

"So far."

"Meaning?"

"The usual components of pipe bombs, things like gunpowder, gelignites, and low-strength dynamite, aren't powerful enough. They only reach forces of one thousand meters per second. That doesn't create enough shock to produce twinning, but it's plenty of force to cause havoc on an aircraft. So lack of twinning doesn't rule out a detonation." He emptied the fork. "And there's plenty of evidence of an explosion."

At that moment Ryan's cell phone rang. He listened, and replied in clipped French. Though I understood his words, they made little sense without the benefit of the Quebec end of the conversation.

"So the NTSB isn't much further ahead than it was last week. Something blew inside the rear of the plane, but they have no idea what or why."

"That's about it," McMahon agreed. "Though the rich husband has been ruled out as a suspect. Turns out the guy was a candidate for priesthood. Made a quarter-million-dollar donation to the Humane Society last year when they found his lost cat."

"And the Sri Lankan kid?"

"The uncle is still broadcasting in Sri Lanka, and there have been no threats, notes, public statements, nothing from anyone over there. That angle looks like a dead end, but we're still checking."

"Has the investigation been handed over to the FBI?"

"Not officially. But until terrorism is ruled out, we're not going away."

Ryan ended his phone conversation and fumbled for a cigarette. His face was fixed in an expression I couldn't read. Remembering my Danielle blunder, I didn't ask.

McMahon had no such compunction.

"What's happened?"

After a pause, "Pepper Petricelli's wife is missing."

"She took off?"

"Maybe."

Ryan lit up, then scanned the table for an ashtray. Finding none, he jammed the match into his sweet potato pudding. There was an awkward silence before he continued.

"A crackhead named André Metraux was busted for possession yesterday in Montreal. Being unenthused about a long separation from his pharmaceuticals, Metraux offered to flip for consideration."

Ryan drew deeply, then blew smoke through both nostrils.

"Metraux swears he saw Pepper Petricelli at a

steak house in Plattsburgh, New York, last Saturday night."

"That's impossible," I burst out. "Petricelli is dead. . . ." My voice trailed off on the last word.

Ryan's eyes did a long sweep of the diner, then came back to rest on mine. In them I saw pure agony.

"Four passengers remain unidentified, including Bertrand and Petricelli."

"They don't think— Oh, my God, what *do* they think?"

Ryan and McMahon exchanged glances. My heartbeat quickened.

"What is it you're not telling me?"

"Don't go schizoid. We're not keeping things from you. You've had a rough day, and we thought it could wait until tomorrow."

I felt anger coalesce like fog inside my chest.

"Tell me," I said evenly.

"Tyrell attended the briefing today to present an updated trauma chart."

I felt miserable at being excluded, and lashed out. "*There's* a news story."

"He says he has remains that don't fit anyone on the manifest."

I stared at him, too surprised to speak.

"Only four passengers remain missing. All were in the left rear of the plane. Their seats were pretty much pulverized, so it's to be expected the occupants did not fare well."

Ryan drew on his cigarette again, exhaled.

"Twenty-two A and B were occupied by male students. Bertrand and Petricelli were behind them in row twenty-three. Tyrell claims to have tissue fitting none of the eighty-four passengers already identified, and none of these four."

"Such as?"

"A shoulder fragment with a large tattoo."

"Someone could have gotten a tattoo right before the flight."

"A portion of jaw with elaborate bridgework."

"Fingerprints," McMahon added.

I took a moment to digest this.

"What does it mean?"

"It could mean a lot of things."

McMahon caught Cynthia's eye and signaled for the check.

"Maybe the biker boys got a stand-in and Petricelli really was enjoying a porterhouse in New York last weekend." Ryan's voice was tempered steel.

"What are you implying?"

"If Petricelli wasn't on that plane it means one of two things. Either Bertrand was persuaded by greed or force to make a career change . . ."

Ryan took one last pull and added his butt to the sweet potatoes.

". . . or Bertrand was murdered."

Back in my room, I treated myself to a long hot bubble bath, followed by a talcum powder chaser. Only slightly relaxed, but smelling of honeysuckle and lilac, I propped myself in bed, raised my knees to my chest, pulled up the blankets, and turned on my phone. I'd missed seventeen calls. Finding no familiar numbers, I dumped the messages and made a call I'd been putting off.

Though fall break had ended and university classes had resumed the day before, I'd requested continued leave after finding the decomp stain at the courtyard house. I hadn't actually said it, but neither had I corrected my chair's assumption that I was still involved in victim processing. In a sense, I was.

But today's media delirium had made me apprehensive. Taking a deep breath, I scrolled to Mike Perrigio's number and hit "dial." I was about to click off after seven rings, when a woman picked up. I asked for Mike. There was a long pause. I could hear a lot of racket in the background, a child crying.

When Mike came on, he was brusque, almost cold. My classes were covered. Keep checking in. Dial tone.

I was still staring at the phone when it rang again.

The voice was totally unexpected.

Larke Tyrell asked how I was. He'd heard I was back in Bryson City. Could I meet with him the next day? Zero-nine-hundred at the family assistance center? Good, good. Take care.

Again, I sat staring at the little black handset, not knowing whether to feel crushed or buoyed. My boss at the university obviously knew of the news coverage. That had to be bad. But Larke Tyrell wanted to talk. Had the chief ME come around to my position? Had this other errant tissue persuaded him that the great foot controversy did not involve crash remains?

I reached for the chain on the bedside lamp. Lying in a silence filled with crickets, I felt that my issues were at last being resolved. I was confident of vindication, and never questioned the venue or purpose of the morning's meeting.

That was a mistake.

17

THE FIRST THING I NOTICED ON OPENING MY EYES was a sheet of paper wedged against the braided rug.

The clock said seven-twenty.

Throwing back the covers, I retrieved the paper and scanned the contents. It was a fax containing six names.

Shivering in panties and T-shirt, I checked the header information: *Sender: Office of the Attorney General, State of Delaware. Recipient: Special Agent Byron McMahon. Subject: H&F, LLP.*

It was the list of H&F officers. McMahon must have forgotten to mention it the night before and had slipped it under my door. I read the names. Nothing clicked.

Chilled through, I tucked the fax into the outer pocket of my computer case, ran on tiptoes into the bathroom, and hopped into the shower. Reaching for the shampoo, I suffered my first defeat of the day.

Damn! I'd left my groceries in Luke Bowman's truck.

Filling the empty shampoo container with water, I gave my hair a low-lather scrub. After blowing it dry and applying makeup, I slipped on khakis and a white cotton blouse, then checked my image.

The woman in the mirror looked appropriately prim, but a bit too casual. I added a cardigan, buttoned at the top as Katy had instructed. Wouldn't want to look like a dork.

I checked again. Stylish but professional. I hurried downstairs.

Too tense for breakfast, I threw down coffee, fed Boyd the dregs from the Alpo bag, had a nervous tinkle, and collected my purse. I'd just crossed the front door threshold when I stopped short.

I had no wheels.

I was standing on the porch, looking good but feeling panicky, when the door flew open and a boy of about seventeen emerged. His hair was dyed blue and shaved to a single strip running from his forehead to the nape of his neck. His nose, eyebrows, and earlobes displayed more metal than a Harley shop.

Ignoring me, the young man clumped down the stairs and disappeared around the house.

Seconds later, Ryan appeared, blowing steam across the top of a mug.

"What's up, buttercup?"

"Who the hell was that kid?"

"The studded Smurf?" He took an experimental sip. "Ruby's nephew, Eli."

"Nice look. Ryan, I hate to ask, but I have a meeting with Tyrell in twenty minutes and just realized I have no car."

He dug into a pocket and tossed me his keys.

"Take mine. I'll ride with McMahon."

"Are you sure?"

"You're not on the rental contract. Don't get arrested."

In the past, family assistance centers were established near accident sites in order to facilitate the transfer of records. This practice was abandoned once psychologists began to recognize the emotional impact on relatives of being in such proximity to the death scene.

The FAC for Air TransSouth 228 was at a Sleep Inn in Bryson City. Ten rooms had been converted into offices by replacing beds and armoires with desks, chairs, telephones, and laptops. It was here that antemortem records had been collected, briefings had been held, and families had been informed of identifications.

All that was finished now. With the exception of a single pair, the rooms that had once swarmed with grieving relatives, NTSB personnel, medical examiner interviewers, and Red Cross representatives had reverted to their original function.

Security was also not what it had been. Pulling

into the lot, I was surprised to see journalists chatting and drinking from Styrofoam cups, obviously awaiting a breaking story.

So intent was I on a timely arrival, it never crossed my mind that the story was me.

Then, a cameraman shouldered his minicam.

"There she is."

Other cameras went up. Microphones shot out, and shutters clicked like gravel in a power mower.

"Why did you move remains?"

"Did you tamper with disaster victim packets?"

"Dr. Brennan . . ."

"Is it true that evidence is missing from cases you processed?"

"Doctor . . ."

Strobes flashed in my face. Microphones nudged my chin, my forehead, my chest. Bodies pressed against me, moved with me, like a tangle of seaweed clinging to my limbs.

I kept my eyes straight, acknowledging no one. My heart hammered as I pushed forward, a swimmer struggling toward shore. The distance to the motel seemed oceanic, insurmountable.

Then, I felt a strong hand on my arm, and I was in the lobby. A state trooper was locking the glass doors, glaring at the mob outside.

"You all right, ma'am?"

I didn't trust my voice to reply.

"This way, please."

I followed to a bank of elevators. The trooper waited

with hands clasped, feet spread as we ascended. I stood on rubbery legs, trying to recompose my thoughts.

"How did the press find out about this?" I asked.

"I wouldn't know that, ma'am."

On the second floor, the trooper walked to Room 201, squared his shoulders to the wall beside the door.

"It's not locked." He fixed his eyes on something that was not me.

Drawing two steadying breaths, I turned the knob and entered.

Seated behind a desk on the far side of the room was North Carolina's second in command. Of a zillion thoughts winging through my mind at that moment, this is the one I remember: Parker Davenport's color had improved since I'd seen him on the day of the crash.

To the lieutenant governor's left sat Dr. Larke Tyrell, to his right, Earl Bliss. The ME looked at me and nodded. The DMORT commander's eyes wouldn't meet mine.

"Dr. Brennan, please have a seat." The lieutenant governor gestured to an armchair directly in front of the desk.

As I sat, Davenport leaned back and laced his fingers on his vest. The view behind him was spectacular, a Smoky Mountain postcard in explosive fall color. Squinting into the glare, I recognized my disadvantage. Had Tyrell been in charge, I'd have known the seating arrangement was strategy. I wasn't sure Davenport was that smart.

"Would you like coffee?" Davenport asked.

"No, thank you."

Looking at Davenport, I had difficulty imagining how he had lasted so long in public office. He was neither tall nor short, dark nor fair, smooth nor craggy. His hair and eyes were nondescript brown, his speech flat and without inflection. In a system that elects its leaders based on looks and eloquence, Davenport was clearly a noncontender. In a word, the man was unmemorable. But perhaps this was his greatest asset. People voted for Davenport, then forgot him.

The lieutenant governor unlaced his fingers, examined his palms, then looked at me.

"Dr. Brennan, some very disturbing allegations have been brought to my attention."

"I'm glad we're meeting to clear this up."

"Yes." Davenport leaned into the desk and opened a folder. To its left lay a videocassette. No one spoke as he selected and perused a document.

"Let's get right to the meat of this."

"Let's."

"Did you enter the site of the Air TransSouth crash on October fourth prior to the arrival of NTSB or medical examiner officials?"

"Since I was in the area, Earl Bliss asked me to stop by." I looked at the DMORT commander. His eyes remained on the hands in his lap.

"Did you have official orders to go there?"

"No, sir, but—"

"Did you falsely identify yourself as an official representative of the NDMS?"

"No, I did not."

Davenport checked another paper.

"Did you interfere with local authorities in their search-and-recovery efforts?"

"Absolutely not!" I felt heat rise up my neck and into my face.

"Did you order Deputy Anthony Skinner to remove protective covering from a crash victim, knowing there was risk of animal predation?"

"That's standard protocol."

I turned to Earl and Larke. Neither man was looking at me. Stay calm, I told myself.

"It is alleged that you broke *protocol*," Davenport emphasized my word, "by removing remains prior to documentation."

"That was a unique situation requiring immediate action. It was a judgment call, which I explained to Dr. Tyrell."

Davenport leaned farther forward, and his tone grew hard.

"Was stealing those remains also a judgment call?"

"What?"

"The case to which we refer is no longer at the morgue."

"I know nothing about that."

The insipid brown eyes narrowed.

"Really."

Davenport picked up the cassette, crossed to a TV/VCR unit, and inserted it. When he hit "play," a ghostly, gray scene filled the screen, and I knew instantly I was viewing a surveillance tape. I recognized the highway and the entrance to the morgue parking lot.

Within seconds my car entered the frame. A guard waved me away. Primrose appeared, spoke to the guard, tapped her way to the car, and handed me a bag. We exchanged a few words, then she patted my shoulder, and I drove off.

Davenport hit "stop" and rewound the tape. As he returned to his chair, I looked at the other two men. Both were studying me, their faces unreadable.

"Let me summarize," said Davenport. "Following a highly irregular sequence of events, the specimen in question, the specimen that you claim to have wrested from coyotes, is now missing."

"What does that have to do with me?"

Davenport picked up another paper.

"Early Sunday morning, a data-entry technician named Primrose Hobbs removed fragmented human tissue bearing morgue number 387 from a refrigerated trailer containing cases in process. She then proceeded to the admitting section and withdrew the disaster victim packet associated with those remains. Later that morning, Miss Hobbs was seen transferring a package to you in the morgue parking lot. That transaction was recorded, and we have just observed it."

Davenport drilled me with a look.

"Those remains and that packet are now gone, Dr. Brennan, and we believe you have them."

"I would strongly suggest you speak with Miss Hobbs." My voice dripped icicles.

"That was, of course, our first endeavor. Unfortunately, Miss Hobbs has not reported to work this week."

"Where is she?"

"That is unclear."

"Has she checked out of her motel?"

"Dr. Brennan, I realize that you are a board-certified forensic anthropologist of international stature. I am aware that you have consulted to Dr. Tyrell in the past, as well as to coroners worldwide. I am told that your credentials are unimpeachable. That makes your behavior in this matter all the more puzzling."

Davenport turned to his companions, as if enlisting support.

"We don't know why you've developed an obsession with this case, but it is clear that your interest has gone far beyond what is professional or ethical."

"I've done nothing wrong."

For the first time, Earl spoke.

"Your intentions may be honorable, Tempe, but unauthorized removal of a victim shows very poor judgment."

He dropped his eyes and flicked a nonexistent particle from his pants.

"And is a felony," Davenport chimed in.

I spoke to the DMORT commander.

"Earl, you know me. You know I would never do that."

Before Earl could reply, Davenport exchanged the paper in his hand for a brown envelope, and shook two photos from it. He glanced at the larger, laid it on the desk, then pushed it toward me with one finger.

For a moment I thought it was a joke.

"That is you, Dr. Brennan, is it not?"

Ryan and I were eating hot dogs across from the Great Smoky Mountains Railroad Depot.

"And Lieutenant-Detective Andrew Ryan from Quebec." He pronounced it Qwee-bec.

"What is the relevance of this, Mr. Davenport?" Though my face was burning, I kept my voice frigid.

"Exactly what is your relationship with this man?"

"Detective Ryan and I have worked together for years."

"But I am correct in assuming that your relation-ship extends beyond the professional, am I not?"

"I have no intention of answering questions about my private life."

"I see."

Davenport pushed the second photo across the desk.

I was too stunned to speak.

"I surmise from your reaction that you know the gentleman pictured with Detective Ryan?"

"Jean Bertrand was Ryan's partner." Shock waves were passing through every cell in my body.

"Are you aware that this Bertrand is being investigated in conjunction with the Air TransSouth crash?"

"Where is this going?"

"Dr. Brennan, I shouldn't have to spell it out. Your"—he feigned indecision over word selection—"colleague has ties to a principal suspect. You yourself have acted"—again the careful search—"erratically."

"I have done nothing wrong," I repeated.

Davenport tilted his head and twisted his mouth, neither smiling nor grimacing. Then he sighed, indicating what a burden this was for all.

"Perhaps, as Mr. Bliss has suggested, your only offense has been one of misjudgment. But in tragedies of this nature, with so much media attention, and so many grieving families, it is of utmost importance that those involved avoid even the appearance of impropriety."

I waited. Davenport began gathering papers.

"Reports of suspected misconduct are being lodged with the National Disaster Medical System, the American Board of Forensic Anthropology, and the Ethics Committee of the American Academy of Forensic Sciences. The chancellor of your university will also be informed."

Cold fear shot through me.

"Am I suspected of committing a crime?"

"We must consider every possibility, painstakingly and impartially."

Something snapped. I shot to my feet, fingers tightening into fists.

"There's nothing impartial about this meeting, Mr. Davenport, and you have no intention of treating me fairly. Or Detective Ryan. Something's wrong, very wrong, and I've been set up as some sort of scapegoat."

Tears burned the backs of my lids. It's the glare, I told myself. Don't you dare cry!

"Who turned this meeting into a publicity circus?"

Red splotches appeared in Davenport's cheeks, looking oddly out of place in the bland complexion.

"I have no idea how the press found out about this meeting. The leak did not come from my office."

"And the surveillance photo? Where did that order originate?"

Davenport did not answer. The room was deathly quiet.

I uncurled my fingers and drew a deep breath. Then I impaled Davenport with a look.

"I perform my duties scrupulously, ethically, and out of concern for both the living and the dead, Lieutenant Governor Davenport." I kept my voice level. "I do not deviate from protocol. Dr. Tyrell knows that and Mr. Bliss knows that."

My eyes moved to Larke, but he looked away. Earl's attention remained focused on his pants. I turned back to Davenport.

"I don't know what's going on, or why it's going on, but I will find out."

I pointed a finger to emphasize every word.

"I . Will. Find. Out."

With that, I turned and walked from the room, quietly closing the door behind me. The trooper trailed me down the corridor, into the elevator, and across the motel lobby.

The parking lot was an encore of my arrival. Though my escort defended one flank, I was accosted on all others. Cameras rolled, microphones jabbed, and strobes flashed. Questions were shouted in the round. Pushing forward, head down, arms clasped to my chest, I felt more trapped than I had by the coyote pack.

At Ryan's car, the trooper restrained the onslaught with both arms while I unlocked and opened the door. Then he bullied the crowd back, and I broke free and shot onto the highway.

As I drove, my face cooled and my pulse normalized, but a million questions swirled in my brain. How long had I been under surveillance? Could this explain the ransacking of my room? How far would they go? Why?

Would they be back?

Who were "they"?

My eyes flew to the rearview mirror.

Where in God's name was that foot? Had someone actually taken it? If so, for what purpose?

How did they know it was gone? Who had wanted that foot on Monday? Why?

Where was Primrose Hobbs?

The lieutenant governor's office was not typically included in the disaster inquiry loop. Why was Davenport taking such an interest?

Could I actually be facing criminal charges? Should I obtain counsel?

I was completely absorbed in these questions, driving robotically, seeing and responding to my surroundings, but registering nothing on a conscious level. I don't know how far I'd driven when a loud whoop sent my eyes back to the rearview mirror.

A police cruiser rode my bumper, headlights flashing like a strobotron.

18

I SLOWED AND PULLED ONTO THE SHOULDER. THE cruiser followed.

Traffic whizzed by, normal people on their way to normal places.

I was staring in the rearview mirror when the cruiser's door opened and Lucy Crowe climbed out. My first reaction was relief. Then she put on her hat, squared it carefully, suggesting this was not a social call. I wondered if I should get out too, decided to stay put.

Crowe walked to my car, looking tall and powerful in her sheriff's livery. I opened the door.

"Mornin'," she said, giving her inverted nod.

I nodded back.

"New car?" She spread her feet and placed hands on her hips.

"Borrowed. Mine took an unscheduled sabbatical."

Crowe was not asking for a license or posing the

usual questions, so I assumed this was not a traffic stop. I wondered if I was about to be arrested.

"Got something you're probably not going to want to hear."

The radio on her belt sputtered, and she adjusted a knob.

"Daniel Wahnetah turned up last night."

I almost couldn't ask.

"Alive?"

"Very. Knocked on his daughter's door around seven, had dinner with the family, then went home to bed. Daughter called me this morning." She spoke loudly over the rush of traffic.

"Where was he for three months?"

"West Virginia."

"Doing what?"

"She didn't offer that."

Daniel Wahnetah was not dead. I couldn't believe it.

"Any developments on George Adair or Jeremiah Mitchell?"

"Not a word."

"Neither really fits the profile." My voice was tight.

"Guess this doesn't help you much."

"No."

Though I'd never allowed myself to say it, I'd been counting on the foot belonging to Wahnetah. Now I was back to zero.

"But I am happy for the Wahnetah family."

"They're good people."

She watched my fingers worrying the steering wheel.

"I heard about the news report."

"My phone's ringing so much it's now off. I just left a meeting with Parker Davenport, and there was a crazy media scene outside the Sleep Inn."

"Davenport." She hooked an elbow over the top of the car door. "There's a real peckerwood."

"What do you mean?"

She looked up the road, then back at me. Sunlight glinted off her aviator shades.

"Did you know that Parker Davenport was born not far from here?"

"No, I didn't."

She was quiet a moment, lost in memories that were hers alone.

"I take it you don't like the man."

"Let's just say his poster's never going to hang above my bed."

"Davenport told me that the foot is now missing and accused me of taking it." I had to pause to keep the tremor from my voice. "He also said that a data technician who helped me take measurements has also disappeared."

"Who's that?"

"An elderly black lady named Primrose Hobbs."

"I'll ask around."

"You know this is all bullshit," I said. "What I can't figure out is why Davenport is gunning for me."

"Parker Davenport has his own mind about things."

A truck rumbled by, blasting us with a wave of hot air. Crowe straightened.

"I'm going to talk with our DA, see if I can't inspire a push for that warrant."

Something suddenly struck me. Though Larke Tyrell had cited trespass when he'd banished me from the investigation, the issue of the courtyard house hadn't been raised today.

"I tracked down the owners."

"I'm listening."

"The property has belonged to an investment group called H&F since 1949. Before that it was owned by Edward E. Arthur, before that Victor T. Livingstone."

She shook her head.

"You're talking way before my time."

"I've got a list of the H&F officers in my room. I could bring it by your office after I check on my car."

"I need to swing by Fontana when I'm done with the DA. We've got Fox Friggin' Mulder over there thinks he's found an alien." She looked at her watch. "I should be back by four."

I drove back to High Ridge House, feeling feverish with anxiety. To work off the tension I offered Boyd a jog. I also felt I should make up for breakfast. Not one for grudges, he accepted with enthusiasm.

The road was damp from yesterday's rain, and our feet made soft popping sounds on the muddy gravel. Boyd panted and his tags jingled. Jays and sparrows were the only other creatures breaking the stillness.

The view was another Impressionist tableau, an endless expanse of valleys and hills polished and buffed by a brilliant morning sun. But the wind had shifted overnight and now carried an edge. Each time we moved into shadow, I sensed winter and shortening days.

The exercise calmed me, but not much. As I climbed the stairs to Magnolia, my chest tightened at the memory of Monday's intrusion. Today my door was closed, my belongings intact.

I showered and put on fresh clothes. As I turned on the phone it rang in my hand. I answered with rigid fingers. Another journalist. I hung up and dialed Pete.

As usual, a machine took the call. Though I was anxious for an opinion on my legal situation, I knew it was useless to try his other numbers. Pete had both car and cell phones, but rarely recharged either. If he did progress that far, he'd forget to turn the unit on, or he'd leave it on a dashboard or bedroom dresser.

Frustrated, I dug out McMahon's fax, stuffed it in my purse, and headed downstairs.

I was making an egg salad sandwich when Ruby backed through the swinging door into the kitchen, a blue plastic laundry basket in her arms. She wore a white blouse, fake pearls, sweatpants, socks, and slippers, and her hair roll looked freshly lacquered. Her appearance suggested a morning outing, followed by a change from the waist down.

"Can I do that for you?" she asked.

"I'm fine."

She set down the basket and walked to the sink, slippers flapping against her heels.

"I'm real sorry about your room."

"I had nothing of value up there."

"Someone must have come in while I was to market." She picked up a dish towel, sniffed it. "Sometimes I wonder what the world's coming to. The Lord—"

"These things happen."

"We've never had stealing in this house." She turned to me, the towel twisted between her hands. "I don't blame you for being angry."

"I'm not angry at you."

She took a quick breath, opened her mouth, closed it. I had the impression she was about to say something, changed her mind, wary of how the telling might impact her life. Good. I was too strung out for sympathetic listening.

"Can I get you a drink?"

"Do you have lemonade?"

She tossed the towel into her basket and crossed to the refrigerator. Withdrawing a plastic pitcher, she filled a glass and set it next to my sandwich.

"And that television business and all."

"All through school, I was never once voted most popular."

I smiled, not wanting Ruby to see how agitated I was. The gesture must have looked as strained as it felt.

"It isn't funny. You shouldn't let them do this."

"I can't control the press, Ruby."

She got a paper plate, placed my sandwich on it. "Cookies?"

"Sure."

She added three sugar cookies, then looked straight into my eyes.

"'Blessed are ye when men shall revile you, and persecute you, and shall say all manner of evil against you falsely.'"

"The people who matter know these accusations are false." Keep cool.

"Then maybe you need to be controlling someone else."

She hoisted the basket onto her hip and left without a backward glance.

Hoping for more rational conversation, I went outside to lunch with Boyd. I was not disappointed. The chow inhaled the cookies, then watched without comment as I ate the sandwich and considered my options.

Arriving at the garage, I learned that the problem with my car was minor, but a pump was required. The absent letter, either P or T, was in Asheville, and would try to obtain the part. Assuming that mission went well, repairs could be finished the next afternoon.

Could be. I noticed that the Chevy, Pinto, and pickups remained exactly where they'd been the day before.

I checked the time. Two-thirty. Crowe wouldn't be back yet.

Now what?

I requested a phone directory and was handed a

1996 edition, dog-eared and reeking of petroleum products. Two hands were required to part the pages.

While there was no entry for the Eternal Light Holiness-Pentecostal House of God, I did find a listing for L. Bowman on Swayney Creek Road. P/T knew the intersection but could provide nothing more. I thanked him and returned to Ryan's car.

Following P/T's instructions, I headed out of town. As he'd predicted, Swayney Creek dead-ended into Highway 19 between Ela and Bryson City. I stopped at a filling station to ask directions to Bowman's house.

The attendant was a kid of about sixteen with greasy black hair, separated down the crown and tucked behind the ears. White flecks littered his part like snowflakes along a muddy creek.

The kid put down his comic and glanced at me, his eyes scrunched as though sensitive to light. Picking a cigarette from a scalloped metal dish, he drew deeply, then jerked his chin in the direction of Swayney Creek.

"It's about two miles north." Smoke billowed out with his answer.

"Which side?"

"Look for a green mailbox."

Walking out, I felt squinty eyes on my back.

Swayney Creek was a thin black tongue that dropped sharply after leaving the highway. The road descended for the next half mile, then leveled off and passed through a long stretch of mixed-conifer forest. A creek ran along one side, the water so clear I could see individual pebbles littering the bottom.

Driving north, I passed few signs of habitation. Then the road curved east, climbed slightly, and I spotted an opening in the trees, a rusty green mailbox to its right. Drawing close, I saw the name "Bowman" carved on a plaque hung below the box with two short segments of chain.

I turned onto the dirt lane and crept forward, hoping I had the right Bowman. Pine, spruce, and hemlock towered above, choking off all but a few shoots of sunlight. Fifty yards up, Luke Bowman's house squatted like a solitary sentinel guarding the forest road.

The reverend lived in a weathered frame bungalow, with a porch at one end and a shed at the other. Together they were stacked with enough firewood to heat a medieval castle. Bright turquoise awnings angled over windows to either side of the front door, looking as out of place in the gloom as the Golden Arches on a synagogue.

The "front yard" was black with shade and carpeted with a thick mat of leaves and pine needles. A gravel path crossed it, leading from the door to a rectangle of gravel at the road's end.

I pulled next to Bowman's pickup, cut the engine, and turned on my phone. Before I could get out, the front door opened and the reverend appeared on the stoop. Again, he was dressed in black, as though wanting to remind even himself of the soberness of his calling.

Bowman didn't smile, but his face relaxed when he recognized me. I climbed out of the car and walked up the path. Small brown mushrooms bordered each side.

"I'm sorry to disturb you, Reverend Mr. Bowman. I left a shopping bag in your truck."

"You surely did. It's in the kitchen." He stepped back. "Please, come inside."

I brushed past him into a dim interior heavy with the odor of burned bacon.

"Would you like something to drink?"

"No, thank you. I can't stay."

"Please, have a seat."

He gestured into a small living room crammed with furniture. The pieces looked as though they'd been purchased by the roomful, then placed exactly as on the showroom floor. Only closer together.

"Thanks."

I sat on a brown velour sectional, the centerpiece of a three-piece grouping still covered in plastic. Though the weather was cool the windows were open, and the perfectly matched brown plaid curtains billowed inward with the breeze.

"I'll get your things."

He disappeared and a door opened, allowing the muted voices, bongs, and applause of a television game show to drift out. I looked around.

The room was devoid of personal items. There were no wedding or graduation pictures. Not one snapshot of the kids at the beach or the dog in a party hat. The only images were of haloed persons. I recognized Jesus, and a chap I thought might be John the Baptist.

After several minutes, Bowman returned. The plastic slipcover crackled as I rose.

"Thank you."

"It was a pleasure, Miss Temperance."

"And thank you again for yesterday."

"I was glad to help. Peter and Timothy are the best mechanics in the county. I've taken my trucks to them for years."

"Reverend Mr. Bowman, you've lived here a long time, haven't you?"

"All my life."

"Do you know anything about a lodge house with a courtyard near the spot where the plane went down?"

"I remember my daddy talking about a camp out that way near Running Goat Branch, but never a lodge."

I had a sudden thought. Shifting the bag onto my left hip, I dug out McMahon's fax and handed it to Bowman.

"Are any of these names familiar to you?"

He unfolded and read the paper. I watched closely, but saw no change in his expression.

"Sorry."

He handed back the fax, and I returned it to my purse.

"Have you ever heard of a man named Victor Livingstone?"

Bowman shook his head.

"Edward Arthur?"

"I know an Edward Arthur lives over near Sylva.

Used to be Holiness, but left the movement years ago. Brother Arthur used to claim he was led to the Holy Ghost by George Hensley himself."

"George Hensley?"

"The first man to take up serpents. Brother Arthur said they made acquaintance during Reverend Hensley's time in Grasshopper Valley."

"I see."

"Brother Arthur's got to be close to ninety by now."

"He's still alive?"

"As God's holy word."

"He was a member of your church?"

"He was one of my father's flock, as devoted a man as ever breathed God's air. Army changed him. Kept the faith for a few years after the war, then just stopped following the signs."

"When was that?"

"Around forty-seven or forty-eight. No. That's not right." He pointed a gnarled finger. "The last service Brother Arthur attended was for Sister Edna Farrell's passing. I recall that because Papa had been praying for the renewal of the man's faith. About a week after the funeral Papa paid Brother Arthur a visit, and found himself preaching down the barrel of a gun. After that, he give up."

"When did Edna Farrell die?"

"Nineteen forty-nine."

Edward Arthur had sold his land to the H&F Investment Group on April 10, 1949.

19

I FOUND EDWARD ARTHUR IN A VEGETABLE PATCH
behind his log cabin. He wore a wool plaid shirt over
denim coveralls, rubber boots, and a ragged straw
hat that might once have belonged to a gondolier. He
paused when he saw me, then went back to turning
dirt.

"Mr. Arthur?" I asked.

The old man continued jabbing a pitchfork at the
ground, then pushing on it with a shaky foot. He had
so little strength the prongs barely penetrated, but he
repeated the movement again and again.

"Edward Arthur?" I spoke more loudly.

He didn't answer. The fork made a soft thud each
time he thrust it at the soil.

"Mr. Arthur, I can see that you're busy, but I'd like
to ask you a few questions."

I set my face in what I hoped was an encouraging
smile.

Arthur straightened as best he could and walked to a wheelbarrow loaded with rocks and dead vegetation. When he removed his shirt I saw scrawny arms and hands covered with liver spots the size of lima beans. Exchanging the pitchfork for a hoe, he tottered back to the row where he'd been working.

"I'd like to ask you about a piece of property near Running Goat Branch."

For the first time Arthur looked at me. His eyes were rheumy, the rims red, the irises so pale they were almost colorless.

"I believe you used to own acreage in that vicinity?"

"Why you coming to me?" His breathing sounded wheezy, like air being sucked through a filter.

"I'm curious about who bought your land."

"Are you FBI?"

"No."

"You one of them crash people?"

"I was with the investigation, but I'm not any longer."

"Who sent you here?"

"No one sent me, Mr. Arthur. I found you through Luke Bowman."

"Whyn't you put your questions to Luke Bowman?"

"Reverend Mr. Bowman didn't know anything about your land, except that it might have been a campground at one time."

"That's what he said, was it?"

"Yes, sir."

Arthur pulled a parrot-green kerchief from a pocket and ran it across his face. Then he dropped the hoe and hobbled toward me, his back as rounded as a turkey vulture's. When he drew close I could see coarse white hair sprouting from his nostrils, neck, and ears.

"Can't say much about the son, but Thaddeus Bowman was as pesky a man as ever drew air. Ran a hallelujah house for forty years."

"You were one of Thaddeus Bowman's followers?"

"Till I learnt all that casting out o' demons and speaking in tongues was a heap of horseshit."

Arthur hawked up phlegm and spat into the dirt.

"I see. You sold your land after the war?"

He went on as if I hadn't spoken.

"Thaddeus Bowman kept hounding me to repent, but I was on to other things. The damned fool wouldn't accept my leavin' until I put it to him from the business end of a squirrel rifle."

"Mr. Arthur, I'm here to ask about the property you bought from Victor Livingstone."

"Didn't buy no property from Victor Livingstone."

"Records indicate Livingstone transferred title to you in 1933."

"I was nineteen in 1933. Got myself married."

This seemed to be going nowhere.

"Did you know Victor Livingstone?"

"Sarah Masham. She died in birthing."

His answers were so disjointed I wondered if he was senile.

"The seventeen acres was our weddin' present. They got a word for that."

The creases around his eyes deepened with concentration.

"Mr. Arthur, I'm sorry for taking you away from your garden, bu—"

"Dowry. That's the word. It was her dowry."

"What was her dowry?"

"Ain't you asking 'bout that land t' Running Goat?"

"Yes, sir."

"Sarah's daddy give it to us. Then she died."

"Victor Livingstone was your wife's father?"

"Sarah Masham Livingstone. That was my first wife. We was married three years when she passed. Wasn't but eighteen. Her daddy was so tore up, he went and died, too."

"I'm so sorry, Mr. Arthur."

"That's when I lit outta here and threw in with George Hensley over t' Tennessee. He's the one got me to taking up serpents."

"What happened with the Running Goat property?"

"City fella asked if he could rent it, run a little camp. I wanted nothing to do with the place, so I said hell, yes. Seemed like easy money."

Again he cleared his throat and spat.

"It was a campground?"

"They came up for huntin' and fishin', but you ask me, it was mostly to hide from their womenfolk."

"Was there a house?"

"They stayed with tents and campfires and all, till I

built the lodge." He shook his head. "Beats me what some fools consider fun."

"When did you build the lodge?"

"Before the war."

"Did it have a walled courtyard?"

"What the hell kinda question is that?"

"Did you build a stone wall and make a court-yard?"

"I wasn't puttin' up no friggin' Camelot."

"You sold the land in 1949?"

"Sounds right."

"The year you broke with Thaddeus Bowman."

"Eyeh."

"Luke Bowman remembered that you left his father's congregation right after Edna Farrell died."

Again the eyes creased.

"You implyin' something, young lady?"

"No, sir."

"Edna Farrell was a fine Christian lady. They should have done better by her."

"Would you mind telling me who bought the camp?"

"Would you mind tellin' me why you're wantin' to know my business?"

I was quickly revising my estimate of Edward Arthur. Because he was old and taciturn I had presumed his faculties might be dulled. The man in front of me was as cagey as Kasparov. I decided to play it straight.

"I'm no longer involved in the crash investigation

because I've been accused of acting improperly. The charges are false."

"Eyeh."

"I believe there's something wrong in that lodge, and I want to know what. The information may help clear my name, but I think my efforts are being blocked."

"You been there?"

"Not inside."

He started to speak, but a gust of wind grabbed his hat and sent it reeling across the garden. Purple lips drew back against toothless gums, and a scarecrow arm shot out.

Bolting, I overtook the hat and pinned it with a foot. Then I brushed it clean and carried it back to Arthur.

The old man shivered as he took the boater and pressed it to his chest.

"Would you like your shirt, sir?"

"Turnin' cold," he said, and started for the wheelbarrow.

When he'd finished buttoning, I helped him gather his tools and store them with the wheelbarrow in a shed behind the cabin. As he closed the door, I reposed my question.

"Who bought your land, Mr. Arthur?"

He clicked the padlock, tugged it twice, and turned to face me.

"You'd best stay clear of that place, young lady."

"I promise you, sir, I won't go there alone."

Arthur regarded me for so long, I thought he wasn't going to answer. Then he stepped close and raised his face to mine.

"Prentice Dashwood."

He spat "Prentice" with such force that saliva misted my chin.

"Prentice Dashwood bought your land?"

He nodded, and the watery old eyes darkened.

"The devil hisself," he hissed.

When I phoned Crowe's office, a deputy informed me that the sheriff was still in Fontana. I sat a moment, clicking my keys on the steering wheel and staring at Arthur's cabin.

Then I started the car and pulled out.

Though fat, black-green clouds were rapidly gathering, I drove with the windows down, the air buffeting my face. I knew wind would soon whip the trees, and rain would wash across the pavement and down the mountain face, but for the moment the air felt good.

Taking Highway 19, I headed back toward Bryson City. Two miles south of town I spotted a small wooden sign and turned off onto a gravel road.

The Riverbank Inn lay a quarter mile down the road, on the banks of the Tuckasegee River. It was a one-story, yellow stucco affair built in a 1950s ranch design. Its sixteen rooms stretched to the left and right of a central office, each with its own front entrance and porch in back. A plastic jack-o'-lantern grinned from every stoop, and an electrified skeleton hung from a tree outside the main entrance.

Clearly, the inn's appeal lay in setting and not in decorating or architectural style.

Pulling up outside the office, I saw only two other vehicles, a red Pontiac Grand Am with Alabama plates, and a blue Ford Taurus with North Carolina plates. The cars were parked in front of units two and seven.

As I passed the skeleton, it gave a warbly moan, followed by a high-pitched mechanical laugh. I wondered how often Primrose had to endure the display.

The motel lobby had the same feel as High Ridge House. A strand of bells hanging on the door, chintz curtains, knotty pine. A plaque welcomed me, and introduced the owners as Ralph and Brenda Stover. Another jack-o'-lantern smiled from the counter.

A man in a Redskins jersey sat beside Jack, leafing through a copy of *PC World.* He looked up when I jingled in, and smiled at me across the lobby. I assumed this was Ralph.

"May I help you?" Ralph had thinning blond hair, and his skin was pink and Simonize shiny.

"I'm Dr. Tempe Brennan," I said, extending a hand.

"Ralph Stover."

As we shook, his medical ID bracelet jangled like the bells on the door.

"I'm a friend of Primrose Hobbs," I said.

"Yes?"

"Mrs. Hobbs has been staying here for the past two weeks?"

"She has."

"She's working with the crash investigation."

"I know Mrs. Hobbs." Ralph's smile never wavered.
"Is she in?"

"I can ring her room if you'd like."

"Please."

He dialed, listened, replaced the receiver.

"Mrs. Hobbs is not answering. Would you like to
leave a message?"

"I take it she has not checked out."

"Mrs. Hobbs is still registered."

"Have you seen her today?"

"No."

"When did you last see her?"

"I can't possibly keep track of all our guests."

"Mrs. Hobbs hasn't been to work since Sunday,
and I'm concerned about her. Could you please tell
me what room she's in?"

"I'm sorry, but I can't do that." The smile widened.
"Policy."

"She could be ill."

"The maid would report a sick guest."

Ralph was as polite as a policeman on a traffic
stop. O.K. I can do polite.

"This is really important." I placed a palm lightly
on his wrist and looked into his eyes. "Can you tell
me what Mrs. Hobbs drives so I can see if her car is
in your lot?"

"No, I cannot."

"Can we go together to check her room?"

"No."

"Will you go while I wait here?"

"No, ma'am."

Pulling back my hand, I tried another tack.

"Would Mrs. Stover remember when she last saw Mrs. Hobbs?"

Ralph laced his fingers and laid his hands on the magazine. The hair on his forearms looked pale and wiry against the calamine-pink skin.

"You are asking the same questions the others asked, and my wife and I will give you the same answers we gave to them. Unless served with an official warrant we will open no room, and divulge no information about any guest." His voice was buttery smooth.

"What others?"

Ralph drew a long, patient breath.

"Is there anything else I can help you with?"

I honed my voice to scalpel sharp.

"If Primrose Hobbs comes to any harm because of your *policy,* you'll wish you'd never sent away for that hotel-motel management course."

Ralph Stover's eyes narrowed but the smile held firm.

I pulled a business card from my purse and jotted down my cell phone number.

"If you have a change of heart, give me a call."

I turned and strode toward the door.

"You have a nice day, ma'am."

I heard the flip of a magazine page, the jangle of a bracelet.

Gunning the engine, I raced from the lot, sped up the highway, and pulled onto the shoulder fifty yards north. If I knew human nature, curiosity would drive Stover to Primrose's room. And he would go there immediately.

Hurriedly locking the car, I sprinted back to the Riverbank turnoff and cut into the woods. Then I picked my way forward, paralleling the gravel road, until I had a clear view of the motel.

My intuition was right on. Ralph was just arriving at unit four. He checked to his left, then his right, unlocked the door, and slipped inside.

Minutes passed. Five. Ten. My breathing slowed to normal. The sky darkened and the wind picked up. Overhead, pines arched and dipped, like ballerinas doing arm positions *sur les pointes.*

I thought about Primrose. Though we'd known each other for years, I knew very little about the woman. She had married, divorced, had a son somewhere. Beyond that, her life was a blank. Why was that? Had she been unwilling to share, or had I never bothered to ask? Had I treated Primrose like one of the many who pass time with us, delivering our mail, typing our reports, cleaning our houses, while we pursue our own interests, oblivious to theirs?

Perhaps. But I knew Primrose Hobbs well enough to be certain of one thing: She would never willingly leave a job unfinished.

I waited. Lightning streaked from an eggplant cloud,

illuminating its interior like a million-watt artery. Thunder rumbled. The storm was not far off.

Finally, Stover emerged, pulled the door shut and jiggled the knob, then hurried up the sidewalk. When he was safely inside the office, I began circling, keeping my distance and using the trees for cover. The back of the inn stretched ahead of me on one side, the river on the other, trees between them. I moved through the trees to a point I estimated was opposite unit four, then paused to listen.

Water boiling over rocks. Boughs swishing in the wind. A train whistle. Valves slamming inside my chest. Thunder, louder now. Quicker.

I crept to the edge of the tree line and peeked out.

A row of wooden porches projected from the back of the motel, each with a black wrought-iron numeral nailed to its railing. My instincts had been good again. Only five yards of grass separated me from unit four.

I took a deep breath, darted across the gap, and double-stepped the four risers. Dashing across the porch, I reached out and yanked the screen door. It opened with a grating squeak. The wind had suddenly calmed, and the sound seemed to shatter the heavy air. I froze.

Stillness.

Sliding between the screen and inner door, I leaned close and peered through the glass. Green-and-white gingham blocked my view. I tried the knob. No go.

I eased the screen door closed, moved to the window, and tried again. More gingham.

Noticing a gap where the lower border met the sill, I placed my palms on the window frame and pushed up. Tiny white flakes fluttered down around my fingers.

I pushed again, and the window jogged upward an inch. Again I froze. In my mind I heard an alarm, saw Ralph burst from the office with a Smith & Wesson.

Turning palms up, I wriggled my fingers into the gap.

What I was doing was illegal. I knew that. Breaking into Primrose's room was precisely the wrong move given my present situation. But I needed to assure myself that she was all right. Later, if it turned out that she wasn't, I needed to know that I had done what I could to help her.

And, to be honest, I needed to do this for myself. I had to find out what had happened to that foot. I had to track Primrose down and show that panel of men that they were wrong.

I spread my feet and pushed. The window opened another inch.

I heard the first *patta-patta-pat* as fat drops slapped the floorboards. Dime-sized blotches multiplied and merged around my boots.

I manipulated the window another two inches.

It was then that the storm broke. Lightning streaked, thunder cracked, and rain fell in torrents, turning the porch into a shimmering rink.

I abandoned the window and pressed my body to the wall, hoping for protection from the overhang. Within seconds water soaked my hair and dripped from my ears and nose. My clothes molded to me like papier-mâché on a wire frame.

Millions of drops cascaded off the roof and the porch. They bit into the lawn, met up, and coursed in channels between the blades of grass. They formed a river in the gutter above my head. Wind slapped leaves against the wall and my legs, sent others twirling across the ground. It carried the scent of wet earth and wood, of numberless creatures hunkered into burrows and nests.

Shivering, I waited it out, my back against the stucco, hands under armpits. I watched drops bead a spider-web, build, then bow the fibers. Its maker watched too, a small brown bundle on an outer filament.

Islands were born. Continental plates shifted. A score of species disappeared from the planet forever.

Suddenly my cell phone shrilled, the sound so unexpected I almost jumped from the porch.

I clicked on.

"No comment!" I shrieked, expecting another reporter.

Lightning shot straight to the treetops. Thunder snapped.

"Where the hell are you?" said Lucy Crowe.

"The storm came up quickly."

"You're outside?"

"Are you back in Bryson City?"

"I'm still out at Fontana Lake. Do you want to ring me when you've gotten inside?"

"That could be a while." I had no intention of telling her why.

Crowe spoke to someone else, came back on the line.

"Afraid I've got more bad news for you."

I heard voices in the background, then the crackle of a police radio.

"Looks like we've found Primrose Hobbs."

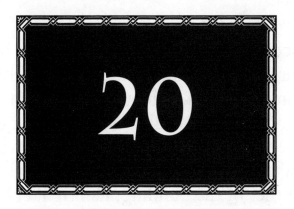

20

WHILE I WAS MEETING WITH OUR ESTEEMED LIEU-
tenant governor and friends, the owners of a marina
were finding a body.

As was their custom, Glenn and Irene Boynton
rose at dawn and dealt with the morning rush, renting
equipment, selling bait, filling coolers with ice, sandwiches, and canned drinks. When Irene went to check
on a bass boat returned late the previous day, an odd
rippling drew her to the end of the dock. Peering into
the water, the woman was terrified to see two lidless
eyes staring back.

Following Crowe's directions, I found Fontana
Lake, then the narrow dirt track leading to the marina.
The rain had tapered off, though the leaves overhead
were still dripping. I wound through puddles toward
the lake, my tires throwing up a spray of mud and
water.

As the marina came into view, I saw a wrecker, an

ambulance, and a pair of police cruisers bathing a parking area in oscillating red, blue, and yellow light. The marina stretched along the shore on the lot's far side. It consisted of a dilapidated rental office–gas station–general store, with narrow wooden piers jutting into the water at both ends. A wind sock fluttered from a corner of the building, its bright colors jauntily snapping in the breeze, jarringly at odds with the grim scene on the ground below.

A deputy was interviewing a couple in jean shorts and windbreakers on the southernmost pier. Their bodies were tense, their faces the color of pale putty.

Crowe stood on the office steps talking to Tommy Albright, a hospital pathologist who occasionally did autopsies for the medical examiner. Albright was wrinkled and scrawny, with sparse white hair combed straight across his crown. He'd been making Y-incisions since the Precambrian, but I'd never worked with him.

Albright watched me approach then held out a hand.

We shook. I nodded to Crowe.

"I understand you knew the victim."

Albright tipped his head in the direction of the ambulance. The doors stood open, revealing a shiny white pouch lying on a collapsible gurney. Bulges told me the body bag was already occupied.

"We pulled her out just before the storm broke. Are you willing to try a quick visual?"

"Yes."

No! I didn't want to do this. Didn't want to be here. Didn't want to identify Primrose Hobbs's lifeless body.

We walked to the ambulance and climbed in back. Even with the doors open the smell was noticeable. I swallowed hard.

Albright unzipped the bag and the odor rolled over us, a nauseating cocktail of stagnant mud, seaweed, lake creatures, and putrefying tissue.

"I'd guess she was in the water two or three days. She's not scavenged too badly."

Holding my breath, I looked into the bag.

It was Primrose Hobbs, but it wasn't. Her face was bloated, her lips swollen like those of a tropical fish in an aquarium. The dark skin had sloughed in patches, revealing the pale underside of her epidermis, and giving her body a mottled appearance. Fish or eels had devoured her eyelids, and nibbled her forehead, cheeks, and nose.

"Won't be too much problem with cause," said Albright. "Course, Tyrell will want a full autopsy."

Primrose's wrists were wrapped with electrical tape, and I could see a thin wire embedded in her neck.

I tasted bile, swallowed hard.

"Garroted?"

He nodded. "Bastard wrapped the line around her throat, then tightened it in back with some kind of tool. Very effective in cutting off the windpipe."

I placed a hand over my nose and mouth and leaned in. Jagged lines scored the flesh on one side of Primrose's neck, scratched by her nails as she clawed for life with her bound hands.

"It's her," I said, lunging from the ambulance. I needed air. Miles and oceans of fresh air.

Hurrying to the far end of the unoccupied pier, I stood a moment, arms wrapped around my middle. A boat whined in the distance, grew loud, receded. Waves lapped below my feet. Frogs croaked from the weeds lining the shore. Life continued, oblivious to the death of one of its creatures.

I thought about Primrose, pictured her hobbling out to our final meeting in the morgue parking lot. A sixty-two-year-old black woman with a nursing degree, a weight problem, proficiency at cards, and a fondness for rhubarb crumble. There. I did know something about my friend.

My chest gave a series of heaves.

Steady.

I pulled a ragged breath.

Think.

What could Primrose have done, known, or seen that could have brought such violence down on her? Was she killed because of her involvement with me?

Another tremor. I gulped air.

Or was I magnifying my own role? Was her death random? We Americans are the world's leading producers of homicide. Was Primrose Hobbs bound and strangled for nothing more than her car? That made no sense. Not the garroting and the duct tape. This was a planned murder and she was the intended victim. But why?

Hearing doors slam, I turned. The attendants were climbing into the front of the ambulance. Seconds later, the engine revved, and the vehicle crawled up the dirt road.

Good-bye, old friend. If I brought you to this, please, please, forgive me. My lower lip trembled, and I bit down hard.

You will not cry. But why not? Why hold back tears of mourning for a good and gentle person?

I looked out across the lake. The sky was clearing, and the pines on the far shore stood out blue-black against the first pink rays of dusk. I recalled something else.

Primrose Hobbs loved sunsets. I gazed at the sunset and wept until I felt angry. Beyond angry. I felt a hot, red rage burning inside me.

Bridle it, Brennan. Use it.

Vowing to find answers, I drew a deep breath and walked up the pier to rejoin Crowe and Albright.

"What did she drive?" I asked.

Crowe consulted a spiral pad.

"Blue Honda Civic. Ninety-four. North Carolina plates."

"It's not parked at the Riverbank Inn."

Crowe looked at me strangely.

"Car could be on its way to Saudi Arabia by now," said Albright.

"I told you that the victim was helping me with my investigation."

"I'll want to talk to you about that." Crowe.

"Find anything here?" I asked.

"We're still looking."

"Tire tracks? Footprints?" I knew it was stupid as soon as I said it. The rain would have obliterated such impressions.

Crowe shook her head.

I scanned the pickups and SUVs left behind by fishermen and pleasure boaters. Two sixteen-foot aluminum outboards bobbed in their slips.

"Any permanent tie-ups at the marina?"

"It's strictly a rental business."

"That means a lot of people coming and going every day. Pretty busy spot for a body dump."

"Rentals are due back by eight P.M. Apparently things quiet down after that."

I indicated the couple with the putty faces. They were alone on the dock now, hands in their pockets, unsure what they were supposed to do next.

"Are those the owners?"

"Glenn and Irene Boynton. They say they're here every night until eleven, return around six in the morning. They live up the road."

Crowe indicated the dirt track.

"They claim to notice cars at night. Worry about kids messing with their boats. Neither one heard or saw a thing over the past three days. For what that's worth. A perp wouldn't exactly advertise that he was using your dock to off-load a corpse."

The celery eyes appraised the scene, came back to me.

"But you're right. This would be an odd choice. There's a small road kisses the shore about a half mile up from here. We're thinking that was the toss-in point."

"Two, three days seems a little long for the currents to carry her here," added Albright. "Body may have deadheaded awhile."

"Deadheaded?" I snapped, furious at his callousness.

"Sorry. Old logging term. Refers to snagged timber."

I was almost afraid to ask the next question.

"Was she sexually assaulted?"

"Clothing's on, underwear's in place. I'll test for semen, but I doubt it."

We stood silent in the gathering dusk. Behind us, the docks creaked and settled against the waves. A cold breeze blew off the water, carrying the scent of fish and gasoline.

"Why would someone garrote an old lady?" Though I spoke aloud, the question was really for me, not my companions.

"Why do these sick bastards do any of the things they do?" Albright replied.

I left them and walked toward Ryan's car. The ambulance and wrecker were gone, but the cruisers remained, pulsing blue light across the muddy lot. I sat a moment, staring at the hundreds of prints left by the feet of ambulance attendants, wrecker operators, police, the pathologist, and myself. Primrose's last disaster scene.

I turned the key and headed back toward Bryson City, tears coursing down my cheeks.

When I checked my messages later that evening, I found one from Lucy Crowe. I returned her call and told her everything I knew about Primrose Hobbs, ending with our Sunday-morning rendezvous at the morgue.

"And that foot and all its paperwork are now missing?"

"So I was told. Primrose was probably the last person to see the stuff."

"Parker Davenport told you she signed it out. Did she sign it back in?"

"Good question."

"Tell me about security."

"All DMORT and ME personnel have IDs, as do the people from your department and the Bryson City PD who work security. A guard checks IDs at the perimeter fence, and there's a sign in/sign out sheet inside the morgue. A color-coded dot goes on your badge each day."

"Why?"

"In case someone manages to duplicate the ID, they'd have no way of knowing that day's color."

"What about after hours?"

"By now there's probably a smaller crew left at the morgue, mostly records and computer staff, some medical personnel. There'd be no one there at night except your deputy or a Bryson City cop."

I pictured the lieutenant governor with his videocassette.

"There is a surveillance camera on the gate."

"What about the computers?"

"Every VIP user has a password, and only a limited number of people can enter or delete data."

"Assuming Hobbs returned it, where would that foot have been?"

"At the end of the day everything goes into reefer trucks marked 'unprocessed,' 'in process,' or 'identified.' Cases are located with a computer tracking system."

"How hard would it be to break in?"

"High school kids have hacked the Pentagon."

I heard distant conversation, like voices drifting through a wormhole in space.

"Sheriff, I think Primrose Hobbs was murdered because of that foot."

"Or the thing could be a biological specimen."

"A woman examines an object which is the subject of controversy, that object disappears, and the woman turns up dead three days later. If there's no link it's one hell of a coincidence."

"We're looking at every angle."

"Have you learned why no one reported her missing?"

"Apparently, parts of the operation are shifting to Charlotte. When Hobbs failed to show at the morgue on Monday, her coworkers figured she had gone there. Folks in Charlotte assumed she was still in Bryson City. She was in the habit of phoning her son on Saturdays, so he had no clue that anything was amiss."

I wondered about Primrose's son. Was he married? A father? In the army? Gay? Were mother and child close? Occasionally my work casts me as the bearer of life's most terrible news. In one visit, families are shattered, lives forever altered. Pete had said that most marine officers in Vietnam days would rather engage the enemy than visit a home in middle America to deliver a message of death. I wholeheartedly shared those sentiments.

I imagined the son's face, blank at first, confused. Then, with comprehension, agony, grief, the pain of an open wound. I closed my eyes, sharing at that moment his crushing despair.

"I dropped in at the Riverbank Inn."

Crowe's voice brought me back.

"After the marina, I swung by for a chat with Ralph and Brenda," she said. "They admitted they hadn't seen Hobbs since Sunday, but didn't consider it odd. She'd left without explanation twice during her stay, so they assumed she'd gone off again."

"Gone off where?"

"They figured she was visiting family."

"And?"

"Her room suggested otherwise. All her toiletries were there, toothbrush, dental floss, face cream, the things a woman takes when she travels. Her clothes were still in the dresser, suitcase empty under the bed. Her arthritis medication was sitting on the nightstand."

"Purse? Car keys?"

"Negative. Looks like she may have left the room on her own, but she wasn't planning to be away overnight."

Crowe listened while I described my own visit to the inn, leaving out nothing but my larcenous intentions.

"Why do you suppose Ralph went into her room?"

"Your intuition may have been right. Curiosity. Or maybe he knows more than he's letting on. Maybe he wanted to get something out. I don't have that yet, but we *will* be watching Mr. Stover. We'll also talk to anyone acquainted with the victim, look for witnesses who might have seen her during the time she was missing. You know the drill."

"Round up the usual suspects."

"In Swain County, that ain't many."

"Was there nothing in that room to suggest where she might have gone? An address? A map? A toll ticket?"

The line hummed.

"We found two numbers next to the phone."

As she read the digits, my stomach tightened.

The first rang at High Ridge House. The second rang the cellular on my belt.

An hour later I lay in bed, trying to sort and evaluate what I knew.

Fact: My mysterious foot did not belong to Daniel Wahnetah. Possibility: The foot came from a corpse at the courtyard house. The ground stain contained volatile fatty acids. Something had decomposed there. Possibility: The foot came from Air TransSouth 228. Biohazard containers and other problem body parts had been recovered near the wreckage.

Fact: The foot and its dossier were now missing. Possibility: Primrose Hobbs had kept the material. Possibility: Primrose Hobbs had returned the material, which was then taken by someone else.

Fact: The remains of Jean Bertrand and Pepper Petricelli had not been identified. Possibility: Neither man was on the plane. Possibility: Both the detective and his prisoner were on board, their bodies pulverized by the explosion.

Fact: Jean Bertrand was now a suspect.

Fact: A witness claimed to have seen Pepper Petricelli in upstate New York. Possibility: Bertrand had been turned. Possibility: Bertrand had been burned.

Fact: I had been accused of stealing evidence. Possibility: I was no longer trusted because of my relationship with Andrew Ryan, Bertrand's SQ partner. Possibility: I was being set up as a scape-

goat to prevent me from participating in the investigation. But which investigation, the plane crash or
the courtyard house? Possibility: I was at risk.
Somebody had tried to run me down and had
trashed my room.

A tickle of fear. I held my breath, listening. Silence.

Fact: Primrose Hobbs had been murdered. Possibility: Her death was a random act of violence. More
likely: Her death was related to the missing foot.

Fact: Edward Arthur obtained the property at Running Goat Branch in 1933 through his marriage to
Sarah Livingstone. He rented it as a campground,
then built a lodge, then sold the land in 1949 to a
man named Prentice Dashwood, but title was taken
in the name of H&F Investment Group, LLP. Arthur
had not erected any stone walls or a courtyard. Who
was Prentice Dashwood?

I turned on the lamp, retrieved McMahon's
Delaware fax, and scurried back to bed, my lips chat-
tering. Huddled under the covers, I reread the names.

W. G. Davis, F. M. Payne, C. A. Birkby, F. L. Warren, P. H. Rollins, M. P. Veckhoff.

The only name that was remotely familiar was that
of Veckhoff. A Charlottean named Pat Veckhoff had
served in the North Carolina senate for sixteen years.
He had died suddenly the previous winter. I wondered if there was a link to the M. P. Veckhoff on the
list.

Returning the room to darkness, I lay back and
searched for connections among the things I knew. It

« 311 »

was hopeless. Images of Primrose kept disrupting my concentration.

Primrose at her computer, glasses on the end of her nose. Primrose in the parking lot. Primrose at the scene of a commuter plane crash, 1997, Kinston, North Carolina. Primrose across a card table, playing bid whit. Primrose in Charlotte. The Presbyterian Hospital cafeteria. I was eating vegetarian pizza made with canned peas and asparagus. I remembered hating the pizza, but not why I had met Primrose there.

Primrose lying in a body bag.

Why, dear God?

Was she carefully chosen, researched, stalked, then overpowered as part of an elaborate plan? Or was she selected by chance? Some psycho's sick impulse. The first blue Honda. The fourth woman to exit the mall. The next black. Was death part of the plan, or did things go badly wrong, spinning out of control to one irreversible moment?

Violence against women is not a recent phenomenon. The bones of my sisters litter history and prehistory. The mass grave at Cahokia. The sacred cenote at Chichén Itzá. The Iron Age girl in the bog, hair shorn, blindfolded and leashed.

Women are conditioned to be wary. Walk faster at the sound of footsteps. Peek through the hole before opening the door. Stand by the controls in the empty elevator. Fear the dark. Was Primrose simply another marcher in a random parade of female victims?

Who was I kidding? I knew the reason. Had no doubt.

Primrose Hobbs had been killed because she fulfilled a request. My request. She had accepted a fax, taken measurements, and provided data. She had helped me, and in doing that she had threatened someone.

I'd gotten her involved, and that someone had butchered her for it. The guilt and sorrow formed a physical weight pressing on my chest.

But how had Primrose posed a threat? Had she uncovered something that I did not know? Had she realized the significance of that discovery, or had she been unaware of its importance? Had she been silenced for what she knew, or for what someone feared she would figure out?

And what about me? Was I also a threat to some homicidal madman?

My thoughts were interrupted by a soft wailing from below. Throwing back the covers, I pulled on jeans and a sweatshirt and slipped into my deck shoes. Then I tiptoed through the silent house and out the back door.

Boyd was sitting beside his doghouse, nose pointed at the night sky. On seeing me, he sprang to his feet and waggled the entire back half of his body. Then he dashed to the fence and went bipedal. Leaning on forepaws, he stretched his neck and gave a series of yips.

I reached over and scratched his ears. Boyd lapped my hand, giddy with excitement.

When I entered the pen and leashed him, the dog went hyperactive, spinning and kicking up dirt.

"Be cool." I pointed a finger at his snout. "This is against the rules."

He looked at me, tongue dangling, eyebrows dancing. I led him across the yard and into the house.

Moments later we lay in the dark, Boyd on the carpet beside my bed. I heard him sigh as he settled chin on forepaws.

I fell asleep with my hand on his head.

21

THE NEXT MORNING I WOKE EARLY, FEELING COLD
and empty but unsure why. It came to me in a thick,
dreadful wave.

Primrose was dead.

The combined agonies of loss and guilt were
almost paralyzing, and I lay still a long time, wanting
nothing to do with the world.

Then Boyd nuzzled my hip. I rolled over and
scratched his ear.

"You're right, boy. Self-pity does no one any good."

I rose, threw on clothes, and sneaked Boyd out to
his run. During my absence a note appeared on the
door to Magnolia. Ryan would be spending another
day with McMahon and wouldn't need his car. The
keys I'd left on his bureau were now on mine.

When I turned on my phone, I had five messages.
Four journalists and P & T. I called the repair shop,
dumped the rest.

The job was taking longer than anticipated. The car should be ready by tomorrow.

We'd gone from "could" to "should." I was encouraged.

But what now?

An idea rose from deep in my past. The favorite refuge of a worried or restless little girl. It couldn't hurt, and I might uncover something useful.

And for a few hours, at least I would be anonymous and inaccessible.

Following toast and Frosted Flakes, I drove to the Marianna Black Public Library, a one-story redbrick box at the corner of Everett and Academy. Cardboard skeletons flanked the entrance, each with a book held in its hands.

A tall, spindly black man displaying several gold teeth occupied a counter at the main entrance. An older woman worked beside him, securing a chain of orange pumpkins above their heads. Both turned when I entered.

"Good morning," I said.

"Good morning." The man showed a mile of precious metal. His lilac-haired companion eyed me suspiciously.

"I'd like to look at back issues of the local paper." I smiled disarmingly.

"The *Smoky Mountain Times*?" asked Mrs. Librarian, laying down her staple gun.

"Yes."

"How far back?"

"Do you have material from the thirties and forties?"

Her frown deepened. "The collection begins in 1895. It was the *Bryson City Times* back then. A weekly. The older publications are on microfilm, of course. You can't view the originals."

"Microfilm will be fine."

Mr. Librarian began opening and stacking books. I noticed that his nails were buffed, his clothes immaculate.

"The viewer is in the overflow room, beside the genealogy section. You may only have one box at a time."

"Thank you."

Mrs. Librarian opened one of two metal cabinets behind the counter and withdrew a small gray box. "I'd better explain the machine."

"Please, you mustn't bother. I'll be fine. I'm familiar with microfilm viewers."

I read her expression as she handed me the microfilm. A civilian loose in the stacks. It was her worst nightmare.

Settling at the machine, I checked the box's label: *1931–1937.*

An image of Primrose flashed into my mind, and tears blurred my vision.

Stop. No grieving.

But why was I here? What was my objective? Did I have one, or was I merely hiding out?

No. I had a goal.

I was still convinced that the courtyard property

lay at the center of my problems, and wanted to learn more about who had been associated with it. Arthur had told me he'd sold his land to one Prentice Dashwood. But beyond that, and the names on McMahon's fax, I was unsure what I was looking for.

In truth, I held little hope of finding anything helpful but had run out of ideas. And I had to do something about the charges against me. I couldn't return to Charlotte until my car was repaired, and I was barred from any other form of inquiry. What the hell. History should teach something.

A poster had decorated Pete's office during his stint in uniform, guiding words embraced by JAG attorneys uncommitted to the military system: *Indecision Is the Key to Flexibility.*

If the maxim was good enough for officer-lawyers of the United States Marine Corps, it seemed good enough for me. I'd look for everything.

I inserted the film and wound it through the viewer. The machine was a hand-crank model, probably manufactured before the Wright brothers went flying at Kitty Hawk. Text and pictures swam in and out of focus. Within minutes I felt a headache begin to organize.

I flicked through spool after spool, making trip after trip to the front desk. By the late 1940s, Mrs. Librarian relented and allowed me a half dozen boxes at a time.

I skimmed over charity events, car washes, church socials, and local dramas. The crime was mostly petty, involving traffic offenses, drunk and disorderly, missing property, and vandalism. Births, deaths, and weddings were announced, garage and barn sales advertised.

The war had claimed a large number from Swain County. From '42 to '45 the pages were filled with their names and photos. Each death was a feature story.

Some citizens did manage to die in their beds. In December of 1943, the passing of Henry Arlen Preston was front-page news. Preston had been a lifelong resident of Swain County, an attorney, judge, and part-time journalist. His career was recounted in radiant detail, the highlights being a term in Raleigh as a state senator, and the publication of a two-volume work on the birds of western North Carolina. Preston died at the age of eighty-nine, leaving behind a widow, four children, fourteen grandchildren, and twenty-three great-grandchildren.

The week following Preston's death, the *Times* reported the disappearance of Tucker Adams. Two column inches on page six. No photo.

The obscure little notice touched something in me. Had Adams enlisted secretly, then died overseas as one of our many unknowns? Had he returned, surprised his neighbors with tales of Italy or France, then gone on to live his life? Had he fallen from a cliff? Run off to Hollywood? Though I searched for a follow-up, nothing more on Adams's disappearance was reported.

The rugged terrain had also claimed its victims. In 1939 a woman named Hilda Miner left home to deliver a strawberry pie to her granddaughter. She never arrived, and the pie tin was discovered beside the swollen Tuckasegee River. Hilda was presumed drowned, though her body was not located. A decade later the same waters took Dr. Sheldon Brodie, a biologist at Appalachian State University. A day after the professor's body washed up, Edna Farrell was thought to have fallen into the river. Like Miner, Farrell's remains were never found.

I leaned back and rubbed my eyes. What had the old man said about Farrell? They should have done better by her. Who were "they"? Done better in what way? Was he referring to the fact that Farrell's body wasn't recovered? Or was he unhappy with the quality of Thaddeus Bowman's memorial service?

In 1959 the fauna claimed a seventy-four-year-old Cherokee named Charlie Wayne Tramper. Two weeks after his disappearance, Charlie Wayne's rifle turned up in a remote valley on the reservation. Bear tracks and spoor suggested the cause of death. The old man was buried with full tribal ceremony.

I'd worked on victims of bear attacks, and knew what had remained of Charlie Wayne. I shook the image from my mind.

The list of environmental hazards courtesy of Mother Nature went on. In 1972 a four-year-old girl wandered from a campground in Maggie Valley. The little body was dragged from a lake the following day. The next winter two cross-country skiers froze to death when caught in a sudden blizzard. In 1986 an apple farmer named Albert Odell went searching for morels and never returned.

I found no reference to Prentice Dashwood, to the Arthur property, or to the officers of the H&F Investment Group. The closest I came was a May 1959 spread on a fiery crash on Highway 19. Six hurt, four killed. Pictures showed tangled wreckage. Dr. Anthony Allen Birkby, sixty-eight, from Cullowhee, died three days later of multiple injuries. I took note. Though the name was not uncommon, one C. A. Birkby was listed on McMahon's fax.

By noon, my head pulsed and my blood sugar had dropped to a level incapable of sustaining life. I slipped a granola bar from my purse, did a stealthy peel, and munched quietly as I cranked my zillionth spool through the viewer.

Issues from recent years were not yet on microfilm, and by midafternoon I was able to switch to hard copy. But the headache had already escalated from a minor disturbance to major pain that swirled across my frontal, temporal, and occipital lobes and pulsed at an epicenter behind my right eye.

Final stretch. The tough get going. Bring it home. Remember the Gipper.

Shit.

I was flipping through papers from the current year, scanning headlines and photographs, when a name caught my eye. George Adair. The missing fisherman.

The coverage of Adair's disappearance was detailed, giving the exact time and place of the fatal fishing trip, a description of the victim, and an itemized account of what he was wearing, right down to his high school ring and St. Blaise medal.

Another childhood flashback. The parish priest. The blessing of throats on St. Blaise Day. What was the story? Blaise was reputed to have saved a child from choking on a fish bone. The medal made sense. Crowe said Adair complained of throat problems.

Adair's companion was interviewed, as were his wife, friends, former employer, and priest. A grainy picture was printed beside the story, the pendant clearly visible around his neck.

Who was Crowe's other missing person? I searched my pounding brain. Jeremiah Mitchell. February. I moved back almost eight months and began a more careful perusal. Small things began to connect.

Jeremiah Mitchell's disappearance was reported in one short paragraph. On February 15 a seventy-two-year-old black male left the Mighty High Tap and walked into oblivion. Anyone having information blah, blah, blah.

Old ways die hard, I thought, feeling a prickle of anger. White man goes missing: feature story. Black man goes missing: blurb on page seventeen. Or maybe it was station in life. George Adair had a job, friends, family. Jeremiah Mitchell was an unemployed alcoholic who lived alone.

But Mitchell had once had kin. A follow-up

appeared in early March, again a single paragraph, seeking information and citing the name of his maternal grandmother, Martha Rose Gist. I stared. How far back had I seen that name?

I returned to the boxes, jumping the microfilm weeks at a turn. The obituary appeared on May 16, 1952, along with six inches in the arts column. Martha Rose Gist had been a potter of local fame. The article included a picture of a beautifully decorated ceramic bowl, but none of the artist.

Damn!

Checking to be sure the overflow room was empty, I clicked on my cell. Six messages. Ignoring them, I dialed Crowe's number, muffling the beeps with my jacket.

"Sheriff Crowe."

I didn't bother announcing myself.

"Are you familiar with Sequoyah?" I asked in a loud whisper.

"Are you in church?"

"The Bryson City library."

"Iris catches you, she'll rip off your lips and feed them to her shredder."

I assumed Iris was the lilac-haired dragon I'd met at the entrance.

"*Sequoyah?*"

"Sequoyah invented an alphabet for the Cherokee language. Hang around long enough and someone will buy you an ashtray decorated with the symbols," she said.

"What was Sequoyah's family name?"

"You want my final answer?"

"I'm serious."

"Guess."

"This is important," I hissed.

"His name was Guess. Or Gist, depending on the transliteration. Why?"

"Jeremiah Mitchell's maternal grandmother was Martha Rose Gist."

"The potter?"

"Yes."

"I'll be damned."

"You know what that means?"

I didn't wait for her answer.

"Mitchell was part Cherokee."

"This is a library!"

Iris's words scorched the side of my face.

I held up a finger.

"Hang up instantly!" She spoke as loud as a human can without using the vocal cords.

"Is there a newspaper printed on the reservation?"

"The *Cherokee One Feather.* And I think there's a tribal photo archive at the museum."

"Gotta go." I disconnected and shut off the power.

"I'm going to have to ask you to leave." Iris stood with hands on hips, the gestapo protectress of the printed word.

"Shall I return the boxes?"

"That will not be necessary."

. . .

It took three stops to find what I needed. A trip to the offices of the *Cherokee One Feather,* located in the Tribal Council Center, revealed that the paper had only been in print since 1966. While there had been a predecessor publication years before, *The Chero-kee Phoenix,* the current staff had no photos or back issues in their possession.

The Cherokee Historical Association had pictures, but most had been taken as promotional shots for the outdoor theatrical production *Unto These Hills.*

I hit pay dirt at the Museum of the Cherokee Indian, directly across the street. When I repeated my request, I was taken to a second-floor office, issued cotton gloves, and allowed to graze through their photo and newspaper archives.

Within an hour I had confirmation.

Martha Rose Standingdeer was born in 1889 on the Qualla Boundary. She wed John Patrick Gist in 1908 and gave birth to a daughter, Willow Lynette, the following year.

At the age of seventeen, Willow married Jonas Mitchell at the AME Zion Church in Greenville, South Carolina. Their wedding portrait shows a deli-cate girl in a cloche veil and Empire gown, a bou-quet of daisies in her hands. At her side stands a man with skin much darker than that of his bride.

I studied the picture. Though rawboned and homely, Jonas Mitchell was appealing in a strange sort of way. Today, he might have modeled for Benet-ton ads.

Willow Mitchell gave birth to Jeremiah in 1929, died of tuberculosis the following winter. I found no mention of Jonas or his son after that date.

I sat back, processing what I'd learned.

Jeremiah Mitchell was at least one half Native American. He was seventy-two years old when he disappeared. The foot must surely be his.

My deductive centers logged in immediately. The dates didn't correlate.

Mitchell went missing in February. The VFA profile gives a postmortem interval of six to seven weeks, placing the death in late August or early September.

Maybe Mitchell survived the night of the Mighty High Tap. Maybe he ventured off, then returned and died of exposure six months later.

Ventured off?

On a trip.

A seventy-two-year-old alcoholic with no car or money?

It happens.

Uh-huh. Died of exposure in the summer?

I sat, stumped and frustrated by a million facts I couldn't integrate.

Hoping pictures would be more headache friendly, I switched to the photo archives.

Again, small things caught my attention.

I'd gone through fifty or sixty folders when an eight-by-ten black-and-white aroused my interest. Flower-draped casket. Mourners, some in broad-shouldered baggy suits, others in traditional Cherokee dress. I flipped to the back. A yellowed label identified the event in faded ink: *Charlie Wayne Tramper Funeral. May 17, 1959.* The old man who had gone missing and been killed by a bear.

My gaze roved over the faces, then froze on one of two young men standing apart from the crowd. I was so surprised I gasped.

Though forty years younger, there was no mistaking that face. He would have been in his late twenties in 1959, newly arrived from England. A professor of archaeology at Duke. An academic superstar about to fade.

Why was Simon Midkiff at Charlie Wayne Tramper's funeral?

My eyes slid right, and this time the gasp was audible. Simon Midkiff was standing shoulder to shoulder with a man who would later rise to the office of lieutenant governor.

Parker Davenport.

Or was it? I stared at the features. Yes. No. This man was much younger, thinner.

I hesitated, looked around. No one had poked through this file for half a century. It wasn't stealing. I would return the print in a few days, no damage done.

I slipped the photo into my purse, returned the folder to its drawer, and bolted.

Outside, I dialed Raleigh Information, requested a number for the Department of Cultural Resources, then waited while the connection was made. When a voice answered I asked for Carol Burke. She came on in less than ten seconds.

"Carol Burke."

"Carol, this is Tempe Brennan."

"Good timing. I was just about to close it up for the day. Are you planning to dig up another graveyard?"

Among its many duties, the North Carolina Department of Cultural Resources is responsible for heritage preservation. When development involving state or federal moneys, permits, licenses, or lands is proposed, Carol and her colleagues order surveys and excavations to determine if prehistoric or historic sites will be threatened. Highway projects, airport work, sewer lines—without their clearance, no ground is broken.

Carol and I met in the days when archaeology was my main focus. Twice Charlotte developers had retained me to help relocate historic cemeteries. Carol had overseen both projects.

"Not this time. I'd like information."

"I'll do my best."

"I'm curious about the site Simon Midkiff is digging for you."

"Currently?"

"Yes."

"He's not doing anything for us at the moment. At least nothing of which I'm aware."

"Isn't he excavating in Swain County?"

"I don't think so. Hold on."

By the time she returned, I'd walked to Ryan's car and opened the door.

"Nope. Midkiff hasn't worked for us in over two years and isn't likely to any time soon because he still owes us a site report from his last contract."

"Thanks."

"I wish all my requests were this simple."

I'd barely put down the phone when it rang again. A journalist from the *Charlotte Observer.* A reminder of my continuing notoriety. I clicked off without comment.

A thousand cranial vessels pulsed in my skull. Nothing made sense. Why had Midkiff lied? Why had he and Davenport attended the Tramper funeral? Did they know each other back then?

I needed aspirin. I needed lunch. I needed an objective listener.

Boyd.

After popping two Bayers, I collected the chow, and we set forth. Boyd rode with his head out the passenger window, nose to the air, twisting and turning to suck in every discernible odor. Watching him at the Burger King drive-through, I thought of the squirrel, then the wall at the courtyard house. Just *what* had his former owner trained him to find?

Suddenly, I had an idea. A place to picnic and check out names.

The Bryson City Cemetery is located on Schoolhouse Hill, overlooking Veterans Boulevard on one side, a mountain valley on the other. The drive took seven minutes. Boyd did not understand the delay and kept prodding and licking the food bag. By the time I pulled into the cemetery, the cardboard tray was so soggy I had to carry it with two hands.

Boyd dragged me from stone to stone, peeing on several, then kicking back divots with his hind feet. Finally, he stopped at a pink granite column, turned, and yipped.

Sylvia Hotchkins
Entered this world January 12, 1945.
Left this world April 20, 1968.
Taken too early in the spring of her life.

Sixty-eight was a rough year for all of us, Sylvia.

Certain she would enjoy the company, I settled at the base of a large oak shading Sylvia's grave and ordered Boyd to sit beside me. He complied, his eyes fixed on the tray in my hands.

When I withdrew a burger, Boyd sprang to his feet.

"Sit."

He sat. I peeled off the paper and gave him the burger. He rose, separated it into components, then ate the meat, bun, and lettuce-tomato garnish sequentially. Finished, he focused on my Whopper, muzzle spotted with ketchup.

"Sit."

He sat. I spread fries on the grass and he began picking them delicately off the surface so they wouldn't sink between the blades. I unwrapped my Whopper and slipped a straw into my drink.

"Now here's the deal."

Boyd glanced up, went back to the fries.

"Why would Simon Midkiff have gone to the funeral of a seventy-four-year-old Cherokee killed by a bear in 1959?"

We both ate and thought about that.

"Midkiff is an archaeologist. He might have been researching the Eastern Band Cherokee. Maybe Tramper was his guide and historian."

Boyd's attention shifted to my burger. I replenished his potatoes.

"O.K. I'll buy that."

I took a bite, chewed, swallowed.

"Why was Parker Davenport there?"

Boyd looked at me without raising his head from the fries.

"Davenport grew up near here. He probably knew Tramper."

Boyd's ears flicked forward, back again. He finished the last of his fries and stared at mine. I flipped him a few.

"Perhaps Tramper and Davenport had mutual friends on the reservation. Or maybe Davenport was already building a political base in those days."

I threw out another half dozen fries. Boyd reengaged.

"How about this? Did Davenport and Midkiff know each other back then?"

Boyd's head came up. His eyebrows spun and his tongue dropped.

"If so, how?"

He cocked his head and watched as I finished my burger. I tossed him the rest of my fries, and he ate them as I sipped my Diet Coke.

"Here's the big one, Boyd."

I gathered wrappers and bunched them with the remains of the tray. Seeing no more food, Boyd flopped onto his side, sighed loudly, and closed his eyes.

"Midkiff lied to me. Davenport wants my head on a spike. Is there a link?"

Boyd had no answer.

I sat with my back to the oak, absorbing warmth and light. The grass smelled freshly mown, the leaves dry and sun-baked. At one point Boyd rose, turned four times, then resettled at my side.

A short time later a man came over the crest of the hill, leading a collie on a length of rope. Boyd sat up and barked at the dog but didn't make an aggressive move. The late-afternoon sunshine was mellowing woman and beast. Reeling him in, I got to my feet.

As dusk gathered, we strolled among the gravestones. Though I spotted no one from the H&F list, and no Dashwoods, I did find markers with familiar names. Thaddeus Bowman. Victor Livingstone and his daughter, Sarah Masham Livingstone. Enoch McCready.

I remembered Luke Bowman's words, and wondered what had caused the death of Ruby's husband in 1986. Instead of answers, I was finding more questions.

But one mystery was solved. One missing person found. Turning to go, I stumbled across an unadorned slab in the cemetery's southernmost corner. Its face was inscribed with a simple message.

Tucker Adams
1871–1943
R.I.P.

22

LEAVING THE CEMETERY, I DROVE TO HIGH RIDGE House, settled Boyd for the night, and returned to my room, unaware that it would be my busiest telephone evening since junior high.

I'd hardly hit the power switch when Pete called.

"How's Big B?"

"Enjoying the mountain food and fauna. Are you back in Charlotte?"

"Hung up in the Hoosier state. Is he straining your patience?"

"Boyd has a unique take on life."

"What's new?"

I told him about Primrose.

"Oh, babe, I'm really sorry. Are you O.K.?"

"I'll be fine," I lied. "There's more."

I summarized the interrogation with Davenport, and listed the complaints the lieutenant governor planned to file.

"Sounds like a mainline mind fuck."

"Don't try to impress me with legal jargon."

"This has to be politically motivated. Any conjectures as to why?"

"He doesn't like my hair."

"I do. Did you establish anything more about the foot?"

I told him about the histological age estimate, about the racial classification, and about the formerly and currently missing Daniel Wahnetah and Jeremiah Mitchell.

"Mitchell sounds like a winning candidate for the foot."

I described the photo of Charlie Wayne Tramper's funeral and my phone call to Raleigh.

"Why would Midkiff lie to you about doing a dig?"

"He doesn't like my hair. Should I get an attorney?"

"You have one."

"Thanks, Pete."

Next, it was Ryan. He and McMahon had finished late and would be returning to the reassembly site at dawn, so they were overnighting in Asheville.

"Problems with your phone?"

"The media are scenting blood in the water, so I've had it turned off. Besides, I spent a lot of the day in the library."

"Learn anything?"

"Mountain life is hard on old folks."

"What do you mean?"

"I don't know. Seems like a lot of seniors drown, freeze to death, or end up in the food chain around here. I'll take the flatlands, thanks. What goes with the investigation?"

"The chemical guys are picking up weird traces."

"Explosives?"

"Not necessarily. I'll fill you in tomorrow."

"Have Bertrand and Petricelli been found?"

"No."

Lucy Crowe beeped in at that point, and I clicked over. She had little to report and no warrant.

"The DA doesn't want to second-guess the magistrate without something more solid."

"What the hell do these people want? Miss Scarlet in the library, candlestick in hand?"

"She finds your argument contradictory."

"Contradictory?"

"The VFA profile says something died during the summer. Mitchell disappeared in February. Madam Prosecutor is convinced the stain is from an animal. Says you can't bust in on a citizen for aging meat in his backyard."

"And the foot?"

"Crash victim."

"Anything on Primrose's murder?"

"Turns out Ralph Stover is no hayseed. The gentleman owned a company in Ohio, holds patents on a number of microchips. In eighty-six Ralph under-

KATHY REICHS

went a metamorphosis following a cardiac event. He sold out for megabucks and bought the Riverbank. Been a country motel owner ever since."

"Any police record?"

"Two DWIs back in the seventies, otherwise the guy's clean."

"Does it make sense to you?"

"Maybe he watched too many *Newhart* reruns, dreamt of being an innkeeper."

The next to ring was my friend at Oak Ridge. Laslo Sparkes asked if I'd be available in the morning. We made a date for nine o'clock. Good. Maybe he had some more results from the soil samples.

The final call came from my department chair. He opened by apologizing for his abruptness Tuesday night.

"My three-year-old put our kitten in the Kenmore to dry it after a fall into the toilet. My wife had just rescued the poor thing, and everyone was hysterical. Kids crying. Wife crying, trying to get the cat to breathe."

"How awful. Is it all right?"

"The little guy pulled through, but I don't think he's seeing too well."

"He'll come around."

There was a pause. I could hear his breath against the receiver.

"Well, Tempe, there's no easy way, so I'm just going to say it. The chancellor asked me to meet with him today. He's received a complaint about your behavior during the crash investigation and has decided to suspend you pending a full inquiry."

I remained silent. Nothing I was doing in Bryson City was under the auspices of the university, though I was on its payroll.

"With pay, of course. He says he doesn't believe a word of it but has no choice in the matter."

"Why not?" I already knew the answer.

"He's afraid of the negative publicity, feels he has to protect the university. And apparently the lieutenant governor is on his case directly and being a real hard-ass about this."

"And, as everyone knows, the university is funded by the legislature." My hand was clenched on the phone.

"I tried every argument I could think of. He wouldn't budge."

"Thanks, Mike."

"You're welcome back in the department anytime. You could file a grievance."

"No. I'm going to sort this out first."

I went through my bedtime ritual with toothpaste, soap, Oil of Olay, hand cream. Cleansed and lubricated, I turned off the lights, crawled under the blankets, and screamed as loud as I could. Then I hugged knees to chest and for the second time in two days began to cry.

It was time to give up. I'm not a quitter, but I had to face reality. I was getting nowhere. I'd uncovered nothing persuasive enough to obtain a warrant, discovered little at the courthouse, struck out with the newspapers. I'd stolen from a library and had almost committed breaking and entering.

It wasn't worth it. I could apologize to the lieutenant governor, resign from DMORT, and return to my normal life.

My normal life.

What *was* my normal life? Autopsies. Exhumations. Mass fatalities.

I am constantly asked why I've chosen such a morbid vocation. Why I work with the mutilated and decomposed.

Through time and introspection, I have come to understand my choices. I want to serve both the living and the dead. The dead have a right to be identified. To have their stories drawn to a close and to take their places in our memories. If they died at the hands of another, they also have a right to have those hands brought to account.

The living as well deserve our support when the death of another alters their lives: The parent desperate for news of a missing child. The family hopeful of remains from Iwo Jima or Chosin or Hué. The villagers bereft at a mass grave in Guatemala or Kurdistan. The mothers and husbands and lovers and friends dazed at an overlook in the Smoky Mountains. They have a right to information, explanations, and also a right to have murderous hands brought to account.

It is for these victims and the mourners that I tease

posthumous tales from bones. The dead will remain dead, whatever my efforts, but there have to be answers and accountability. We cannot live in a world that accepts the destruction of life with no explanations and no consequences.

Of course, an ethics violation would end my career in forensics. If the lieutenant governor had his way, I would effectively be barred from pursuing my profession. An expert witness under an ethical cloud is roadkill on cross-examination. Who would have confidence in any opinion of mine?

Anger replaced self-pity. I would not be driven out of forensics by unfounded accusations and innuendo. I couldn't give in. I had to prove that I was right. I owed it to myself. Even more, I owed it to Primrose Hobbs and her mourning son.

But how?

What to do?

I tossed and turned, feeling like that spider in the rain. My world was under attack by forces stronger than me, and I lacked the power to keep it together.

Sleep finally came, but there was no relief.

When agitated, my brain weaves thoughts into psychedelic collages. All night disjointed images floated in and out of focus.

I was in the incident morgue, sorting body parts. Ryan ran past. I called out, asking what had happened to the foot. He didn't stop. I tried to chase him, but my feet wouldn't move. I kept shouting, reached out, but he drew farther and farther away.

Boyd raced around a cemetery, a dead squirrel hanging from his mouth.

Willow Lynette Gist and Jonas Mitchell posed for a wedding picture. In her hand the Cherokee bride clutched the foot I'd taken from coyotes.

Judge Henry Arlen Preston held a book out to an old man. The man started to walk away, but Preston followed, insisting he take the offering. The old man turned and Preston dropped the book. Boyd snatched it up and ran down a long gravel road. When I caught up and took the object from him, it was no longer a book but a stone tablet, the name "Tucker Adams" carved on its face, and 1943, the year they both died, one a prominent citizen, the other obscure.

Simon Midkiff sat on a chair in the P & T garage office. Next to him was a man with long gray braids and a Cherokee headband.

"Why are you here?" Midkiff asked me.

"I can't drive," I replied. "There was a crash. People were killed."

"Is Birkby dead?" asked gray braids.

"Yes."

"Did they find Edna?"

"No."

"They won't find me either."

Gray braid's face morphed into that of Ruby McCready, then into the bloated features of Primrose Hobbs.

I screamed and my head jerked from the pillow. My eyes flew to the clock. Five-thirty.

Though the room was chilly, my back was slick with perspiration, my hair plastered to my head. I threw back the covers and ran on tiptoes for a drink of water. Gazing into the mirror, I rolled the glass across my forehead.

I returned to the bedroom and flicked on a light. The window was opaque with predawn blackness. Frost spiderwebbed the corners of the glass.

I pulled on sweats and socks, took out a tablet, and settled at the table. After dividing several sheets into thirds, I began writing down images from my dream.

Henry Arlen Preston. The coyote foot. The braided old man in Cherokee headgear. Had that been Charlie Wayne Tramper? I wrote the name, followed by a question mark. Edna Farrell. Tucker Adams. Birkby. Jonas and Willow Mitchell. Ruby McCready. Simon Midkiff.

Next, I added what I knew about each character.

Henry Arlen Preston: Died 1943. Age eighty-nine. Attorney, judge, writer. Birds. Family man.

Coyote foot: Elderly male. Native-American ancestry. Height approximately five foot six. Dead last summer. Found near Arthur/H&F property. Trans-South passenger?

Charlie Wayne Tramper: Cherokee. Died 1959. Age seventy-four. Bear attack. Midkiff and Davenport attended the funeral.

Edna Farrell: Died 1949. Holiness follower. Drowned. Remains not recovered.

Tucker Adams: Born 1871. Disappeared then died, 1943.

Anthony Allen Birkby: Died 1959. Car crash. C. A. Birkby on list of H&F officers.

Jonas Mitchell: African American. Married Willow Lynette Gist. Father of Jeremiah Mitchell.

Willow Lynette Gist: Daughter of Martha Rose Gist, Cherokee potter. Mother of Jeremiah Mitchell. Died of TB, 1930.

Though he wasn't in the dream, I made out a slip for Jeremiah Mitchell. African American–Cherokee. Born 1929. Loner. Disappeared last February.

Ruby McCready: Alive and well. Husband Enoch dead, 1986.

Simon Midkiff: Doctorate from Oxford, 1955. Duke, 1955 to 1961. University of Tennessee, 1961 to 1968. Attended Tramper funeral in 1959. Knew Davenport (or was at least at the same funeral). Lied about working for Department of Cultural Resources.

When I'd finished I spread the slips on the table and studied them. Then I began arranging them according to different criteria, starting with gender. The piles were very lopsided, the smaller containing only Edna Farrell, Willow Lynette Gist, and Ruby McCready. I created a slip for Martha Rose Gist. Nothing seemed to connect the women.

Next I tried race. Charlie Wayne Tramper and the Gist-Mitchell lineage went into one pile, along with the coyote foot. I began a chart and drew a line between Jeremiah Mitchell and the foot.

Age. Again I was struck by the number of old people. Though Henry Arlen Preston had managed to die in bed, appropriate, perhaps, for a distinguished judge, few others on the list had had that luxury. Tucker Adams, seventy-two. Charlie Wayne Tramper, seventy-four. Jeremiah Mitchell, seventy-two. I made out a slip for the missing fisherman, George Adair, sixty-seven. All were old.

The window was moving from black to pewter. I decided to sort by birth dates. Nothing. I tried death dates.

Judge Henry Arlen Preston passed away in 1943. According to his tombstone, Tucker Adams also died in 1943. I remembered the feature article on Preston, the brief inside report on Adams's disappearance less than a week later. I placed their slips together.

A. A. Birkby died in 1959. Charlie Wayne Tramper died in 1959. When was the wreck in which Birkby died? May. The same month Charlie Wayne went missing.

Oh?

I paired the slips.

Edna Farrell died in 1949. Hadn't someone drowned just the day before?

Sheldon Brodie, professor of biology at Appalachian State University. Brodie's body was found. Farrell's wasn't.

I made a slip for Brodie and set it with the one for Edna Farrell.

I stared at the three sets of paired slips. Was it a pattern? Someone is killed or dies, within days another death occurs? Were people dying in pairs?

I started a list of questions.

Edna Farrell's age?

Earlier drowning. Strawberry pie. Age? Date?

Tucker Adams's cause of death?

Jeremiah Mitchell, February. George Adair, September. Others?

The room was the color of the rising sun, and I could hear bird sounds through the closed window. A rectangle of light fell across the table, illuminating my questions and scribbled notes.

I stared at the paired slips, feeling there was something else. Something important. Something my subconscious had not had time to place in the collage.

Laslo was devouring biscuits and gravy when I arrived at the Everett Street Diner. I ordered pecan pancakes, juice, and coffee. While we ate, he told me about the conference he was going to attend at UNC-Asheville. I told him about Crowe's inability to obtain a search warrant.

"So the good old boys are skeptical," he said, nodding to the waitress that he had finished.

"And girls. The DA is a woman."

"Then this may not help."

He pulled a paper from his briefcase and handed it to me. As I read, the waitress refilled our cups. I looked up when I'd finished.

"Basically the report agrees with what you told me on Monday at your lab."

"Yes. Except for the part about the caproic and heptanoic acid concentrations."

"The conclusion that they look unusually high."

"Yes."

"What does that mean?"

"Elevated levels of the longer-chained VFAs usually mean the corpse has been exposed to cold, or that it underwent a period of decreased insect and bacterial activity."

"Does that alter your estimate of time since death?"

"I still think decomposition began in late summer."

"Then what's the significance?"

"I'm not sure."

"Is this a common finding?"

"Not really."

"Great. That will convert the disbelievers."

"Maybe this will be more helpful."

This time he took a small plastic vial from his briefcase.

"I found this when filtering the rest of your soil sample."

The container held a tiny white chip, no larger than a grain of rice. I unscrewed the cap, slid the object onto my palm, and studied it closely.

"It's a fragment of tooth root," I said.

"That's what I thought, so I didn't treat it with anything, just brushed off the dirt."

"Holy shit."

"That's what I thought."

"Did you take a peek under the scope?"

"Yep."

"How does the pulp chamber look?"

"Chock-full."

Laslo and I signed evidence transfer forms and I packed the vial and report into my briefcase.

"Could I ask you one last favor?"

"Absolutely."

"If my car is ready, could you help me return the one I'm driving, then take me to the shop where mine is being fixed?"

"No problem."

When I called P & T an automotive miracle had occurred: The repairs were complete. Laslo followed me to High Ridge House, delivered me to P & T, then went on to his conference. After a brief discussion of pumps and hoses with one of the letters, I paid the bill and slid behind the wheel.

Before leaving P & T, I turned on my phone, scrolled through my programmed numbers, and hit "dial."

"Charlotte-Mecklenburg Police Department Crime Laboratory."

"Ron Gillman, please."

"Who's calling, please?"

"Tempe Brennan."

He came on in seconds.

"The infamous Dr. Brennan."

"You've heard."

"Oh yes. Will we be printing and booking you here?"

"Very funny."

"I suppose it's not. I won't even ask if there's anything to it. Are you getting things cleared up?"

"I'm trying. I may need a favor."

"Shoot."

"I have a tooth fragment I want profiled for DNA. Then I want that profile compared to one you've done on a bone sample from the Air TransSouth crash. Can you do that?"

"I don't see why not."

"How soon?"

"Is this urgent?"

"Very."

"I'll put it on a fast track. When can you get the new sample to me?"

I looked at my watch.

"Two o'clock."

"I'll call over to the DNA section right now, smooth the way. See you at two."

I turned the key and swung into traffic. There were a couple more things I needed to do before leaving Bryson City.

23

THIS TIME THE LILAC DRAGON WAS BY HERSELF.

"Just need to check a couple of details on microfilm," I said, beaming my most winning smile.

Her face did a ménage à trois of emotions. Surprised. Suspicious. Stern.

"It would be very, very helpful if I could take several reels at a time. You were so kind about that yesterday."

Her face softened somewhat. Sighing loudly, she went to the cabinet, removed six boxes, and placed them on the counter.

"Thank you so much," I purred.

Crossing toward the overflow room, I heard a stool squeak, and knew she was craning in my direction.

"Cellular phones are strictly prohibited in the library!" she hissed to my retreating back.

Unlike my prior visit, I whipped through the spools, taking notes on specific items.

In less than an hour I had what I needed.

Tommy Albright was not in, but a drawly female voice promised to deliver my message. The pathologist rang back before I'd hit the outskirts of Bryson City.

"In 1959 a Cherokee named Charlie Wayne Tramper died in a bear attack. Would a file that old still exist?"

"Maybe, maybe not. That was before we centralized. What do you need to know?"

"You remember the case?" I couldn't believe it.

"Hell, yes. I poked through what was left of that ole boy."

"Which was?"

"I've seen my share of bear bait, but Tramper was the worst. Those little bastards tore the bejeezus out of him. Carried his head clean off."

"The skull was not recovered?"

"No."

"How did you ID him?"

"Wife recognized the rifle and clothing."

I found the Reverend Luke Bowman gathering fallen branches in his shadowy front yard. Save for the substitution of a black windbreaker, he was dressed exactly as on our previous meetings.

Bowman watched me pull next to his pickup, added

his armful to a pile beside the drive, and approached my car. We spoke through the open window.

"Good morning, Miss Temperance."

"Good morning. Beautiful day for yard work."

"Yes, ma'am, it is." Fragments of bark and dry leaves clung to his jacket.

"Could I ask you something, Reverend Mr. Bowman?"

"Of course."

"How old was Edna Farrell when she died?"

"I believe Sister Farrell was just shy of eighty."

"Do you remember a man named Tucker Adams?"

His eyes narrowed, and the tip of his tongue slid across his upper lip.

"Adams was elderly, died in 1943," I prompted.

The tongue disappeared and a gnarled finger sighted on me. "I surely do. I was ten years old when that old fellow wandered off from his farm. I helped search for him. Brother Adams was blind and half deaf, so the whole community pitched in."

"How did Adams die?"

"Everyone assumed he just died in the woods. We never found him."

"But his grave is in the cemetery on Schoolhouse Hill."

"No one's buried there. Sister Adams put the headstone up a couple years after her husband went missing."

"Thank you. You've been very helpful."

"I see the boys got your car to running."

"Yes."

"Hope they didn't charge too much."

"No, sir. It seemed fair."

I pulled into the sheriff's department lot directly behind Lucy Crowe. She parked her cruiser, then waited with hands on hips as I turned off the engine and retrieved my briefcase. Her face looked drawn and cheerless.

"Rough morning?"

"Some morons stole a golf cart from the country club, left it a mile up Conleys Creek Road. Two seven-year-olds found the thing and ran it into a tree. One's got a broken collarbone, the other a concussion."

"Teenagers?"

"Probably."

We spoke as we walked.

"Anything new on the Hobbs murder?"

"One of my deputies was working security Sunday morning. He remembers seeing Hobbs enter the morgue around eight, remembers you. The computer shows she checked the foot out at nine-fifteen, back in at two."

"She kept it that long after talking to me?"

"Apparently."

We climbed the steps and were buzzed through the outside door, then again through a barred prison gate. I followed Crowe down a corridor and across an outer workroom to her office.

"Hobbs signed out of the morgue at three-ten. A

guy from Bryson City PD was working the afternoon shift. He doesn't recall seeing her leave."

"What about the surveillance camera?"

"This is beautiful."

Crowe unclipped a radio from her belt, placed it on
a cabinet, and dropped into her chair. I took one of
those opposite the desk.

"The thing went out around two Sunday afternoon,
stayed down until eleven Monday morning."

"Did anyone see Primrose after she left the
morgue?"

"Nope."

"Did you discover anything in her room?"

"The lady was fond of Post-its. Phone numbers.
Times. Names. Lots of notes, mostly work-related."

"Primrose was always losing her glasses, wore
them on a cord around her neck. She worried about
being forgetful." I felt a cold spot in my chest. "Any
clue about her destination Sunday afternoon?"

"Not a word."

A deputy entered and placed a paper on the sheriff's desk. She glanced at it briefly, back to me.

"I see your wheels are running again."

My Mazda was the talk of Swain County.

"I'm heading down to Charlotte, but I want to
show you a couple of things before I go."

I handed her the purloined photo of the Tramper
funeral.

"Recognize anyone?"

"I'll be goddamned. Parker Davenport, our venerable lieutenant governor. The little twerp looks like he's fifteen." She returned the print. "What's the significance?"

"I'm not sure."

Next, I handed her Laslo's report, waited while she read.

"So the DA was right."

"Or I was right."

"Oh?"

"How about this scenario? Jeremiah Mitchell died after leaving the Mighty High Tap last February. His body was stored in a freezer or refrigerator, removed, then placed outside later."

"Why?" She tried to keep the skepticism out of her voice.

I withdrew the notes I'd taken at the library, took a deep breath, and began.

"Henry Arlen Preston died here in 1943. Three days later a farmer named Tucker Adams disappeared. He was seventy-two. Adams's body was never found."

"What does that have to d—"

I held up a hand.

"In 1949 a biology professor named Sheldon Brodie drowned in the Tuckasegee River. A day later Edna Farrell disappeared. She was around eighty. Her body was never found."

Crowe picked up a pen, placed the tip on the blotter, and slid it end over end through her fingers.

"In 1959 Allen Birkby was killed in an automobile accident on Highway 19. Two days after the wreck

Charlie Wayne Tramper disappeared. Tramper was seventy-four. His body was recovered, but it was badly mangled, the head missing. The ID was strictly circumstantial."

I looked up at her.

"That's it?"

"What day did Jeremiah Mitchell disappear?"

Crowe dropped the pen, opened a drawer, and withdrew a file.

"February fifteenth."

"Martin Patrick Veckhoff died in Charlotte on February twelfth."

"Lots of people die in February. It's a lousy month."

"The name 'Veckhoff' is on the list of H&F officers."

"The investment group that owns that weird property near Running Goat Branch?"

I nodded.

"So is 'Birkby.'"

She leaned back and rubbed the corner of one eye. I pulled out Laslo's find and set it in front of her.

"Laslo Sparkes found this in the dirt we collected near the wall at the Running Goat house."

She studied but did not reach for the vial.

"It's a tooth fragment. I'm taking it to Charlotte for DNA testing to establish whether it goes with the foot."

Her phone rang. She ignored it.

"You need to get a reference sample for Mitchell."

She hesitated a moment. Then, "I can look into it."

"Sheriff."

The kiwi eyes met mine.

"This may be bigger than Jeremiah Mitchell."

Three hours later Boyd and I were crossing Little Rock Road, heading north on I-85. The Charlotte skyline rose in the distance, like a stand of saguaro in the Sonoran Desert.

I pointed the highlights out to Boyd. The giant phallus of the Bank of America Corporate Center. The syringelike office building on The Square housing the Charlotte City Club, with its circular green cap of a roof and antenna sticking straight up from the center. The jukebox contour of One First Union Center.

"Look at that, boy. Sex, drugs, and rock and roll."

Boyd raised his ears but said nothing.

While Charlotte's neighborhoods may be small-town cozy, its downtown is a city of polished stone and tinted glass, and its attitude toward crime is au courant. The Charlotte-Mecklenburg Police Department is housed in the Law Enforcement Center, an enormous concrete structure at Fourth and McDowell. The CMPD employs approximately 1,900 officers and 400 unsworn support personnel, and maintains its own crime laboratory, second only to that of the SBI. Not bad for a populace of less than 600,000.

Exiting the expressway, I cut across downtown and pulled into the visitors' lot at the LEC.

Officers entered and left the building, each uniformed in deep blue. Boyd growled softly as one crossed close to the car.

"See the emblem on the shoulder patch? It's a hornet's nest."

Boyd made a yodel-like noise but kept his nose at the window.

"During the Revolutionary War, General Cornwallis encountered such pockets of intense resistance in Charlotte that he branded the area a hornet's nest."

No comment.

"I have to go inside, Boyd. You can't."

Disagreeing, Boyd stood.

I promised to be gone less than an hour, gave him my last emergency granola bar, cracked the windows, and left him.

I found Ron Gillman in his corner office on the fourth floor.

Ron was a tall, silver-haired man with a body that suggested basketball or tennis. The only blemish was a Lauren Hutton gap in his upper dentition.

He listened without interrupting as I told him my theory about Mitchell and the foot. When I'd finished, he held out a hand.

"Let's see it."

He slipped on horn-rimmed glasses and studied the fragment, rolling the vial from side to side. Then he picked up the phone and spoke to someone in the DNA section.

"Things move faster if the request comes from here," he said, replacing the receiver.

"Fast would be good," I said.

"I've already checked on your bone sample. That's done, and the profile's gone into the database we set up for the crash victims. If we get results on this"—he indicated the vial—"we'll feed them in and search for a hit."

"I can't tell you how much I appreciate this."

He leaned back and placed his hands behind his head.

"You really put your finger in someone's eye, Dr. Brennan."

"Guess I did."

"Any thoughts as to whose?"

"Parker Davenport."

"The lieutenant governor?"

"That's the one."

"How did you rile Davenport?"

I turned palms up and shrugged.

"It's hard to help if you're not forthcoming."

I stared at him, torn. I'd shared my theory with Lucy Crowe. But that was Swain County. This was home. Ron Gillman directed the second largest crime lab in the state. While the force was funded locally, money came to it via federal grants administered in Raleigh.

Like the ME. Like the university.

What the hell.

I gave him a condensed version of what I'd told Lucy Crowe.

"So you think the M. P. Veckhoff on your list is state senator Pat Veckhoff from Charlotte?"

I nodded.

"And that Pat Veckhoff and Parker Davenport are tied together in some way?"

Another nod.

"Davenport and Veckhoff. The lieutenant governor and a state senator. That's heavy."

"Henry Preston was a judge."

"What's the link?"

Before I could answer, a man appeared in the doorway, the name "Krueger" embroidered above the pocket of his lab coat. Gillman introduced Krueger as the technical leader of the DNA section. He, along with another analyst, examined all DNA evidence at the lab. I rose and we shook hands.

Gillman handed Krueger the vial and explained what I wanted.

"If there's something there, we'll get it," he said, giving a thumbs-up gesture.

"How long?"

"We'll have to purify, amplify, document all along the way. I might be able to give you a verbal in four or five days."

"That would be great." Forty-eight hours would be great, I thought.

Krueger and I signed evidence transfer forms, and he disappeared with the specimen. I waited as Gillman took a call. When he hung up, I asked a question.

"Did you know Pat Veckhoff?"

"No."

"Parker Davenport?"

"I've met him."

"And?"

"He's popular. People vote for him."

"And?"

"He's a royal pain in the ass."

I produced the Tramper funeral photo.

"That's him. But it was a long time ago."

"Yes."

He handed back the picture.

"So what's your explanation for all this?"

"I don't have one."

"But you will."

"But I will."

"Can I help?"

"There is something you can do for me."

I found Boyd curled in granola crumbs, sound asleep. At the sound of the key, he shot to his feet and barked. Realizing this was not a sneak attack, he placed one forepaw on each front seat and wagged his hips. I slid behind the wheel, and he began removing makeup from the side of my face.

Forty minutes later I pulled up at the address Gillman had found for me. Though the residence was only ten minutes from downtown, and five minutes from my condo at Sharon Hall, it had taken that long to work through my usual Queens Road confusion.

Charlotte's street names reflect its schizoid personality. On the one hand the street-naming approach was simple: They found a winner and stuck with it. The city has Queens Road, Queens Road West, and Queens Road East. Sharon Road, Sharon Lane, Sharon Amity, Sharon View, and Sharon Avenue. I've sat at the intersection of Rea Road and Rea Road, Park Road and Park Road. There was also a biblical influence: Providence Road, Carmel Road, Sardis Road.

On the other hand, no appellation seemed adequate for more than a few miles. Streets change names with whimsy. Tyvola becomes Fairview, then Sardis. At one point Providence Road reaches an intersection at which a hard right keeps one on Providence; going straight places one on Queens Road, which immediately becomes Morehead; and going left puts one on Queens Road, which immediately becomes Selwyn. The Billy Graham Parkway begets Woodlawn, then Runnymede. Wendover gives rise to Eastway.

The Queens sisters are the most evil by far. I give visitors and newcomers one driving rule of thumb: If you get onto anything named Queens, get off. The policy has always worked for me.

Marion Veckhoff lived in a large stone Tudor on Queens Road East. The stucco was cream, the woodwork dark, and each downstairs window was a latticework of lead and glass. A neatly trimmed hedge bordered the property, and brightly colored flowers crowded beds along the front and sides of the house. A pair of enormous magnolias all but filled the front yard.

A lady in pearls, pumps, and a turquoise pants suit was watering pansies along a walk bisecting the front lawn. Her skin was pale, her hair the color of ginger ale.

With a warning to Boyd, I got out and locked the door. I shouted, but the woman seemed oblivious to my presence.

"Mrs. Veckhoff?" I repeated as I drew close.

She spun, spraying my feet with her hose. Her hand jerked, and the water was redirected onto the grass.

"Oh, dear. Oh, my. I'm so sorry."

"It's no problem at all." I stepped back from the water puddling the flagstone. "Are you Mrs. Veckhoff?"

"Yes, dear. You're Carla's niece?"

"No, ma'am. I'm Dr. Brennan."

Her eyes went slightly out of focus, as if consulting a calendar somewhere over my shoulder.

"Did I forget an appointment?"

"No, Mrs. Veckhoff. I wondered if I might ask you a few questions about your husband."

She recentered on me.

"Pat was a state senator for sixteen years. Are you a reporter?"

"No, I'm not. Four terms is quite an achievement."

"Being in public office took him away from home too much, but he loved it."

"Where did he travel?"

"Raleigh, mostly."

"Did he ever visit Bryson City?"

"Where's that, dear?"

"It's in the mountains."

"Oh, Pat loved the mountains, went there whenever he could."

"Did you travel with your husband?"

"Oh no, no. I have the arthritis, and . . ." Her voice trailed off, as though uncertain where to go with the thought.

"Arthritis can be very painful."

"Yes, it surely is. And those trips were really Pat's time with the boys. Do you mind if I finish my watering?"

"Please."

I walked beside her as she moved along the pansy beds.

"Mr. Veckhoff went to the mountains with your sons?"

"Oh, no. Pat and I have a daughter. She's married now. He went with his chums." She laughed, a sound halfway between a choke and a hiccup. "He said it was to get away from his women, to put the fire back into his belly."

"He went to the mountains with other men?"

"Those boys were very close, been friends since their school days. They miss Pat terribly. Kendall, too. Yes, we're getting old. . . ." Again her voice tapered into silence.

"Kendall?"

"Kendall Rollins. He was the first to go. Kendall was a poet. Do you know his work?"

I shook my head, outwardly calm. Inside my heart

was thumping. The name "Rollins" was on the H&F list.

"Kendall died of leukemia when he was fifty-five."

"That's very young. When was that, ma'am?"

"Nineteen eighty-six."

"Where did your husband and his friends stay in the mountains?"

Her face tensed, and the comma of skin under her left eye jumped.

"They had some kind of lodge. Why are you asking about all this?"

"A plane crashed recently near Bryson City, and I'm trying to learn what I can about a nearby property. Your husband might have been one of the owners."

"That terrible affair with all those students?"

"Yes."

"Why do young people have to die? A young man was killed flying to my husband's funeral. Forty-three years old." Her head wagged.

"Who was that, ma'am?"

She looked away.

"He was the son of one of Pat's friends, lived in Alabama, so I'd never met him. Still, it broke my heart."

"Do you know his name?"

"No."

Her eyes would not meet mine.

"Do you know the names of the others who went to the lodge?"

She began fidgeting with the nozzle.

"Mrs. Veckhoff?"

"Pat never talked about those trips. I left it to him. He needed privacy, being in the public eye so much."

"Have you ever heard of the H&F Investment Group?"

"No." She remained focused on the hose, her back to me, but I could see tension in her shoulders.

"Mrs. Veck—"

"It's late. I have to go inside now."

"I'd like to find out if your husband had an interest in that property."

Twisting off the spray, she dropped the hose and hurried up the walk.

"Thanks for your time, ma'am. I'm sorry to have kept you so long."

She turned with the door half open, one veiny hand on the knob. From inside the house came the soft bong of Westminster chimes.

"Pat always said I talk too much. I denied it, told him I was just the friendly type. Now I think he was probably right. But it gets lonely being by yourself."

The door closed, and I heard a bolt slide into place.

It's O.K., Mrs. Veckhoff. Your answers were bullshit, but they were charming bullshit. And very informative.

I dug a card from my purse, wrote my home address and number on it, and stuck it into the doorjamb.

24

IT WAS PAST EIGHT WHEN MY FIRST VISITOR ARRIVED.

After leaving Mrs. Veckhoff, I'd bought a rotisserie chicken at the Roasting Company, then collected Birdie from my neighbor. The three of us had shared the fowl, Bird's tail fluffing like a feather duster each time Boyd moved in his direction. I was scraping plates at the sink when I heard the knock.

Pete stood on the back stoop, a bouquet of daisies in one hand. As I opened the door, he bowed at the waist and proffered the flowers.

"On behalf of my canine associate."

"Not necessary, but appreciated." I held open the door, and he went past me into the kitchen.

Boyd bounded over at the sound of Pete's voice, dropped snout onto front paws, rump in the air, then began cavorting around the kitchen. Pete clapped and called his name. Boyd went berserk, barking and racing in circles. Birdie bolted.

"Stop. He'll scratch the floor."

Pete took a chair at the table and Boyd moved beside him.

"Sit."

Boyd stared at Pete, eyebrows dancing. Pete tapped the dog's rump, and Boyd sat, chin upon his master's knee. Pete began a two-handed ear scratch.

"Got any beer?"

"Root beer."

"Right. How'd you two get along?"

"Fine."

I opened and placed a Hire's in front of him.

"When did you get back?" Pete lowered and tipped the bottle so Boyd could drink.

"Today. How did things go in Indiana?"

"The local arson investigators were about as sophisticated as the Bobbsey twins. But the real problem was the liability insurance adjuster representing the roofer. His client was working on a roof patch with an acetylene torch in the exact area where the fire started."

He wiped the mouth of the bottle with his hand and drank.

"This asshole knew the cause and origin. We knew the cause and origin. He knew we knew it. We knew he knew we knew, but his official position was that they needed additional investigation."

"Will it go to court?"

"Depends on what they offer." He lowered the root

beer again, and Boyd slurped. "But it was good to have a break from chow breath, here."

"You love that dog."

"Not as much as I love you." He gave me his "Goofy Pete" grin.

"Hmm."

"Any progress on your DMORT problems?"

"Maybe."

Pete looked at his watch.

"I want to hear all about it, but right now I'm bushed."

He drained the bottle and stood. Boyd shot to his feet.

"I think I will mosey with my dog."

I watched them leave, Boyd dancing around Pete's legs. When I turned, Birdie was peering in from the hall doorway, feet positioned for a quick retreat.

"Good riddance" is what I said. Miffed is what I felt. The damn dog hadn't looked back once.

Birdie and I were watching *The Big Sleep* when the second knock sounded. I was in a T-shirt, panties, and my old flannel robe. He was in my lap.

Ryan stood on the doorstep, face ashen in the porch light. I avoided repeating my usual opener. He'd tell me soon enough why he was in Charlotte.

"How did you know I'd be here?"

He ignored my question.

"Spending the evening by yourself?"

I tipped my head. "Bacall and Bogart are in the study."

I opened the door, as I had for Pete, and he brushed past me into the kitchen. I smelled cigarette smoke and perspiration, and assumed he'd driven straight from Swain County.

"Will they mind if I make it a foursome?" Though his words were light, his face told me his heart was not.

"They're flexible."

He followed me to the den, and we settled at opposite ends of the couch. I clicked off the TV.

"Bertrand's been ID'ed."

I waited.

"Mostly dental. And some other"—His Adam's apple rose and fell—"fragments."

"Petricelli?"

He shook his head, a short, tight gesture.

"They were seated at ground zero, so Petricelli may be vapor. What they found of Bertrand was two valleys over from the main site." His voice was tight and shaky. "Embedded in a tree."

"Has Tyrell released the body?"

"This morning. I'm escorting it to Montreal on Sunday."

I wanted to wrap my arms around his neck, to press my cheek to his chest and stroke his hair. I didn't move.

"The family wants a civil ceremony, so the SQ's organizing a funeral for Wednesday."

I didn't hesitate.

"I'm going with you."

"That's not necessary." He kept opening and closing one hand around the other. His knuckles looked hard and white as a row of pebbles.

"Jean was my friend, too."

"It's a long trip."

His eyes glistened. He blinked, leaned back, and ran both hands up and down his face.

"Would you like me to go?"

"What about this pissing match with Tyrell?"

I told him about the tooth fragment, held back the rest.

"How long will the profiling take?"

"Four or five days. So there's no reason I have to stay here. Would you like me to go?"

He looked at me, and a wrinkle formed at the corner of his mouth.

"I have a feeling you will, anyway."

Knowing he would spend the next two days arranging transport for Bertrand's casket and meeting with McMahon at FBI headquarters, Ryan had booked a room at the Adams Mark Hotel near uptown. Or perhaps he had other reasons. I didn't ask.

The next day I researched names on the H&F list, and learned only one thing. Once outside my own lab my investigative skills are limited.

Encouraged by my success in Bryson City, I spent a library morning with back issues of the *Charlotte*

Observer. Though a mediocre public official, State Senator Pat Veckhoff had been a model citizen. Otherwise, I discovered zilch.

The Internet produced a few references to the poetry of Kendall Rollins, the poet Mrs. Veckhoff had mentioned. That was it. Davis. Payne. Birkby. Warren. They were common names, leading into labyrinths of useless information. The Charlotte White Pages listed dozens of each.

That evening, I took Ryan to dinner at the Selwyn Pub. He seemed withdrawn and preoccupied. I didn't push.

Sunday afternoon Birdie went to Pete, and Ryan and I flew to Montreal. What remained of Jean Bertrand traveled below in a glossy metal casket.

We were met at Dorval Airport by a funeral director, two hearse attendants, and four uniformed officers of the Sûreté du Québec. Together we escorted the body into town.

October can be glorious in Montreal, with church spires and skyscrapers piercing a crisp, blue sky, the mountain burning brightly in the background. Or it can be gray and cheerless, with rain, sleet, or even snow.

This Sunday the temperature flirted with freezing, and dark, heavy clouds hung over the city. Trees looked stark and black, lawns and parkways frosted white. Burlap-wrapped shrubs stood guard outside homes and businesses, floral mummies bundled against the cold.

It was past seven by the time we delivered Bertrand to an Urgel Bourgie in St-Lambert. Ryan and I parted ways, he being taken to his condo at Habitat, I to mine in Centre-ville.

Arriving, I threw my overnighter on the bed, turned on the heat, checked my answering machine, and then the refrigerator. The former was full, flashing like a blue light at a Kmart special. The latter was empty, stark white walls and smeared glass shelves.

LaManche. Isabelle. Four telemarketers. A McGill graduate student. LaManche.

Digging a jacket and gloves from the hall closet, I walked to Le Faubourg for provisions.

By the time I returned, the condo had warmed. I built a fire anyway, needing its comfort more than its heat. I was feeling as down as I had at Sharon Hall, haunted by the specter of Ryan's mysterious Danielle, saddened by the prospect of Bertrand's funeral.

As I stir-fried scallops and green beans, sleet began ticking against the windows. I ate at the hearth, thinking of the man I'd come to bury.

The detective and I had worked together over the years, when murder victims caused our paths to cross, and I'd come to understand certain things about him. Incapable of deviousness, he'd seen the world in black and white, with cops on one side of a moral line, criminals on the other. He'd had faith in the system, never doubting it would sort the good guys from the bad.

Bertrand had visited me here the previous spring, devastated by an incomprehensible break with Ryan. I pictured him sitting on my couch that night, wretched with anger and disbelief, not knowing what to say or do, the same feelings now overpowering Andrew Ryan.

After dinner, I loaded the dishwasher, stoked the fire, then took the handset to the sofa. Mentally switching to French, I dialed LaManche's home number.

My boss said he was glad I'd come to Montreal, even though the circumstances were so sad. There were two anthropology cases at the lab.

"Last week a woman was found, nude and decomposed, wrapped in a blanket in Parc Nicholas-Veil."

"Where is that?"

"The far northern edge of the city."

"CUM?"

The Communauté Urbaine de Montréal Police, or Montreal Urban Community Police, have jurisdiction over everything on the island of Montreal.

"*Oui.* Sergent-détective Luc Claudel."

Claudel. The highly regarded bulldog of a detective who would grudgingly work with me, but remained unconvinced that female forensic anthropologists were helpful to law enforcement. Just what I needed.

"Has she been ID'ed?"

"There is a presumptive identification, and a man has been arrested. The suspect is claiming she fell, but Monsieur Claudel is suspicious. I would like you to examine the cranial trauma." LaManche's French, always so proper.

"I'll do it tomorrow."

The second case was less urgent. A small plane had crashed two years earlier near Chicoutimi, the copilot never found. A segment of diaphysis had recently washed up in that vicinity. Could I determine if the bone was human? I assured him I could.

LaManche thanked me, asked about the Air TransSouth recovery, and expressed sorrow over Bertrand's death. He did not inquire about my problems with the authorities. Surely the news would have reached him, but he was too discreet to raise a painful subject.

The telemarketers I ignored.

The graduate student had long since obtained the needed reference.

My friend Isabelle had hosted one of her soirees the previous Saturday. I apologized for missing her call, and her dinner party. She assured me there would be another soon.

I had just replaced the handset when my cell phone rang. I sprinted across the room and dug it out, once again vowing to find a better storage location than my purse. It took a moment for the voice to register.

"Anne?"

"What are you doing?" she asked.

"Finalizing world peace. I just got off the phone with Kofi Annan."

"Where are you?"

"Montreal."

"Why the hell are you back in Canada?"

I told her about Bertrand.

"Is that why you sound so bummed?"

"Partly. Are you in Charlotte? How was London?"

"What does that mean? Partly?"

"You don't want to know."

"Of course I do. What's wrong?"

I unloaded. My friend listened. Twenty minutes later I took a breath, not weeping but close.

"So the Arthur property and unidentified foot issue are separate from the crash complaint issue?"

"Sort of. I don't think the foot came from anyone on the flight. I have to prove that."

"You think it's this Mitchell character who's been missing since February?"

"Yes."

"And the NTSB still doesn't know what took that plane out?"

"No."

"And all you know about this property is that some guy named Livingstone gave it as a wedding gift to some guy named Arthur who sold it to some guy named Dashwood."

"Uh-huh."

"But the deed is in the name of an investment group, not Dashwood."

"H&F. In Delaware."

"And some of the officers' names match up to the

names of people who died right before local seniors went missing."

"You're good."

"I took notes."

"Sounds ridiculous."

"Yes. And you have no idea why Davenport is on a tear for you?"

"No."

Silence hummed across two countries.

"We heard about some lord in England named Dashwood. A friend of Benjamin Franklin's, I think."

"That should crack this wide open. How *was* London?"

"Great. But too much the ABC tour."

"ABC tour?"

"'Another bloody cathedral.' Ted likes history. He even dragged me through a bunch of caves. When will you be back in Charlotte?"

"Thursday."

"Where are we going for Thanksgiving?"

Anne and I met when we were young and pregnant, I with Katy, she with her son, Brad. That first summer we'd all packed up and taken the babies to the ocean for a week. We'd been going to one beach or another every summer and Thanksgiving ever since.

"The kids like Myrtle. I like Holden."

"I want to try Pawleys Island. Let's have lunch. We'll discuss it and I'll tell you all about my trip. Tempe, things will get back to normal. You'll see."

I fell asleep listening to sleet, thinking of sand and palmetto, and wondering if I had any chance at all of having a normal life again.

The Laboratoire de Sciences Judiciaires et de Médecine Légale is the central medico-legal and crime laboratory for the province of Quebec. It is located on the top two floors of the Édifice Wilfrid-Derome, known to locals as the Sûreté du Québec, or SQ building.

By nine-thirty Monday morning I was in the anthropology-odontology lab, having already attended the morning staff meeting, and collected my *Demande d'Expertise en Anthropologie* request form from the pathologist assigned to each case. After determining that the copilot long-bone shaft actually came from the lower leg of a mule deer, I wrote a brief report and turned to Claudel's lady.

I arranged the bones in anatomical order on my worktable, did a skeletal inventory, then checked indicators of age, sex, race, and height for consistency with the presumed ID. This could be important, since the victim had been toothless, and dental records did not exist.

I broke at one-thirty and ate my bagel with cream cheese, banana, and Chips Ahoy! cookies while watching boats sailing under cars driving over the Jacques Cartier Bridge far below my office window. By two I was back with the bones, and by four-thirty I had finished my analysis.

The victim *could* have shattered her jaw, orbit, and cheekbone and smashed the depressed fractures into her forehead by falling. From a hot air balloon or high-rise building.

I called Claudel and left a verbal opinion of homicide, locked up, and went home.

I spent another night by myself, cooking and eating a chicken breast, watching a rerun of *Northern Exposure,* reading a few chapters of a novel by James Lee Burke. It was as though Ryan had dropped from the planet. I was asleep by eleven.

The next day was spent documenting the battered lady: photographing my findings with regard to biological profile and photographing, diagramming, describing, and explaining the injury patterns on her skull and face. By late afternoon I'd compiled a report and left it in the secretarial office. I was removing my lab coat when Ryan appeared at my office door.

"Need a lift to the funeral?"

"Rough couple of days?" I asked, taking my purse from the bottom desk drawer.

"There's not a lot of sunshine in the squad."

"No," I said, meeting his gaze.

"I'm completely jammed up with this Petricelli thing."

"Yes." My eyes never left his.

"Turns out Metraux isn't quite so sure about eye-balling Pepper."

"Because of Bertrand?"

He shrugged.

"These bastards will dime their own mothers for an afternoon out."

"Risky."

"As tap water in Tijuana. Do you want the ride?"

"If it's not too much trouble."

"I'll pick you up at eight-fifteen."

Since Sergent-détective Jean Bertrand had died while on duty, he was given full state honors. La Direction des Communications of the Sûreté du Québec had informed every police force in North America, using the CPIC system in Canada and the NCIC system in the United States. An honor guard flanked the casket at the funeral parlor. The body was escorted from there to the church, from the church to the cemetery.

While I had expected a large turnout, I was astounded by the mass of people who showed up. In addition to Bertrand's family and friends, his fellow SQ officers, members of the CUM, and many from the medico-legal lab, it looked like every police department in Canada, and many in the United States, had sent representatives. French and English media sent reporters and TV crews.

By noon, the bits of Bertrand that passed for his corpse lay in the ground at the Notre-Dame-des-Neiges Cemetery, and Ryan and I were winding our way down the mountain toward Centre-ville.

"When do you fly out?" he asked, splitting off Côte-des-Neiges onto rue St-Mathieu.

"Eleven-fifty tomorrow morning."

"I'll pick you up at ten-thirty."

"If you're aspiring to a position as my chauffeur, the pay is lousy."

The joke plunged to its death before I'd finished saying it.

"I'm on the same flight."

"Why?"

"Last night the Charlotte PD busted an Atlanta lowlife named Pecan Billie Holmes."

He dug a pack of du Maurier's from his pocket, tapped one out on the steering wheel, and placed it between his lips. After lighting up with one hand, he inhaled, then blew smoke through both nostrils. I lowered my window.

"Seems the Pecan had a lot to say about a certain telephone tip to the FBI."

25

THE NEXT FEW DAYS FELT LIKE A PLUNGE ON THE Mind Eraser at Six Flags. After weeks of the slow climb, suddenly everything broke. But there was nothing amusing about the ride.

It was late afternoon when Ryan and I touched down in Charlotte. In our absence, fall had caught on, and a strong breeze flapped our jackets as we walked to the parking garage.

We drove directly downtown to the FBI office at Second and Tryon. McMahon had just returned from interviewing Pecan Billie Holmes at the jail.

"Holmes was coked to the eyeballs when they hauled his butt to the bag last night, yelling and screaming, offering to roll over on everything back to a Little League game his team threw in the fourth grade."

"Who is this guy?" Ryan.

"A thirty-eight-year-old three-time loser. Hangs on the fringes of the Atlanta biker scene."

"Hells Angels?"

McMahon nodded.

"He's not a full patcher, doesn't have the brains of a banana Popsicle. The club tolerates him as long as he's useful."

"What was Holmes doing in Charlotte?"

"Probably here for a Rotary luncheon," McMahon said.

"Does Holmes really know who phoned in the bomb tip?" I asked.

"At four A.M. he had an inside track. That's why the arresting officers phoned us. By the time I got there, a night's sleep had dulled the Pecan's enthusiasm for sharing."

McMahon lifted a mug from his desk, swirled and examined the contents as one might a stool sample.

"Fortunately, at the time of his arrest the scumbag was on probation for bouncing rubber all over Atlanta. We were able to persuade him that full disclosure was in his own best interest."

"And?"

"Holmes swears he was present when the scheme was hatched."

"Where?"

"The Claremont Lounge in midtown Atlanta. That's about six blocks from the pay phone where the call was made."

McMahon set down the mug.

"Holmes says he was drinking and snorting blow with a couple of Angels named Harvey Poteet and Neal Tannahill. The boys were talking about Pepper Petricelli and the crash when Poteet decided it would be cool to diddle the FBI with a false lead."

"Why?"

"Barstool brilliance. If Petricelli was alive, it would scare him into silence. If he'd gone down with the plane, a message would go out. Talk and the brothers erase you from the planet. A freebie."

"Why would these assholes talk business in front of an outsider?"

"Poteet and Tannahill were doing lines in Holmes's car. Our hero was out cold in the backseat. Or so they thought."

"So the whole thing was a hoax," I said.

"Appears so." McMahon moved the mug beyond the edge of the blotter.

"Metraux's backing off on his Petricelli sighting," Ryan added.

"There's a surprise."

Down the hall a phone rang. A voice called out. Heels clicked down the corridor.

"Looks like your partner and his prisoner just got on the wrong flight."

"So the Sri Lankans are clean, Simington is up for Humanitarian of the Year, and the Angels are nothing but merry pranksters. We're back to square one with a blown plane and no explanation." Ryan.

"I got a call from Magnus Jackson as I was leaving Bryson City. He claims his investigators are picking up evidence of slow burning."

"What kind of evidence?" I asked.

"Geometric burn patterns on debris."

"Which means?"

"Fire prior to the explosion."

"A mechanical problem?"

McMahon shrugged.

"They can separate precrash from postcrash burning?" I pushed.

"Sounds like crap to me."

McMahon grabbed the mug and got out of his chair.

"So the Pecan may be a hero."

Ryan and I stood.

"And Metraux's not finding a seller's market," said Ryan.

"Ain't life grand."

I hadn't told Ryan about Parker Davenport's insinuations concerning himself and Bertrand. I did so now, outside the Adams Mark Hotel. Ryan listened, hands tight on his knees, eyes straight ahead.

"That rat-brained little prick." Headlights moved across his face, distorting lines and planes rigid with anger.

"This should dampen that line of reasoning."

"Yes."

"I'm sure Davenport's reaming me has nothing to

do with you or Bertrand. That was a sidebar to his real agenda."

"Which is?"

"I have every intention of finding out."

Ryan's jaw muscles bunched, relaxed.

"Who the fuck does he think he is?"

"Powerful people."

His palms rubbed up then down his jeans, then he reached over and took my hand.

"Sure I can't buy you dinner?"

"I need to collect my cat."

Ryan dropped my hand, flipped the handle, and got out of the car.

"I'll call you in the morning," I said.

He slammed the door and was gone.

Back at the Annex, my answering machine flashed four messages.

Anne.

Ron Gillman.

Two hang-ups.

I dialed Gillman's pager. He phoned back before I'd filled Birdie's bowls.

"Krueger says you've got a match on the DNA."

My stomach and tonsils changed places.

"He's sure?"

"One chance in seventy godzillion of error. Or whatever figures those guys throw around."

"The tooth and foot come from the same person?" I still couldn't believe it.

"Yes. Go get your warrant."

I dialed Lucy Crowe. The sheriff was out, but a deputy promised to find her.

There was no answer in Ryan's room.

Anne picked up on the first ring.

"Figure out who your bomber is?"

"We figured out who it isn't."

"That's progress. How about dinner?"

"Where's Ted?"

"At a sales meeting in Orlando."

My cupboard would have made Mother Hubbard proud. And I was so agitated I knew sitting at home would be sheer torture.

"Foster's in thirty minutes?"

"I'll be there."

Foster's Tavern is a subterranean hideaway with somber wood paneling and tufted black leather rising to midwall. A carved bar wraps around one end, battered tables fill the other. Blood cousin to the Selwyn Avenue Pub, the tavern is small, dark, and flawlessly Irish.

Anne had the Guinness stew and Chardonnay. Were I in the game, I'd have gone for a black and tan, but Anne always had Chardonnay. I ordered corned beef and cabbage, a Perrier with lime. Normally I ask for lemon, but the green seemed more fitting.

"So who's been ruled out?" Anne asked, fingertipping a speck from her wine.

"I can't really discuss that, but there's other progress I can tell you about."

"You've figured out the early temperature history of the solar system."

She flicked the particle. Her hair looked blonder than I remembered.

"That was last week. Did you lighten your hair?"

"A mistake. What's this progress?"

I told her about the DNA hit.

"So your foot belongs to whoever went soupy inside the wall."

"And it wasn't any jive deer."

"Who was it?"

"I'll bet the farm it was Jeremiah Mitchell."

"The black Cherokee."

"Yes."

"Now what?"

"I'm waiting for a call from the Swain County sheriff. With the DNA match, a warrant should be a piece of cake. Even from that medieval moron of a magistrate."

"Nice alliteration."

"Thanks."

Over dinner, we decided on Wild Dunes at Thanksgiving. The rest of the time Anne described her trip to England. I listened.

"Did you see *anything* besides cathedrals and monuments?" I asked when she paused for breath.

"Caves."

"Caves?"

"Totally bizarre. This guy named Francis Dash-wood had them dug sometime in the eighteenth century. He wanted a Gothic atmosphere, so he had this corny three-sided stone structure built around the entrance. Cathedral windows, doors, and arches, a stone-bordered portal in the center, and a black wrought-iron fence at each side. Creates a sort of courtyard. Gothic chic, complete with souvenir shop, café, and white plastic tables and chairs for the thirsty medieval tourist."

She took a sip of wine.

"You enter the caves through a long white tunnel with a low, rounded ceiling."

"Why white?"

"It's all fake. The caves were chiseled out of chalk."

"Where are they?"

"West Wycombe in Buckinghamshire. It's about an hour's drive northwest of London. Someone told Ted about the place, so we had to stop off on our way to Oxford." She rolled her eyes. "Tempe, these caves are mondo bizarro. Passages meander all over the place, with little rooms and crannies and side branches. And they're filled with all sorts of creepy carvings."

"Creepy?"

"Most of the engravings look like the work of kids, but they're way too grotesque."

"Like what?"

"A face with a cross gouged into its forehead,

another wearing a sorcerer's hat, the mouth and eyes perfect O's."

She gave what she must have considered a ghostly grimace.

"Tunnels split, then rejoin, then change direction for no reason. There's a Banqueting Hall, and a River Styx, complete with fake stalactites, that you have to cross to enter a chamber called the Inner Temple. My personal favorite was a winding passage to nowhere stuffed with tacky mannequins of Dashwood and his cronies."

"Why did Dashwood dig the caves?"

"Maybe he had more money than brains. The guy's mausoleum is there, too. Looks like the Coliseum."

She drained her wine, swallowed quickly as another idea struck her.

"Or maybe Frank was an eighteenth-century Walt Disney. Planned to make millions opening the place as a tourist attraction."

"Didn't they provide an explanation?"

"Yeah. Outside the cave there's a long brick corridor with wall hangings that give the history. I was taking pictures, so I didn't read them. Ted did."

She rechecked her glass, found it still empty.

"Just down the road, there's an elaborate English manor called Medmenham Abbey. The place was built by twelfth-century Cistercian monks, but Dashwood bought and renovated it to use as a country getaway. Gothic walls, crumbling entrance with engraved motto arching above."

She said this in a breathy voice, moving her hand in a semicircle above her head. Anne is a real estate agent and sometimes describes things in Realtorese.

"What did the motto say?"

"Damned if I know."

Coffee arrived. We added cream, stirred.

"After our phone conversation the other day, I kept thinking about this guy Dashwood."

"The name Dashwood is not uncommon."

"How common is it?"

"I can't quote numbers."

"Do you know anyone named Dashwood?"

"No."

"Uncommon enough."

It was hard to maneuver around that.

"Francis Dashwood lived two hundred and fifty years ago."

She was in midshrug when my cell phone rang. I clicked on quickly, apologizing with a grimace to the other patrons. While I find cell phones in restaurants the height of rudeness, I hadn't wanted to chance missing Lucy Crowe's call.

It was the sheriff. I talked as I hurried outside. She listened without interrupting.

"That's good enough for a warrant."

"What if this asshole still won't issue?"

"I'm going to drop by Battle's house right now. If he stonewalls, I'll think of something."

When I returned to the table, Anne had ordered another glass of Chardonnay and a stack of photos had appeared. I spent the next twenty minutes admiring shots of Westminster, Buckingham Palace, the Tower, the Bridge, and every museum in greater London.

It was almost eleven when I pulled in at Sharon Hall. As I swung around the Annex, the headlights picked up a large brown envelope on my front stoop. I parked in back, cut the engine, and cracked a window.

Only crickets and traffic noises on Queens Road.

I sprinted to the back door and slipped inside. Again, I listened, wishing Boyd were with me.

Nothing cut the silence but the whir of the refrigerator, the hammering of Gran's mantel clock.

I was about to call Birdie when he appeared in the doorway, stretching first one hind leg, then the other.

"Was someone here, Bird?"

He sat and gazed at me with round yellow eyes. Then he licked a forepaw, dragged it across his right ear, repeated the maneuver.

"Obviously you're not worried about intruders."

I crossed to the living room, put my ear to the door, then stepped back and turned the knob. Birdie observed from the hall. No sign of any person. I took the package inside and locked the door behind me.

Birdie watched politely.

My name was written on the envelope in a swirly, feminine hand. There was no return address.

"It's for me, Bird."

No reply.

"Did you see who left it?"

I shook the package.

"Probably not the way the bomb squad would do it."

I tore a corner and peeked inside. A book.

Ripping open the envelope, I withdrew a large, leather-bound journal. A note was taped to the front cover, penned on delicate peach stationery by the same hand that had placed my name on the outer packaging.

My eyes raced to the signature.

Marion Louise Willoughby Veckhoff.

26

Dr. Brennan,

I am a useless old woman. I have never had a job or held office. I have not written a book or designed a garden. I have no gift for poetry, painting, or music. But I was a loyal and obedient wife all the years of my marriage. I loved my husband, supported him unquestioningly. It was the role to which my upbringing led me.

Martin Patrick Veckhoff was a good provider, a loving father, an honest businessman. But, as I sit, deafened by the silence of another sleepless night, questions burn inside my heart. Was there another side to the man I lived with for almost six decades? Were there things that weren't right?

I am sending you a diary that my husband kept under lock and key. Wives have a way, Dr. Brennan, wives alone with time on their hands. I found the diary years ago, returned to it again and again, listened, followed the news. Kept silent.

The man killed on the way to Pat's funeral was Roger Lee Fairley. His obituary gives the date. Read the journal. Read the clippings.

I'm not sure what it all means, but your visit frightened me. These past few days I have peered deep into my soul. Enough. I cannot endure one more night alone with the dread.

I am old, soon to die. But I ask one thing. If my suspicions prove correct, do not disgrace our daughter.

I apologize for my rudeness on Friday last.
   Regretfully,
   Marion Louise Willoughby Veckhoff

Burning with curiosity, I double-checked the security system, made myself a cup of tea, and took everything to my study. After collecting notebook and pen, I opened the journal, removed and upended an envelope I found stuck between the pages.

Neatly trimmed clippings fluttered to my desk, some without identification, others from the *Charlotte Observer,* the *Raleigh News & Observer,* the *Winston-Salem Journal,* the *Asheville Citizen-Times,* also known as "the Voice of the Mountains," and the *Charleston Post and Courier.* Most were obituaries. A few were feature stories. Each reported the death of a prominent man.

The poet Kendall Rollins succumbed to leukemia on May 12, 1986. Among those surviving Rollins was his son, Paul Hardin Rollins.

The small hairs on my neck reached for the ceiling. P. H. Rollins was on the list of H&F officers. I made note.

Roger Lee Fairley died when his small plane went down in Alabama eight months back. O.K., that's what Mrs. Veckhoff said. I jotted the name and date. February 13.

The oldest item described the 1959 highway accident that killed Anthony Allen Birkby.

The other names meant nothing. I added them to my list, along with their dates of death, laid the clippings aside, and turned to the diary.

The first entry was made on June 17, 1935, the last in November 2000. Flipping through the pages, I could see that the handwriting changed several times, suggesting multiple authors. The final three decades were chronicled in a taut, cramped script almost too small to read.

Martin Patrick Veckhoff was tightly wrapped, indeed, I thought, returning to the first page. For the next two hours I plowed through the faded script, now and then glancing at my watch, distracted by thoughts of Lucy Crowe.

The journal contained not a single proper name. Codes or nicknames were used throughout. Omega. Ilus. Khaffre. Chac. Itzmana.

I recognized an Egyptian pharaoh here, a Greek letter there. Some handles sounded vaguely familiar, others not at all.

There were financial accounts: money in, money out. Repairs. Purchases. Awards. Demerits. There were descriptions of events. A dinner. A business meeting. A literary discussion.

Beginning in the forties another type of entry began to appear. Lists of code names, followed by sets of strange symbols. I flipped through several. The same players reappeared year after year, then disappeared, never to be seen again. When one went out, a new one came in.

I counted. There were never more than eighteen names on any of these rosters.

When I finally leaned back, my tea was cold, and my neck felt as though it had been hung from a line and allowed to dry in the wind. Birdie was asleep on the love seat.

"All right. Let's go at it the other way round."

The cat stretched but didn't open an eye.

Using the dates I'd taken from Mrs. Veckhoff's clippings, I fast-forwarded through the journal. A list of code names was entered four days after Birkby's car crash. Sinuhe appeared for the first time, but Omega was missing. I scanned subsequent lists. Omega was never mentioned again.

Had Anthony Birkby been Omega?

Using this hypothesis, I flashed ahead to 1986.

Within days of Kendall Rollins's death, a list appeared. Mani replaced Piankhy.

Heart beating slightly faster, I continued with the clipping dates.

John Morgan died in 1972. Three days later, a list. Arrigatore checked in. Itzmana vanished.

William Glenn Sherman died in 1979. Five days later Veckhoff recorded a list. Ometeotl debuted. Rho was history.

Every death notice clipped by Mrs. Veckhoff was followed within days by a code name list. In each instance, a regular disappeared, and a newcomer joined the roster. Matching clippings with journal entries, I correlated code names with real names for everyone dead since 1959.

A. A. Birkby: Omega; John Morgan: Itzmana; William Glenn Sherman: Rho; Kendall Rollins: Piankhy.

"But what about the early years?"

Bird had no idea.

"O.K., back the other way."

I flipped to a clean page in my notebook. Every time an entry showed the replacement of one code name with another, I noted the date. It didn't take long.

In 1943, Ilus was replaced by Omega. Could that have been the year Birkby joined H&F?

In 1949, Narmer took over for Khaffre.

Pharaoh in, pharaoh out. Was it some sort of Masonic group?

I moved forward, added the year for each list.

Nineteen fifty-nine, 1972, 1979, 1986.

I stared at the years. Then I flew to my briefcase, pulled out other notes, and checked.

"Sonofabitch!"

I looked at my watch: 3:20 A.M. Where the hell was Lucy Crowe?

To say I rested poorly would be like saying Quasimodo had a bad back. I tossed and turned, hovering on the edge but never moving into real sleep.

When the phone rang I was already up, sorting laundry, sweeping the patio, snipping dead leaves, drinking cup after cup of coffee.

"Did you get it?" I almost shrieked.

"Repeat the punch line."

"I can't tie up the line, Pete."

"You have call waiting."

"Why are you phoning at seven in the morning?"

"I have to return to Indiana to reinterview Itchy and Scratchy."

It took me a moment to connect.

"The Bobbsey twins?"

"I've downgraded them. I'm calling to tell you that Boyd will be furloughed to the Granbar Kennel."

"What? The towels were too rough here?"

"He didn't want to impose."

"Isn't Granbar awfully expensive?"

"Knowing I'm in Big Law, Boyd has come to expect a certain lifestyle."

"I could work him in."

"You like that dog," he wheedled.

"That dog is a moron. But there's no reason to lay out bucks when I'm still stuck with five pounds of Alpo."

"The Granbar staff will be crushed."

"They'll work through it."

"I'll bring him by in an hour."

I was spray-cleaning the inside of the trash can when the phone rang again. Lucy Crowe's voice was taut with frustration.

"It's still no go with the magistrate. I don't get it. Frank's usually reasonable, but he got so angry this morning I thought he was going to have a heart attack. I backed off because I was afraid I'd kill the weasel."

I told her what I'd found in the Veckhoff diary.

"Can you check on MPs from seventy-two and seventy-nine?"

"Yeah."

A long silence rolled down from the highlands. Finally, "I noticed a metal bar when we were out at that place, lying in the dirt by the front porch."

"Oh?" My burglary tool.

Another pause.

"If wreckage is discovered on property within reasonable proximity of an airplane crash, my office has jurisdiction during the period of active recovery."

"I see."

"Only for matters relating directly to the crash. To

check for survivors who might have crawled off, for example. Maybe died under the house."

"Or inside the courtyard."

"Anything suspicious found while inside, I'd need a regular warrant."

"Of course."

"There are still two passengers unaccounted for."

"Yes."

"Did that bar look like wreckage to you?"

"Could have been a piece from the cabin floor."

"That was my impression. Guess I'd better take a look."

"I can be there by two."

"I'll wait."

By three, Boyd and I were in the backseat of a Jeep, Crowe at the wheel, a deputy riding shotgun. Two others were behind us in a second vehicle.

The chow was as pumped as I was, though for different reasons. He rode with his head out the window, nose twisting like a weather vane in a tropical storm. Now and then I'd push down on his haunches. He'd sit, rise immediately.

The radio sputtered as we raced along the county road. Passing the Alarka Fire Department, I noted that only one reefer truck and a few cars were parked in the lot. A Bryson City cruiser guarded the entrance, its driver bent over a magazine spread across the steering wheel.

Crowe took the blacktop to its end, then the Forest

Service road, where I'd left my car three weeks earlier. Ignoring the cutoff to the crash site, she proceeded another three quarters of a mile and turned onto a different logging trail. After crawling upward for what seemed like miles, she stopped, studied the forest to either side, advanced, repeated the process, then took us off road. Our backup followed closely.

The Jeep bounced and pitched, branches scraping its top and sides. Boyd pulled in like a box turtle, and I yanked my arm from the window ledge. The dog whipped his head from right to left, spraying saliva on everyone. The deputy pulled a hanky from his pocket and wiped his neck but said nothing. I tried to remember his name. Was it Craig? Gregg?

Then the trees stepped back, yielding to a narrow dirt track. Ten minutes later, Crowe braked, alighted, and swung back what looked like an entire thicket. When we proceeded, I could see that what she'd moved was a gate, entirely overgrown with kudzu and ivy. Moments later the Arthur house came into view.

"I'll be goddamned," said the deputy. "This place in the 911 book?"

"Listed as abandoned," said Crowe. "I never knew it was here."

Crowe pulled to the front of the house and honked twice. No one appeared.

"There's a courtyard around to the side." Crowe nodded in that direction. "Tell George and Bobby to cover that entrance. We'll enter in front."

They got out, simultaneously releasing the safety

clips on their guns. As the deputy walked back to the second Jeep, Crowe turned to me.

"You stay here."

I wanted to argue, but her look told me no way.

"In the Jeep. Until I call you."

I rolled my eyes but said nothing. My heart was hammering, and I shifted about more than Boyd.

Crowe sounded another long blast on the horn while scanning the upper windows of the house. The deputy rejoined her, a Winchester pump held diagonally across his chest. They crossed to the house and climbed the steps.

"Swain County Sheriff's Department." Her call sounded tinny in the thin air. "Police. Please respond."

She banged on the door.

No one came forth.

Crowe said something. The deputy spread his feet and raised the shotgun, and the sheriff began hammering the door with her boot. There was no give.

Crowe spoke again. The deputy replied, keeping the barrel of his weapon trained on the door.

The sheriff walked back to the Jeep, sweat dampening the carrot frizz escaping her hat. She rummaged in back, returned to the porch with a crowbar.

Wiggling the tip between two shutters, she applied the full force of her body weight. A more earnest rendition of my own jimmying act.

Crowe repeated the movement, adding a Monica Seles grunt. A panel yielded slightly. Sliding the bar farther into the crack, she heaved again, and the

shutter flew back, hitting the wall with a loud crash.

Crowe laid down the bar, braced herself, then smashed a foot through the window. Glass shattered, sparkled in the sun as it showered the porch with jagged shards. Crowe kicked again and again, enlarging the opening. Boyd urged her on with excited barks.

Crowe stood back and listened. Hearing no movement, she poked her head inside and called out again. Then the sheriff unholstered her gun and disappeared into darkness. The deputy followed.

Centuries later the front door opened, and Crowe stepped onto the porch. She waved a "come on" gesture.

I leashed Boyd with clumsy hands and wrapped the loop around my wrist. Then I dug a Maglite from my pack. Blood pounded hard below my throat.

"Easy!" I aimed a finger at his nose.

He practically dragged me out of the Jeep and up the steps.

"The place is empty."

I tried to read Crowe's face, but it was registering nothing. No surprise, disgust, uneasiness. It was impossible to guess her reaction or emotion.

"Better leave the dog here."

I tied Boyd to the porch railing. Clicking on the flashlight, I followed her inside.

The air that hit me was not as musty as I expected. It smelled of smoke and mildew and something sweet.

My olfactory lobe scanned its database. Church.

Church?

The lobe separated into components. Flowers. Incense.

The front door opened directly into a parlor that spanned the entire width of the house. Slowly, I swept my light from right to left. I could make out sofas, armchairs, and occasional tables, grouped in clusters and draped with sheets. Floor-to-ceiling bookshelves covered two sides.

A stone fireplace filled the room's northern wall, an ornate mirror decorated its southern. In the dim glass I could see my beam slide among the shrouded shapes, our own two images creeping with it.

We progressed slowly, taking the house a room at a time. Dust motes swirled in the pale yellow shaft, and an occasional moth fluttered across like a startled animal in headlights on a two-lane blacktop. Behind us, the deputy held his shotgun raised. Crowe clutched her gun double-handed, close to her cheek.

The parlor opened onto a narrow hallway. Staircase on the right, dining room on the left, kitchen straight ahead.

The dining room was furnished with nothing but a highly polished rectangular table and matching chairs. I counted. Eight at each side, one at each end. Eighteen.

The kitchen was in back, its door standing wide open.

Porcelain sink. Pump. Stove and refrigerator that

had seen more birthdays than I had. I pointed to the appliances.

"Must be a generator."

"Probably downstairs."

I heard the sound of voices below, and knew her deputies were in the basement.

Upstairs, a hallway led straight down the middle of the house. Four small bedrooms radiated from the central artery, each with two sets of homemade bunks. A small spiral staircase led from the end of the hall to a third-floor attic. Tucked under the eaves were two more cots.

"Jesus," said Crowe. "Looks like Spin and Marty at the Triple R."

It reminded me of the Heaven's Gate cult in San Diego. I held my tongue.

We were circling back down when either George or Bobby appeared on the main staircase at the far end of the hall. The man was flushed and perspiring heavily.

"Sheriff, you gotta see the basement."

"What is it, Bobby?"

A bead of sweat broke from his hairline and rolled down the side of his face. He backhanded it with a jerky gesture.

"I'll be goddamned if I know."

A SET OF WOODEN STAIRS SHOT STRAIGHT FROM THE kitchen down to an underground cellar. The sheriff ordered Deputy Nameless to remain topside while the rest of us went down.

Bobby led, I followed, Crowe brought up the rear. George waited at the bottom, flashlight darting like a klieg on opening night.

As we descended, the air went from cool to refrigerator cold, and murky dimness gave way to pitch-black. I heard a click behind me, saw Crowe's beam at my feet.

We gathered at the bottom, listening.

No scurrying feet. No whirring wings. I aimed my light into the darkness.

We were in a large windowless room with a plank ceiling and cement floor. Three sides were plaster, the fourth formed by the escarpment at the back of the house. Centered in the cliff-side wall was a heavy wooden door.

When I stepped backward, my arm brushed fabric. I spun and my beam swung down a row of pegs, each holding an identical red garment. Handing my flashlight to George, I unhooked and held one up. It was a hooded robe, the type worn by monks.

"Holy mother of Jesus." I heard Bobby wipe his face. Or cross himself.

I retrieved my flash, and Crowe and I probed the room, spotlighted by George and Bobby.

A full sweep produced nothing indigenous to a basement. No worktable. No Peg-Board hung with tools. No gardening equipment. No laundry tub. No cobwebs, mouse droppings, or dead crickets.

"Pretty damn clean down here." My voice echoed off cement and stone.

"Look at this." George angled his beam to where plaster met ceiling.

A bearlike monster leered from the darkness, its body covered with gaping, bloody mouths. Below the animal was one word: *Baxbakualanuxsiwae.*

"Francis Bacon?" I asked, more to myself than to my companions.

"Bacon painted people and snarling dogs, but never anything like this." Crowe's voice was hushed.

George moved his light to the next wall, and another monster stared down. Lion mane, bulging eyes, mouth wide to devour a headless infant gripped between its hands.

"That's a bad copy of one of Goya's Black Paintings," Crowe said. "I've seen it in the Prado in Madrid."

The more I got to know the Swain County sheriff, the more she impressed me.

"Who is that creep?" George asked.

"One of the Greek gods."

A third mural depicted a raft with billowed sail. Dead and dying men littered the deck and dangled overboard into the sea.

"Enchanting," said George.

Crowe had no comment as we crossed to the rock wall.

The door was held in place by black wrought-iron hinges, drilled into stone and cemented in place. A segment of chain connected a circular wrought-iron handle to a vertical steel bar adjacent to the frame. The padlock looked shiny and new, and I could see fresh scars in the granite.

"This was added recently."

"Step back," Crowe ordered.

As we withdrew, our beams widened, illuminating words carved above the lintel. I played my light over them.

Fay ce que voudras

"French?" Crowe asked, sliding her flashlight into her belt.

"Old French, I think. . . ."

"Recognize the gargoyles?"

A figure decorated each corner of the lintel. The male was labeled "Harpocrates," the female "Angerona."

"Sounds Egyptian."

Crowe's gun exploded twice, and the smell of cordite filled the air. She stepped forward, yanked, and the chain slithered loose. There was no resistance when she lifted the latch.

She pulled on the handle and the door opened outward. Cold air rolled over us, smelling of dark hollows, sightless creatures, and epochs of time underground.

"Maybe it's time to bring him down," said Crow.

I nodded, and double-stepped up the stairs.

Boyd showed his usual exuberance at being included, prancing and snapping the air. He lapped my hand, then danced beside me into the house. Nothing on the ground floor dampened his delight.

Starting down the basement steps, I felt his body tense beside my leg.

I added an extra coil to the wrap around my hand, and allowed him to pull me down the steps and across toward Crowe.

Three feet short of the door he exploded, lunging and barking as he had at the wall. Cold prickled up my spine and across my scalp.

"All right, keep him over there," said Crowe.

Grabbing his collar with both hands, I dragged Boyd back and gave Bobby the leash. Boyd continued to growl loudly and attempted to pull Bobby forward. I rejoined Crowe.

My flash revealed a cavelike tunnel with a series of alcoves to either side. The floor was dirt, the ceiling and walls solid rock. Height to the tunnel's arched top was approximately six feet, width was about four feet. Length was impossible to tell. Beyond five yards, it was a black hole.

My pulse had not slowed since I'd entered the house. It now went for a personal best.

Slowly we crept forward, our beams probing the floor, the ceiling, the walls, the recesses. Some were nothing more than shallow indentations. Others were good-sized caves with vertical metal bars and central gates at their mouths.

"Wine cellars?" Crowe's question sounded muffled in the narrow space.

"Wouldn't there be shelving?"

"Check this out."

Crowe illuminated a name, then another, and another, chiseled the length of the tunnel. She read them aloud as we progressed.

"Sawney Beane. Innocent III. Dionysus. Moctezuma. . . . Weird bedfellows. A pope, an Aztec emperor, and the party meister himself."

"Who's Sawney Beane?" I asked.

"Hell if I kno—"

Her beam left the wall and shot straight into nothing. She threw out an arm, catching me across the chest. I froze.

Our lights leapt to the dirt at our feet. No drop-off.

We rounded the corner and inched forward, sweeping our beams from side to side. I could tell from the sound of the air that we had entered a large chamber of some sort. We were circling its perimeter wall.

The names continued. Thyestes. Polyphemus. Christie o' the Cleek. Cronus. I recognized no one from Veckhoff's diary.

Like the tunnel, the chamber gave onto a number of alcoves, some with bars, others ungated. Directly opposite our entrance point we found a wooden door, similar to that at the head of the tunnel, and secured with the same chain-and-padlock arrangement. Crowe dealt with it in the same way.

As the door swung inward, cold, foul air slithered out. Behind me I could hear Boyd barking as if possessed.

The odor of putrefaction can be altered by the mode of death, sweetened by some poisons, tinted with pear or almond or garlic by others. It can be retarded by chemicals, augmented by insect activity. But the essence is unmistakable, a heavy, fetid mix that heralds the presence of rotting flesh.

Something dead lay in that alcove.

We entered and circled left, keeping to the wall as we had in the outer chamber. Five feet in, my beam caught an irregularity on the floor. Crowe saw it at the same time.

We focused our lights on a patch of coarse, dark soil.

Wordlessly, I handed my Maglite to Crowe and

pulled a collapsible spade from my backpack. Keeping my left hand on the stone wall, I squatted and scraped at the ground with the side of the blade.

Crowe holstered her gun, hooked her hat to her belt, and trained twin beams on the ground before me.

The stain gave way easily, revealing a boundary between freshly turned earth and hard-packed floor. The smell of decay increased as I lifted soil and laid it to the side.

Within minutes I hit something soft and pale blue.

"Looks like denim." Crowe's eyes glistened, and her skin gleamed amber in the pale yellow light.

I followed the faded fabric, lengthening the opening.

Levi's, contoured around a scarecrow leg. I worked my way down to a shriveled brown foot, angled ninety degrees at the ankle.

"That's it." Crowe's voice caused my hand to jump.

"What?"

"This is no airplane passenger."

"No."

"I don't want a bad crime scene. We're shut down until I have a warrant."

I didn't argue. The victim in that pit deserved to have his or her story told in court. I would do nothing to compromise a potential prosecution.

I rose and tapped my spade against the wall, carefully removing adhering soil. Then I folded the blade, stuck it in my pack, and reached for my light.

On the hand off, the beam shot across the alcove and glinted off something in the farthest recess.

"What the hell's that?" I asked, squinting into the dark.

"Let's go."

"We should hit your magistrate with everything we can."

I picked my way toward the point where I'd seen the flash. Crowe hesitated a moment, followed.

A long bundle lay tucked against the base of the wall. The bundle was wrapped in shower curtains, one transparent, one translucent blue, and tied with several lengths of rope. I approached and ran my light over the surface.

Though blurred by layers of plastic, I could make out details in the clear upper half. Matted hair, a red plaid shirt, ghostly white hands bound at the wrists. I pulled gloves from my pack, snapped them on, and gently rolled the bundle.

Crowe's hand flew to her mouth.

A face, purple and bloated, eyes milky and half closed. Cracked lips, a bulging tongue pressed to the plastic like a giant leech.

Noticing an oval object at the base of the throat, I brought my light close. A pendant. I pulled out my knife and slit the plastic. The hiss of escaping gas was followed by an overpowering stench of putrefaction. My stomach recoiled, but I didn't pull back.

Holding my breath, I teased back the plastic with the tip of the knife.

A male silhouette was clearly visible on a small silver medal, arms crossed piously at the throat.

Engraved letters formed a halo around the head. I held the light obliquely to bring out the name.

Saint Blaise.

We had found the missing fisherman with the ailing throat. George Adair.

This time I suggested a different route. Crowe agreed. Leaving Bobby and George to secure the site, the sheriff and I drove to Bryson City and pulled Byron McMahon from a football game he was watching on the parlor TV at High Ridge House. Together we prepared an affidavit, which the special agent took directly to a federal magistrate judge in Asheville.

In less than two hours McMahon called Crowe. Based on the probability of a hate crime, and on the possible involvement of federal lands, due to the proximity of a reservation and national parks, a search warrant had been issued.

It fell to me to phone Larke Tyrell.

I found the ME at home, and, from background noise, guessed he was involved with the same football game.

Though Larke's words were cordial, I could tell my call unnerved him. I did not take time to assuage his anxiety, or to apologize for the lateness of the hour.

The ME listened while I explained the situation. Finally, I stopped. Silence stretched so long I thought we'd been disconnected.

"Larke?"

When he spoke again, his tone had changed.

"I want you to handle this. What do you need?"

I told him.

"Can you pick it up at the incident morgue?"

"Yes."

"Do you want personnel?"

"Who's still there?"

"Maggie and Stan."

Maggie Burroughs and Stan Fryeburg were death investigators with the Office of the Chief Medical Examiner in Chapel Hill, deployed to Bryson City for the processing of Air TransSouth 228. Both were graduates of my body recovery workshop at the university, and both were excellent.

"Tell them to be ready at seven."

"Roger."

"This has nothing to do with the plane crash, Larke."

"I know that. But these are dead bodies in my state."

There was another long pause. I heard an overwrought announcer, a cheering crowd.

"Tempe, I—"

I did not help him out.

"This has gone too goddamned far."

I listened to a dial tone.

What the hell did that mean?

I had other things to worry about.

The next day I was up at dawn, at the Arthur house by seven-thirty. The scene had been transformed overnight. A sheriff's deputy now stood guard at the kudzu gate, others at the front and back doors. A generator had been activated, and every light in the house was on.

When I arrived, George was helping McMahon load books and papers into cardboard boxes. Bobby was covering the mantel with white powder. As I passed on my way to the kitchen, McMahon winked and wished me good luck.

I spent the next four days like a miner, descending to the basement at dawn, surfacing at noon for a sandwich and coffee, then descending again until after dark. Another generator and lights were brought in to illuminate my underground world, so day and night became indistinguishable.

Tommy Albright arrived on the morning of day one. After examining and photographing the bundle I was certain contained George Adair, he released the body for transport to the Harris Regional Hospital in Sylva.

While Maggie worked the decomp stain inside the courtyard wall, Stan helped me photograph the cellar floor. Then we exhumed the alcove burial, slowly exposing the corpse, recording body position and grave outline, and screening every particle of dirt.

The victim lay facedown on a gray wool blanket, one arm twisted beneath the chest, the other curled around the head. Decomposition was advanced, the organs soup, the head and hands largely skeletonized.

When the remains were fully uncovered and documented, we began removal. Transferring the cadaver to a body bag, I noted that the left pants leg was badly torn, the leg missing below the knee.

I also noticed concentric fractures in the right temporo-parietal region of the skull. Linear cracks radiated up the sides of the central depression, turning the whole into a spiderweb of fragmented bone.

"Somebody really blasted this guy." Stan had stopped screening to look at the skull.

"Yes."

My outrage was building as it always did. The victim had been dealt a skull-shattering blow, then dumped in a hole like last year's mulch. What kind of monster did such things?

Another thought pierced through my anger.

This corpse was buried only inches below the ground surface. Though putrefied, considerable soft tissue remained, indicating a relatively recent death. Did earlier victims lie beneath? In other alcoves? I kept my eyes and mind open.

Maggie joined us in the basement on day two, having excavated a ten-foot square to a depth of twelve inches around and below the courtyard stain. Though the job was tedious, her efforts paid off. Two isolated teeth turned up in the screen.

While Stan finished sifting dirt from the alcove burial, Maggie and I probed every inch of the cellar floor, testing for the presence of buried objects and for differences in soil density. We found eight suspicious locations, two in the original alcove, two in the main chamber, and four in a dead-end tunnel off the chamber's west side.

By late afternoon we'd dug a test trench at each location. The suspect spots in the main room yielded only sterile soil. The other six sites produced human bone.

I explained to Stan and Maggie how we would proceed. I would request help from the sheriff's department with photography and screening. Stan would continue in the alcove. Maggie and I would begin with the tunnel sites.

I directed my crew with professional detachment, the calm of my voice and the composure of my face wildly out of sync with my pounding heart. It was my worst nightmare. But what *was* that nightmare? How many more bodies would we unearth, and why were they there?

Maggie and I were excavating the first two tunnel disturbances when a figure appeared at the entrance, caught between our spots and a light in the main chamber. I couldn't make out the silhouette, and wondered if a member of the transport team was coming to ask a question.

One step and I knew.

Larke Tyrell walked toward me, gait precise, back ramrod straight. I rose but did not greet him.

"I've been trying your portable."

"The press have me on autodial."

He did not pursue it.

"What's the count?"

"At this point, two decomposed bodies and two skeletons. There's bone in at least four other locations."

His eyes moved from my face to the pits where Maggie and I were uncovering skeletons, each with tightly flexed limbs.

"They look like prehistoric bundle burials."

"Yes, but they're not."

His gaze swung back to me.

"You would know that."

"Yes."

"Tommy sent the two decomps to Harris Regional, but they're not going to want their autopsy room tied up. I'll order everything transferred to the incident morgue and keep the place operational for as long as you need."

I did not reply.

"You will do this?"

"Of course."

"Everything is under control?"

"Here it is."

"I'm looking forward to your report."

"I have excellent penmanship."

"I thought you'd like to know that the last of the Air TransSouth passengers has been identified."

"Petricelli and the students in 22A and B?"

"Petricelli, yes. And one of the students."

"Only one?"

"Two days ago the young man assigned to seat 22B phoned his father from Costa Rica."

"He wasn't on the plane?"

"While in the waiting area, a man offered him a thousand bucks for his boarding pass."

"Why didn't he come forward earlier?"

"He was in the rain forest and completely cut off, never heard about the crash until he returned to San José. Then he hesitated a few days before calling home, knowing the jig was up for torpedoing the semester."

"Who is the substitute passenger?"

"The unluckiest bastard in the universe."

I waited.

"A tax accountant from Buckhead. We found him through a thumbprint."

He looked at me a very long moment. I stared back. The tension between us was palpable.

"This is not the place, Tempe, but we do need to talk. I am a fair man, but I have acted unfairly. There have been pressures."

"Complaints."

Though Maggie kept her eyes down, the rhythm of her trowel changed. I knew she was listening.

"Even wise people make unwise choices."

With that, he was gone.

Again, I wondered what he meant. Whose unwise choices? Mine? His? Someone else's?

The next forty-eight hours were spent with trowels and brushes and human bones. My team dug and documented while Crowe's deputies hauled and sifted dirt. Ryan brought me coffee and doughnuts and news of the crash. McMahon brought me reports on the operation upstairs. I gave him Mr. Veckhoff's diary, and explained my notes and theories during lunch breaks.

I forgot the names engraved in stone. I forgot the strange caricatures watching silently from walls and ceilings. I forgot the bizarre underground chambers and caves in which I worked.

We recovered eight people in all, the last on Halloween.

The following day we learned who blew up Air TransSouth 228.

28

"A PIPE. THE KIND THAT YOU PUT IN YOUR MOUTH and smoke."

McMahon nodded.

"In a checked bag." My voice registered my incredulity.

"An airline employee remembers telling this guy arriving at the last moment that his duffel was too large for the overhead bin and he would have to check it. The guy was sweaty and distracted, and pulled off his sport jacket and stuffed it into the duffel before giving it to a baggage handler. They're saying he left a hot pipe in the pocket of the jacket."

"What about smoke detectors? Fire detectors?"

"Baggage compartments don't have them."

Ryan, McMahon, and I were seated in folding chairs in a briefing room at NTSB central. I could see Larke Tyrell at the end of our row. The front of the room was filled with personnel of the response and investigative teams, the back crammed with journalists.

Magnus Jackson was making a statement, projecting visuals onto a screen behind him.

"Air TransSouth 228 was brought down by an unpredictable confluence of events resulting in fire, explosion, depressurization, and in-flight breakup. In that order. I'll take it step by step, take questions when I'm done."

Jackson worked the keys of a laptop, bringing up a diagram of the passenger cabin.

"On October fourth, at approximately eleven forty-five A.M. passenger Walter Lindenbaum presented himself to Air TransSouth agent James Sartore for boarding of Flight 228. Agent Sartore had just announced last call for boarding and stated that Mr. Lindenbaum was extremely agitated, concerned that his late arrival had caused the forfeiture of his seat.

"Mr. Lindenbaum had two bags, a small one and a larger canvas duffel. Agent Sartore informed Mr. Lindenbaum that there was no overhead space left for the duffel and that it was too large to fit under the seat. He tagged the bag and told Lindenbaum to leave it on the jetway and the baggage handler would take care of it. Mr. Lindenbaum then removed a knitted fabric sport jacket, put it in the duffel, and boarded the aircraft."

Jackson brought up a credit card receipt.

"Mr. Lindenbaum's credit card records reflect the purchase of a one-liter bottle of 151-proof Demerara rum on the evening prior to flight."

More keystrokes, and the receipt was replaced by several views of a charred canvas bag.

"The Lindenbaum bag and its contents, *and these objects alone, of all the artifacts recovered from the crash"*—the phrase emphasized by a hard look to the audience—"manifest geometric burn patterns showing symmetry and more combustion inside than outside."

He traced the patterns with his laser pointer.

"Interviews with family members have disclosed that Walter Lindenbaum was a pipe smoker. He was of the habit when entering a no-smoking area of slipping his pipe into his pocket and relighting it later. All evidence points to the presence of a smoldering pipe in the pocket of the Lindenbaum jacket when that jacket went into the cargo bay."

A murmur spread through the back of the room. Hands shot up and questions were shouted. Jackson ignored them as he projected additional pictures of burned clothing, unfolded then folded.

"Inside the baggage compartment, fragments of smoldering tobacco and ash spilled from the pipe bowl and communicated incandescent combustion to surrounding fabrics in the bag, generating what we call a hot spot."

More shots of burned canvas and clothing.

"Let me repeat. Geometric burn patterns have been found on no other items recovered from the wreckage. I'm not going to go into it here, but the press release explains how evidence of slow burning of folded clothes inside the bag cannot be explained by anything that occurred *after* a midair explosion."

The next visual showed smoke-blackened fragments of glass.

"Mr. Lindenbaum's rum bottle. Inside the loosely packed duffel, smoke spread at a temperature consistent with that of the localized combustion, a temperature warmer than the bottle and its contents, which were not involved in the combustion process. The bottle remained intact, and smoke was deposited on it. These deposits, seen in this view, have been analyzed by our lab. The products of decomposition present in the smoke are consistent with the point of origin as I am describing it. Traces of tobacco smoke were positively identified on the bottle, among other traces, especially since forensic analysis also disposed of unburned tobacco strands in the pipe bowl as reference."

Jackson switched to a diagram of the plane.

"In the Fokker-100, fuel lines run under the cabin floor, above the baggage compartments, from wing tanks to aft-mounted engines."

He traced the route with his pointer, clicked to a close-up of a fuel line, then zoomed in on a fitting.

"Our structures team has found evidence of a fatigue crack in a fuel line fitting where it passes through the bulkhead at the rear of the baggage compartment. In all likelihood, this crack was generated by a flawed through-fitting acting as a stress riser."

A magnified image of a hairline fracture filled the screen.

"Heat from the incandescent combustion in Mr. Lindenbaum's duffel aggravated the crack, allowing minute quantities of vaporized fuel to dissipate from the line into the hold."

He brought up a dirty and discolored chunk of metal casting.

"Localized heat degradation, manifested in localized discoloration, is clearly recognizable on the fuel line at the point of failure due to heat exposure. I'll go to simulation now."

Keys clicked, the screen went blank, then filled with an animation of an F-100 in flight. Time ticked in one-second increments at the top of the screen.

The Lindenbaum duffel could be seen high in the left rear of the baggage compartment, immediately below seats 23A and B. I watched it ooze from pink, to salmon, to red, a cold lump in the pit of my stomach.

"Incandescent combustion in the duffel," Jackson narrated. "A first ignition sequence."

Pale blue specks began to seep from the bag.

"Smoke."

The particles formed a fine, transparent mist.

"The baggage compartment is pressurized the same as the passenger cabin, meaning it is supplied with air containing an adequate proportion of oxygen. The significance is that there is a lot of warm air moving around down there."

The mist slowly dispersed. Red colored the ends of the Lindenbaum suitcase.

"Though it was contained at first, the smoke eventually spread from the duffel. The heat eventually pierced, and then there was a development to laminar flaming combustion outside the duffel, igniting the suitcases on each side and giving off dense smoke."

Tiny black dots appeared at a fuel line running along the inner wall of the baggage compartment. I stared, mesmerized, as the dots multiplied and slowly descended, or were entrained in the ambient air movement.

"Then began the second ignition sequence. When fuel began to dissipate out of the pressurized line, the quantity was so minute it vaporized and mixed with the air. As the fuel expanded in a vapor state it sank, since fuel fumes are heavier than ambient air. At that point an odor would have been present and easily detected."

Traces of blue appeared in the passenger cabin.

"Smoke seeped into the cabin through the ventilation, heating, and air-conditioning system, and eventually to the exterior via the pressurization outflow valve."

I thought of Jean Bertrand. Had he noticed the odor? Seen the smoke?

There was a flash, red spread outward from the Lindenbaum suitcase, and a jagged hole appeared in the rear of the baggage compartment.

"Twenty minutes and twenty-one seconds into the flight, vaporized fuel crossed a wire bundle, which apparently contained some arcing wires, and ignited in a deafening detonation. This explosion can be heard on the cockpit voice recorder."

I remembered Ryan's account of the pilot's last words, felt the same helplessness he had described.

"The circuit failed."

I thought of the passengers. Had they felt the shock? Heard the explosion? Did they realize they were going to die?

"The initial explosion blew from the pressurized baggage compartment into the unpressurized fuselage behind, and air loads began tearing parts from the plane. At that point, more fuel escaped from the line and flaming fire ensued in the hold."

Jackson identified items as they separated and fell to the ground.

"Skin from the aft fuselage. Speed brakes."

The room was deathly quiet.

"Air loads then blew up through the vertical tail and dislodged the horizontal stabilizer and elevators."

The plane in the animation pitched nose down and plunged toward the ground, the passenger cabin still intact. Jackson hit a key and the screen went blank.

No one seemed to breathe or move. Seconds passed. I heard a sob, or perhaps only a deep breath. A cough. Then the room exploded.

"Mr. Jackson—"

"Why weren't smoke detect—"

"Mr. Jack—"

"How long—"

"I'll take questions one at a time."

Jackson pointed to a woman with Buddy Holly frames.

"How long would it have taken to raise the temperature in the duffel to the point of fire?"

"Let me clarify one thing. We're talking about incandescence, a glowing type of combustion generated when the little oxygen available comes in direct contact with a solid, like coals or embers. This is not flaming combustion. In a small volume like the bag's interior, incandescence could be quickly established and maintained at around five hundred to six hundred degrees Fahrenheit."

His finger found another journalist.

"How could the rum bottle survive the fire in the bag?"

"Easy. On the other end of the temperature spectrum, incandescence can reach eleven hundred to twelve hundred degrees Fahrenheit, the temperature of a lit pipe or cigarette. That's hardly enough to alter a glass bottle containing liquid."

"And the smoke deposits would remain on the bottle?"

"Yes. Unless it was subjected to a very intense and sustained fire, which was not the case, as it occurred inside the suitcase."

The finger moved.

"The metal fatigue marks survived as well?"

"To melt steel you need temperatures of twenty-five hundred degrees Fahrenheit or more. Beach marks, your typical evidence of fatigue, generally survive fires of the intensity I'm describing."

He pointed to a reporter from the *Charlotte Observer.*

"Did the passengers know what was happening?"

"Those seated close to the flash point would have felt the shock. Everyone would have heard the explosion."

"What about smoke?"

"Smoke would have seeped into the passenger cabin via the heating and air-conditioning system."

"Were the passengers conscious the whole time?"

"The type of combustion I've described can give off noxious gases which may affect people very quickly."

"How quickly?"

"The old, the young, perhaps as fast as ninety seconds."

"Could these gases have gotten into the passenger compartment?"

"Yes."

"Have traces of smoke or noxious gases been found in the victims?"

"Yes. Dr. Tyrell is going to make a statement shortly."

"With so much smoke, how can you be sure about the source of the deposits on the rum bottle?" The questioner looked about sixteen.

"Fragments of the Lindenbaum pipe were recovered, and reference studies were conducted using unburned strands of tobacco adhering to the inside of the bowl. The deposits on the bottle were the by-products of the combustion of that tobacco."

"How could there have been a fuel leak?" Shouted from the back.

"When fire broke out in the hold, flame impingement affected only a segment of the fuel line. This pulled the wall of the line, or induced a stress that opened very slightly the seed failure."

Jackson called on a reporter who looked and sounded like Dick Cavett.

"Are you telling us that the initial fire did not directly cause the explosion?"

"Yes."

"What caused the explosion?" he persisted.

"An electrical failure. That's the second ignition sequence."

"How sure can you be?"

"Reasonably certain. When electricity sparks an explosion, the electrical energy is not lost, it must ground. Damage due to electrical grounding has been identified on the same segment of fuel line. Such damage is normally seen on copper items and rather seldom on steel parts."

"I can't believe that the fire in the suitcase didn't cause the explosion." Cavett made little attempt to hide his skepticism. "Wouldn't that be more normal?"

"Your question makes sense. It's really what we thought at first, but you see, the fumes are not yet mixed enough with air at such short distance from the source of emission. The fumes must mix before ignition can occur, but when it does, the blast is deafening."

Another hand.

"Was the analysis done by certified fire and explosion specialists?"

"Yes. Outside experts were brought in."

Another questioner stood.

Eighty-eight people were dead because one man was preoccupied about losing his seat. The whole thing was a tragic mistake.

I looked at my watch. Crowe would be waiting.

Feeling numb, I slipped from the room. I had victims waiting whose deaths were not due to simple carelessness.

The reefer trucks were gone from the grounds of the Alarka Fire Department. The lot held only the company's displaced engines and the vehicles of those assisting me. A single deputy guarded the entrance.

Crowe was there when I arrived. Seeing me, she climbed from her cruiser, collected a small leather case, and waited. The sky was pewter, and a cold wind was tearing through the gorge. Gusts teased her hat brim, subtly reshaping it around her face.

I joined her, and we entered what was now a different type of incident morgue. Stan and Maggie worked at autopsy tables, arranging bones where crash victims recently had lain. Four tables held unopened cardboard boxes.

I greeted my team and hurried to the cubicle I was using as an office. As I exchanged my jacket for a lab coat, Crowe took the chair opposite my desk, zipped open the case, and withdrew several folders.

"Nineteen seventy-nine came up zilch. All MPs accounted for. There were two from 1972."

She opened the first folder.

"Mary Francis Rafferty, white female, age eighty-one. Lived alone over in Dillsboro. Her daughter checked on her every Saturday. One week Rafferty wasn't in her home. Never seen again. It was presumed she wandered off and died of exposure."

"How often have we heard that?"

She went to the next folder.

"Sarah Ellen Deaver, white female, age nineteen. Left home to go to her job at a convenience store on Highway 74. Never got there."

"I doubt we've got Deaver out there. Anything from Tommy Albright?"

"George Adair's positive," Crowe confirmed.

"Dental?" I asked.

"Yes." Pause. "You know that first alcove burial was missing its left foot?"

"Albright phoned me."

"Jeremiah Mitchell's daughter thought she recognized some of the clothing. We're getting blood from a sister."

"Albright asked me to cut bone samples. Tyrell's promised to rush them through. Did you check the other dates?"

"Albert Odell's family provided the name of his dentist."

"He's the apple farmer?" I asked.

"Odell's the only MP still out from eighty-six."

"Many dentists don't keep records past ten years."

"Dr. Welch didn't sound like the brightest bulb in the marquee. I'm driving over to Lauada this afternoon to see what he has."

"What about the others?" I knew what her answer would be even as I asked the question.

"The others will be tough. It's been over fifty years for Adams and Farrell, over forty for Tramper."

She withdrew three more folders and laid everything on my desk.

"Here's what I've managed to dig up." She stood. "I'll let you know what I get from the dentist."

When she'd gone I spent a few moments perusing the folders. The one for Tucker Adams contained only the press items I'd already seen.

Edna Farrell's record was a little better, and included handwritten notes taken at the time of her disappearance. There was a statement by Sandra Jane Farrell, giving an account of Edna's last days and a detailed physical description. Edna had fallen from a horse as a young woman, and Sandra described her mother's face as "lopsided."

I snatched up a black-and-white snapshot with

scalloped edges. Though the image was blurry, the facial asymmetry was obvious.

"Way to go, Edna."

There were photos of Charlie Wayne Tramper, and his disappearance and death were reported in several newspaper articles. Otherwise, there was little in the way of written information.

The following days were like the first I'd spent at the Alarka Fire Department, living with the dead from dawn until dusk. Hour after hour I sorted and arranged bones, determined sex and race, estimated age and height. I searched for indicators of old injury, past illness, congenital peculiarity, or repetitive movement. For each skeleton I built as complete a profile as was possible working from remains devoid of living tissue.

In a way, it was like processing a crash, where names are known from the passenger roster. Based on Veckhoff's diary, I was convinced I had a limited population because the dates entered in his lists matched precisely the disappearance dates of seniors from Swain and adjoining counties: 1943, Tucker Adams; 1949, Edna Farrell; 1959, Charlie Wayne Tramper; 1986, Albert Odell.

Believing them to be the earliest in time, we started with the four tunnel burials. While Stan and Maggie cleaned, sorted, numbered, photographed, and X-rayed, I studied bones.

I found Edna Farrell early. Skeleton number four

was that of an elderly female whose right cheekbone and jawbone deviated sharply from the midline due to fractures that had healed without proper intervention.

Skeleton number five was incomplete, lacking portions of the rib cage, arms, and lower legs. Animal damage was extensive. Pelvic features told me the individual was male and old. A globular skull, flaring cheekbones, and shoveling on the front teeth suggested Native-American ancestry. Statistical analysis placed the skull squarely in the Mongoloid camp. Charlie Wayne Tramper?

Number six, the most deteriorated of the skeletons, was that of an elderly Caucasoid male who had been toothless at the time of his death. Save for a height estimate of over six feet, I found no unique markers on the bones. Tucker Adams?

Skeleton number three was that of an elderly male with healed fractures of the nose, maxilla, third, fourth, and fifth ribs, and right fibula. A long, narrow skull, Quonset hut nasal bridge, smooth nasal border, and anterior projection of the lower face suggested the man was black. So did the Fordisc 2.0 program. I suspected he was the 1979 victim.

Next, I examined the skeletons found in the alcove with Mitchell and Adair.

Skeleton number two was that of an elderly white male. Arthritic changes in the right shoulder and arm bones suggested repeated extension of the hand above the head. Apple picking? Based on the state of preservation, I guessed this individual had died more recently than those buried in the tunnel graves. The apple farmer, Albert Odell?

Skeleton number one was that of an elderly white female with advanced arthritis and only seven teeth. Mary Francis Rafferty, the woman from Dillsboro whose daughter had found her mother's house empty in 1972?

By late afternoon Saturday, I felt confident I had matched the bones with their proper names. Lucy Crowe helped by finding Albert Odell's dental records, the Reverend Luke Bowman by remembering Tucker Adams's height. Six foot three.

And I had a pretty good idea as to manner of death.

The hyoid is a small, horseshoe-shaped bone embedded in the soft tissue of the neck, high up behind the lower jaw. In the elderly, whose bones are often brittle, the hyoid fractures when its wings are compressed. The most common source of compressive force is strangulation.

Tommy Albright phoned as I was preparing to close up.

"Find any more hyoid fractures?"

"Five out of the six."

"Mitchell, too. He must have put up a helluva fight. When they couldn't strangle him, they smashed his head in."

"Adair?"

"No. But there's petechial hemorrhage."

Petechiae are minute blood clots that appear as

dots in the eyes and throat, and are strong indicators of asphyxiation.

"Who the hell would want to strangle old people?"

I did not answer. I'd seen other trauma on the skeletons. Trauma I found puzzling. Trauma I would not mention until I understood more.

When he hung up, I went to burial four, picked up the thighbones, and brought them to the magnifier light.

Yes. It was there. It was real.

I collected the femora from every skeleton, and took the bones to a dissecting scope.

Tiny grooves circled each right proximal shaft and ran the length of each linea aspera, the roughened ridge for muscle attachment on the back side of the bone. Other gashes ran horizontally, above and below the joint surfaces. Though the number of marks varied, their distribution was consistent from victim to victim.

I cranked the magnification as high as it would go.

When I focused, the grooves crystallized into sharp-edged crevices, V-shaped in cross section.

Cut marks. But how could that be? I'd seen cut marks on bone, but only in cases of dismemberment. Except for Charlie Wayne Tramper and Jeremiah Mitchell, these individuals had been buried whole.

Then why? And why only the right femora? *Was* it only the right femora?

I was about to begin a reexamination of every bone when Andrew Ryan burst through the door.

Maggie, Stan, and I looked up, startled.

"Have you been listening to the news?" Ryan asked, flushed and perspiring despite the coolness.

We shook our heads.

"Parker Davenport was found dead about three hours ago."

"Dead?"

Emotions snapped inside me. Shock. Pity. Anger. Wariness.

"How?"

"A single bullet to the brain. An aide found him at his home."

"A suicide?"

"Or a setup."

"Is Tyrell doing the post?"

"Yeah."

"Has it hit the media?"

"Oh, yeah. They're pissing their pants for information."

Relief. The pressure would lift from me. Guilt. A man is dead and you think first of yourself.

"But the thing's wrapped tighter than the U.S. war plan."

"Did Davenport leave a note?"

"None found. What's up here?" He gestured toward the autopsy tables.

"Got some time?"

"The crash was due to carelessness and mechanical failure." He spread his arms. "I'm a free man."

The wall clock said seven forty-five. I told Stan and Maggie to call it a day, then led Ryan to my cubicle and explained the Veckhoff diary.

"You're suggesting that random elderly persons were murdered following the deaths of prominent citizens?" He tried but failed to keep the skepticism from his voice.

"Yes."

"And no one noticed."

"The disappearances weren't frequent enough to suggest a pattern, and the selection of aged victims created less of a ripple."

"And this granny-napping has been going on for half a century."

"Longer."

It did sound preposterous, and this made me edgy. When edgy, I get mouthy.

"And gramps was fair game, too."

"And the perps used the Arthur house to dispose of the bodies."

"Yes, but for more than just disposing."

"And this was some sort of group in which everyone had a code name."

"Has," I snapped.

Silence.

"Are you talking cult?"

"No. Yes. I don't know. I don't think so. But I do think the victims were used in some sort of ritual."

"Why is that?"

"Come with me."

I walked him from table to table, making introductions and pointing out details. Finally, I took him to the dissecting scope and focused the lens on Edna Farrell's right femur. When he'd studied it, I inserted one of Tucker Adams's thighbones. Rafferty. Odell.

The pattern was unmistakable. Same nicks. Same distribution.

"What are they?"

"Cut marks."

"As in knife?"

"Something with a sharp blade."

"What do they mean?"

"I don't know."

Each bone made a soft thunk as I replaced it on the stainless steel. Ryan watched me, his face unreadable.

My heels clicked loudly as I crossed to the sink, then walked to my cubicle to remove my lab coat and put on my jacket. When I returned, Ryan was standing over the skeleton I believed to be the apple farmer, Albert Odell.

"So you know who they are."

"Except for that gentleman." I indicated the elderly black male.

"And you think they were strangled."

"Yes."

"What the hell for?"

"Talk to McMahon. That's police work."

Ryan followed me out to the parking lot. As I was sliding behind the wheel, he shot off one more question.

"What kind of twisted mutant would snatch old people, choke them to death, and play with their bodies?"

The answer would come from an unexpected source.

Back at High Ridge House, I made myself a ham salad sandwich, grabbed a bag of Sunchips and a handful of sugar cookies, and headed out to dine with Boyd. Though I apologized profusely for my negligence over the past week, his eyebrows barely moved, and his tongue remained firmly out of sight. The dog was annoyed.

More guilt. More self-censure.

After giving Boyd the sandwich, chips, and cookies, I filled his bowls with water and chow, and promised him a long walk the following day. He was sniffing the Alpo as I slipped away.

I reprovisioned myself and took the snack to my room. A note lay on the floor. Based on the mode of delivery, I suspected it had come from McMahon.

It had. He asked that I stop by FBI headquarters the next day.

I wolfed down my dinner, took a hot bath, and phoned a colleague at UNC-Chapel Hill. Though it was past eleven, I knew Jim's routine. No morning classes. Home around six. After dinner, a five-mile run, then back to his archaeology lab until 2 A.M. Except when excavating, Jim was nocturnal.

After greetings and a brief catch-up, I asked for his help.

"Doing some archaeology?"

"It's more fun than my usual work," I said non-committally.

I described the strange nicks and striations without revealing the nature of the victims.

"How old is this stuff?"

"Not that old."

"It's odd that the marks are restricted to a single bone, but the pattern you're describing sounds suspicious. I'm going to fax you three recent articles and a number of my own photos."

I thanked him and gave him the morgue number.

"Where is that?"

"Swain County."

"You working with Midkiff?"

"No."

"Someone told me he was digging up there."

Next, I phoned Katy. We talked about her classes, about Boyd, about a skirt she'd seen in the Victoria's Secret catalog. We made plans for the beach at Thanksgiving. I never mentioned the murders or my growing trepidation.

After the phone call, I climbed into bed and lay in the dark, visualizing the skeletons we'd recovered from the cellar. Though I'd never seen an actual case, I knew in my heart what the strange marks meant.

But why?

I felt horror. I felt disbelief. Then I felt nothing until the sun warmed my face at 7 A.M.

Jim's photos and articles lay on the fax machine when I arrived at the morgue. *Nature, Science,* and *American Antiquity.* I read each and studied his pictures. Then I reexamined every skull and long bone, taking Polaroids of anything that looked suspicious.

Still, I could not believe it. Ancient times, ancient peoples, yes. These things didn't happen in modern America.

A sudden synapse.

One more phone call. Colorado. Twenty minutes later, another fax.

I stared at it, the paper trembling slightly in my hand.

Dear God. It was undeniable.

I found McMahon at his temporary headquarters in the Bryson City Fire Department. As with the incident morgue, the function of the FBI office had changed. McMahon and his colleagues had shifted their focus from crash to crime scene investigation, their paradigm from terrorism to homicide.

Space formerly occupied by the NTSB was now empty, and several cubicles had been merged to create what looked like a task force squad room. Bulletin boards that had once featured the names of terrorist groups and militant radicals now held those of eight murder victims. In one cluster, the positive IDs: Edna Farrell. Albert Odell. Jeremiah Mitchell. George Adair. In another, the unknown and those still in question: John Doe. Tucker Adams. Charlie Wayne Tramper. Mary Francis Rafferty.

Though every name was accompanied by a date of disappearance, the amount and type of information varied considerably from board to board.

On the opposite end of the room, more boards displayed photos of the Arthur house. I recognized the attic cots, the dining room table, the great room fireplace. I was examining shots of the basement murals when McMahon joined me.

"Cheerful stuff."

"Sheriff Crowe thought that was a copy of a Goya."

"She's right. It's *Saturn Devouring His Children.*"

He tapped a photo of the raft scene.

"This one's by Théodore Géricault. Know him?"

I shook my head.

"It's called *The Raft of Medusa.*"

"What's the story?"

"We're checking."

"Who's the bear?"

"Same answer. We ran the name but came up with zip. Can't be that many Baxbakualanuxsiwaes out there."

He removed a thumbtack with his nail and handed me a list.

"Familiar with anyone on the playbill?"

"The names from the tunnel walls?"

"Yeah. Special Agent Rayner's working them."

Three folding tables lined the back of the room. One held a computer, the others cardboard boxes, each marked with date and provenance: *Kitchen drawer L3. Living room, north wall bookcase.* Other boxes were stacked on the floor.

A young man in shirtsleeves and tie worked at the computer. I'd seen him at the Arthur house, but we hadn't met. McMahon gestured from the agent to me.

"Roger Rayner, Tempe Brennan."

Rayner looked up and smiled, then went back to his monitor.

"We've nailed a few of the more obvious players. The Greek and Roman gods, for example."

I noted comments following some names. Cronus. Dionysus. The Daughters of Mineus. The Daughters of Pelias. Polyphemus.

"And the pope and the Aztec emperor popped right up. But who the hell is Dasakumaracarita? Or Abd al-Latif? Or Hamatsa?" He pronounced the names syllable by syllable. "At least I can say 'Sawney Beane' or 'John Gregg.'"

He ran a hand through his hair and it did its rooster thing.

"I figured an anthropologist might recognize some obscure goddess or something."

I was staring at one name, my nerve cells tingling. Hamatsa.

Moctezuma. The Aztecs.

Saturn devouring his children.

"Is there somewhere we can talk in private?" My voice sounded high and shaky.

McMahon gave me an odd look, then led me into an adjacent cubicle.

I took a moment to collect my thoughts.

"What I'm about to say is going to sound ludicrous, but I'd like you to hear me out."

He leaned back and laced his fingers across his paunch.

"Among the Kwakiutl of the Pacific Northwest, the Hamatsa were a society of tribal elite. Young men who hoped to become Hamatsa went through a lengthy period of isolation."

"Like fraternity pledges."

"Yes. During their time in the forest the initiates would periodically appear on the outskirts of the village, demented and screaming, charge in, bite flesh from the arms and chests of those unfortunate enough to be present, then disappear back into the woods."

McMahon's eyes were on his hands.

"Shortly before the end of his exile, each initiate was brought a mummy that had been soaked in salt water, cleaned, and split open. The initiate was expected to smoke-cure the corpse for the final ritual."

I swallowed.

"During that ritual the aspirant and senior members of the brotherhood devoured portions of the corpse."

McMahon did not look at me.

"Are you familiar with the Aztecs?"

"Yes."

"They appeased their gods through the ritual eating of human beings."

"Cannibalism?"

McMahon's eyes finally met mine.

"On a grand scale. When Cortés and his men entered Moctezuma's capital, Tenochtitlán, they found mounds of human skulls in the city square, others impaled on spikes. Their estimate was over one hundred thousand."

Silence. Then, "Saturn ate his children."

"Polyphemus captured Ulysses and dined on his crew."

"Why the pope?"

"I'm not sure."

McMahon disappeared, returned in a moment.

"Rayner's looking him up."

He looked at a note, scratched a clump of hair.

"Rayner found the Géricault painting. It's based on the 1816 wreck of a French frigate, *La Méduse*. According to the story, survivors ate the dead while stranded at sea."

I was about to show McMahon my own findings when Rayner appeared in the doorway. We listened as he read from scribbled notes.

"I don't think you want the old boy's entire résumé, so I'll give you the highlights. Pope Innocent III is best known for organizing the Fourth Lateran Council in twelve fifteen A.D. Anyone who was anyone in Christendom was told to get his butt to this meeting."

He looked up.

"I'm paraphrasing. With all the honchos convened, Innocent decreed that henceforth the words *hoc est corpus meum* were to be taken literally, and the faithful were required to believe in transubstantiation. That's the idea that, at Mass, the bread and wine are changed into the body and blood of Christ."

He looked up again to see if we were with him.

"Innocent decreed that the act isn't symbolic, it's real. Apparently this question had been debated for about a thousand years, so Innocent decided to settle the issue. From then on, if you doubted transubstantiation, you were guilty of heresy."

"Thanks, Roger."

"No problem." He withdrew.

"So what's the link?" McMahon asked.

"Innocent defined the most sacred ceremonial act of Christianity as true God-eating. It's what anthropologists call ritual anthropophagy."

A childhood memory. A nun in traditional habit, crucifix on her breast, chalk on her hands.

"Do you know the origin of the word *host*?"

McMahon shook his head.

"*Hostia*. It means 'sacrificial victim' in Latin."

"You think we're dealing with some fringe group that gets high on cannibalism?"

I took a steadying breath.

"I think it's much worse than that."

"Worse than what?"

We both turned. Ryan stood in the spot recently occupied by Rayner. McMahon gestured at a chair.

"Worse than drooling over myths and allegorical paintings. I'm glad you're here, Ryan. You can verify what I'm about to describe."

I pulled Jim's photos from my briefcase and handed the first to McMahon.

"That is the reconstructed leg bone of a red deer. The gashes were made with a sharp instrument, probably a stone knife. Notice how they cluster around the tendon and ligament attachment points, and at the joints."

McMahon passed the photo to Ryan, and I handed him several more.

"Those are also animal bones. Notice the similar distribution of cut marks and striations."

Next picture.

"Those are fragments of human bone. They were recovered from the same cave in southeastern France where the animal bones were found."

"Looks like the same pattern."

"It is."

"Meaning?"

"Butchery. The bones were stripped of flesh and cut or twisted apart at the joints."

"How old is this stuff?"

"One hundred thousand to one hundred and twenty thousand years. The site was occupied by Neanderthals."

"Is this relevant?"

I gave him several more prints.

"Those are also human bones. They were recovered at a site near Mesa Verde, in southwestern Colorado."

"Anasazi?" Ryan asked, reaching for a photo.

"Yes."

"Who are the Anasazi?" McMahon.

"Ancestors of groups like the Hopi and Zuni. This site was occupied by a small group around 1130 to 1150 A.D., during a period of extreme drought. A colleague from Chapel Hill did the digging. These are his photos. At least thirty-five adults and kids were butchered. Notice that the pattern is identical."

I fed them another photo.

"Those are stone tools found in association with the human bones. Tests confirmed the presence of human blood."

Another.

"That ceramic cooking pot held the residue of human tissues."

"How can they be sure these marks aren't caused by abrasion? Or by animals? Or by some sort of burial ritual? Maybe they cut up the dead to prepare them for the afterlife. That could explain the bloody tools and pot."

"That was exactly the argument until this was discovered."

I passed them another photo.

"What the hell is that?" McMahon gave it to Ryan.

"After seven people were killed, cooked, and eaten in a small underground room at this site, one of the diners squatted over the cold hearth and defecated."

"Holy shit."

"Exactly. Archaeologists call preserved feces coprolites. Biochemical tests showed traces of digested human muscle protein in this particular beauty."

"Could the protein have gotten there by some other route?"

"Not myoglobin. Tests also showed this guy had eaten almost nothing but meat for eighteen hours prior to his grand gesture."

"That is great stuff, Tempe, but I've got eight stiffs and a pack of reporters breathing down my neck. Other than perps with a morbid taste in art and literature, how is this relevant? You're showing me people who have been dead for centuries."

I placed three more photos on his desk.

"Ever heard of Alfred G. Packer?"

He glanced at his watch, then at the pictures.

"No."

"Alfie Packer is reputed to have killed and eaten five people in Colorado during the winter of 1874. He was tried and convicted of murder. The victims were recently exhumed and analyzed."

"What the hell for?"

"Historic accuracy."

Ryan circled behind McMahon. As the two men studied the bones of the Packer victims, I got up and spread my Polaroids across the desk.

"I took these at the morgue this morning."

Like spectators at a tennis match, their eyes shifted among the Neanderthals, the Anasazi, the Packer victims, and my Polaroids. For a very long time no one spoke.

McMahon broke the silence.

"Jesus, Mary, and Joseph in a bloody pear tree."

30

N O ONE HAD ANYTHING TO ADD TO THAT.

"Who the hell are these lunatics?" Ryan's question broke the silence.

McMahon responded.

"The H&F Investment Group is buried under more layers than Olduvai Gorge. Veckhoff's dead, so he's not talking. Following up on your suggestion, Tempe, we tracked down Rollins and Birkby through their fathers. Rollins lives in Greenville, teaches English at a community college. Birkby owns a chain of discount furniture stores, has homes in Rock Hill and Hilton Head. Each gentleman tells the same story: inherited his interest in H&F, knows nothing about the property, never visited there."

I heard a door open, voices in the corridor.

"W. G. Davis is a retired investment banker living in Banner Elk. F. M. Payne is a philosophy professor at Wake Forest. Warren's an attorney in Fayetteville.

We found the counselor on his way to the airport, had to spoil his little getaway to Antigua."

"Do they admit to knowing one another?"

"Everyone tells the same story. H&F is strictly business, they never met. Never set foot on the property."

"What about prints inside the house?"

"The recovery team lifted zillions. We're running them but it will take time."

"Any police records?"

"Payne, the professor, was busted for pot in seventy-four. Otherwise, nothing came up. But we're checking every cell these guys have ever shed. If one of them peed on a tree at Woodstock, we'll get a sample. These assholes are dirty as hell, and they're going down for murder."

Larke Tyrell appeared in the doorway. Deep lines creased his forehead. McMahon greeted him, went in search of additional seating. Tyrell spoke to me.

"I'm glad you're here."

I said nothing.

McMahon returned with a folding metal chair. Tyrell sat, his spine so erect it made no contact with the backrest.

"What can I do for you, Doc?" McMahon.

Tyrell removed a handkerchief, wiped his fore-head, then refolded the linen in a perfect square.

"I have information that is highly sensitive."

The Andy Griffith eyes shifted from face to face, but he did not say the obvious.

"I'm sure you are all aware that Parker Davenport died of a gunshot wound yesterday. The wound appears to be self-inflicted, but there are disturbing elements, including an extremely high level of trifluoperazine in his blood."

We all looked blank.

"The common name is Stelazine. The drug is used in the treatment of psychotic anxiety and agitated depressions. Davenport had no prescription for Stelazine, and his doctor knows of no reason he would be taking it."

"A man in his position wouldn't have trouble getting what he wanted." McMahon.

"That's true, sir."

Tyrell cleared his throat.

"Minute traces of trifluoperazine were also detected in the body of Primrose Hobbs, but immersion and decomposition had complicated the picture, so a definitive finding was not possible."

"Does Sheriff Crowe know this?" I asked.

"She knows about Hobbs. I'll tell her about Davenport when I leave here."

"Stelazine wasn't found among Hobbs's belongings."

"Nor did she have a prescription."

My stomach tightened. I had never seen Primrose take so much as an aspirin.

"Equally disturbing are phone calls made by Davenport on the evening of his death," Larke went on.

Tyrell handed McMahon a list.

"You may recognize some of the numbers."

McMahon scanned the printout, then looked up.

"Sonofabitch. The lieutenant governor phoned the H&F officers just hours before blowing his brains out?"

"What?" I blurted.

"Or had them blown out." Ryan.

McMahon passed me the list. Six numbers, five names. W. G. Davis, F. M. Payne, F. L. Warren, C. A. Birkby, P. H. Rollins.

"What was the sixth call?"

"The number traces to a rented cabin in Cherokee. Sheriff Crowe is checking it out."

"Tempe, show Dr. Tyrell what you just showed me."

McMahon reached for his phone.

"It's time to run these bastards to ground."

Larke wanted to examine the marks firsthand, so we went straight to the morgue. Though I'd had nothing since coffee at seven, and it was after one, I had no appetite. I kept seeing Primrose, wondering what she'd discovered. What threat she'd posed. And a new question: Was her murder linked to the death of the lieutenant governor?

Larke and I spent an hour going over the bones, the ME looking and listening closely, now and then asking a question. We'd just finished when my cell phone rang.

Lucy Crowe was in Waynesville but had something she needed to discuss. Could we meet around nine at High Ridge House? I agreed.

As we were disconnecting she asked a question.

"Do you know an archaeologist named Simon Midkiff?"

"Yes."

"He may be involved with this H&F bunch."

"Midkiff?"

"His was the sixth number Davenport dialed before his death. If he tries to contact you, agree to nothing."

As we talked, Larke photocopied the pictures and articles. When he was done, I told him what Crowe had said. He posed a single question.

"Why?"

"Because they're crazy," I answered, still distracted by Crowe's comment about Midkiff.

"And Parker Davenport was one of them."

He slid the photocopies into his briefcase, impaled me with exhausted eyes.

"He tried professional sabotage to keep you from that house." Larke swept an arm in the direction of the tables. "To divert you from this."

I did not reply.

"And I was suckered in."

Still, I remained silent.

"Is there anything I can say to you?"

"There are things you can say to my colleagues."

"Letters will go to the AAFS, the ABFA, and the NDMS immediately." He grabbed my wrist. "And I will phone the head of each organization first thing Monday to explain personally."

"And the press?" Though I knew he was suffering, I could force no warmth into my voice. His disloyalty had hurt me, professionally and personally.

"That will come. I must determine how best to handle it."

Best for whom? I wondered.

"If it's any consolation, Earl Bliss acted on my orders. He never believed anything against you."

"Most who know me did not."

He released my arm but his eyes held firm. Overnight he'd come to look like a tired old man.

"Tempe, I was trained as a military man. I believe in respecting the chain of command and carrying out the lawful orders of my superiors. That predisposition led me not to question things I should have questioned. The abuse of power is a terrible thing. Failure to resist corrupting pressure is equally contemptible. It's time for this old dog to rouse and get off the porch."

I felt a deep sadness as I watched him leave. Larke and I had been friends for many years. I wondered if we could ever be friends again.

As I made coffee, my thoughts shifted to Simon Midkiff. Of course. It all made sense. His intense interest in the crash site. The lies about excavating in Swain County. The photo with Parker Davenport at Charlie Wayne Tramper's funeral. He was one of them.

A sudden flashback. The black Volvo that had

almost run me down. The man at the wheel had looked vaguely familiar. Could it have been Simon Midkiff?

I was completing my report on Edna Farrell when my cell phone rang a second time.

"Sir Francis Dashwood was a prolific guy."

The statement came from a different galaxy than the one in which my mind was orbiting.

"I'm sorry?"

"It's Anne. I was organizing stuff from our London trip and came across a pamphlet Ted bought at the West Wycombe caves."

"Anne, this is not—"

"There are gobs of Dashwoods still around."

"Gobs?"

"Descendants of Sir Francis, later known as Lord Le Despencer, of course. Just for fun I popped the name Prentice Dashwood into a genealogical site where I'm registered. I couldn't believe how many hits I got. One was particularly interesting."

I waited.

Nothing.

I cracked.

"Do we do this with twenty questions?"

"Prentice Elmore Dashwood, one of Sir Frank's many descendants, left England in 1921. He opened a haberdashery in Albany, New York, made bundles of money, and eventually retired."

"That's it?"

"During his years in America, Dashwood wrote

and self-published dozens of pamphlets, one of which recounted tales of his great-great-great-something, Sir Francis Dashwood the Second."

"And the other pamphlets?" If I didn't ask, this would take forever.

"You name it. The song lines of the Australian Aboriginals. The oral traditions of the Cherokee. Camping. Fly-fishing. Greek mythology. A brief ethnography of the Carib Indians. Prentice was quite the Renaissance man. He penned three booklets and several articles that focused exclusively on the Appalachian Trail. Apparently Big P was a real mover in getting the trail started back in the twenties."

Oh? A mecca for hikers and trekkers, the AT starts at Mount Katahdin in Maine and runs along the Appalachian ridgeline to Springer Mountain in Georgia. Much of the trail lies in the Great Smoky Mountains. Including Swain County.

"Are you still there?"

"I'm here. Did Dashwood spend time here in North Carolina?"

"He wrote five pamphlets on the Great Smokies." I heard paper rustle. "Trees. Flowers. Fauna. Folklore. Geology."

I remembered Anne's tale of her visit to West Wycombe, pictured the caves under the H&F house. *Could* this guy Anne was talking about be the Prentice Dashwood of Swain County, North Carolina? It was a striking name. Could there be a connection to the British Dashwoods?

"What else did you find out about Prentice Dashwood?"

"Not a thing. But I can tell you that old Uncle Francis hung with a wild crowd back in the eighteenth century. Called themselves the Monks of Medmenham. Listen to the list. Lord Sandwich, who at one point commanded the Royal Navy, John Wilkes—"

"The politician?"

"Yep. William Hogarth, the painter, and poets Paul Whitehead, Charles Churchill, and Robert Lloyd."

"Impressive roster."

"Very. Everyone was a member of Parliament or the House of Lords. Or a poet or whatever. Our own Ben Franklin dropped in now and then, though he was never an official member."

"What did these guys do?"

"Some accounts claim they engaged in satanic rites. According to the current Sir Francis, author of the booklet we picked up on our trip, the monks were just jolly fellows who got together to celebrate Venus and Bacchus. I take that to mean women and wine."

"They held wild parties in the caves?"

"And at Medmenham Abbey. The current Sir Francis admits to his ancestor's sexual frolics but denies the devil worship. He suggests the satanism rumor came from the boys' somewhat irreverent attitude toward Christianity. They also referred to themselves as the Knights of Saint Francis, for example."

I could hear her biting an apple, then chewing.

"Everyone else called them the Hell Fire Club."

The name hit me like a sledgehammer.

"What did you say?"

"The Hell Fire Club. Big in Ireland in the 1730s and 1740s. Same deal. Overprivileged devos mocking religion and getting drunk and laid."

Anne had a way of cutting to the quick.

"There were attempts to suppress the clubs, but they weren't effective. When Dashwood gathered his little group of philanderers, the label Hell Fire naturally transferred."

Hell Fire. H&F.

I swallowed.

"How long is this booklet?"

"Thirty-four pages."

"Can you fax me a copy?"

"Sure. I can get two pages on one sheet."

I gave her the number and went back to my report, forcing myself to concentrate. Within minutes the fax rang, screeched, and bonged, then began to spit out pages. I stayed with my description of Edna Farrell's facial trauma. Some time later the machine reengaged. Again, I resisted the impulse to rush to it and gather Anne's pages.

When I'd completed the Farrell report, I began another, a million thoughts screaming for ascendancy. Though I tried to focus, images broke through again and again.

Primrose Hobbs. Parker Davenport. Prentice Dashwood. Sir Francis. The Hell Fire Club. H&F. Was anything connected? The evidence was growing. There must be a connection.

Had Prentice Dashwood rekindled his ancestor's idea of an elitist boys' club here in the Carolina mountains? Had the members been more than hedonistic dilettantes? How much more? I pictured the cut marks, suppressed a shudder.

At four the guard came in to say that a deputy had fallen sick, another was stranded with a malfunctioning cruiser. Crowe sent her apologies but needed him to control a domestic situation. I assured him I'd be fine.

I worked on, the silence of the empty morgue wrapping around me like a living thing except for the hum of a refrigerator. My breath, my heartbeat, my fingers clicking the keyboard. Outside, branches scraped windowpanes high overhead. A train whistle. A dog. Crickets. Frogs.

No car horns. No traffic noises. No living person for miles.

My sympathetic nervous system kept the adrenaline in front row, center. I made frequent errors, jumped at every squeak and tap. More than once I wished for Boyd's company.

By seven I'd finished with Farrell, Odell, Tramper, and Adams. My eyes burned, my back ached, and a dull headache told me that my blood sugar was in the cellar.

I copied my files to floppy, closed down my laptop, and went to collect Anne's fax.

Though I was anxious to read about the eighteenth-century Sir Francis, I was too tired, too hungry, and too edgy to be objective. I decided to return to High Ridge House, walk Boyd, talk with Crowe, then read the pamphlet in the comfort and safety of my bed.

I was gathering pages when I heard what sounded like gravel crunching.

I froze, listening.

Tires? Footsteps?

Fifteen seconds. Thirty.

Nothing.

"Time to boogie," I said aloud.

Tension made my movements jerky, and I dropped several papers from the basket. Gathering them from the floor, I noticed that one differed. The type was larger, the text arranged in columns.

I flipped through the other pages. Anne's cover sheet. The front of the pamphlet. The rest were brochure text, two pages to a sheet, each numbered sequentially.

I remembered the machine's pause. Could the odd page have arrived as a separate transmission? I looked but found no return fax number.

Taking everything to my office, I placed Anne's material in my briefcase and lay the mismatched sheet on my desk. As I read the contents, my adrenaline rocketed even higher.

The left column contained code names, the middle

one real names. Dates appeared after some individuals, forming an incomplete third column.

Ilus	Henry Arlen Preston	1943
Khaffre	Sheldon Brodie	1949
Omega	A. A. Birkby	1959
Narmer	Martin Patrick Veckhoff	
Sinuhe	C. A. Birkby	
Itzmana	John Morgan	1972
Arrigatore	F. L. Warren	
Rho	William Glenn Sherman	1979
Chac	John Franklin Battle	
Ometeotl	Parker Davenport	

Only one name was unfamiliar. John Franklin Battle.

Or was it? Where had I heard that name?

Think, Brennan. Think.

John Battle.

No. That's not right.

Franklin Battle.

Blank.

Frank Battle.

The magistrate who'd stonewalled the search warrant!

Would a mere magistrate qualify for membership? Had Battle been protecting the H&F property? Had he sent me the fax? Why?

And why was the most recent date more than twenty years old? Was the list incomplete? Why?

Then a terrifying thought.

Who knew I was here?

Alone.

Again I froze, listening for the faintest indicator of another presence. Picking up a scalpel, I slipped from my office to the main autopsy room.

Six skeletons stared upward, fingers and toes splayed, jaws silent beside their heads. I checked the computer and X-ray sections, the staff kitchenette, the makeshift conference room. My heart beat so loudly it seemed to overpower the stillness.

I was poking my head into the men's toilet when my cell phone sounded for the third time. I nearly screamed from the tension.

A voice, smooth as a double latte.

"You're dead."

Then empty air.

31

I CALLED MCMAHON. NO ANSWER. CROWE. DITTO. I left messages: Seven thirty-eight. Leaving Alarka for High Ridge House. Call me.

Picturing the empty lot, the deserted county road, I punched Ryan's number.

Another image. Ryan, facedown on an icy drive. I'd asked for his help that other time in Quebec. It had gotten him shot.

Ryan has no jurisdiction, Brennan. And no personal responsibility.

Instead of "send," I hit the delete button.

My thoughts ricocheted like the metal sphere in a pinball game.

Someone should be told of my whereabouts. Someone I would not be placing in danger.

Sunday night. I dialed my old number.

"Hello." A woman's voice, mellow as a purring cat.

"Is Pete there?"

"He's in the shower."

I heard a wind chime tinkle. A wind chime I'd hung years ago outside my bedroom window.

"Is there a message?"

I clicked off.

"Fuck it," I muttered. "I'll take care of myself."

Slinging purse and laptop over one shoulder, I rewrapped my fingers around the scalpel and readied my keys in the other hand. Then I cracked the door and peered out.

My Mazda was alone with the exiled hook-and-ladder trucks. In the deepening twilight, it looked like a warthog facing off with a herd of hippos.

Deep breath.

I bolted.

Reaching the car, I threw myself behind the wheel, slammed down the locks, revved the motor, and raced from the lot.

When I'd gone a mile, I began to calm, and an ill-focused anger seeped over the fear. I turned it on myself.

Jesus, you're like the heroine in a B-grade movie. One crank call and you scream for the help of a big strong man.

Seeing deer on the shoulder, I checked my speed. Eighty. I slowed, returned to chiding myself.

No one leaped from behind the building, or grabbed your ankle from under the car.

True enough. But the fax was not a crank. Whoever sent that list knew I'd be the one to receive it. Knew I was alone at the morgue.

As I drove through Bryson City, I checked the rearview mirror repeatedly. The Halloween decorations now looked menacing rather than festive, the skeletons and tombstones macabre reminders of the hideous events that had unfolded nearby. I gripped the wheel, wondering if the souls of my skeletal dead wandered the world in search of justice.

Wondering if their killers wandered the world in search of me.

At High Ridge House, I cut the engine and peered down the road I'd just climbed. No headlights wound their way up the mountain.

I wrapped the scalpel in a Wendy's napkin and zipped it into my jacket pocket for return to the morgue. Then I gathered my belongings and dashed to the porch.

The house was quiet as a church on Thursday. The parlor and kitchen were empty, and I passed no one on my way to the second floor. I heard no rustling or snoring from behind Ryan's or McMahon's doors.

I'd barely removed my jacket when a soft knock made me jump.

"Yes?"

"It's Ruby."

Her face was tense and pale, her hair glossier than a page from *Vogue*.

When I opened the door she handed me an envelope.

"This come for you today."

I glanced at the return address. Department of Anthropology, University of Tennessee.

"Thank you."

I started to close the door but she held up a hand.

"There's something you need to know. Something I need to tell you."

"I'm very tired, Ruby."

"It wasn't an intruder that wrecked your room. It was Eli."

"Your nephew?"

"He's not my nephew."

She halted.

"The Gospel of Matthew tells us that whoever shall put away his wife—"

"Why would Eli trash my things?" I was not in the mood for religious discourse.

"My husband left me for another woman. She and Enoch had a child."

"Eli?"

She nodded.

"I wished terrible things for them. I wished them to burn in hell. I thought, if thine eye offend thee, pluck it out. I plucked them from my life."

I heard the muffled sound of Boyd's barking.

"When Enoch passed, God touched my heart. Judge not and ye shall not be judged; condemn not and ye shall not be condemned; forgive and ye shall be forgiven."

She sighed deeply.

"Eli's mother died six years ago. The boy had no one, so I took him in."

Her eyes dropped, returned to mine.

"A man's foes shall be they of his own household. Eli hates me. Takes joy in tormenting me. He knows I take pride in this house. He knows I like you. He was just getting at me."

"Perhaps he just wants attention."

Look at the kid, I thought, but didn't say it.

"Perhaps."

"I'm sure he'll come around in time. And don't worry about my things. Nothing was taken." I changed the subject. "Is anyone else here?"

She shook her head.

"I believe Mr. McMahon's gone off to Charlotte. Haven't seen Mr. Ryan all day. Everyone else has checked out."

Again, I heard barking.

"Has Boyd been a nuisance?"

"Dog's been ornery today. Needs exercising." She brushed her skirt. "I'm off to church. Shall I bring dinner before I leave?"

"Please."

Ruby's roast pork and yam pudding had a calming effect. As I ate, the panic that had sent me racing through the twilight gave way to a dismal loneliness.

I remembered the woman on Pete's phone, wondered why hearing her voice felt like a kick in the gut. I know postcoital somnolence when I hear it, but so what? Pete and I were both adults. I'd left him. He was free to see whomever he pleased.

Condemn not and ye shall rock.

I wondered how I really felt about Ryan. I knew he was a bastard, but at least he was a winsome bastard, though I could do without his smoking. He was smart. He was funny. He was dizzyingly handsome, but completely unaware of his effect on women. And he cared about people.

Lots of people.

Like Danielle.

So why had Ryan's number been one of the first I'd started to dial? Was it just that he was nearby, or was he more than a colleague, a person I would think of for protection or comfort?

I remembered Primrose and was again flattened with remorse. I'd involved my friend and now she was dead. I'd gotten her killed. The guilt was crushing, and I was sure it would follow me the rest of my life.

Enough. Read the letter Ruby brought. It will thank you for the lecture and say it was splendid.

It did. The envelope also contained a copy of the student newsletter with its photo of me and Simon Midkiff. To say I looked tense would be like saying Olive Oyl was on the thin side.

But Simon Midkiff took best of show. I studied his face, wondering what had been in his mind that day. Had he been sent to pump me for information? Had he come on his own? My scientific colleagues often attend one another's lectures. Was it he who had faxed me the code name list? If so, why would he divulge his complicity?

My musings were interrupted by a sharp yip, followed by another.

Poor Boyd. He was the only being on the planet whose loyalty never wavered, and I ignored him. I checked my watch. Eight-twenty. Time for a quick run before Crowe arrived at nine.

I locked my computer and briefcase in the wardrobe in case Eli decided on a return engagement. Then I threw on my jacket, grabbed flashlight and leash, and headed downstairs.

Night had taken full control, ushering in a zillion stars but no moon. The porch lights did little to dispel the darkness. As I crossed the lawn, my limbic system began firing questions.

What if someone is watching?

Like Eli the Avenging Adolescent?

What if the call was not a prank?

Don't be melodramatic, I reasoned. It's the weekend after Halloween, and kids are kicking up their heels. You left messages with McMahon and Crowe.

What if they don't check?

The sheriff will be here in forty minutes.

A stalker might be out there right now.

What could happen in the company of a seventy-pound chow?

That seventy-pound chow yipped again, and I sprinted the last few yards to his pen. Hearing footsteps, he placed forepaws on the chain-linking and raised himself to a bipedal stance.

When he recognized me, Boyd went ballistic, pushing back, bounding forward, jumping up, and pushing off the fence again. He repeated the cycle several times, like a hamster on a wheel, then stood again on hind feet, threw back his head, and barked steadily.

Saying doggy things, I ruffled his ears and clipped on the leash. He nearly dragged me chowside in his lunge toward the gate.

"We're only going to the end of the property," I warned, leveling a finger at his nose.

He cocked his head, twirled the brows, and yipped once. When I lifted the latch, he bounded out and raced in circles, nearly toppling me.

"I envy your energy, Boyd."

He lapped my face as I disentangled the leash from between his legs, then we started up the road. Light from the porch barely reached the edge of the lawn, and within ten yards I clicked on my flash. Boyd stopped and growled.

"It's a flashlight, boy."

I reached down and patted his shoulder. He rotated his head and licked my hand, then doubled back, did a little dance, and pressed his body against my legs.

I was about to move on when I felt him tense. His head dropped, his breathing changed, and a low rumble rose from his throat. He did not respond to my touch.

"What is it, boy?"

More rumbling.

"Not another dead squirrel."

I reached out to stroke him and felt hackles. Not good. I tugged the leash.

"Come on, boy, we're turning back."

He would not move.

"Boyd."

The growl grew deeper, more savage.

I aimed my light where Boyd was staring. The beam crawled over tree trunks and was sucked into dead zones of blackness between.

I yanked the leash harder. Boyd whipped left and barked. I swept my light in that direction.

"This isn't funny, dog."

Then my eyes made out a form. Or had it been a trick of shadow? In the moment I glanced down at Boyd, what I thought I'd seen vanished. Or had it been there at all?

"Who's there?" Fear crimped my voice.

Nothing but crickets and frogs. A fallen tree lodged against one still standing groaned and creaked in the air.

Suddenly I heard movement behind me. Footfalls. The rustling of leaves.

Boyd turned and snapped, lunging as far as the leash would allow.

"Who's there?" I repeated.

A silhouette emerged from the trees, denser than the surrounding night. Boyd snarled and tore at the leash. The dark shape moved toward us.

"Who is it?"

No answer.

I thrust the flashlight and leash into one hand and reached for my cell phone with the other. Before I could autodial, it slipped from my shaking fingers.

"Stay back!" It was almost a shriek.

I raised the light to shoulder level. As I was readjusting the leash for better control, about to reach for the phone, my grip loosened. Boyd broke free and charged, teeth gleaming, a fierce growl rumbling from his throat.

In an instant the silhouette altered shape. An arm uncurled.

Boyd leaped.

A flash. A deafening crack.

The dog bounced off the silhouette, dropped to the ground, whimpered, and lay still.

"Boyd!"

Tears ran down my cheeks. I wanted to tell him I'd take care of him. Tell him he'd be all right, but my body was paralyzed with fear, and no words came from my mouth.

The form moved swiftly toward me now. I turned to run. Hands grabbed me. I twisted, wrenched free. The shadow coalesced into a man.

He hit me with his full weight, his shoulder beneath my armpit. The shock of the impact sent me falling sideways.

The last thing I remembered was breath on my

face, sprawling. Then the crack of my skull against igneous rock.

The dream was frightening. An airless place. I couldn't move. I couldn't see. Then something stroked my cheek.

I opened my eyes to a reality more hellish than any nightmare.

My mouth was stuffed and wrapped with tape. I was blindfolded.

My heart shrank in my chest.

I can't breathe!

I tried raising a hand to my face. My wrists were tied over my chest.

The rag filled my mouth with an acrid taste. A tremor began below my tongue.

I'm going to vomit! I'm going to choke!

I felt panic, began to shake.

Move!

I tried shifting, and a cocoon of fabric moved with me. I smelled dust and mildew and spoiled vegetation.

I kicked out, thrust with my head.

The movement shot arrows through my brain. I lay still, waiting for the pain to subside.

Breathe through your nose. In. Out. In. Out.

The throbbing lessened slightly.

Think!

I was imprisoned in some sort of bag. My hands and feet were bound. But where was I? How had I gotten here?

Disjointed memories. The morgue. The empty county road. Ruby's troubled face. Primrose Hobbs.

Boyd!

Oh, dear God. Not Boyd! Had I killed the dog, too?

In. Out.

I rolled my head and felt a lump the size of a plum. Another wave of nausea.

In. Out.

More synapses.

The attack. The faceless form.

Simon Midkiff? Frank Battle? Could my captor be the moron magistrate?

I twisted my wrists, trying to loosen the tape. More nausea.

Clamping my teeth, I rolled onto my side. If I did vomit, I didn't want to aspirate the contents.

The movement made my stomach heave. I filled my lungs and the contractions receded.

I lay rigid, listening. I had no idea how long I'd been unconscious, or how I'd arrived at my present location. Was I still in the woods at High Ridge House? Had I been taken elsewhere? Was my attacker just feet away?

My heart rate slowed by a nanosecond, and cogent thought began to creep back.

It was then the thing crawled across my cheek. I heard dry insect sounds, felt movement in my hair, then the tickle of antennae on my skin.

A scream formed in my throat. I rolled back and

forth, batting at my face, my hair. Blinding pain seared my brain, and my innards jammed up against the back of my throat.

Quiet! One functioning brain cell commanded.

Cockroaches! The others shrieked.

I tugged at my jacket, tried to pull it up over my head. It wouldn't go.

Lie still!

My heart hammered the order against my ribs.

Be still. Be still. Be still.

Slowly, I calmed, and reason returned.

Get out.

Run.

But not into another trap.

Think.

Listen.

Bare branches hissing in the wind. A chirp. Leaves skittering across the ground.

Forest sounds.

I peeled back a layer of sound.

Water swirling around rocks.

River sounds.

Another layer.

Far away and barely there, a loonlike wail followed by a strange giggle.

Gooseflesh spread across my arms and up my throat.

I knew where I was.

I STRAINED, BARELY BREATHING. HAD I REALLY heard what I thought I had? Minutes crept by. Doubt crept in. Then it sounded again, faint and surreal.

An undulating moan, a high-pitched laugh.

The electric skeleton!

I was not far from the Riverbank Inn. Where Primrose had stayed. Where she had never been seen again.

I pictured Primrose's bloated face, saw the gouges left by underwater feeders.

I lay bound, gagged, and blindfolded in a sack beside the Tuckasegee River!

I had to break free!

My skull pounded from its encounter with the rock. The rag cut off my air, and tasted of garbage and filth. The duct tape burned my cheeks and lips, and fired splinters of light up my optic nerve.

And I could hear the swish of roaches on my nylon

jacket, feel their movement in my hair and on my jeans.

My thoughts flew in a thousand directions.

Again, I listened. Hearing no indicators of a human presence, I began manipulating my bindings, breathing steadily through my nose.

My stomach swirled, my mouth grew dry.

Millennia passed. The tape loosened a millimeter.

Tears of frustration welled behind my mashed lids. No weeping!

I kept at my ankles and wrists, yanking, twisting, tugging, stopping periodically to monitor for sound outside my bag.

Roaches scuttled across my face, their feet feathery on my skin.

Go away! I screamed in my mind. *Get the fuck off!*

I struggled on. Sweat dampened my hair.

My mind soared like a nocturnal bird, and I looked down on myself, a helpless larva on the forest floor. I pictured the blackness around me and wished for the safety of a familiar night haven.

A twenty-four-hour coffee shop. A tollbooth. A precinct house. A nurses' station in a sleeping ward. An ER.

Then I remembered.

The scalpel!

Could I reach it?

I drew my knees to my chest, scrunching the hem of my jacket as far up as possible. Then I jerked my elbows across the nylon, raising my hips each time.

Blindly I inched the pocket forward, gauging its progress by touch.

Reading my clothing like a Braille map, I located the nylon loop attached to the pull tab and grasped it between the fingertips of both hands.

I held my breath, applied downward pressure.

My fingers slid down the nylon and off the end.

Damn!

I tried again, with the same result.

Over and over I repeated the maneuver, fishing, squeezing, pulling, until my hand cramped and I wanted to scream.

New plan.

Pressing the zipper tab to my thigh with the back of my left hand, I bent my right wrist and tried to hook a finger through the loop. The angle was too shallow.

I bent my hand farther. No go.

Using the fingers of my left hand, I placed pressure on my right, increasing the backward angle. Pain screamed up the tendons of my forearm.

As I thought my bones would snap, my index finger found the loop and slipped through. I tugged gently. The tab gave, and my bound wrists followed it down. With the zipper open, it was easy to slide the fingers of one hand into the pocket and withdraw the scalpel.

Carefully cradling my prize, I rolled onto my back and wedged the instrument against my stomach. Then I peeled off the napkin by rolling the scalpel between my hands. Rotating the blade toward my body, I began sawing the tape that bound my wrists. The scalpel was razor sharp.

Easy. Careful. Don't carve your wrist.

In less than a minute my hands were free. I reached up and tore the bindings from my lips. Flames raced across my face.

Don't scream!

I yanked the rag from my mouth, alternately gulped air and spat. Gagging on my own foul saliva, I sliced through the blindfold circling my head and ripped it from my eyes.

Another burst of fire as skin and some eyebrows went with the tape. With shaking hands, I reached down and freed my ankles.

I was slashing at the bag when a sound paralyzed my arm.

The chunk of a car door!

How far away? What to do? Play dead?

My arm flew, a piston driven by a will of its own.

Feet rustled through leaves. My mind calibrated.

Fifty yards.

I jabbed at the canvas. Up, down. Up, down.

The rustling grew louder.

Thirty yards.

I thrust my boots into the opening, thrashed out with all my strength. The tearing sounded like a shriek in the stillness.

The rustling paused, resumed, faster, more reckless.

Twenty yards.

Fifteen.

"Hold it right there."

I pictured the gun, felt bullets slam into my flesh. It didn't matter. I'd either be dead now or dead later. Better to make a fight of it while there was still the chance to resist.

"Don't move."

I flipped around, grabbed the edges I'd torn, and pulled with both hands. Then I lunged headfirst through the opening, tumbled facedown, rolled onto my feet, and stood on rubber legs, trying to focus.

"Madam, you are dead."

I bolted away from the sound of the voice.

Keeping the gurgling of the river to my left, I ran through darkness dense as an endless tunnel, one arm in front of my face. Obstacles leaped at me without warning, forcing my feet on a zigzag path.

Again and again I stumbled on some form of planetary rubble. A rock older than life itself. A fallen trunk. A dead branch. I kept my balance. Burning fear gave rise to strength and speed.

The things of the night seemed to go silent. I heard no buzzing, no chirping, no padding of feet, just my own rasping breath. Behind me, footfalls, thrashing like some giant woodland beast.

Sweat soaked my clothing. Blood pounded in my ears.

My pursuer stayed with me, neither closing in nor falling back. Was he working a home court advantage? Was he the cat, I his mouse? Was he biding his time, confident the prey would be his?

My lungs burned, unable to take in enough air. A stabbing pain ripped my left side. Still, the blind urge to run.

One minute. Three. An eternity.

Then the muscles of my right thigh cramped. I slowed to a limping lope.

The cat slowed, too.

I tried to push on. It was no good. My legs and arms were going dead.

My pace dropped to a trot. Sweat trickled from my forehead and burned my eyes.

I saw the outline of a dark shape in front of my face. My outstretched hand slammed something solid. My elbow folded, and my cheek hit hard. Pain shot through my wrist. Blood moistened my palm and cheek.

With my good hand, I reached out and explored. Solid rock.

I probed farther.

More rock.

My heart shriveled.

I'd run up against a cliff wall. Water to my left. Dense trees to my right.

The cat knew. I had nowhere to go.

Don't panic!

I pulled out the scalpel and held it behind me. Then I turned, back to the wall, and faced my attacker.

He spoke before I saw him.

"Bad routing."

He was breathing hard, and I could smell the rancid odor of sweat and rage.

"Stay away from me!" I yelled with more bravado than I felt.

"Why should I do that?" Taunting.

I knew that voice. The caller at the morgue. But I'd also heard it in person. Where?

Crunching, then a black cutout appeared in the darkness.

"Don't take one step closer," I hissed.

"You're in an odd position to give orders."

"Come near me and I'll kill you." I grasped the scalpel like a lifeline.

"The proverbial rock and hard place, I'd call it."

More crunching. The cutout resolved itself into a man, arm extended in my direction. Broad shoulders, thick arms.

It was not Simon Midkiff.

"Who are you?"

"Surely you know that by now."

I heard the click of a safety uncatching.

"You killed Primrose Hobbs. Why?"

"Because I could."

"And you plan to kill me."

"With the greatest of pleasure."

"Why?"

"Your meddling destroyed a holy thing."

"Who are you?"

"Kulkulcan."

Kulkulcan. It was one I knew.

"The Mayan deity."

"Why settle for a pharaoh or some faggot Greek?"

"Where is the rest of your society of sickos?"

"If it wasn't for that miserable crash you'd never have stumbled onto us. Your busybody intrusiveness uncovered things you had no right to know. It has fallen to Kulkulcan to exact vengeance."

The melodious voice was now tinged with fury.

"It's over for your Hell Fire Club."

"It will never be over. Since the dawn of time the mediocre masses have tried to suppress the intellectually superior. It never works. Conditions can make us dormant, but we reemerge when the climate changes."

To what egomaniacal delusion was I listening?

"It was my time to enter the ranks of the holy," he continued, oblivious to the fact that I hadn't replied. Or indifferent. "I found my offering. I made my sacrifice. I honored the ritual that you have profaned."

"Jeremiah Mitchell or George Adair?"

"Irrelevant. Their names don't matter. I was chosen. I was ready. I followed the way."

Keep him talking, my mind reasoned. Someone knows where you are. Someone is doing something

"Kulkulkan is a creator god. You destroy life."

"Mortals are transient. Wisdom endures."

"Whose?"

"The wisdom of the ages, shown to those worthy to receive it."

"And you ensure its survival through ritual slaughter?"

"The body is a material envelope, of no lasting value. We discard it in the end. But wisdom, strength, the essence of the soul, these are the forces that prevail."

I let him rant on.

"The brightest of the species must be nurtured. Those passing from this earth must yield their mana to those who remain, add to the strength and wisdom of the chosen."

"How?"

"Through blood, heart, muscle, and bone."

Dear God, it was true.

"You think you can increase your IQ by consuming the flesh of others?"

"As flesh wastes away, so does strength. But mind, spirit, intellect, those elements are transferable through the very cells of our bodies."

I clutched the scalpel so tightly my knuckles ached.

"Herodotus told of the eating of kinsmen among the Issedones of Central Asia, who grew strong and ruled. Strabo found it among the Irish clans. Many conquering peoples gained strength through eating the flesh of their enemies. Eat the weak and grow stronger. It's as old as man himself."

I thought of the Neanderthal bones, the victims in the kiva near Mesa Verde. The skeletons in my morgue.

"Why the elderly?"

"The aged hold the greatest reservoirs of wisdom."

"Or do old people simply make easier targets?"

"My dear Miss Brennan. Would you rather that your flesh contribute to the advancement of chosen beings or be consumed by maggots?"

Anger welled, overrode fear.

"You egotistical, demented prick."

"Fee-fi-fo-fum, I smell the blood of an English-man. Be he alive or be he dead, I'll grind his bones to make my bread."

At a distance, the skeleton moaned, cackled.

I was confronted by madness! Who was this man? How did I know him?

I began inching along the wall, holding the scalpel behind me with my right hand, feeling with my left. I'd taken a half dozen steps when a powerful beam shot out of the dark, blinding me like a possum on a backyard fence. I threw up an arm.

"Going somewhere, Miss Brennan?"

In the backglow I could see his lower face, lips drawn back in murderous rage.

Stay away from him!

I pivoted to run, tripped, and fell. As I scrabbled to right myself, the shadow sprang, closed the gap, and a hand reached out and grabbed my ankle. My feet went out from under me again, and my knees cracked against alluvium. The scalpel flew into darkness.

"You goddamn treacherous cow!"

The golden voice was now sizzling with fury.

I kicked out but couldn't break his grip. His fingers were like steel clamping through my jeans.

Never more afraid in my life, I gouged my elbows into the earth, trying to hitch myself forward, kicking out with my free leg. Suddenly, his full weight was on me. A knee pinned my back, and a hand pressed my face into the ground. Dirt and debris filled my nose, my mouth.

I thrashed wildly, kicking and clawing to get out from under him. He'd dropped his flash and it lay on the ground, lighting us like some writhing, two-headed beast. As long as I could move, he would not get that garrote wire around my throat.

My hand touched something jagged and hard, and my fingers closed around it. I twisted my torso and struck out blindly.

I heard the soft thunk of rock against bone, then the metallic clink of steel on granite.

"Bitch!"

He slammed his fist into my right ear. Lightning exploded in my head.

He released his grasp, fumbled to retrieve the gun. I jerked an elbow backward and caught him along the border of his jaw. His teeth cracked and his head flew back.

A shriek like that of a wounded animal.

I pushed with all my strength and his knee slipped off my back. In less than a second I scrambled to my knees and crawled toward the flashlight. He regained his balance and we dived at the same time. I got it.

I swung as hard as I could and connected with his temple. A thump, a grunt, and he fell backward. Clicking off the beam, I lunged toward the trees and crouched behind a pine.

I didn't move. I didn't blink. I tried to reason.

Don't thrash into the trees. Don't turn your back on him. Maybe as he moves you can slip past him, run back toward the inn, scream for help.

Dead calm, broken only by his panting. Seconds passed. Or maybe it was hours. I felt dizzy from the blow to my head, couldn't track time or space or distance.

Where was he?

A voice from near the ground. "I have found the gun, Miss Brennan."

A single shot exploded in the stillness.

"But we both know I don't need it now that that cur of yours is out of the way."

His voice came to me as though under water.

"I'm going to make you pay for this. Really pay."

I heard him rise.

"I have a necklace I want to show you."

I inhaled deeply, trying to clear my head. He was coming at me with the garrote.

Out of the corner of my eye, a glimmer. I turned. Three slivers of light were bobbing toward me. Or was I hallucinating?

"Freeze!" A gravelly female voice.

"Drop it!" Male.

"Stop!" A different male voice.

A muzzle flashed in the darkness in front of me. Two shots rang out.

Return fire from the direction of the voices. The ping of a bullet ricocheting off rock.

A thud, an expulsion of air. The sound of a body sliding down the rock wall.

Running feet.

Hands on my throat, my wrist.

"—pulse is strong."

Faces above me, swimming like a mirage on a summer sidewalk. Ryan. Crowe. Deputy Nameless.

"—ambulance. It's O.K. We didn't hit her."

Static.

I struggled to sit.

"Lie back." Gentle pressure on my shoulders.

"I have to see him."

One circle of light slid to the cliff where my assailant sat motionless, legs stretched in front, back against rock. Slowly, the light illuminated feet, legs, torso, face. I knew who he was.

Ralph Stover, the not-so-happy owner of the River- bank Inn, the man who would not let me into Prim- rose's room. He stared sightlessly into the night, chin forward, brain slowly oozing onto a stain on the rock behind his head.

33

I LEFT CHARLOTTE AT DAWN ON FRIDAY AND DROVE west through heavy fog. The shifting vapors lightened as I climbed toward the Eastern Continental Divide, vanished outside Asheville.

Leaving Highway 74 at Bryson City, I drove up Veterans' Boulevard, past the cutoff to the Fryemont Inn, turned right on Main, and parked opposite the old courthouse, now a senior citizens' center. I sat a moment watching sunlight glisten on its little gold dome, and thought of those seniors whose bones I'd unearthed.

I pictured a tall, gangly man, blind and nearly deaf; a fragile old woman with a crooked face. I imagined them on these same streets all those years ago. I wanted to put my arms around them, to tell each of them that things were being put right.

And I thought about those who had perished on Air

TransSouth 228. So many stories had only begun. Graduations not attended. Birthdays not celebrated. Voyages not taken. Lives obliterated because of one fatal voyage.

I took my time walking to the fire station. I'd spent a month in Bryson City, had come to know it well. I was leaving now, my work completed, but a few questions remained.

When I arrived McMahon was packing the contents of his cubicle into cardboard boxes.

"Breaking camp?" I asked from the doorway.

"Hey, girl, you're back in town." He cleared a chair, gestured me into it. "How are you feeling?"

"Bruised and scraped but fully functional."

Amazingly, I'd sustained no serious injury during my romp in the woods with Ralph Stover. A slight concussion had sent me to the hospital for a couple of days, then Ryan had driven me to Charlotte. Assured I was fine, he'd flown back to Montreal, and I'd spent the rest of the week on the couch with Birdie.

"Coffee?"

"No thanks."

"Mind if I keep working?"

"Please."

"Has someone regaled you with the whole strange tale?"

"There are still gaps. Take it from the top."

"H&F was some kind of hybrid between Mensa and the Billionaire Boys Club. It didn't start out that way, was originally just a bunch of businessmen, doctors, and professors coming to the mountains to hunt and fish."

"Back in the thirties."

"Right. They'd camp on Edward Arthur's land, hunt during the day, drink and party all night. Applaud themselves on their extraordinary intelligence. The group got to be very close over the years, eventually formed a secret society which they called H&F."

"The founding father being Prentice Dashwood."

"Dashwood was the first prior, whatever the hell that means."

"H&F stands for Hell Fire," I said. "Hell Fire Clubs flourished in eighteenth-century England and Ireland, the most famous being the brainchild of Sir Francis Dashwood. Prentice Dashwood of Albany, New York, was a descendant of Sir Francis. Mama was an unnamed Hell Fire lady." I'd done a lot of reading during my time on the couch. "Sir Francis had four sons named Francis."

"Sounds like George Foreman."

"The man was proud of his name."

"Or the least creative progenitor in history."

"Anyway, the original Hell Fires had a healthy skepticism for religion and loved lampooning the church. They referred to themselves as the Knights of Saint Francis, to their parties as 'devotions,' to their steward as 'prior.'"

"Who were these assholes?"

"The rich and powerful of Merry Old England. Ever hear of the Bohemian Club?"

McMahon shook his head.

"It's a highly select, all-male club whose members have included every Republican president since Calvin Coolidge. They gather for two weeks every year at a secluded campground in Sonoma County, California, called the Bohemian Grove."

McMahon paused, a folder in each hand.

"That does ring a bell. The few journalists that have gotten in over the years have been thrown out and their stories killed."

"Yep."

"You're not suggesting our political and industrial bigwigs plot murder at these rendezvous?"

"Of course not. But the concept is similar: powerful men camping in seclusion. Bohemian Club members are even reported to use mock-druidic rituals."

McMahon taped a carton, slid it across the floor, and placed another on his desk.

"We've netted all but one of the H&F members, and we're accumulating the story bit by bit, but it's slow. Needless to say, no one's enthused about talking to us, and everyone is lawyered to the gills. Each of the six officers will be charged with multiple counts of homicide, but it's unclear what the culpability is for the rest of the pack. Midkiff claims only the leaders participated in murder and cannibalism."

"Has Midkiff been given immunity?" I asked.

He nodded. "Most of our info is coming from him."

"He sent the code name fax?"

"Yes. He'd reconstructed what he remembered.

Midkiff left the group in the early seventies, claims he was never involved in any killing. Didn't know about Stover. He says he reached a point last week where he couldn't live with himself anymore."

McMahon began transferring papers from a file cabinet to the box.

"And he was afraid for you."

"Me?"

"You, darlin'."

I took a moment to absorb that.

"Where is he now?"

"The judge didn't think he was a flight risk or in personal danger, so he's out. He's still living in a rental cabin in Cherokee."

"Why did Parker Davenport call Midkiff before shooting himself?"

"To warn him that the lid was about to blow. Apparently the two remained friends after Midkiff withdrew from H&F. It was largely because of the lieutenant governor that Midkiff remained unmolested all these years. Davenport kept the club convinced that Midkiff posed no threat; in return, Midkiff kept his mouth shut."

"Until now."

"Until now."

"What has he told you?"

"H&F had eighteen members at any given time. Of those, six lucky boys made up the inner circle. Very exclusive. Only when a member of that inner circle died was a replacement chosen from the group at large. The initiation banquet was black tie; red, hooded robe; dessert provided by the inductee."

"Human flesh."

"Yes. Remember the Hamatsa you told me about?"

I nodded, too revolted to reply.

"Same deal. Only our gentlemen cannibals restricted themselves to sharing the flesh of one thigh from each victim. It was like a blood brotherhood pact. Though the whole club met regularly at the Arthur house, Midkiff swears that only members of the inner circle knew what really went on at these initiations."

I thought of Ralph Stover's words to me. "I found my offering."

"Tucker Adams was killed in 1943 when inner-circle member Henry Arlen Preston died, and Anthony Allen Birkby joined the elite. When Sheldon Brodie drowned in 1949, Martin Patrick Veckhoff was the new inner-circle choice and Edna Farrell was his victim. Anthony Allen Birkby perished in a car wreck a decade later, his son was given the inner-circle nod, and Charlie Wayne Tramper ended up on the Communion table."

"Wasn't Tramper killed by a bear?"

"Young Birkby may have cheated a bit. The Tramper funeral was where Parker Davenport met Simon Midkiff, by the way. Midkiff knew Tramper through his research on the Cherokee."

"Did Midkiff know what had happened to Tramper?"

"Claims he had no clue."

"How did Midkiff get hooked up with H&F?"

"In 1955 the young professor was newly arrived from England, and had been told to look up Prentice Dashwood, an old family friend. Dashwood recruited Midkiff into H&F."

"He never made it to the inner circle."

"No."

"But Davenport did."

"Following the Tramper funeral, Midkiff gradually introduced Davenport to the brothers. The idea of an intellectual elite appealed to Davenport, and he joined up."

"Even though he was from Swain County, Davenport had never known about the lodge?"

"Not before he joined. Apparently no one did. These guys were amazing at keeping themselves hidden. They'd sneak in and out after dark. Over the years, everyone forgot the place was there."

"Everyone except old Edward Arthur and Luke Bowman's father."

"Right." McMahon perused the contents of a drawer as if unsure whether to pack or discard them.

"And the club put nothing on paper."

"Very little."

He emptied the drawer into the box, reinserted it in the desk, opened another.

"What is all this shit?" He straightened and looked at me. "Continuing with the chronology, John Morgan died in 1972, Mary Francis Rafferty was killed, and F. L. Warren moved up. By this time, Midkiff was getting disenchanted. He quit shortly after that."

"So he may not have been a party to any murders."

"It looks that way. But Davenport's dirty. In 1979 he was chosen to replace William Glenn Sherman in the inner circle. Davenport's canapé was the unidentified black male."

"Was it significant that the victims were drawn from different races and both sexes?"

"The idea was to maximize the breadth of spiritual intake."

"Jesus."

"Kendall Rollins succumbed to leukemia in 1986 and his son Paul took his place."

"Albert Odell was the victim?"

"Correct."

McMahon dumped the second drawer.

"What happened with Jeremiah Mitchell and George Adair?"

"Major fuck-up. When Martin Patrick Veckhoff checked out last February, Roger Lee Fairley was slated for coronation. He was informed of the requirements, and Mitchell was grabbed and killed. Fairley's sudden death on the way to the Veckhoff funeral created a problem, and Mitchell was put on ice while the succession issue was resolved."

"By whom?"

"Ralph Stover was told that it would soon be his turn to move from the outer to the inner circle, was advised of the conditions, and was asked to perform a few extra duties. He stored Mitchell's body in a freezer at the Riverbank Inn."

I suppressed a shudder.

"That's why the volatile fatty acid readings were off."

"Exactly. In early September Stover was officially proposed to succeed Veckhoff, and Mitchell's body was taken back and placed in the courtyard in preparation for an induction ceremony. That's when things began to unravel. Some within the inner circle opposed Stover's promotion, seeing him as too zealous, too unstable. The dispute dragged on, decomposition began, meaning the body couldn't be used for the ritual and the corpse had to be buried in the cave."

"But not before a coyote visitation."

"Bless them."

"Stover did the dirty work again?"

"He's our man."

McMahon upended another drawer, taped the box, and labeled it with a felt-tip pen.

"Anyway, after weeks of wrangling, the Stover faction prevailed. George Adair was abducted on October first. The crash occurred on October fourth."

"I retrieved the foot on October fifth."

He stacked the box with the earlier ones and opened a file drawer.

"As you know, Stover also killed Primrose Hobbs. Lucy Crowe found Stelazine in his apartment at the Riverbank Inn. The prescription was written by a Mexican doctor for none other than Parker Davenport. Stover had four capsules in his pocket Sunday night. The same drug he used on Primrose."

He looked at me.

"She also found a length of wire that matches the garrote from Hobbs's neck."

The cold fist. It still didn't seem possible that Primrose was dead.

"He told me he did it because he could."

"An order may have come from the inner circle, or he may have been acting on his own. Perhaps he feared she'd discovered something. He probably stole her key and password to remove the foot from the morgue and alter the file."

"Has the foot been found?"

"Never will be, I suspect. Hang on."

McMahon disappeared into the hall, returned with two more empty boxes.

"How can so much crap accumulate in one month?"

"Don't forget the rubber snake."

I pointed to an artifact on his desk.

"I'm curious how Crowe found me."

"She and Ryan hit High Ridge House minutes apart Sunday night, well past the time you should have arrived. Finding your car in the lot but no sign of you in the house, they went looking. When they found the dog—"

He glanced up, quickly back to the box. I kept my face neutral.

"Apparently your chow got hold of Stover's wrist before he was shot. Ryan found a medical bracelet with Stover's name on it lying next to the dog's snout. Crowe made the connection based on something Midkiff had told her."

"The rest is history."

"The rest is history."

He threw the snake into the box, changed his mind and took it out.

"Ryan headed back to Quebec?"

"Yes."

Again, I kept my face neutral.

"I don't know the monsieur that well, but his part-ner's death really turfed him."

"Yes."

"Throw in the niece, and I'm amazed the guy held it together."

"Yes." The niece?

"'Danielle the Demon,' he called her."

McMahon crossed to his jacket and tucked the snake into a pocket.

"Said we'd probably read about the kid in the papers one day."

The niece?

I felt a smile tug the corners of my mouth.

At times neutrality is difficult.

I found Simon Midkiff bundled in overcoat, gloves, and muffler, dozing in a rocker on his front stoop. A brimmed cap hid most of his face, and I suddenly thought of another question.

"Simon?"

His head snapped up and the watery eyes blinked in confusion.

"Yes?"

He wiped a hand across his mouth, and a filament of saliva glistened on wool. Removing the glove, he dug under layers of clothing, withdrew glasses, and slid them onto his nose.

Recognition.

"I'm glad to see you are all right." Chains looped to either side of his head, throwing delicate shadows across his cheeks. The skin looked pale and paper-thin.

"Can we talk?"

"Of course. Perhaps we should go inside."

We entered a combination kitchenette–living area with one interior door, which I presumed led to a bedroom and bath. The furnishings were lacquered pine, and looked like they'd come from a home workshop.

Books lined the baseboards, and notebooks and papers covered a table and desk. A dozen boxes were stacked at one end of the room, each marked with a series of archaeological grid numbers.

"Tea?"

"That would be nice."

I watched as he filled a kettle, took Tetley's bags from their paper holders, placed cups on saucers. He seemed frailer than I remembered, more stooped.

"I don't get many visitors."

"This is lovely. Thank you."

He led me to an afghan-draped sofa, placed both

cups on a coffee table made from a slice of tree trunk, and dragged a chair opposite.

We both drank. Outside, I heard the whiney buzz of an outboard motor on the Oconaluftee River. I waited until he was ready.

"I'm not sure how well I can talk about it."

"I know what happened, Simon. What I don't understand is why."

"I wasn't there in the beginning. What I know comes from others."

"You knew Prentice Dashwood."

He leaned back, and his eyes shifted to another time.

"Prentice was an insatiable reader with a staggering array of knowledge. There was nothing that didn't interest him. Darwin. Lyell. Newton. Mendelyev. And the philosophers. Hobbs. Aenesidemus. Baumgarten. Wittgenstein. Lao-tzu. He read everything. Archaeology. Ethnology. Physics. Biology. History."

He interrupted to sip his tea.

"And he was wonderful at spinning yarns. That's how it began. Prentice told stories of his ancestor's Hell Fire Club, describing the members as rakish good fellows who banded together for riotous profanity and intellectual conversation. The idea seemed benign enough. And for a while it was."

His cup trembled in its saucer as he set it down.

"But Prentice had a darker side. He believed that certain human beings were more valuable than others." His voice trailed off.

"The intellectually superior," I prodded.

"Yes. As Prentice aged, his worldview was strongly influenced by his cross-cultural reading on cosmology and cannibalism. His grasp on reality diminished."

He paused, sorting through things he could say.

"It started out as frivolous blasphemy. No one really believed it."

"Believed what?"

"That eating the dead negated the finality of death. That partaking of the flesh of another human being allowed the assimilation of soul, personality, and wisdom."

"Is that what Dashwood believed?"

One bony shoulder shrugged.

"Perhaps he did. Perhaps he simply used the idea, and for the inner circle the actual act, as a way to keep the club intact. Collective indulgence in the forbidden. The in-group, out-group mind-set. Prentice understood that cultural rituals exist to reinforce the unity of those performing them."

"How did it start?"

"An accident."

He sniffed.

"A bloody accident. A young man showed up at the lodge one summer. God knows what he was doing way out there. There was a lot of drinking, a fight, the boy was killed. Prentice proposed that everyone—"

He withdrew a hanky and ran it over his eyes.

"This took place before the war. I learned about it years later when I overheard a conversation that was not for my ears."

"Yes."

"Prentice cut slivers of muscle from the boy's thigh and required everyone to partake. They had no inner-outer-circle distinction back then. It was a pact. Each was a participant and equally guilty. No one would talk about the boy's death. They buried the body in the woods, the following year the inner circle was formed, and Tucker Adams was killed."

"Intelligent men accepted this insanity? Educated men with wives, and families, and responsible jobs?"

"Prentice Dashwood was an extraordinarily charismatic man. When he spoke, everything made sense."

"Cannibalism?" I kept my voice calm.

"Do you have any idea how pervasive the theme of humans eating humans is in Western culture? Human sacrifice is mentioned in the Old Testament, the Rig-Veda. Anthropophagy is central to the plot of many Greek and Roman myths; it's the centerpiece of the Catholic Mass. Look at literature. Jonathan Swift's 'Modest Proposal' and Tom Prest's tale of Sweeney Todd. Movies *Soylent Green; Fried Green Tomatoes; The Cook, the Thief, His Wife, Her Lover;* Jean-Luc Godard's *Weekend.* And let's not forget the children: Hansel and Gretel, the Gingerbread Man, and various versions of Snow White, Cinderella, and Red Riding Hood. Grandma, what big teeth you have!"

He drew a tremulous breath.

"And, of course, there are the participants of necessity. The Donner party; the rugby team stranded in the Andes; the crew of the yacht *Mignonette;* Marten

Hartwell, the bush pilot marooned in the Arctic. We are fascinated by their tales. And we embrace our famous-for-fifteen-minutes serial killer cannibals with even greater curiosity."

Another deep breath, exhaled slowly.

"I can't explain it, don't condone it. Prentice made everything sound exotic. We were naughty boys sharing an interest in a wicked topic."

"Fay ce que voudras."

I recited the words carved above the entrance to the basement tunnel. During my convalescence, I'd learned that the Rabelais quote in sixteenth-century French also graced the archway and fireplaces at Medmenham Abbey.

"'Do what you like,'" Midkiff translated, then laughed mirthlessly. "It's ironic. The Hell Fires used the quote to sanction their licentious indulgence, but Rabelais actually credits the words to Saint Augustine. "'Love God and do what you like. For if with the spirit of wisdom a man loves God, then, always striving to fulfil the divine will, what he wishes should be the right thing.'"

"When did Prentice Dashwood die?"

"Nineteen sixty-nine."

"Was someone killed?" We had found only eight victims.

"There could be no replacement for Prentice. Following his death no one was elevated to the inner circle. The number dropped to six and remained there."

"Why wasn't Dashwood on the fax you sent me?"

"I wrote down what I could recollect. The list was far from complete. I know almost nothing about those who joined after I left. As for Prentice, I just couldn't—" He glanced away. "It was so long ago."

For a long moment, neither of us spoke.

"You really didn't know what was going on?"

"I put it together after Mary Francis Rafferty died in 1972. That's when I withdrew."

"But said nothing."

"No. I give no excuse."

"Why did you tip Sheriff Crowe about Ralph Stover?"

"Stover joined the club after I dropped out. That's why he moved to Swain County. I've always known he was unstable."

I remembered my most recent question.

"Was it Stover who tried to run me down in Cherokee?"

"I heard it was a black Volvo. Stover has a black Volvo. That incident convinced me that he really was dangerous."

I gestured at the boxes.

"You're digging here, aren't you, Simon?"

"Yes."

"Without permission from Raleigh."

"The site is crucial to the lithic assemblage sequence I'm constructing."

"That's why you lied to me about working for the Department of Cultural Resources."

He nodded.

I set down my cup and stood.

"I'm sorry things haven't turned out as you'd hoped." I was sorry, but couldn't forgive what he had known and not reported.

"When the book is published people will recognize the value of my work."

Outside, the day was still clear and cool, with no haze in the valleys or along the ridges.

Twelve-thirty. I had to hurry.

34

THE TURNOUT FOR EDNA FARRELL'S FUNERAL WAS larger than I expected, given that she'd been dead more than half a century. In addition to members of her family, much of Bryson City, and many from the police and sheriff's departments had gathered to lay the old woman to rest. Lucy Crowe came, and so did Byron McMahon.

Stories of the Hell Fire Club now eclipsed accounts of the Air TransSouth crash, and reporters were there from across the Southeast. Eight seniors butchered and buried in the basement of a mountain lodge, the lieutenant governor discredited, and more than a dozen prominent citizens jailed. The media were calling them the Cannibal Murders, and I was forgotten like last year's sex scandal. While I was sorry that I could not shield Mrs. Veckhoff and her daughter from the publicity and public humiliation, I was relieved to be out of the spotlight.

I hung back during the graveside service, thinking of the many exits our departing lives can take. Edna Farrell didn't die in her bed but departed through a much more melancholy door. So did Tucker Adams, at rest under the weathered plaque at my feet. I felt great sadness for these people, so long dead. But I felt comfort in the knowledge that I had helped bring their bodies to this hill. And satisfaction that the killings were at last at an end.

When the mourners dispersed, I approached and laid a small bouquet on Edna's grave. Hearing footsteps behind me, I turned. Lucy Crowe was walking in my direction.

"Surprised to see you back so soon."

"It's my hard Irish head. Impossible to crack."

She smiled.

"It's so beautiful up here." My gaze swept over the trees, the tombstones, the hills and valleys spreading to the horizon like orange velveteen.

"It's why I love the highlands. There is a Cherokee creation myth that tells how the world was created from mud. A vulture flew over, and where his wings beat down, there were valleys. Where his wings rose, there grew mountains."

"You are Cherokee?"

A Crowe nod.

Another question answered.

"How's your situation with Larke Tyrell?"

I laughed.

"Two days ago I received a letter of commendation

from the Office of the Chief Medical Examiner assuming full responsibility for the misunderstanding, exonerating me of any wrongdoing, and thanking me for my invaluable contribution to the Air Trans-South recovery. Copies were sent to everyone but the Duchess of York."

We left the cemetery and walked up the blacktop to our cars. I was inserting my key when she asked another question.

"Did you identify the gargoyles on the tunnel entrance?"

"Harpocrates and Angerona were the Egyptian gods of silence, a reminder to the brothers of their oath of secrecy. Another gimmick borrowed from Sir Francis."

"The names?"

"Literary and historic references to cannibalism. Some are pretty obscure. Sawney Beane was a fourteenth-century cave-dwelling Scot. The Beane family was supposed to have slaughtered travelers and taken them home for supper. Same thing with Christie o' the Cleek. He and his family lived in a cave in Angus and dined on passing travelers. John Gregg kept the tradition alive in eighteenth-century Devon."

"Mr. B?"

"Baxbakualanuxsiwae."

"Very good."

"A Kwakiutl tribal spirit, a bearlike monster whose body was covered with bloody, snarling mouths."

"Patron saint of the Hamatsa."

"That's him."

"And the code names?"

"Pharaohs, gods, archaeological discoveries, characters in ancient tales. Henry Preston was Ilus, the founder of Troy. Kendall Rollins was Piankhy, an ancient Nubian king. Listen to this. Parker Davenport chose the Aztec god Ometeotl, the lord of duality. Do you suppose he was aware of the irony?"

"Ever take a close look at the seal of the State of North Carolina?"

I admitted that I hadn't.

"The motto is from Cicero's 'Essay on Friendship'—'*Esse Quam Videri.*'"

The Coke-bottle eyes held mine.

"'To be rather than to seem.'"

Winding down Schoolhouse Hill, I couldn't help but notice a bumper sticker on the car ahead.

Where will you spend eternity?

Though placed in a broader time frame than I'd been considering, the decal posed the same question that was on my mind. Where would I spend the time ahead? More pointedly, with whom?

During my convalescence, Pete had been caring and helpful, bringing flowers, feeding Birdie, heating soup in the microwave. We'd watched old movies, engaged in long conversations. When he was away, I spent hours recalling our life together. I remembered the good times. I remembered the fights, the minor irritations that simmered, then eventually escalated into full-scale battle.

I had resolved one thing: I loved my estranged husband, and we would always be bound in our hearts. But we could no longer be bound in our beds. While handsome, and loving, and funny, and smart, Pete shared something with Sir Francis and his Hell Fire mates: His hat would always be off to Venus.

Pete was a wall I could beat myself against forever. We made much better friends than spouses, and henceforth, I would keep us that way.

I turned onto Main at the bottom of the hill.

I'd also considered Andrew Ryan.

Ryan the colleague. Ryan the cop. Ryan the uncle.

Danielle was not a paramour. She was a niece. That was good.

I considered Ryan the man.

The man who wanted to suck my toes.

That was very good.

Because of the wound Pete had inflicted, I'd been hovering on the edge of a relationship with Ryan, wanting to get close but keeping my distance, like a moth drawn to a flame. Attracted but afraid.

Did I need a man in my life?

No.

Did I want one?

Yes.

What were the words of the song? I'd rather be

sorry for something I did, than for something that I didn't do.

I'd decided to give Ryan a try and see how it went.

I had one more stop in Bryson City. A stop I couldn't wait to make.

I parked outside a redbrick building at the corner of Slope and the Bryson Walk. When I entered the glass door, a woman in surgical scrubs looked up and smiled.

"Is he ready?"

"Very. Have a seat."

She disappeared, and I settled into a plastic chair in the waiting area.

Five minutes later she led Boyd out. His chest was taped, and one foreleg had been shaved. Seeing me, he gave a little hop, then limped over and placed his head on my lap.

"Is he in pain?" I asked the vet.

"Only when he laughs."

Boyd rolled his eyes upward at me, and the purple tongue dropped out.

"How are you doing, big guy?" I nuzzled his ears and touched my forehead to his.

Boyd sighed.

I straightened and looked at him.

"Are you ready to go home?"

He yipped and his eyebrows danced.

"Let's do it."

I could hear a laugh in his bark.

ABOUT THE AUTHOR

Kathy Reichs is forensic anthropologist for the Office of the Chief Medical Examiner, State of North Carolina, and for the Laboratoire de Sciences Judiciaires et de Médecine Légale for the province of Quebec. She is one of only fifty forensic anthropologists certified by the American Board of Forensic Anthropology and is on the Executive Committee of the Board of Directors of the American Academy of Forensic Sciences. A professor of anthropology at the University of North Carolina at Charlotte, Dr. Reichs is a native of Chicago, where she received her Ph.D. at Northwestern. She now divides her time between Charlotte and Montreal and is a frequent expert witness at criminal trials. Her first novel, *Déjà Dead,* brought Dr. Reichs fame when it became a *New York Times* bestseller and won the 1997 Ellis Award for Best First Novel. *Death du Jour* and *Deadly Décisions* also became international bestsellers. *Fatal Voyage* is her fourth novel featuring Temperance Brennan.